PENGUIN

CW00402647

Praise for Phi

'Sparkling and festive, as satisfying as figgy pudding
and clotted cream – loved it!'
Milly Johnson

'Filled with warm and likeable characters. Great fun!'
Jill Mansell

'Warm and funny and feel-good. The best sort
of holiday read'
Katie Fforde

'A delicious festive treat with as many twists and
turns as a Cornish country lane'
Jules Wake

'A transporting festive romance, full of genuine
warmth and quirky characters'
Woman's Own

'Serious festive escapism . . . like a big warm hug'
Popsugar

'A page-turner of a festive read'
My Weekly

'Gloriously uplifting and unashamedly warm-hearted'
Faith Hogan

'A fantastic setting and intriguing premise, all bound
together by Phillipa Ashley's storytelling talent'
Sue Moorcroft

Also by Phillipa Ashley

About the Author

Phillipa Ashley is a *Sunday Times*, Amazon and Audible bestselling author of uplifting romantic fiction.

After studying English at Oxford University, she worked as a copywriter and journalist before turning her hand to writing. Since then, her novels have sold well over a million copies and have been translated into numerous languages.

Phillipa lives in an English village with her husband, has a grown-up daughter and loves nothing better than walking the Lake District hills and swimming in Cornish coves.

Phillipa Ashley

Escape for Christmas

PENGUIN BOOKS

PENGUIN BOOKS

UK | USA | Canada | Ireland | Australia
India | New Zealand | South Africa

Penguin Books is part of the Penguin Random House group
of companies whose addresses can be found at
global.penguinrandomhouse.com

Penguin
Random House
UK

Published in Penguin Books 2024
003

Copyright © Phillipa Ashley, 2024

The moral right of the author has been asserted

Typeset in 10.4/15pt Palatino LT Pro by JOUVE(UK), Milton Keynes
Printed and bound in Great Britain by Clays Ltd, Elcograf S.p.A.

The authorised representative in the EEA is Penguin Random House Ireland,
Morrison Chambers, 32 Nassau Street, Dublin D02 YH68

A CIP catalogue record for this book is available from the British Library

ISBN: 978–1–804–94554–4

www.greenpenguin.co.uk

MIX
Paper | Supporting
responsible forestry
FSC
www.fsc.org FSC® C018179

Penguin Random House is committed to a
sustainable future for our business, our readers
and our planet. This book is made from Forest
Stewardship Council® certified paper.

For Romilly,
who has brought such joy to our lives.
With love,
Nanny xx

Chapter One

'And you're one hundred per cent certain this isn't the biggest mistake of your life, Soph?'

Sophie Cranford's finger hesitated over the Enter key on her laptop while Vee, her friend and housekeeper, hovered over her shoulder.

'I'm never one hundred per cent sure about anything,' Sophie admitted, but she decided it was now or never, so she uploaded the ad she'd spent hours composing onto the guest-house website.

There was a pause before Vee spoke again. 'Well, you're the boss. You know best, only I've got to admit it's an *unusual* marketing strategy for a cosy guest house. We do normally get a lot of snow in the Lake District over winter, so it is kind of perfect for a Christmas break.'

Sophie fiddled with the pendant at her neck. Vee did have a point, because Sunnyside *was* a dream location for a festive holiday. It was arguably too big to be called a cottage, although it had all the best features of one, from its stone walls and slate roof to its tall chimneys and the wisteria climbing above the door. There were several acres of grounds

1

with a garden, hot tub and a wooden veranda, making it an ideal spot for guests to admire the views over the fells and Lake Windermere below.

In spring, lambs bleated in the fields, wild flowers ran riot in summer, and autumn turned the hillsides russet with bracken. When Sophie had taken over Sunnyside in March earlier that year she'd woken up to snow dusting the fell-tops like icing sugar as she waited for spring to arrive. Now, as the year turned its face towards winter, she could picture her guests crunching through the frosted grass and curling up in front of the fire with a hot chocolate.

In fact Sunnyside was a gingerbread latte of a house, with whipped cream on top and starry sprinkles for good measure. Anyone would be delighted to stay there, including Sophie herself – which was why she hadn't been able to resist buying it, even at the lowest ebb of her life when the people she'd trusted most had shattered her heart like a cheap glass bauble.

Her office chair creaked as she swivelled round to face Vee.

'*Have* I made a terrible mistake?' she asked, her resolve wobbling.

'We-ell,' Vee dithered before continuing, 'if you think people loathe Christmas enough to want to come to an anti-Christmas hotel . . .'

'Sunnyside isn't an anti-Christmas hotel, and the guests don't have to loathe Christmas to book. I just want to provide an alternative way to relax and chill out for people who might not feel like celebrating in the traditional way.

Christmas can be a difficult time for people,' Sophie insisted, trotting out her carefully rehearsed marketing message behind the 'Escape for Christmas' break.

'Sorry,' Vee muttered.

'It's OK,' Sophie said cheerfully, because she didn't want to upset Vee. 'But it's important that people don't get the wrong idea and think that alternative means boring or "Bah, humbug".'

Vee's eyebrows knitted together. 'I'm sure it will be fine . . .'

'I sense a "but".'

'Are you sure that you're not doing this because . . . well, because . . .'

'Spit it out, Vee. You know we can be honest.'

'Because *you* hate Christmas.'

Sophie's stomach knotted. Vee was dangerously close to a sensitive subject. 'I don't hate it.'

Vee raised her Marigold-clad hands in surrender, knowing her friend well enough not to push it. 'OK. OK. I understand. Well, I don't totally get it, but you probably have a point. You should go for it, and I'll support you. I even swear not to wear my Christmas jumper to work.'

'You do what you want to. I'm not out to spoil other people's enjoyment. I only want to offer a unique way of spending the three big days; some respite from the clichéd jollity.'

Vee patted her shoulder. 'It will get easier, Sophie. I promise it will. You've done an amazing job since you came here.

3

No one would ever know you'd never run a guest house before.'

Sophie fought back the tears that were threatening to form. It was really kind of Vee to say that, and perhaps she hadn't given herself enough credit for what she'd achieved in her first seven months of running the B&B.

'Thanks. That means so much to me, coming from a professional. I couldn't have done it without your help.'

Without a lot of people's help, Sophie acknowledged, silently thanking those friends and family who'd been her rock over the past year. Although there were others who had sniggered or had blatantly told her she'd never make it work. Chief among them was Ben, her ex-fiancé, but she supposed she ought to thank the lying git, in a way. Without him cheating on her, she'd never had taken the leap to buy Sunnyside.

The period after the split had almost crushed her, but now she'd achieved her long-held dream of owning a guest house, and in such a beautiful location too. One thing was for sure: the thirty-fourth year of her life had most certainly been the most eventful ever – for all the right and wrong reasons. And even though Vee might be sceptical about her latest plan, she had been one of Sophie's biggest supporters since she'd moved to Sunnyside, becoming a close friend too.

'I'm sure this anti- – I mean "Escape for Christmas" – break will be a big hit,' Vee reassured her, perching on the edge of the desk. 'Look at it this way: the woman who can go from running a Christmas shop to managing a guest house within less than a year can make anything work.'

'Thanks for the vote of confidence,' Sophie said, although the doubting voice in her head was growing louder again. 'There are some similarities, though. I learned to be really good at holding my tongue and smiling while customers gave me their opinions.'

Despite this, she also had to admit that putting up with awkward people for ten minutes in her shop was quite different from having them stay for days in your home.

'Do you ever miss your shop at all?' Vee asked.

Sophie thought for a few moments. There had been times when, cleaning hairs from a shower or mopping up catsick from the guest-lounge carpet, she might, momentarily, have rather been gift-wrapping a Shakespeare bauble for an American tourist.

This time last year she had been the proprietor of a year-round Christmas shop in Stratford-upon-Avon, which was loved by tourists from all over the world who travelled to it. It had been fun and thriving, and she'd been as happy as the jolly elves grinning from the shelves in the July heat.

Until Christmas Eve, when she'd found her ex, Ben, writhing naked on the floor of the stockroom with her best friend, amid a sea of luxury double-strand tinsel.

'No,' she said firmly, deciding that even the yuckiest chore was preferable to staying in a place that had so many painful memories. 'It's true that things happened fast and it's been a bigger change than I ever expected, but life doesn't always run to the schedule you plan.'

'You can say that again,' Vee replied. 'I never thought I'd have two kids within three years! Bloody Kev . . .' She rolled her eyes and Sophie smiled. 'Wouldn't have it any other way now, of course,' she added.

'Neither would I,' said Sophie. 'You know that Ben sneered when he heard I was selling the shop to buy a guest house up here? He thought I was mad and told me he "didn't think it was wise to make any hasty decisions while I was vulnerable".'

'Oh, the cheeky sod!' Vee exclaimed. 'You mean that, after cheating on you, he still thought he had a right to comment on your life choices?'

'I think he was furious that I was selling the shop and flat – *my* shop and flat – and he'd have to find another job. A proper job,' Sophie said. 'But most of all, I think he was shocked that I could possibly make a new life on my own.' She stopped, a lump forming in her throat. As strong and happy as she felt now, talking about it somehow made her feel that little bit smaller and less assured.

It had been so hard to make that decision to move away from the town she'd grown up in and where her support network was. She and Ben had a few joint friends, which had made life awkward for a while after the split. Plus, her parents were understandably worried about her upping sticks to take on a huge new venture.

'I had to do something drastic, for a clean break. I felt that life was telling me that now was the moment I should go for things I'd always fancied trying. Mum and Dad used to bring me up here when I was younger. I didn't always appreciate the scenery then, but on the few occasions I'd persuaded Ben to have a break with me, I felt almost bereft when I had to go home, as I'd felt such a strong connection to the Lakes. It's so majestic and the landscape changes so much, depending on the weather. You never know what you're going to get, and I like that.'

'It's certainly full of surprises,' Vee said wryly. 'Did you ever think of running a B&B together up here?'

'Well, it's funny you should say that. Because as much as I loved the shop, it was always going to be the same, so a few years back I did start to wonder if we should have a change.'

'Were you with *him* then?' Vee asked, curling her lip at the reference to Ben.

'Yes, we'd been working and living together for a couple of years. We managed a long spring weekend in Ambleside a while ago. The woods were filled with bluebells and wild garlic and everywhere looked as if it had been reborn after the winter, if that doesn't sound too airy-fairy.'

'I know exactly what you mean. I could never move,' Vee replied.

'We stayed in a guest house and it was nice, but I kept thinking how I'd have run it differently, although Ben hated the idea.' Sophie glanced out of her window at the sun glittering on the distant lake and felt sadness weigh on her again. 'Sometimes I wonder how long he'd fancied Naomi, and if she was the reason he'd wanted to stay put in Stratford.'

'But then he set about breaking everything anyway.' Vee shook her head disapprovingly.

'Yes . . . and I wasn't going to let him destroy every last part of me. I'll admit I was terrified when I started looking for a business here within days of finding him with Naomi. I needed to take that rage and hurt and turn it into something positive. I just never thought Sunnyside would come up so soon.'

'Clearly you were meant to buy it,' Vee said.

'I think so,' Sophie smiled, feeling a renewed determination to continue making this work.

'Shall I make a cuppa?' Vee offered.

'That would be amazing. I could do with the caffeine hit. I've lain awake for ages composing this ad and thinking about this ad.'

'Done,' said Vee, heading for the kitchen.

Sophie stood up and stretched her back, thinking again of how much her life had changed in the past year.

The speed at which events had moved had left her breathless. In the ten months since her split with Ben, she'd sold her shop and bought Sunnyside. A business acquaintance who owned a boutique in Stratford had always wanted to run the Christmas shop and had made an offer the moment she'd heard it was up for sale.

The very next day Sophie had been alerted by a Lake District estate agent that Sunnyside was going on the market. She'd already viewed – and rejected – several guest houses as being too big, too small or in need of costly renovation, but Sunnyside had only recently been refurbished. Its owners had just finished the makeover when the husband had been offered a lucrative contract in Dubai that was too tempting to turn down.

Sophie didn't have the trouble and expense of having to

do it up and, more importantly, it was an established business with forward bookings, so she could hit the ground running. Otherwise she could never have afforded to take it on. Even so, she'd had to pump the proceeds of her flat and business into Sunnyside and take out a mortgage.

She'd finally moved in at the very start of March, in time for the busy Easter period – a baptism of fire that had left her wondering if she really had been as mad as everyone thought to make so many huge changes in her life in such a short space of time. Her parents had certainly thought so and urged her 'not to rush into something she'd regret'.

Considering they'd been aghast that she'd had her long chestnut curls transformed into a choppy bob after Ben had left, she'd expected her decision to sell up and move north to horrify them. She knew the haircut was the classic 'break-up' behaviour, but didn't care. She'd wanted to try a new style for ages, but Ben had often begged her not to change it. Cutting her hair had felt symbolic of breaking away from him.

Vee returned with two mugs.

'Thanks,' Sophie said, accepting her coffee. 'Don't know what I'd do without you.' She really meant it because it had been a steep learning curve moving from retail to hospitality. She was glad she'd taken advice on running a guest house from her friend, Lyra, who had her own B&B back in Stratford.

Vee laughed. 'Glad we found each other.'

'It was my friend, Lyra, who told me, "Above all else, lovely, find a great cleaner and get some help serving breakfast. Oh, and send the laundry out or you'll be in trouble."' Sophie did a passable imitation of Lyra's Cardiff accent.

Vee laughed. 'I like this Lyra even though I've never met her, and I'm so pleased that Brody's mum told me you were looking for someone to help with the changeovers.'

Brody was Sophie's next-door neighbour, and his mother, Louise, was a stalwart of the local Bannerdale community. While Louise McKenna could be a bit domineering, she knew *everyone*. It was when Sophie visited the guest house for an inspection that she'd bumped into Brody and Louise and had been interrogated – politely, of course – on her plans for Sunnyside.

On hearing that Sophie intended to take it on, Louise had put her in touch with Vee and a number of local suppliers. Sophie had also managed to hire a morose but efficient student called Ricky to help with the breakfasts.

The chimes of the grandfather clock in reception startled them both.

Vee glanced at her watch with a gasp. 'Look at the time! I must go and see how Ricky's getting on with the breakfast room. Oh, and I hate to mention it, but the cats have been sleeping in the window seat of the guest lounge again. We've hoovered and got up most of the fur with that special roller-thing, but . . .'

Sophie groaned. 'Argh, I'm sorry. The door must have been left open again, and you know how they love that sunny spot in the window. I'll stick a notice on the lounge door, asking guests to keep it shut at all times, and I'll try to make sure the cats don't come into the public part of the house.'

Vee crossed her fingers. 'That should work.'

Sophie hoped so. Keeping her duo of mischievous cats in her part of Sunnyside had proved quite a challenge. Her modest flat occupied one side of the ground floor of the property. It had a sitting room, a kitchenette and a bedroom with a tiny en suite. The cats occasionally sneaked into the reception area and guest lounge and, while some visitors adored her pets, others were less keen.

Vee bustled off and Sophie heard her break into a humming of 'Fairytale of New York' before she hastily changed it to 'Summer Nights'.

Now that Sophie was alone in the office, she felt guilty for not being totally honest with Vee. She *did* hate Christmas these days. She hated all the associations of it: like the hurtful memories that flooded back when she heard Mariah Carey telling some loser that all she wanted for Christmas was him . . . Or when she thought of the supermarket shelves and shop windows bedecked with glittery tat, even though she had once been the purveyor of glittery tat and Christmas had been her livelihood.

Any enjoyment of the upcoming festive season had been destroyed by Bloody Ben and by Naomi, the 'best' friend who was meant to be the bridesmaid at their wedding, yet had turned out to be a treacherous snake in the grass. This would be Sophie's first Christmas since the split happened and it was bound to be the most difficult one.

She hadn't always got things right at Sunnyside so far

11

and she was still learning. But she was sure that hosting an 'Escape for Christmas' break wouldn't be the biggest mistake of her life, because that had been falling for her Ben and trusting him with her heart.

She dreaded the thought of spending this Christmas on her own, yet somehow it felt worse to imagine being surrounded by merrymaking family and friends, whose well-meaning pity would just about finish her off. This really was going to be for the best – hopefully it would give her a nice flurry of business to end the year before she planned to close in January for a break; secondly, it would be something completely different this year, which would be exactly what she needed to help her continue to move on.

Sophie refreshed the website and read back the ad she'd spent time crafting. She hoped that somewhere out there were other souls who felt the same as she did. People with bruised hearts, hiding losses behind a forced smile as they sat around the festive dinner table, pulling crackers and trying not to cry or scream.

DESPERATE TO ESCAPE FOR CHRISTMAS?

Do you long to flee the festive season? Can't face another plate of mince pies or rerun of It's a Wonderful Life? *Want to get away from the glitter and the giant snowmen?*
You're in luck!
At the Sunnyside Hotel it might be winter, but it's
never *Christmas!*
We can promise you:

ESCAPE FOR CHRISTMAS

Books in cosy nooks, winter walks and convivial company.
*No tinsel, no turkey and definitely **no** Love Actually!*
If you want to get away from Christmas, if you're a self-confessed
Grinch but love a good time, book now!
Places strictly limited.
To book or to find out more (click here)

PS No Santa hats allowed on the premises.

Chapter Two

15 December

'Deck the halls with boughs of holly. Fa-la-la-la-la . . .'

Sophie gritted her teeth as the carol blared out while she waited in the vet's waiting room with her cat carrier on her lap. Over the top of it, she could see a border collie in a bow tie glaring at a pug in an elf jumper. The teenager next to her had festooned his guinea pigs' cage with tinsel and even the practice manager, the formidable Mrs Hazeldine, was wearing a knitted Rudolph dress with a light-up nose.

Sophie sighed. You'd have thought a vet's surgery would be a refuge from the human festivities, but apparently not.

McKenna's Vets was located in the heart of the large and bustling village of Bannerdale, a twenty-minute journey from Sunnyside. As she'd driven down to the surgery this morning, the pale winter sun had emerged, thawing the early frost and making Lake Windermere sparkle in the morning light. It was another moment when she felt grateful to live in such a beautiful part of the world.

A vet nurse in a headband with antlers returned a chameleon to the man sitting next to Sophie, and who leaned over to the cats. 'Not long now,' she promised.

A door opened and a tall man in blue scrubs and a Santa hat called out cheerfully, 'Jingle and Belle Cranford, please.'

Sophie rose to her feet, trying to ignore the sniggers from the teenage owner of the guinea pigs.

He turned to her with a smirk. 'Are your cats really called Jingle and Belle?'

'Yes,' said Sophie, trying to keep a polite smile in place.

'Why's that then?' he asked.

'Because I had them as kittens from the rescue centre on Christmas Eve.'

'Aw, bless the little fur-babies!' A lady wearing a Russian hat that looked like a racoon poked a finger through the carrier mesh. 'You're *such* lucky kitties to have a cat mum who loves Christmas so much.'

'Thank you,' Sophie said through gritted teeth.

'Jingle and Belle, the vet is ready for you *now*, please,' the vet called again, holding open the door to his consulting room as a hint for her to get a move on.

Sophie hauled the carrier past him and into the room.

'Hello,' he said, as she carefully placed the carrier on the exam table. 'So how are the lucky kitties and their cat mum doing today?' He chuckled.

Sophie groaned. As much as she loved Jingle and Belle, she hated the phrase 'cat mum', mainly because bloody Ben had used it ad nauseam when they first got the kittens. Oh, it had seemed cute at the time; how she'd laughed and called him the Cat Dad. Now she rued the day she'd ever been tempted to give her cats such daft monikers, but the two fluffy bundles were crying out for a festive name when she'd picked them up from the rescue shelter – a small Christmas miracle of her own.

'She's fine, thanks, Brody. How's the most popular vet in the village?'

He rolled his eyes. 'I'm the only vet in the village,' he corrected her, unhooking the catch on the carrier. 'Well, not the only vet; I do have partners. Do you like the hat by the way?'

Sophie hadn't the heart to say she'd gone off Santa hats of any kind. 'It's – very festive.'

'Do you think so? To be honest, I feel a right prat and I'm beginning to suspect it might have attracted fleas, but Cora, our practice manager, insists we all get into the festive spirit. She says it's good PR and it helps the patients feel less nervous.'

'Does it? Jingle and Belle run away if they see tinsel.' An extra excuse not to have any in the guest house – the last time she'd seen tinsel, it was wrapped around Naomi when she caught Ben cheating on her.

'It's for the owners really. It makes us seem more approachable, warm and – er – human.' Brody scratched the back of his neck.

Sophie laughed.

'I don't mind really,' he said unconvincingly as he peered into the carrier door. 'Come on then, you two, let's take a look at you. I'm sure you've been looking forward to your annual check-up *so* much.'

'They can't wait,' Sophie smiled as Jingle sauntered out, while Belle lurked at the back of the carrier.

'Good lad, Jingle,' Brody said, running his hand along

the sleek black fur of Jingle's back. 'Come on, Belle. Be a good girl for Uncle Brody.'

Sophie let out a snicker. Uncle Brody . . . it always made her laugh when he talked to the cats as if he was their favourite uncle.

'She's always been the shy one,' Sophie explained.

However, Belle did eventually emerge from the carrier, allowing Brody to scoop her up in his arms – strong, tanned arms, Sophie couldn't help noticing. Perhaps having to scoop up pets all day brought some benefits, but it was weird to think of Brody like this.

He stared at her. 'What's the matter?'

'Nothing. Only a shiver.'

His brow furrowed with concern. 'You're not getting flu, are you? Mum's only just over it, and half the village seems to have had it.'

'I hope not. Not with the guest house to run, although in my job it would be amazing if I didn't catch something,' Sophie admitted.

'Same,' Brody murmured in agreement as he began expertly examining Belle, while Jingle looked on in contempt. 'Only there's more stuff I can get. Erysipelas and psittacosis . . .' At Sophie's frown, he clarified: 'Better known as parrot fever.'

Her jaw dropped. 'Parrot fever can be caught by humans?'

'Oh yes,' he said solemnly. 'And don't get me started on lumpy wool disease.'

She snorted. 'Now you're making them up!'

'Oh no,' he shook his head before a playful grin broke

out on his face. 'I promise they're all too real, but not dangerous to a healthy human.'

'I'm very glad to hear it,' Sophie said, still giggling.

Jingle let out a loud miaow and Brody returned the dis-
gruntled feline to the back of the table.

'Actually it's the humans who are the filthy disease-
carriers, especially at this time of year,' he joked. 'Now shall
we turn our attention to the most important creatures in the
room?' With Sophie's assistance, Brody managed to weigh
both cats, take their temperatures and give them booster
jabs for cat flu, enteritis and FeLV.

Belle protested more than Jingle, who simply looked out-
raged at the indignities heaped on him.

If Sophie was ever even to contemplate letting a man
near her again, Brody McKenna would come top of the list –
which wasn't difficult, when he was the only man on the
list. He was not merely her vet, but her nearest neighbour. In
fact he was probably the only single man in the village close
to her age.

When she'd first moved into Sunnyside, his black Labrador, Harold, had run straight through the open door of
the guest house, knocking over a vase that Ben's mother
had given them as an anniversary present. Brody had
chased after Harold, apologised endlessly and offered to
pay for the vase. Sophie had refused, admitted she'd always
loathed it and didn't know how it had found its way onto
the removal van.

She'd also instantly warmed to Harold and had been
friends with Brody ever since. Which was fortunate, as

Harold was prone to making frequent breaks for freedom from Brody's smallholding and into the Sunnyside grounds.

Brody stroked both cats' backs. 'Jingle's a handsome boy,' he said admiringly, 'and Belle has a beautiful coat.'

'Thank you,' Sophie said proudly, 'I bet you say that to all the owners.'

Now it was Brody's turn to feign outrage. 'Would I?'

'Yes,' Sophie replied, laughing again.

'Well, they seem absolutely fine.'

Sophie received his verdict with pride, relief and a teeny tinge of disappointment that the appointment was over and now she had no excuse to linger. She found herself racking her brains for a cat health-related question to ask him to prolong their meeting. Failing that, she had a flash of inspiration. 'How's Harold?' she blurted out.

'He's – *Haroldy*. As always,' Brody answered, looking surprised to be asked. 'I'm sorry about his unscheduled visit last week. I heard he helped himself to the remains of a guest's Full English?'

Sophie smiled. 'Luckily the guests had already gone out. I hadn't had a chance to clear the tables when Harold appeared and hoovered up a stray bacon rasher. Ricky took him back to your gate, so we assumed he'd got home safely and well fed.'

Brody rolled his eyes. 'That dog really does think he owns the whole village! Seriously, if he sees food, he eats it. I need to keep a constant check on his diet.'

'Just like me,' Sophie said. 'Although after cooking full

breakfasts for the guests, I find I've mysteriously gone off a fry-up myself.'

'You don't need to watch your diet,' Brody replied.

Sophie cheeks felt warm.

'In my professional opinion. As a vet, that is. Oh, bugger . . .' He squirmed. 'I'm digging a whopping great hole, aren't I?'

'Only the size of Cathedral Cavern,' Sophie teased, unsure whether to be flattered that he'd noticed her figure or whether Brody thought she looked like she needed to look after herself more.

Jingle miaowed loudly and Belle was trying to climb off the table.

'Um, let's have you back in your carrier so you can get home,' Brody muttered, clearly eager to move past any awkwardness.

Sophie opened the door and he shooed Jingle into the carrier while she scooped up Belle, who slunk in next to her brother and eyed Sophie menacingly through the grid.

'Thanks. I'll, um, see you soon,' Brody said, scratching the back of his neck again as Sophie hoisted the carrier off the table and walked towards the door. 'Oh, I almost forgot!' he called after her.

'What?' She turned round, confused because she thought he'd checked everything concerning the cats.

'I'm having a party. Well, it's not an actual party. It's def-initely not *my* party. It's for Mum really. Oh, I'm not explaining this very well, am I?' he mumbled, taking a breath. 'It's her annual Village Do-Gooders' Gathering, though she'd kill me for calling it that. She likes to host it at Felltop Farm because there's a bit more space than at her place.'

That was an understatement. Sophie hadn't been inside Felltop Farm, but she knew it was huge. It was the kind of ancient, rambling Lakeland farmhouse that had wings shooting off in all directions. Outside there were numerous outbuildings and land, where Brody kept a few rare-breed sheep, a donkey and chickens.

Sophie's heart beat faster. A Christmas party – especially of 'Do-Gooders' – was her idea of hell. Brody's company, however, would be a major compensation.

'Oh. OK,' she murmured.

'And I wanted to ask you, but I probably shouldn't . . .'

'*Shouldn't*?' she couldn't help repeating. It was a loaded word that made Sophie's antennae twitch, almost as if he'd thought better of it.

'After seeing your website,' Brody explained. 'And after what Vee told me.'

'What has Vee told you?' she asked, noticing that her voice came out higher than she meant it to. Did Brody – and half the village – know every last detail about the tinsel incident?

'Only that you don't do Christmas, and that's OK,' he said hastily. 'It really is. Lots of people don't, and sometimes I feel like skipping it myself. There's so much pressure on one holiday and it seems to get worse every year.'

'No, really, it's not that I don't do Christmas as such,' Sophie told him, eager to explain sufficiently that he'd

21

understand, but not too much so that she'd have to bare her soul. 'It's more that I – er – spotted a gap in the market for people who want something different. After all, every guest house and hotel in the Lakes is banging on about the log fires and seven-course turkey dinner ... I thought my "Escape" would give Sunnyside a unique selling point.' She was rather proud of herself, thinking she'd managed to sound convincing. 'At least that was the plan.'

'It's a brilliant idea,' Brody added hastily. 'And it's one reason why I thought the party might be a good opportunity for you. There'll be other business people there who you might like to ... bond with. The Traders' Association chair, the director of the Tourist Board, the vicar – not that he'd be any help to Sunnyside – so I thought it might be a useful way to get to know people in an informal setting. But *please* don't feel obliged and, in fact, you can forget I even mentioned it.'

When Brody finally paused for breath, Sophie felt her words stick in her throat, not knowing how to respond. She'd kind of backed herself into a corner, going on about her business reasons for launching the "Escape" ... and now she had little excuse for not attending because, as Brody said, it would offer perfect networking to help her new business.

Argh! Her emotions were like two tug-of-war teams pulling as hard as they could on both sides. It was a proper Christmas do: not a small gathering, but a large formal one with half the village there – exactly the kind of thing she was hoping to avoid this year. Yet Brody would be hosting it and he'd asked her *specially*, even if he'd then tried to un-invite her by telling her to forget it.

Brody was handsome and kind and, if she was being completely honest with herself, was the only man she'd even remotely contemplated getting to know better, since her ex.

'Erm . . .' she said, stalling for time. 'When is this not-a-party happening?'

'The twenty-third of December. You really don't have to come, but you'd be doing me a huge favour and I'd owe you. It would be great to have someone under sixty there, who isn't talking about their pension or what a wonderful man Michael Bublé is.'

Sophie chuckled, although she couldn't help but feel uneasy at the idea of attending a festive party where everyone would be brimming with jollity and asking awkward questions. Especially about her marketing idea.

Since she'd first posted the ad on her website in October, she'd had several local hoteliers asking her why she was hosting an 'anti-Christmas break'. One had even dubbed it an '"I hate Christmas" break', which had sparked Sophie into telling him, in no uncertain terms, that it wasn't any-thing of the kind. She was bound to have gained a reputation as a spiky oddball with some of the Bannerdale diehards, and this would bring her face-to-face with them.

'Of course Harold would love seeing a friendly face too,' Brody said, bringing her back to the matter at hand.

Sophie played along. 'You mean he'd enjoy seeing some-one who lets him have bacon?'

'Naturally.' Brody's caramel-brown eyes focused on Sophie with a sudden seriousness that made her go as gooey as a brownie. 'And I'd love to see your face too, of course.'

'Oh, of course.' She smiled.

She'd dodged so many seasonal invitations already from local acquaintances and business contacts, including an invite to join Vee's family at the lantern parade in the week before Christmas, which was the highlight of the community's festive celebrations, with children carrying home-made lanterns through the streets, carol-singing and a brass band.

Vee had understood ... but Sophie still felt guilty at refusing every invitation. And would it be hard to explain why she'd declined that, but was now accepting this one?

Showing her face at Brody's would tick a box and would have the massive bonus of Brody himself to sugar the pill. On the other hand, she was bound to be asked a lot of personal questions that she didn't want to answer. Not to mention the fact that Christmas parties reminded her of the misery of trying to smile through the festive season for the sake of her parents, after she'd found Ben and Naomi together the night before.

She reminded herself that if it all got too much, home was only a few minutes away.

With a loud miaow, Belle shifted inside the carrier, setting off Jingle and making it wobble in Sophie's arms. The cats were turning restless.

'I'll see what I can do,' she replied hastily. 'I mean, it's very kind of you to ask me and, of course, I'd *love* to see Harold too. If I can make it, I . . . will try. I promise I'll try.'

'You don't have to promise anything,' Brody reassured her, taking the cat carrier from her.

Sophie's shoulders slumped in relief.

'I hope I haven't stressed you out by mentioning it?'

'No! You haven't. I really would like to come . . .'

'Drop in *if* you want to,' he said. 'Now don't give it another thought. If you wouldn't mind opening the door for me, so I can carry the fur-babies out to your car?'

'Really there's no need,' she protested, feeling embarrassed by his attention.

Nonetheless Brody had a firm look in his eye that meant business, so she opened the door and followed him out into the reception area, as the eyes of every owner lasered in on them. Popular though the handsome village vet was, he didn't normally carry pets back to their owners' cars. It wasn't as if Sophie had a broken arm or her cats were heavyweight chonks, so it was obviously special treatment.

Out in the open, she flicked the lock on her pickup and Brody loaded Jingle and Belle onto the floor.

'Thank you,' Sophie said quickly. 'Although we've held you up too long this morning and you'd better get back to work. Your receptionist in the Rudolph jumper looked thunderous when you came out with me.'

'She always looks thunderous. I can never live up to her exacting administrative standards,' Brody replied with a sigh. 'Now, have a safe journey home. I've got to deal with a spaniel's impacted anal glands next, and castrate a Labrador.'

'Delightful! Have a nice day,' Sophie shouted back,

laughing again and realising that Brody seemed to have that effect on her.

With a wave, he walked back through the slush into the surgery while Sophie got into the driver's seat and turned on the engine.

Most of the hilltops were white with snow as Sophie drove back to Sunnyside, but she left the vet's with a warmer glow than she'd experienced since she'd moved to Bannerdale. A lot of that was down to Brody.

Vee was dusting the dining room when Sophie returned. 'Phew, crisis averted,' she declared, flapping the yellow duster in the air.

Sophie's anxiety rose. 'What crisis?'

'Nothing for you to worry about now – I've sorted it. Kev couldn't pick up the kids from judo in the village because he'd forgotten he has mountain-rescue training tonight. I'd already agreed to go to a Christmas lantern-parade meeting, so I couldn't do it. His mum's going to step in, so that's OK.' Vee stopped mid-flow and tutted. 'Sorry to mention the C-word again.'

'Don't worry.' Sophie didn't want Vee to have to tread on eggshells around her. 'I can't avoid it altogether. I'll have guests coming here specifically to enjoy the pre-Christmas festivities right up until Christmas week itself. They'll be talking about it. I can't turn off the carols in the shops, or cancel the lantern parade, or rip all the tinsel off the shelves.' No matter how much she wanted to, she secretly thought. 'But I can control my own little space, so I might keep things more low-key. And I'm so glad you're here to help me. It's going to be a busy time and we're nearly fully booked.'

'You're welcome. I love working here. You're so much better than any of the other bosses I've had before, who were all tossers.'

Sophie had to laugh. 'The bar was set high for me then?'

'No, it wasn't, but really you care about your staff, you pay a fair rate and, if the shit hits the fan, you always try to help.'

'Life's hard enough without making it even tougher for people,' Sophie replied.

'I do appreciate it . . .' Vee's phone rang and she pulled it out of her apron pocket. 'Oh, talking of which. Mind if I get this? It's Kev's mum, so I'd better check she knows what time she needs to be at the village hall.'

'No problem.'

Vee left the office via the rear door that led to the store-rooms and kitchen. Sophie sat down at her desk to enjoy a minute's peace before her guests returned. Four of the five rooms were booked, although all of the guests – three couples and a single man – were out enjoying the rare December sun and winter colours.

Vee worked hard, was flexible and trustworthy, a quality that Sophie valued above all others, after recent experiences in her personal life, which is maybe why they got on so well. In return, Sophie hoped she was flexible on hours, whenever she could be, and had tried to help Vee out during several family emergencies.

If Vee or Ricky was unavailable for any reason, or they

were especially busy, Sophie herself stepped in to help with the cleaning or anything else that needed doing. She used a professional laundry service for the sheets and towels, which helped a lot, but she was ready to muck in when needed.

Through her housekeeper she'd met Vee's husband, Kev, and his friends from the mountain-rescue team. The whole community had opened its arms to this stranger from the south, who was single and naive in the ways of running a guest house in the relative wilds of Cumbria.

Whether by helping Vee, the mountain-rescue team or going to Brody's 'party', Sophie felt she owed it to the community to give a little back, no matter how uncomfortable she might find it.

Chapter Three

'So I need to finalise the guest list for the do.' Louise McKenna's pen was poised ominously over her clipboard.

'Sure,' Brody muttered, busy adding a log to the fire in the snug. Harold was snoozing as close to it as he dared. Both he and Brody liked to spend the winter evenings in the smaller room, with its cast-off furniture and shabby rugs that had been relegated from the much larger sitting room, which they saved for when they had guests, although that was rare these days.

Not counting as a guest, Brody's mother perched on the sofa.

'I've ordered the canapés. I don't have time to be making them myself, so the caterers will deliver late on the afternoon of the party. I've based it on six per person. We have salmon blinis, mini-Yorkshires with beef and horseradish, two vegan options and two sweet ones. How does that sound?'

Sparks flew from the hearth as Brody settled the log on the fire with a poker and a puff of wood-smoke filled the air.

He sat back down in the armchair, trying to give his mother the full attention she deserved, but it was hard to feign interest in party-planning such as canapé choices. He noticed that his mum looked tired underneath her make-up. At sixty-five, she was still a powerhouse, juggling her role as a director of the McKenna family business with numerous activities and community groups. But she was his mum, and he couldn't help worry that she was doing too much and needed to ease up a bit.

'You always sit in your dad's chair,' she remarked with a wistful smile. 'It looks ready to fall apart.'

'Um, I don't mind.' Brody shrugged.

'You will when you fall through the seat. Why don't you let me have it re-upholstered for you? I could arrange it in the New Year?' she offered. 'Call it a late extra Christmas present?'

A spring creaked as Brody shifted in his seat, which didn't help his case. The chair was falling apart, although he felt an ache in his chest at the thought of parting with his beloved armchair, even if only temporarily. He felt close to his father, Ralph, when he sat in it.

His mum had been incredible since his dad had died suddenly of a heart attack when Brody was only seventeen, helping to run the business and support so many worthy causes in the village, but he knew it was also for her, because keeping busy was good for Louise and meant she couldn't wallow.

His father had loved the wingback chair that Brody liked to occupy now. Once Brody had qualified as a vet at twenty-five, his mum had asked him to take on Felltop Farm, preferring to move to a new-build cottage in what she called 'the heart of the action' in Bannerdale. He now owned the house jointly with her and was gradually paying her off. It had meant he could get on the property ladder, and his mum could have a fresh start, away from a place that was too big for her and filled with too many memories.

'True,' he said, seeing the tenderness behind her eyes and that she was trying to do something thoughtful concerning the chair. She might try to manage him too much, yet Brody understood that it was her way of showing she cared. 'Good idea at some point, but *I'll* pay.'

'I was going to treat you,' she said.

'No,' he replied firmly, wanting complete control over the process so that he could steel himself and do it when he felt ready.

'OK. I know that look. It was the same one your father used to roll out when he was about to dig his heels in with me. As you're busy, I'll leave it with you, shall I, and then remind you after Christmas?'

'Thanks.' Brody leaned back in the chair, silently hoping it would still feel the same chair when it returned from its makeover. *If* he ever got round to arranging it.

His mum sighed triumphantly. 'Wow, that was easier than I thought. I was expecting a battle lasting for months, at least.'

'I hate to be predictable,' he said, suspecting the chair saga would go on for months, with a bit of luck.

'Shame we can't sort it before the party, but I've got a nice chenille throw that will hide it.'

'The guests won't come in here, will they?' Brody was

31

unable to hide his dismay. 'I thought this was going to be Harold's haven.'

'Harold can go . . . wherever. We need all the rooms open, for guests to mingle around, and in tip-top shape. Don't worry, I've got a plan,' she said, tapping the clipboard with her pen. 'On that note, here's the schedule for the party day. I'll come round at lunchtime while you're at work, with Samira from swimming. She's a whizz at the decor for these kinds of things.'

Brody listened, knowing he wasn't required to answer anyway.

'Your job will be collecting the booze from the wine merchant on your way home from the surgery,' his mother went on. Brody nodded, just so she'd think he was engaged on the subject. 'We can keep it in one of the outhouses until it's time to serve it. You don't have the fridge space anyway. The caterers are loaning us some glasses and china. They said not to worry if anything gets broken because they'll bring spares.'

Brody felt his phone buzz against his thigh. It must have slipped between the cushion and the frame of the chair. His fingers itched. He ought to answer it. It might be urgent, because he was on-call this evening.

His mum looked at him sharply. 'Brody, did you get all that? Are you listening?'

'Yes, I got it all. Six canapés, pick up the booze. Don't worry about breaking anything because it doesn't matter.'

'Well, I wouldn't actively *try* to break anything. It's only

32

that Oliver said not to worry if anyone does have a mishap. Caterers expect that sort of thing.'

Brody grinned. 'Mum, it'll be fine. Don't stress so much. It's only a few drinks for a few friends, not hosting royalty at Downton Abbey.'

She rolled her eyes. 'Don't stress? You can say that because you're not organising a drinks gathering for sixty of Bannerdale's most influential members of the community. I have to stress about it! You can't simply let an event like that happen. You have to be prepared in advance, and check and double-check the details. By the way, do you have enough diesel for the emergency generator, just in case?'

'I think so.'

'*Think* isn't good enough.' His mum scribbled on her clipboard sheet. 'Here, I've added it to your personal list of responsibilities.' She showed it to him. At the top it read: *BRODY: TO DO*. It was underlined and was twice as long as he had imagined. The last item was: *Check toilets are respectable!*

He groaned. 'Oh, Mum, I don't need it . . .'

'I work from a list, so I'm damn sure you do. You can't bumble through life.'

'I don't bumble. I run a busy vet's practice.'

'Correction: Cora Hazeldine runs the practice. You do the . . .' she didn't bother hiding her shudder, 'unpleasant stuff.'

'You mean the unpleasant stuff that keeps animals healthy?'

His mother wrinkled her nose. 'All that stuff involving plastic gloves going where the sun doesn't shine and – the horrible things.'

Brody knew what his mother meant; there were really difficult parts of his job, and the worst was helping animals have a peaceful end to minimise their suffering.

'Mother, the plastic gloves and horrible stuff go with the territory. I can hardly avoid either, if I want to do my best by the animals and their owners.'

'You didn't have to do it. You could have had a nice cushy time running the business, which would have been much more conducive to family life. All these long hours on-call.' She carried on as if she held his career responsible for not having a grandchild yet.

Brody tamed a flare of annoyance into a weary sigh. 'But I didn't *want* to. It didn't appeal to me. I love animals and I want to help them. Uncle Trevor is much better at being a business mogul than I am. I'd never have felt passionate about agricultural machinery, the way he does, and as a result I'd have bankrupted a successful company within six months.'

Brody had been earmarked by his dad to take over McKenna Machinery, even though from a young age he'd shown way more interest in the livestock on the farms than in the tractors and combines and had wanted to study veterinary medicine at university instead of engineering. His father was only just coming round to the idea when he passed away, which made Brody regret that Ralph never got a chance to see what a good vet he made now.

'Hmm.' His mother rested the clipboard in her lap. 'I suppose you're right. Look, I'm sorry if you think I'm nagging you, and it wasn't fair to mention the business. It's a manic time of year and I'm tired and stressed . . .'

'No wonder. Organising this do on top of everything else.' Brody took the clipboard from her and tore off his to-do list, to show willing. 'I really appreciate all the hard work and effort you put in. I know it's going to be a triumph and I won't forget my part of the bargain. I'll check the generator and diesel tonight as soon as you've gone, while I'm feeding the menagerie.'

She raised her eyebrows. 'Are you trying to get rid of me?'

'Would I?' He patted her arm. 'Stay there. I'll make a cup of tea.'

'Just a quick one. I've got a Christmas supper with the wild swimmers this evening and I ought to go home and get changed first.'

'You look great as you are, to me. Is that a new jumper?'

'Ha-ha. I told you I had it the last time I saw you. Maybe I will go straight from here. It's only at the pub – nothing too fancy.'

Brody went into the kitchen and made the tea in a pot for a change. He usually lobbed a bag in any old mug, but tonight he added the teapot, two mugs and a carton of milk to a tray. Just in time he remembered the box of mince pies that a grateful client had made for him, so he put a few on a plate.

His mother was a tour de force and Brody was in constant awe of her, when he wasn't frustrated by her attempts to

35

manage him. On this occasion he had to admit that she was probably right to organise him. Sixty people for drinks and canapés in the farmhouse was a pretty big deal, especially when many of them were community and business leaders who were used to professionally planned events.

The farmhouse was spacious, with several reception rooms, but it could also be cold and draughty, with its low ceilings and panelled walls. However, once it was decorated and the fires were lit, it would feel very homely and a characterful place for entertaining. Even as a child, he'd loved every quirk and dusty corner of it, grateful to still be able to live in his childhood home. Living at Felltop helped him feel closer to his father and perhaps, one day, he might be able to bring up children of his own here.

When he returned from the kitchen, his mother was scrolling through her phone, but put it down on the lamp table as he entered the room. Her eyebrows lifted in shock as he placed the tray on the table. 'Wow, an actual teapot and mince pies! To what do I owe this honour?'

'I know you like things served in the proper way.'

'It's a step up from a chipped mug with an ad for worming tablets on the side and, my word, you've been baking too?'

'Not quite, they were a present from a client. She has a rabbit called Earl Grey, appropriately enough.'

'Earl Grey . . . it makes a change from Peter, I suppose. The mince pies look lovely, but if you don't mind, I'll take one home for tomorrow, because I don't want to spoil my dinner.' His mother sipped her tea. 'Not bad.'

'Thanks.'

She peered around the room over the top of her cup. 'You know, this is a big place for you to rattle around in on your own.'

'I'm not on my own – I have Harold,' Brody insisted wearily, having heard similar comments before and knowing where this was going. 'And to be fair, you did suggest that I should live here instead of you, Mum.' He bit into a mince pie to avoid meeting her eye.

'That was when I thought there'd be you and a family in it,' his mother said, then smiled. 'But let's hope that might be going to change in the not-too-distant future.'

Brody choked, then coughed.

'Are you OK?'

'J-just the mince-pie crumbs,' he said, gulping his tea. He rested his plate on the table. 'I've been thinking . . .' he said, jumping in to change the subject before she could press him any further. 'I don't think you and Samira should take on the job of decorating this place for the party on your own. I want to help.'

'You *do*?' Louise sounded surprised at his sudden enthusiasm.

'Yes, it's not fair on you, and I ought to take responsibility for my own house. Gather some greenery. Light the fires. Hang some tinsel.'

She laughed. 'That's very noble of you. The greenery would be great, thanks. And if you can keep Harold under some vestige of control, that would help.'

At the mention of his name, Harold opened one eye, but

immediately closed it again. He wasn't a fan of mince pies unless they had actual mince in them.

'I'll leave the surgery early and come home to join you,' Brody said, crossing his heart. 'Promise.'

'Thank you, that would be much appreciated.'

She finished her tea and got up. Brody followed her into the hall, Harold trotting after them, his paws clattering on the stone flags.

'I see he's making sure I'm really off the premises,' she said, with a stern glare for their canine security man, and a peck on the cheek for Brody.

'Harold just wants to say goodbye properly,' Brody lied, knowing that the Labrador recognised he'd be able to go outside with Brody as soon their visitor had left and was eager for his evening walk.

'Hmm . . .' She zipped up her puffer coat and collected her scarf from Brody. 'Oh, I almost forgot to mention, I saw Sophie in the village this morning. I had a few words with her while we were queuing in the bakery. She was buying a load of croissants for her guests. She told me she'd been to see you or, rather, her cats had.'

'Yes, it was their annual check-up today.' He shrugged on his old Barbour and a pair of muddy Hunters from inside the porch, deciding that leaving himself would be the only way to get his mother out.

'Hmm, she's a nice girl. Pretty in an English-rose way, and very polite, but also, don't you think, a little bit *odd*?'

Brody decided it was best just to grunt in agreement, even though 'pretty in an English-rose way' implied that

Sophie was some kind of delicate flower, which she very much wasn't. On the contrary, he admired the spark in her green eyes and the courage she'd shown in moving to the Lakes to start a new business. There was surely some story behind that, but he never felt like it was his place to ask.

'"Odd" in what way?' he asked, even though the comment had rankled with him.

'Well, I asked her if she was looking forward to Christmas, and you'd think I'd asked her if she was looking forward to the dentist's. Her face was an absolute picture. Then I remembered she's the one who's been advertising the anti-Christmas holiday . . .'

Brody's heart sank. 'It's not exactly anti-Christmas. I think it's more of an alternative Christmas. From what I've heard,' he added. He didn't want his mother to know that he'd leapt to Sophie's defence, in case she read too much into it, but he'd also corrected one of the local hoteliers who had sneered about Sophie down the pub the other day.

'Whatever it's called,' his mum said. 'Imagine being so against the festive season that you want to spend it with a bunch of strangers who can't stand to see other people enjoying themselves. It really is so sad. I wonder what's happened to that girl to make her so hostile to it all?'

'I've no idea, Mum. She didn't tell me about her tragic past, as you imagine it, while I was sticking a thermometer up her cats' bums this morning.'

'Brody!' Louise cried. 'Do you have to be quite so graphic?'

He grinned, thrilled that his shock tactic had worked. 'Sorry.'

Harold let out a low woof, which Brody knew meant: hurry up and get rid of her, so I can go out for my evening walk.

His mother shook her head. 'You're not sorry at all. Anyway I might see you at the lantern parade, although I've been roped into manning the WI tombola in the church hall, so who knows?' She patted Harold's head. 'Try to stay out of trouble until then.'

'Who? Me or the dog?' Brody quipped, opening the oak front door for her.

'Both of you!' she called back.

He stood on the doorstep, seeing his mum off, with Harold by his side.

'Don't forget the diesel!' she called through the car window. Finally she drove out of the gates to the yard into the sleet.

Brody walked around the side of the farm to the rear outbuildings.

'Come on, let's deal with the "menagerie",' he said to Harold, using the word that his mother had always used to describe his succession of pets and strays over the years.

Anyone would think he owned a full-on zoo, Brody thought wryly as he strode across his cobbled yard, and not simply two sheep and a donkey, all of which he'd acquired by accident in the past couple of years. The Jacob sheep had arrived after a client, who owned a smallholding, had had to go into a nursing home. Their previous owner had died, so Brody had taken on Jackie and Jill, who'd been beloved family pets.

He'd been called out to Gabriel, the donkey, by a local and found the poor creature in a sorry state of neglect by the river, his owner having abandoned him. Now both Gabriel and the sheep seemed to live quite happily together in the field that separated Felltop from Sunnyside, which was just as well. Gabriel had a cosy shelter, created from an old stable block at the end of Brody's cobbled yard. The donkey could wander in whenever he wanted, and the sheep had also been brought in out of the cold. Tonight was definitely a night to keep them all inside, out of this freezing night air.

He tipped some fresh feed in the donkey's manger and filled the sheep's trough with corn.

Even when he'd had a stressful or exhausting day at work, he found it therapeutic to care for his charges. He loved the scent of them, and the connection he felt when stroking or checking them over. He didn't even mind the heavy work or clearing out the stable. OK, mucking out wasn't the most fun, but it kept him warm on a cold day and took him away from worries about the practice and his personal life. Feeding and cleaning out the animals was simple and straightforward, unlike the rest of his life these days.

He stood back, watching the animals eating – having a donkey and two admittedly grown-up lambs in a stable felt very seasonal.

Gabriel started to tuck in. Brody patted his back, feeling the warmth of the animal's body. 'Good lad, Gabe. I don't blame you, staying inside in this weather. I'd be the same.'

Sophie drifted into his mind. What a pity she was so against Christmas.

'So the chances of her coming to the party aren't great, mate,' he said aloud to Gabriel, who carried on eating his dinner. 'And I oughtn't to feel disappointed about that, but I do.'

His voice echoed around the cold stone of the stable. Perhaps his mother was right: he had lived alone for too long at Felltop Farm, if the only conversations he had were with his animals. Yet Brody couldn't see a way of that changing soon.

Chapter Four

A few wispy flakes of snow were falling as Sophie snuggled into the window seat of her sitting room, pulling a fleecy blanket over her legs and holding a mug of hot chocolate. Jingle and Belle had been very reluctant to venture out and spent most of the day curled up in their radiator cradles or on the heated airer in the utility room.

Since her visit to the vet's a few days before she'd been busy, though not as rushed off her feet as during the summer season, when the guest house had been fully booked for weeks on end. The constant changeovers, breakfasts and guests to greet had been exhausting and, in the busiest period, she'd fallen into bed after dark, waking up early at sunrise.

Even though she loved hosting her guests, her first season had been draining. She'd told herself that she'd be fine if she kept busy and was surrounded by people, but she'd often felt quite lonely, especially at first. Gradually, though, without her even noticing, her heart ached less and she found Ben intruding into her thoughts less frequently.

When she did get some free time, she'd head out for long

walks on the fells or for trips into the village, grateful for how things had turned out after all, giving her the chance to live her dream.

The walks were one of the main reasons guests came to stay. In fact she had two rooms currently occupied by couples who were keen walking companions. They'd taken advantage of a clear day to rise before dawn and climb Helvellyn that morning, leaving details of their route with Sophie in case they got into difficulty, as per mountain-rescue advice to all walkers. You couldn't rely on a mobile signal in the mountains, though it was a fine day, so the hill would probably be swarming with walkers and they'd be unlikely to be without help, if they did have an accident.

With the house empty, Sophie allowed herself a short break and wanted to double-check she'd got all her plans in place for her Christmas escapees. Although she had sophisticated booking apps on her laptop and phone, there was always the possibility that the Internet might go down in bad weather. Or the app cease to work. Or both. Years of experience in retail had taught her always to have a back-up plan, and so Sophie was prepared.

She flipped open a notebook with the names, addresses, phone numbers and emails of all her guests, plus any special requests. As this was her first time hosting a 'full board' experience, she was also using the notebook to work out her menus, entertainment and any other requirements. Since advertising the Escape, four of the five rooms were booked, which was one in the eye for the negative people who had doubted she'd get any guests at all.

A few locals had sneered at her ad, mostly owners of other accommodation who'd questioned the wisdom of swimming against the tide of seasonal offerings, particularly in Sophie's first year of running the business, and needing to build repeat guests. Sophie had explained her reasons, taking great pride in telling them that four of the five rooms were already booked. She hoped that she might get another booking in the couple of weeks left before Christmas, so that Sunnyside would be fully occupied. That would be a nice way to finish off her first year.

Sipping her hot chocolate, she read through her notes again, in case she'd missed anything:

Room 1: Amber Smith. From Edinburgh. On her own. Online booking. Requested a quiet room with a view.

Fortunately, she thought, all the rooms had gorgeous views.

Room 2: Una and Hugo Hartley-Brewer. A phone booking. Brummie accents. Address in a Warwickshire village: not that far from Stratford.

Sophie would have something in common with them and it would be a conversation starter, being from a similar part of the world, but there was always the risk of them knowing someone she did. She added a note to herself:

Don't mention the shop, if possible.

45

She'd need to steer the conversation onto other subjects, because the last thing she wanted was to have to explain everything to strangers. Hopefully her guests would be more interested in chatting to each other than to her. They were well aware that the break would be sociable, with a communal Christmas Eve supper and Christmas Day buffet lunch, plus breakfast and supper on Boxing Day.

Sophie was sure she'd be collapsed in her flat by then, but hopefully the guests would be happy, although there was one she was a little worried about:

Room 3: Mrs Agatha Freeman. On her own. Phone booking. Living in Cambridge, so will have a very long journey. Probably desperate to see hills after all those flat fens? Polite but brisk and not inclined to chit-chat. Slightly scary – <u>former headmistress</u>?

Sophie smiled. She rather enjoyed finding out if her expectations of the guests matched the real thing. Sometimes they did, but often she was surprised, and she found it interesting getting to meet people from such varied walks of life.

Room 4. Suzanne Haughton Smith. Another solo traveller. Address in Truro.

Jingle yawned loudly, showing an impressive set of fangs.

Sophie worked her way through the list of food and drink she would need, until her mobile rang and her mother's face popped up on the screen.

'Hello, Mum? Are you OK?'

'Yes. Why wouldn't I be?' her mum asked.

'Only I thought you'd be at work,' Sophie explained, noting that at this time her mother was usually manning reception in the local doctor's surgery.

'I'm using up my holiday and taking a few days off. Are you cleaning rooms?'

'No, I'm planning what holiday food' – she almost said 'Christmas' – 'to get for the guests.'

Her mum sighed. 'You should be the one who's pampered at Christmas, not your guests. You need to sit back and relax and let someone else wait on you, after the year you've had.'

Sophie prepared for battle. 'I don't want all that fuss, Mum. I can't face it. I've explained already.'

'I know, love, but your dad and I are worried about you,' her mum said softly.

'Don't be. I'm spending Christmas exactly how I want to: by not having one.'

'Is it a good idea to avoid it?'

Sophie briefly glanced out of her window, with the snow-topped mountains beyond. She found it calming to look at them.

'I promise I'm not avoiding it, just spending it in a different way. I want to keep busy and it should be fun. We're having a paella on Christmas Day and flamenco dancing on

47

Christmas Eve, plus I'll see you before the New Year. I'm looking forward to seeing you all and catching up with Lyra and some of my other friends, if they're around.'

'Well, if you change your mind, love, you know where we are.'

'I won't change my mind, Mum. I can't change it, because I'll have a full house of guests. But I promise I'll call you later in the day,' Sophie assured her.

'Can we send you photos? Rob and Fliss are bringing the new baby. You'll miss seeing him.'

A lump formed in Sophie's throat. Oh no, she might cry. Reminding her that her new nephew was joining them for Christmas was a cruel blow. She loved her brother and his growing family, but she didn't want her family feeling sorry for her.

As they spoke, Belle stretched and deftly made her way along various pieces of furniture to the window seat. She sat at one end, watching Sophie with narrowed golden eyes. Sophie reached out and stroked the cat's fur.

'Sophie?' Her mum said gently. 'Are you OK?'

'Y-yes. I'm fine.' She blinked back tears. 'Look, I'll be back for a longer visit in the New Year and we can all get together and have a lovely lunch and I can see Alfie then.'

'OK. I'll arrange it now. I'll cook a—'

'Not turkey, Mum, please!'

'I was going to say I'll cook that nice mushroom-and-Stilton puff-pastry thing you all like.'

'Of course, then you don't have to make something separate for Fliss. I should get back to things, but I'll speak to you soon,' she promised, then hung up after they'd said their goodbyes.

Her mum mentioning cooking reminded Sophie of how much she had on her own plate. She took a deep breath to calm herself down, telling herself that she'd chosen this path, this place, she was in control and she could do this.

After the call ended, Sophie went to check that the cats weren't in the guest areas. Vee had finished the changeovers and taken the dirty linen to the laundry, and the dishwasher was churning away. All was right with the world – apart from the fact that Sophie still hadn't responded to Brody's invitation.

Next she headed for the office to deal with the admin. The answerphone was flashing, which was pretty unusual these days. Most of her bookings came from her website and from booking agencies, but some guests still liked to phone to ask questions about the rooms and facilities and to get a better feel for her as an owner.

She listened to the message before she could tackle her emails.

'Hello.' A softly spoken man with a slightly unusual accent that she couldn't place greeted her. One moment he sounded pure North London, the next pure Rome. 'Do you still have a room available for the Christmas break? I mean, the "*Escape* for Christmas" break. Oh, yeah. My name's – it's Nico Lombardi.' He left his number, speaking so quickly that Sophie could barely understand it.

Luckily her telephone-message deciphering skills had

been honed over years of running the shop and working out garbled messages from all over the world, demanding 'bare-bottom baubles' (flat-bottomed, it turned out) and 'hairy tinsel'.

Sophie called him straight back.

'Nico,' he barked, sounding agitated.

'Mr Lombardi. It's Sophie Cranford from Sunnyside Guest House in the Lake District. You left me a message?'

'Did I? Oh yeah. Sorry. Work is hectic.' A warmth crept into his voice, realising who was calling. 'Yes, am I too late? I bet I'm too late. I tried to get on the website at work – not that I should – but the Internet went down. IT are fixing it. Nightmare!'

'I bet,' said Sophie patiently.

'Anyway, I need to get away. From Christmas, I mean. And I saw this when I googled alternative Christmas breaks,' he explained, talking as quickly as he did on his phone message.

'You're in luck. We do still have one room available, though I have someone else interested in it,' Sophie replied, crossing her fingers that he'd confirm because of her little white lie.

'Brilliant. I'll have it.'

'I'd need to take full payment now,' she told him.

'Great, happy to pay now. I don't care.'

'Oh, OK.' She'd never known a guest show such enthusiasm for parting with their cash. It seemed too good to be true. In fact . . . 'Before I take your booking, you're aware that this isn't a traditional Christmas break?' she said firmly, so that Nico couldn't interrupt or dash off. 'We're providing food and entertainment from Christmas Eve until after breakfast on 27 December, but the . . . celebrations will be *very* different from the usual. Just in case you were expecting turkey and carols. The details are on the website, in case you want to have a look when the Internet is back up and then ring me again?'

'I don't care if you're sending us all out to build our own igloos and hunt a seal for lunch,' Nico insisted. 'I need to book somewhere for Christmas and *fast*.'

That sounded a bit odd, but if he was happy to pay up front, then a booking was a booking.

'Right . . . well, I would have to insist on full payment in case you cancelled at such short notice.'

'I won't cancel. I've got my card ready, if we can do that now,' Nico said hurriedly.

'Of course,' she replied brightly.

Sophie took the card details and sent him a confirmatory email, which he'd hopefully receive when his Wi-Fi was working again.

She added him to her online booking system – and to her notebook too:

> *Room 5. Nico Lombardi. Italian? Not quite sure why he's coming?*

Her guests' personal lives were none of her business, even if some of them seemed intent on making it so. She'd joked to Vee that she could make a good living as a blackmailer if the B&B failed. But with every month that had a good occupancy rate, those worries were pushed to the back of her mind.

Now that all the rooms were full, she could finalise her plans. She fired off an email to the flamenco troupe to make sure they were still coming, ordered an extra delivery of logs for the fire and made a start on the special welcome gift-packs for the guests' rooms.

This Escape had to be a success. She'd staked so much on it and was determined to prove to everyone that she wasn't the only person in the world who wanted to move away from the traditional Christmas, with all of its associations.

Sophie was also beginning to realise that she could be successful on her own, and one day would be able to achieve her other dreams too, like starting a family.

From now on, she should try to focus on the future and all the things she'd achieved in her new home. In the short term, that meant deciding whether to go to Brody's party. After all, he had been sympathetic to her need to move away from a traditional Christmas, and he seemed a decent guy. Perhaps he really was one of the good ones.

While Sophie wasn't sure she could face too much festive bonhomie, she didn't want to let him down. After all, Brody had said she'd be doing him a favour . . .

Chapter Five

Brody drummed his fingers on the Defender's steering wheel. It was mid-afternoon, but already going dark. He'd been called out to attend a difficult birth of a foal at a remote farm. Mother and baby were now doing well, but the call-out had gone on for longer than he'd expected and he was now on his way back to the surgery.

McKenna's was a mixed practice, and Brody was proud that it was still independent. As clinical director, he led a small team of three veterinary surgeons supported by five vet nurses, two receptionists and two animal care assistants. While he might technically be the 'boss', he always mucked in with everyone else. He loved the variety of his job and the fact that one day he might be vaccinating lambs, and the next treating a guinea pig's ear infection.

Today, as he was driving back, he felt drained. Yes, the foal birth had gone well, but earlier he'd had to give a peaceful end to a lovely old dog, a 'Heinz 57', as his owner had called him, a mix of Jack Russell and indeterminate parentage. At fifteen, the old chap had done very well and had lived a good life with his doting owner, but he had a large untreatable tumour. Brody knew it was the right thing to do, but that part of the job never got any easier. In fact since he'd had Harold, who was now four, Brody had found this aspect even harder. He'd also felt bad that the practice was decorated for Christmas and music was playing in the waiting room as he'd escorted the owner to his car.

Life could be cruel, and there was no getting away from it. Maybe Sophie was onto something, because not everyone wanted festive merriment shoved down their throats all the time. The foal birth should have lifted his spirits and reminded him of the cycle of life, but as the dusk descended on this shortest day of the year, he felt gloomy. Normally he loved the lantern parade, but for once he was in no mood for it today. Other problems were also weighing on his mind and they weren't going to go away, either.

Finally he reached the outskirts of the village, where every cottage and guest house was lit up or had a twinkling tree in the window, ready for the spectacle to begin. He was beginning to think he might make the parade after all, when red lights ahead forced him to brake and he ground to a halt.

The opposite side of the road was already closed off, but he was trapped in the long queue of traffic, which was moving forward at a snail's pace, as visitors descended in their droves and tried to find spaces in the car parks. When the queue ground to a complete halt next to a small trading estate, Brody feared there was now gridlock in the village. He was venting his frustration with a few choice words when he looked out of his window and noticed a pickup truck in the car park at the entrance to the trading estate.

Sophie's vehicle was parked – or, more accurately, stuck with a flat tyre – outside the laundry that served the local hotels and holiday cottages. Sophie was standing there, scrolling through her phone. Brody made a snap decision, turning out of the queue and into the laundry's car park.

He got out of the car and walked briskly over to her. 'You OK? Is there anything I can do to help?'

She glanced up, clearly taken aback. Her nose was red at the tip, as if she'd been standing outside for a long time. Even so, he thought she still looked great, though now was clearly not the time to mention such a thing. Even if he'd dared.

'If you mean can you help me change the wheel, that would have been great, but unfortunately it's not as simple as that.' She nodded at the truck's twisted wheel rim. 'I hit a huge pothole in the lane, and I think it must have wrecked the actual wheel frame. I've spoken to the local garage, but they can't get to me while the lantern parade is going on and the village is gridlocked.'

'Hmm. No one's going anywhere for a while, I'm afraid.'

Sophie put her phone in her pocket. 'A long while, in my case. The garage isn't sure it will be able to reach me until tomorrow now. Both their tow-trucks are out and I'm not part of a rescue service. Ha-ha, I decided to save my money, but that doesn't seem to have done me any good.'

'Bummer,' said Brody, torn between offering to help and not trying to interfere. 'Do you mind leaving the truck here tonight? I guess you'll need to get home somehow?'

She shook her head. 'You don't have to. I was just going to call a taxi. Hopefully my phone battery will hold out,' she protested.

'I'm not going to leave you alone here, standing out-side in the cold. Come with me to the surgery – we can wait there, warming up with a hot drink, and I have a phone charger lying around somewhere,' he said, coming up with a good plan.

'I don't want to ruin your evening. Aren't you supposed to be going to the parade?' Sophie said, seeming hesitant.

'I was. I still *am*, hopefully. I arranged to meet some of the staff from work there, but I'm running late.'

'Oh. I – I don't want to spoil your evening or be in the way.'

'Of the patients?' he joked. 'I shouldn't think they'll com-plain, as long as you don't mind a few yappy dogs and vocal cats. We have a couple of convalescents staying overnight, you see.'

'I don't mind. Where's Harold?'

'I came straight from a call-out, but it's better he's left at home tonight. He'd be too excited by all the people and other dogs. Shall we go? These queues will only get worse. Bloody Christmas, eh? Always comes at the most inconveni-ent time of year.'

'It's not funny,' Sophie replied, yet she was smiling as she said it. 'OK, thanks for the offer.'

She climbed into Brody's Defender and fastened her seatbelt. 'How are you going to reach the surgery? It's gridlocked.'

'Oh, I'll think of something,' he said, feeling far less con-fident than he sounded.

The car crawled a few more yards. Sophie was explaining

that she'd been on her way to the laundry to pick up the linen for her Christmas guests when she'd hit the pothole.

'Something felt wrong, but I thought it was better to get down the hill rather than block the lane. By the time I reached the laundry, I realised the wheel was completely shot.'

'These potholes are a nightmare,' Brody mumbled, distracted as he spotted a tall, willowy figure in a hi-vis jacket making his way up the line of traffic. He opened the window and hailed the man. 'Hey, Carl!'

Carl jogged up to the window. 'Well, hello, stranger. You're cutting it fine for the parade.'

'I was on midwife duties to a mare up at High Top,' Brody replied.

Carl grinned. 'Lucky you. Are you hoping to reach the surgery?'

'Well, I *was* . . . though it's not looking very promising.'

'How would you like it if I waved my magic wand and made it possible?' Carl joked.

'I'd be very grateful if you could.'

'Then your wish is my command!' he declared. 'Wait a second.' He strode off.

'Thanks, mate.'

'Who's that?' Sophie was intrigued.

'That's Carl, he's my best mate. Have you not met him? He runs the Magpie gift shop next to the bank in Bannerdale.'

'Ah, of course. How did I not recognise him?' Sophie responded, 'though the Santa hat threw me.'

'Yeah, it makes him look even taller,' Brody said, amused.

His mood had definitely improved in the five minutes since he'd picked up Sophie.

Carl was six and half feet tall and cut an imposing figure wherever he went. He also got things done. He jogged back, shifted a few cones and beckoned Brody onto the closed side of the road.

'Thanks. I owe you one,' Brody said with a grin, noting the glares of the queuing motorists.

'I'll remember that. See you later maybe, though I'm on bloody traffic duty until it starts.'

'We'll have to catch-up properly over Christmas.'

'I'd have thought you'd have been otherwise engaged,' Carl said with a smirk, before having to stop a BMW that was trying to edge around the barrier. 'No, my friend, you can't drive up here. It's officials only.'

Relieved that he didn't have to answer Carl's remark, or wait in the queue, Brody drove up the coned-off road and turned into the car park behind the surgery. The lights were on because two of the vet nurses were on late duty.

'Come in,' he gestured to Sophie, punching his code into the rear door. He ushered her ahead.

Her green eyes became wide and he saw her briefly wrinkle her nose. It was slightly less red now, though her eyes were still as gorgeous.

'That's the delightful aroma of guinea pig,' said Brody. 'We have one in, after a small op.'

She looked around, eyes like saucers. 'I've never been behind the scenes. Is that a *snake*?'

'Yes,' Brody went towards the cage. 'Sir Hiss has had stomatitis. It's a mouth infection.'

'That sounds nasty. Poor Sir Hiss. Will he be OK?'

'Yes, with the help of antibiotics, he's on the mend. He's a lovely chap. I'd get him out and introduce you properly, but he's resting now.'

'Erm, he's very ... handsome – but I think I'll stick to cats,' she whispered and quickly moved away.

Brody swallowed. He was thinking of an excuse to get out of the parade and stay with her. He probably shouldn't have invited her into the practice, but how could he have left her in the dark, cold night, trapped in a laundry car park on the outskirts of the village? He would have done the same for anybody he knew.

One of the animal care assistants walked into the recovery area.

'Oh, hello,' she said, clearly surprised to see Brody there, and with a client who didn't appear to have a pet with her.

'Hi,' Sophie said cheerfully.

'Sophie's car broke down. She's going to wait here until the parade's over and she can get a lift home,' he replied, knowing the nurse would be wondering why he'd brought a client into the staff area.

'OK ...' the nurse smiled again, before attending to one of the cages.

'Here's the staffroom,' he said, enjoying Sophie's reactions to his place of work. It was so familiar to him, but it must seem strange to a lay person, and he felt proud of the practice he'd managed to build up here. 'Please, help yourself to coffee. I'm just going to get changed.'

Brody was keen to get out of the old cords and sweatshirt he'd been wearing all day. He freshened up in the Gents, then half gassed himself with body spray before changing into the spare jeans and jumper that he always kept in his locker.

Through the open window, he could hear the sounds of Christmas music and a Tannoy. He glanced at his watch. The parade would be starting soon.

When he returned, Sophie was perched on a stool in the staffroom, sipping a coffee. 'I wasn't sure if you wanted one, but I made you one anyway.'

'Thanks,' said Brody, realising he'd have to make it a quick drink, because he'd had a message from some of the other staff asking where he was. 'I – um – hope you don't mind, but I have to go. I won't be more than an hour.'

Sophie put down her mug in horror. 'Oh no, please don't rush on my account,' she insisted, her cheeks flushing at the thought of causing him any trouble.

'I don't want to leave you hanging around here. You must have so much to do before your . . .' he almost said 'Christmas', but checked himself in time, 'before your next guests arrive.'

She smiled. 'Thanks, but I'll be fine. In fact when my phone has charged up, I can call a taxi.'

'OK. If you want to, but it's no trouble. You know,' he took a breath, attempting a very long shot, 'you could always come to the lantern parade with me?'

Sophie stared at him as if he'd suggested jumping naked into the lake together.

'OK. Probably a terrible idea. Forget I said it,' he mumbled, feeling like an idiot for bringing it up.

'No. I can't. I mean, it's not a *terrible* idea,' she said. 'If I'm honest, Vee had already invited me and I'd turned her down, because I thought I'd be busy preparing for the guests; but if I'm already stuck, it seems silly to sit in here on my own.'

'Well, I'm not the best company, but hopefully we can have a better time out there together than you would have in here with Sir Hiss, the guinea pig and a castrated pug.'

Sophie grinned. 'Well, the bar was set high, so it's a lot of pressure on you. As long as you know what you're getting yourself into.'

If only . . . Brody thought to himself. 'Let's go. The parade has already left the community hall and will be coming past in ten minutes.'

A few moments later they were weaving through the crowds in the street, already jammed with locals and visitors. Brody instantly had goosebumps. The whole village was buzzing with excitement and anticipation. Little ones sat on their dads' shoulders, while older kids and adults were bedecked in LED glow-necklaces. The aroma of hot food and mulled wine made his stomach rumble. He hadn't had dinner yet.

His stomach growled again. 'Have you eaten?' he asked Sophie.

'I grabbed a stale croissant for lunch,' she said. 'But that seems ages ago. I'm starving.'

'Me too.' He nodded at a stall set up in front of the local bakery a few yards away along the street. 'Fancy a hot dog? There's just time before the parade starts.'

'Won't your friends be looking for you?'

'There's no chance of finding them in these crowds. We've arranged to at outside the Red Lion after the parade passes by.'

'Well, in that case, my treat. It's the least I can do.' Sophie wandered over to the stall.

'Thanks.' Brody grinned when she handed him a hot dog loaded with spiced Cumberland sausage and onion relish.

Sophie licked her lips. 'This is the best hot dog I've ever had.'

It was also the best one Brody had ever eaten, even better than they'd tasted when he was a kid. Sophie seemed OK so far. Despite what she'd said about 'finding a gap in the market' as motivation for her 'Escape for Christmas', he wasn't sure he was hearing the whole story. This evening could be the ideal opportunity to find out more about her.

Chapter Six

It never ceased to amaze Brody how popular a parade of people carrying lanterns on sticks was, even in an age of hyperreal computer games, blockbuster movies and AI.

In the past ten minutes more and more people had crowded onto the pavements, almost spilling into the roadway. Fortunately, the marshals made sure there was space for the parade to get through.

'I'd really no idea the event was so huge,' Sophie said, in between bites

'Oh yes. It's one of the biggest days of the year for Bannerdale, if not *the* biggest. Everyone looks forward to it and I always loved it, growing up. My dad was a fire marshal and Mum used to help at the community hall, with the lantern workshops.' Brody gave a thought to his mother and her tombola and smiled. She'd run it for years, and the parade had given them both so many happy memories.

'So you took part when you were young?' she asked.

'Of course. I was a kid once, you know.'

Her eyes sparkled with mischief. 'Actually, that's easy to imagine.'

'Some would say I've never grown up. Although I was always a bit alternative. While most of the kids made bells, stars and angels, I had to be different. One year I made an owl, and another time I constructed a shark.'

'A shark? Very festive!'

'I thought it was cool. At the time.' At Sophie's amused smile, Brody grinned. 'Another time I made a Herdwick sheep and a rabbit. My final creation was an octopus, which took ages. The workshop leader was fuming because it needed so much willow engineering to help it stay up. He thought it was a liability because, in those days, the lanterns had real tea lights in them.'

'Very impressive,' Sophie said.

'See, we've got more in common than you think. I was doing my own unconventional Christmas celebrations, before you,' he joked and she laughed.

Brody noticed a smudge of ketchup at the side of Sophie's lips from the hot dog. He agonised over whether to mention it, then decided that Sophie was the kind of person who would appreciate honesty. Along with that thought came a large side-order of guilt.

'What's the matter?' she asked, clearly sensing him staring at her.

Brody parked the troublesome pang at the corner of his mind. 'Nothing, except you have ketchup on your mouth.'

'Do I?' She screwed up her nose in embarrassment and started to rub her lips with her finger. 'Has it gone?' she asked.

Resisting the urge to wipe away the remaining trace himself, he said, 'Almost, just a bit – um, there.' He pointed his finger as close as he dared to her cheek.

She rubbed the last smear away. 'Gone now?'

'Yes,' he replied, rather disappointed to surrender his excuse to look at her.

Sophie glanced away, perhaps aware that he'd held her gaze a little too long. 'It's started,' she murmured.

Excitement rippled through the crowds, and people turned almost as one to look down the street to where a glow of waving lights was now visible. A shiver of anticipation ran down Brody's spine, no different to when he was young.

'They're coming,' he said, unable to keep the excitement from his voice. It was one of his favourite traditions and he'd barely missed any parades, apart from when he'd become a teenager and it wasn't cool to take part. He'd secretly missed making his lantern and joining the procession with his friends. Even when he'd been away at Edinburgh, studying to be a vet, he'd always come home in time to watch the procession.

Sophie nodded by his side. Her lips were pressed together in uncertainty, and the relaxed fun of the past half-hour had suddenly ebbed away. Was this actually quite an ordeal for her and she was trying to hide how she really felt about being plunged into the thick of the festivities?

Suddenly a hush descended on the crowd as the first of the children walked by, carrying home-made lanterns attached to poles. It brought a lump to Brody's throat to watch the families bearing the lanterns they'd worked so hard to make through the streets of the village. Seeing them reminded him of the special memories he'd shared with his own dad over the years here. Since losing him, the parade had taken on a new poignancy, and this time of year always made you think more about those who were no longer here.

Sophie turned to him, her eyes glistening with unshed tears. 'I'd no idea it was this touching.'

He must have a piece of grit in his own eye . . . He must find his mum for a word, if he could. She'd be bound to have her own memories, even if she'd keep them to herself.

'Oh, look, that's Vee's two! They look so cute.'

The two children, a boy of four and a girl of six, carried lanterns in the shape of a star and a bell. Their mother, whom Brody recognised but didn't know well, was beside them, keeping an eye on them. A few of the tinier children were being carried on parents' shoulders or were holding hands with an older sibling.

But sweet as the children were, Brody couldn't help stealing a look at Sophie. Her smile had melted away, her lips were pressed together and her eyes were glistening.

'Are you OK?' he asked.

'Yes. Yes, I just . . .' She hesitated. 'Seeing all the children – I'm being silly.'

'No, you're not. It makes me emotional, and always brings up memories of being here with my dad and makes me miss him.'

'Oh, I'm sorry. It's a difficult time of year for so many, isn't it, and you can't help but think how things have changed? But it's so nice to see everyone. It's just the kids – they're all so wide-eyed and innocent. It's great to see them enjoying Christmas with such pure pleasure. It must be wonderful to help the children make the lanterns, and to join the parade with them.'

Brody had sensed there was a wistfulness about Sophie, a sadness hidden under a mask of practical cheerfulness, which she'd probably hidden for a long time. He'd worn that mask himself, after his father had died and he was trying to fit in at university as a student. Even while he'd been drinking and laughing, he was still grieving the loss of his dad.

People wore masks all the time, for different reasons. He hoped he hadn't put Sophie in a difficult position by inviting her along, as he didn't want to upset her. Should he even have suggested that she come with him?

'Do you want me to take you home?' he asked as the last of the children went by, their lanterns swinging in the darkness. People were starting to disperse.

'No. No, I'm *fine*,' she insisted, her defences back in place. 'And I'm glad I didn't miss it. Thank you for bringing me along.'

Brody heaved a silent sigh of relief, even if he knew Sophie was putting on a front. He didn't want her to leave yet. 'I'm pleased you decided to give it a try, even if you had to lose a wheel in the process.'

'Honestly, I did almost stay in with Sir Hiss,' she said.

'Tough call: me or Sir Hiss,' he replied. Before he could say anything else, Brody heard his name being shouted and spotted his friends. 'Er, I think I can see some of the practice team over there.' He spoke more gruffly than he'd intended.

'Oh, I—'

'D'you still fancy a quick drink before we go home?' he asked. 'You probably know a couple of them already. There's Rudolph, aka Cora, and some of the vet nurses. Carl's on marshalling duty, but he might join us later.'

'I'd like to . . .' she began, but they were interrupted by Vee bounding up.

'Sophie!' Vee tapped her on the shoulder. 'You're the last person I expected to see here!'

'I didn't plan to be,' Sophie said hastily. 'The wheel on the truck's damaged, and I was stuck at the laundry. Brody was passing and gave me a lift.'

'That was lucky then. He's like me – Christmas-obsessed – so I can see how he charmed you into coming.'

'I wouldn't say "obsessed",' Brody began, trying to sound amused.

'You've never missed a parade,' Vee said. 'Kev told me you used to come home for it from uni, when everyone else stayed there partying and drinking, like normal students.'

'Dad died only a couple of months after I'd finished my A-levels, so I thought I should come home for the parade at Christmas, to keep Mum company,' Brody replied.

'And that was a really lovely thing to do. I was only joking,' Vee said kindly. 'Look, we're going to the Banner-dale Bakery Café, if you both want to drop by later. They're open late for hot chocolates and reindeer cookies.'

'I hope there's no reindeer in them,' Brody said.

Vee and Sophie burst out laughing before Sophie said, 'I'll see you later.'

'Thanks for the offer, but I'm meeting Carl and some mates at the pub,' Brody replied.

'Lucky you. It's strictly soft stuff for us this evening,' Vee said, walking off with an eye-roll, trying to explain to the kids that hot punch didn't have anything to do with bashing people.

'Kids, eh?' Brody said. 'I'm joking. It's great to see them enjoying the parade.'

'Yeah. They're a handful, but Vee and Kev are so good with them. They're marvellous parents.'

'I can see that. I always wonder how people manage working full-time and bringing up a family,' Brody said.

'You find a way, I suppose. It's one reason Vee and I clicked. She stays longer than she has to, if I need extra help, and I'm more than happy to fit in with her childcare. I still haven't forgotten the time the village school closed because of floods and her kids came up to Sunnyside and "helped", which meant they tried to dust the cats.'

Brody roared. 'Ouch! Sounds like fun,' he said, imagining the scene and enjoying how the memory had infused Sophie's expression with happiness. It was as if her own lantern had been kindled. And he realised, by the high that he was riding, so had his.

'They ran off and didn't come back until kibble time, but we had a great day.'

'I bet. I must admit that when young pet owners come into the surgery, it can be an extra-special challenge. It's rewarding to see the kids learning about their pets and caring for them, but it can be heartbreaking too when the animals get ill.'

'I'd never thought of that.'

'It's part of the job,' he said, recalling his experience earlier that afternoon. He wouldn't mention that now. It would burst the bubble they'd created: a glorious, yet fragile orb of connection. But he had to get one thing straight while he had the chance.

'You know what Vee said just now,' he said. 'I'm not actually Christmas-obsessed. I can see why people – many people – might want to forget about it. Families, life, relationships . . . are complicated, and I've sometimes thought of skipping the whole thing myself, so I hope I didn't make you feel uncomfortable by bringing you along this evening.'

Sophie frowned.

'Brody, firstly, you didn't force me. I didn't have to get in your car. I didn't have to leave the surgery. I could have stayed with Sir Hiss. I could have found Vee and hung out with her. I chose to come out here with you and I really enjoyed myself. I have loved . . . seeing how much joy Christmas brings to everyone here. And don't feel bad about liking Christmas,' she said. 'I used to love it myself. Once.'

Once? The word seemed to hang in the air between them, like the key to unlocking a door that Sophie had closed on her previous life.

'Brody! You made it. I'd given up on you, frankly. You're so disorganised,' Cora suddenly shouted.

'Thank you,' Brody replied, not feeling grateful towards his practice manager, who had borne down on him with half a dozen more of his colleagues.

'You had us worried for a moment,' one of the animal assistants declared. 'Thought it would be the first time you missed it.'

'No way,' Brody said firmly.

'More importantly, how did the foal birth go?' Cora asked solemnly.

'Mum and foal were both doing well when I left.'

Having dealt with her boss, Cora lasered in on Sophie. 'Oh, hello – Sophie Cranford, isn't it?'

'Yes . . .' Sophie replied. 'Cora, isn't it?'

Cora's eyebrows shot into her hairline. 'You know my name?'

'Of course,' Sophie said pleasantly.

Brody became a bystander now that Cora was in full swing.

'Don't you run the anti-Christmas hotel? Shouldn't have thought this was your thing.'

'It's not anti-Christmas. I'm just offering an alternative festive celebration, catering for people who want something different.'

'You're Jingle and Belle's mum, aren't you?' one of the vet nurses put in, with a smile. Brody silently thanked her for rescuing Sophie from Cora's blunt attentions. 'They're such gorgeous cats. I love their fluffy little faces.'

Another nurse jumped in, and Brody was silently grateful they'd changed the subject.

'Thanks. They have their moments, but I love them too,' Sophie replied.

'Why are your cats named after a Christmas song?' Cora began, but Brody leapt in.

'Shall we go to the pub?' he suggested, to enthusiastic mumblings of agreement. 'I'll be with you in a second,' he went on, waiting for Cora and the others to head across the road to the pub. 'I'm sorry Cora gave you the third degree,' Brody said to Sophie. 'She's a very efficient practice manager, but she can be spiky.'

'It's fine. I can stick up for myself, Brody,' Sophie insisted, although now a silence stretched between them. 'Um, it's really kind of you to invite me to the pub, but I think I can see Vee over there with the kids. She really wanted me to come and, now that I have, I feel I ought to spend some time with her and the family.'

Brody's festive spirit went down the drain. He'd been so looking forward to spending more time with her.

'OK,' he said, with a smile that he hoped treaded a fine line between disappointment and polite acquiescence. 'The offer of a lift still stands, though. As I'm heading in your direction.

She nodded. 'Thanks, and I might still need one, even if Vee offers. Felltop is a bit out of her way, but she might relish the chance to get out of bath and bedtime for once.'

'Oh. OK, you've got my mobile number?' he offered.

'Actually I don't have your number. Just the surgery one,' Sophie realised. Normally they'd bumped into each other on walks or near their respective houses.

'Right. OK. Of course.' Until this evening, Brody realised, they'd only been neighbours. Tonight they were friends . . .

A few moments later they'd exchanged numbers and Sophie was making her way over to Vee and her family. Brody watched them embrace, before he trudged up the steps into the pub. It was then that he remembered Sophie still hadn't said whether or not she'd be coming to the party. And, his conscience whispered, perhaps he shouldn't want her to.

Chapter Seven

'Thanks for the lift,' Sophie said as Brody dropped her off outside the house. The full moon was shining through a break in the clouds, revealing snow on the high fells and the silvery lake down below in the valley.

'You're welcome. Oh, and if you need a lift back to your car tomorrow, I'm going down there around seven-thirty, if that's not too early?'

'I'll need to get the car towed first thing, so that would be a help.'

'OK.' He seemed about to ask her something else. 'See you in the morning then.'

She'd had such a great evening. Brody was not only handsome, but was a nice guy – just the type she didn't think was out there, after the heartbreak she'd gone through. Tonight had proved that not only could she get through a festive event, but she could enjoy herself. 'Oh and, Brody, I will try to pop in for the party. For a short time. If that's OK?'

'It's more than OK. It would be good to see you there.'

He grinned before driving off with a final wave. It was much colder up on the fellside than in town and Sophie hurried towards the house. After the bright lights, festivities and crowds at the parade – and the company – the isolation struck her for the first time.

When she opened the door, two pairs of yellow eyes glowed in a shaft of moonlight that spilled into the hall. A flick of a switch and she blinked in the bright hall pendant light, while the cats wound themselves around her legs.

She bent to stroke them and Jingle miaowed in protest at Sophie for daring to be out of the house for so long, while Belle slipped away from her caress, turning tail as her way of showing disapproval for their mum spending a rare evening out.

'You two! I couldn't help being late back tonight. I'll get your dinner now,' she said, feeling guilty that she'd been unable to feed them their evening kibble while she'd been enjoying her hot dog at the parade. The memory of Vee's excited kids and Brody's company rekindled a warm glow that combated the chilly embrace of the house. She'd enjoyed the evening way more than she'd expected. Was it possible that a teeny part of her still had room in her heart for some seasonal jollity?

The kitchen was warm from the Aga as she poured kibble into the cat bowls and then turned her attention to the answerphone, which was beeping from her office. There were two messages.

The first was from Lyra, whom Sophie rang back and they arranged to meet up when Sophie went back to Stratford in between Christmas and New Year.

'How's the "Escape for Christmas" break going?' Lyra asked. 'Hold on! I need to shut the office door. Two of the guests are a bit pissed and are murdering carols in the reception area. I can't be arsed to sort them out yet.'

Sophie laughed. She'd already had to deal with the odd 'merry' guest. 'It's all pretty good. In fact I'm now fully booked.'

'Awesome! I'm made up for you. I think it's a brilliant idea, and I might steal it next year if you don't mind.'

'Of course I don't mind. You've helped me so much.'

Lyra chuckled. 'All I've done is offer unsolicited advice. Now tell me more about your plans.'

After twenty minutes they ended the conversation, with Sophie feeling buoyant after a nice evening out, followed by a good chat with her old friend. She couldn't wait to catch up in person after Christmas.

She turned her attention to the next message, which was from her mother, saying that she couldn't reach Sophie on her mobile and asking her to call when she had a chance. Her mum must have phoned when Sophie's battery was flat at the laundry.

Sophie curled up on her sitting-room sofa and called her mum on WhatsApp and waited for her to appear.

'Oh, Sophie! Hold on, I'll fetch Dad. He's in the garage again,' her mother said impatiently. 'Hold on.'

Sophie sighed. It was always the same; she had to wait for them both to squash up on the sofa, so they could all see and hear each other. Yet seeing them gave her a warm glow, all the same. They'd been a major support to her during the split and afterwards, and she knew they missed and worried about her, even if she was thirty-four and a business owner.

'Hello, love.' Her father squeezed into the shot, next to her mum.

'We couldn't get you earlier.' Her mother sounded worried for a moment.

'Sorry, my car broke down while I was at the laundrette and my phone battery was flat, but my neighbour picked me up. Then we were stuck in Bannerdale during the lantern parade, which closes the roads, and I've only just got home.'

'Boo to the truck, but hurrah for your neighbour,' her mum said.

'Were you actually at this lantern parade?' her father asked.

'Yes. It's a tradition in the village. The children walk through the streets carrying home-made willow lanterns. Vee's family were there too.'

'It sounds lovely,' her mother said. 'And very Christmassy . . .'

'It is,' Sophie said, as her parents exchanged glances of amazement that she'd attended such a festive celebration.

'I'm glad you had a good time, and I'm sorry about the truck,' her father said. 'What's wrong with it?'

'I hit a huge pothole and the wheel buckled. My neighbour's giving me a lift back into town tomorrow, and the garage will sort it out once they're able to tow it.'

'I hope they do it before Christmas,' her mum said.

'So do I, because I'm expecting a full house of guests.'

Sophie crossed her fingers, because she'd be in trouble if her pickup was off the road for more than a day. She'd have to hire a replacement, which would cost a bomb, *if* there was a vehicle available in the holiday season. 'The local garage is good. They'll fix it as a priority, I'm sure.' She sounded way more confident than she felt. 'So how are you?' she asked. 'Everything OK?'

Again her parents looked at each other in a way that made Sophie worry there was something going on.

'Yes. Everything is fine. We're all fine, as are your brother and the kids.'

'But . . .' Sophie murmured, sensing there was something they weren't telling her.

'We've agonised over this. I don't want to spoil your Christmas – or your festivities – especially when it sounds like you've had such a lovely evening.'

Her heart raced. 'What is it, Mum?'

'I'm not sure I should say now – I don't want to spoil things and upset you. It's so nice seeing you more like your old self again,' her mum said.

'I'll be fine, but you have to tell me now. I'll be more worried if you don't,' Sophie persuaded her.

Her mum took a deep breath. 'It's Ben and Naomi. They're expecting a baby.'

Sophie's jaw hit the floor and her stomach churned. 'Expecting whose baby?' she said, slightly hysterically. 'Is Santa delivering it? Or the postman?'

'Ben's baby. Well, hers. I assume it's his. Oh, Sophie. We

were worried you'd react like this. I'm sorry. We shouldn't have told you until after Christmas.'

Sophie felt icy cold and a bit sick, but most of all she was angry with herself for feeling anything at all, as far as Ben was concerned.

'No. You did the right thing,' she replied, her stomach churning.

Her mother held her father's hand. 'I'm sorry I've upset you. Dad told me to wait until after Christmas, but I was worried you'd see what Ben's up to online and that he'd post about the baby, or that one of your old mates would tell you.'

'I try not to see Ben online,' Sophie said, still trying to process the news that the man who'd claimed it was far too soon to start a family with her had started one with her former friend, not long after Sophie had gone. 'I un-friended and blocked Ben, but you're right, I might have heard from one of my friends at home.' She forced down her emotions, determined not to show her parents she was upset. 'When did you find out?' She was curious to know.

'One of my art-group pals is friendly with Ben's mother and she'd heard it from her. Apparently they've only just started telling people, but I knew it wouldn't be long until you found out somehow. Naomi's four months gone.'

'*Four?*' Sophie exclaimed.

'Yes.'

They'd wasted no time then, Sophie thought. Eight months after she and Ben split up, Naomi must have been pregnant. Was it planned? Or a 'happy accident'? Sophie felt the sting of tears in her eyes and a wave of anger bearing down on her.

'I'm so sorry. It must be a shock,' her father said kindly.

'Yes . . . I mean, no. Nothing that snake does shocks me any longer. Actually snakes are OK,' she said, thinking back to poor old Sir Hiss curled up in his cage at the vet's. 'Ben's . . . a slimy, lying cockroach!'

'Your dad used some even stronger words about him, when he first heard.'

He nodded silently to show his solidarity.

'I can imagine,' Sophie murmured, though she couldn't, because her gentle, quiet father rarely swore or lost his temper. She smiled at him. 'I love you both and I'm grateful you told me first. It's strange to hear, but we're all moving on. Ben and Naomi clearly are, and so am I, so I don't want you to worry that this is going to set me back.'

'I'm so proud of you,' her mother said. 'And perhaps it is for the best that you're out of the way and making a new life. I'm sorry for making you feel guilty earlier.'

'You just concentrate on making this Christmas escape a success for your guests and we'll speak soon, then see you in the New Year,' her dad reminded Sophie, lifting her spirits. 'Bye, love . . .'

'Bye.' With a wave, they ended the call.

What a day! Talk about a rollercoaster. First the car, then a lovely evening with Brody, and now this fresh twist. Sophie put down the phone and hugged her knees, feeling a tight knot of pain inside her, exactly as she had for weeks after she'd first found Ben and Naomi shagging in the shop. The temptation to shout, 'I hate you, Ben!' was strong, but what would be the point? It would only scare the cats, and it meant that Ben and Naomi had won.

She tried to refocus on the positive. Ben had already shown why he didn't deserve her, so her dad was right – she had to keep going and continue to put all her energies into the business. The truck could be fixed. In a few days she'd have a full house of guests for her first festive season – and she'd achieved that in her own unique way, despite the naysayers. She'd started and made a success of a new business and now lived in a stunning location.

Gradually her breathing eased and the knot of hurt waned to a bearable ache. This was where she belonged now. Ben and Naomi were part of her history, even if that history was proving harder to shake off than she'd hoped.

Brody picked her up at seven-thirty sharp and they drove off into the dark Lakeland morning to the laundry. Sophie had left a message for the local garage the previous evening before going to bed and followed it up with a phone call on the way to the village. The mechanic assured her he would be out in his tow-truck as soon as possible.

'Here we go,' Brody said, parking next to the pickup as the first glow of daylight appeared over the western fells. 'Let me know if you have any problems or the garage doesn't turn up. I know the mechanic. His kids have seven guinea pigs between them, so he needs to keep me and my friends sweet.'

'Seven?' Sophie said and then, 'Thanks for the offer, but you've already been a huge help and you must have a busy day at the surgery, so don't want to keep you from it.'

'Yeah, I guess so, but I mean it. If you needed a lift home or anything, I'm always here to help.'

She smiled, grateful for the kindness he'd shown her. 'I will. I promise.'

'OK. Well, if not, I'll see you at mine tomorrow for the party?' He was clearly keen to know that Sophie hadn't had second thoughts and was still coming.

'Yes, I'll be there. What time does it start?'

'People will probably rock up from around seven, but drop in any time. It usually goes on until eleven-ish. That's when I'll start collecting up the glasses and offering to fetch the stragglers' coats. You can turn up any time you want to.'

Sophie laughed. 'OK, well, I'll probably pop in near the start, I promise.' She hesitated before asking, 'Are you sure there isn't anything I can do to help? Bring a bottle or some crisps?'

He laughed. 'Thanks for the offer. Mum has caterers doing the food, and it's my job to collect the booze tomorrow afternoon. That and "making sure the loos look respectable".'

'I know that job well.' Sophie giggled. 'Vee and Ricky are coming in to help with breakfast and cleaning on Christmas Eve morning, but after that I'm on my own until the guests leave on the twenty-seventh of December – dealing with anything and everything that might go wrong. I think I'll be very happy to see the back of them by then and have a few days off!'

'I'm on emergency cover most of the time,' Brody said. 'We take it in turns each year.'

'What are you doing for Christmas Day?' she asked. 'Will you be spending it here at Felltop Farm or at your mother's?'

'I haven't been informed yet, but rest assured someone will have plans for me.' Brody's tone surprised her by its bitterness.

'You could always take Harold out for a walk, if it gets too much,' she suggested lightly.

'I *could*. Or I might be called out, which may be the only escape I get,' he muttered, before a brief smile flickered across his face and he said briskly, 'Well, I really must be getting on – busy day and all that. My first appointment is at eight-thirty, and Cora will be having kittens. Not that it's anatomically possible, of course, but . . .'

Sophie grinned. 'I'd like to see it.'

'I wouldn't! Bye!' He drove off, with a wave, leaving Sophie perplexed.

After he'd gone, she waited for the tow-truck to arrive, still puzzling over Brody's cryptic remarks about being told what to do over the festive season, and most of all puzzling about her own reactions to him.

She loved the way he ran his hands through his tousled hair, the colour of espresso coffee, and she liked the cleft in his chin and the whole self-deprecating charm. He adored animals, and his patients adored him. Brody seemed a thoroughly nice guy, and yet so had Ben. He'd shed his nice-guy disguise as fast as the decs off a Christmas tree on Twelfth Night. Could she ever risk being hurt like that again, no matter how much of a 'good guy' Brody seemed?

Chapter Eight

The next day was 23 December – the day of Brody's party – and it was just thirty hours until Sophie's escapees arrived.

Luckily the local garage had managed to fix the wheel while Sophie did a tour of the village shops, looking for any last-minute bits and pieces to give Sunnyside a fiesta, rather than festive, feel.

It hadn't been easy, with the shops rammed with traditional decorations, and she was glad she'd already ordered some items online. Her new cocktail glasses and shaker looked great when arranged on the honesty bar alongside a selection of mixers and spirits, with a price list in a notebook, where people could sign for what they'd drunk. If they could remember . . .

She picked up some staples in the village supermarket that morning, but the bulk of her main shop was already on order at the farm shop, ready to be collected tomorrow, early on Christmas Eve morning.

By lunchtime she was back home, to find Vee having made a start on the dining room and guest lounge. The bedrooms were ready to welcome guests, with a small gift of Spanish *turrón* nougat placed on each pillow, along with a programme of events.

Not for the first time, Sophie had butterflies in her stomach at the prospect of hosting such a comprehensive – and unusual – break. Expectations were bound to be high and she only hoped she could live up to them. Instead of a traditional tree, she'd ordered a large inflatable palm for the dining room. It was bigger than she'd expected and, even using an electric pump, it was hard work to inflate it and set it up.

'For God's sake don't let the cats get their claws on that!' Vee cried when the palm was in place.

'I dread to think of the bang if they do.' Sophie shuddered. 'Must brief everyone to shut the dining-room door at all times. It does look very . . . celebratory, though, don't you think?'

'I love it,' Vee replied enthusiastically. 'Makes me want to put my shades on and start singing "Livin' la Vida Loca".'

Encouraged, Sophie unboxed the rest of the 'tropical-pool party kit': several inflatable parrots, beach balls and flamingos, which she blew up and arranged around the guest lounge. She could hear Vee humming the Ricky Martin pop classic in the dining room and smiled, hoping it would bring a different kind of joy to her guests.

'I might be "anti-Christmas", but I'm not anti-fun!' she joked, standing back to admire their efforts. Vee handed her a mug of coffee and a cranberry brownie.

'It's a festive brownie, but pretend it isn't,' Vee told her, with a wicked gleam. 'I made some for the kids' last-day-at-school party, but kept a few for myself.'

Sophie took a bite. 'This is really good; maybe I should

get you baking for the guests too.' She frowned at the parrots and flamingos perched over the bar. 'Are there flamingos in Spain? I definitely don't think they have parrots. I can't decide whether it looks bonkers or cool.'

'Both,' said Vee with glee. 'It's hilarious. With the grief I've had to deal with about presents, nativity costumes and who's cooking what and when, and with whom, on the big day, I might escape here myself.'

'I'd love that,' Sophie replied. 'But that's not a hint. I want you to have a lovely regular Christmas with your family.'

'What is a "regular" Christmas?' Vee asked. 'No one has a perfect day, do they? 'There's always tension and stress at some point – families falling out or missing loved ones they've lost. I bet thousands of people would love to escape and spend their holiday drinking cocktails with a giant palm tree and an inflatable parrot.'

'Don't forget the flamenco troupe,' Sophie said.

'Are they an actual genuine flamenco troupe?' Vee asked. 'Are they staying in the village?'

'They all live fairly locally. They're a new troupe formed by the Anglo-Spanish club in Kendal. There are only six of them, and apparently they all either have Spanish heritage or are married to Spanish partners. They seemed very keen, and happy to get the guests up and dancing. I didn't think they'd want to come out, but of course there's very little demand for a fledgling flamenco group on Christmas Eve, especially around here.'

'I can't think why!' Vee chuckled, tucking into the remains of her brownie.

Although they were new and keen, the dancers had obviously still needed a fee, which Sophie had had to factor into her prices. Her weekend would cost as much as staying in a boutique hotel for a traditional Christmas, so it had to work.

She had almost finished her brownie too. 'We need to clear the furniture back, ready for the show. I'm thinking of putting people in two rows to create more room, with the dancers at the front. Luckily flamenco doesn't take up much room and they only have a guitarist, not a full band.'

'Good idea, but you'll have to rearrange the tables for Christmas Day breakfast.'

'I'll manage somehow. Maybe someone will offer to lend a hand.'

'You could always ask one of the neighbours to help?' Sophie noticed the twinkle in Vee's eye when she said this.

'If you mean Brody, I expect he'll be far too busy on Christmas Eve. The practice is open until four, and then I think he's doing family stuff.'

'With his mother?'

Sophie shrugged. 'I don't know. He hasn't gone into detail. He just implied he'd be very busy over Christmas. I'm not expecting to see him tomorrow after the party.'

'So you *are* going to his party tonight?' She whistled. 'You're highly honoured. Only the great and good are invited to the McKennas' Christmas-drinks do.'

'Really? Well, I'm neither, so I don't know why I've made the list.' Sophie laughed. 'I'll pop in for half an hour, out of politeness. It could be good for the business to do a bit of networking too.'

'Oh, of course,' Vee replied, putting on her serious face. 'Nothing whatsoever to do with a certain dishy vet.'

Sophie snatched up her plate and mug. 'Nothing whatsoever! Now I think I'd better start moving the furniture around in here for the flamenco night.'

Vee gave a mock salute. 'Hint taken. What next?'

'Just sweeping up the hot-tub area. And please thank Kev for doing all the safety checks on the outdoor lighting and hot tub.' In his day job, when he wasn't volunteering for the mountain-rescue team, Vee's husband was an electrician, which had proved very useful when Sophie needed any work doing. Kev always found time to fit her in, at reasonable prices too. Once again, Sophie said a silent prayer for her good fortune in finding Vee and Kev. They were real diamonds.

Outside, the sun was already dipping towards the horizon and dusk would fall well before 4 p.m. She cast a critical eye over the hot-tub area. The tub had been freshly installed, if a little stark and unwelcoming, when she'd taken over the guest house. She'd proceeded to put her own stamp on it, installing lights in the hot-tub area, around the trunks of the apple tree and along the veranda. In these northern climes, with frequent frosts and the possibility of snow from November to April, there was no place for the tender plants she'd nurtured in the sunny patio behind the Stratford shop. However, she'd found some hardy potted shrubs from the garden centre and had threaded fairy lights through the leaves. Even if guests wouldn't be sitting on the terrace, they could use the hot tub or enjoy the sight of the twinkling garden from inside.

She'd also picked up several LED signs in a bargain shop a few weeks back. No one wanted pink and lime-green signs declaring *Cocktails* and *Tropical Vibes*. There were major advantages to shopping out of season.

A rogue thought entered Sophie's head: of her and Brody in the hot tub. Alone. Sipping cocktails and wearing not a lot . . .

Vee soon sloshed a bucket of cold water over that thought. 'Penny for them?'

'What?' Sophie said. 'I was – er – just checking everything was in hand.'

'Chill. It looks fantastic,' she said. 'You know, if you weren't fully booked, I might check myself in and tell Kev and the kids I'm escaping for Christmas myself. I came out to tell you I'm done, and I'm off to pick the kids up. Have a good time tonight.' She raised a cheeky eyebrow. 'Try to behave in front of the Bannerdale royalty.'

'I'll do my best,' Sophie promised, laughing even though a flutter of nerves had already taken flight in her stomach. She wasn't sure whether they'd been set off by the thought of having to survive a Christmas party or the idea of spending another evening with Brody.

At seven-ten Sophie walked across the field from Sunnyside to Felltop Farm, with her torch. As soon as she reached the gate into the stable yard she turned off the beam, because every downstairs window in the house was lit up, and the sound of music and conversation was spilling out into the yard. The normally quiet farmhouse had come alive.

The back door to the boot-room was open. Although she'd had conversations with Brody out in the yard – usually when they'd bumped into each other while they were both out walking – she'd never been inside the old house itself. She really ought to go up to the front door and knock, like every other guest, yet it felt strange when the rear door was open and she could slip in there with less fuss.

Harold solved her dilemma, barking loudly and bounding up to her. She laughed when she saw his red bow tie. A moment later Brody himself emerged and met her halfway to the door.

'Oh, hello there!' The surprise in his voice; perhaps he hadn't expected her to actually come. Harold woofed again in greeting.

'Hi. I – took a shortcut, but wasn't sure if I should use the front door.'

'Back door is fine for friends,' he said, then pushed a lock of hair sheepishly off his face. 'Bugger! You've never actually been inside, have you?'

Sophie could have replied that she'd never been invited, and realised once again that they'd only been acquaintances until a few days previously. She felt her cheeks heat up as she shook her head. It was a good job it wasn't daylight, so Brody couldn't see her blushing like a teenager.

'Anyway, come in,' he went on. 'The party's just getting

into the swing of things. If you can call it swinging, with the vicar and Brian from the Traders' Association here – not swinging in the sense of people hooking up. It's not that kind of party . . . Argh! Please, ignore me. It's already been a long day.'

'I'll try to banish that image!' Sophie said, with a giggle at the thought of the strait-laced, fussy Brian and the vicar picking keys out of a bowl. 'And I still think I ought to have brought wine,' she said awkwardly, feeling rude for not bringing anything.

'There's plenty inside, and Mum and her friend have just brought the sausage rolls out of the oven, so your timing couldn't be better. The caterers seem to have supplied enough food to feed the whole of Bannerdale.'

'Sounds good. I didn't have any dinner.'

'Wise choice. We need all the mouths we can feed.'

Brody ushered her through a boot-room stacked with coats, hats, wellies, umbrellas and other paraphernalia. He opened a door onto a blast of heat and savoury aromas. The kitchen was huge, twice the size of the one at Sunnyside. There was a range cooker, a modern electric oven and a large, scrubbed oak table that was covered in platters of canapés, sausage rolls and mini-sandwiches.

Sophie spotted four other doors leading off the kitchen, one of which was open and looked like a pantry full of jars and pans.

Several women she didn't recognise bustled in and out, picking up trays of food. They were all in sparkly tops and satin jumpsuits and clearly hadn't walked through a field to reach the farm, like she had. They were so intent on collecting the food that they didn't seem to have noticed her and Brody.

'Can I get you a drink?' Brody offered, moving to a corner of the kitchen stocked with bottles and cans. 'Wine? Fizz? Beer?'

'Fizz, please, if there's one open,' she said.

Brody picked up a bottle of prosecco, found a flute and filled it.

'Thanks,' Sophie replied, taking a sip while observing the scene.

Yet another woman in heels and satin palazzo pants walked in. 'Martina! Louise is asking if we can put another tray of sausage rolls in the oven. They need warming through!'

'No one likes a lukewarm sausage roll . . .' Brody whispered to Sophie while opening a bottle of lager.

'Oh no,' she said, suppressing another giggle. 'I – er – hadn't realised it was quite so formal. The dress code, I mean.'

'It's not,' Brody assured her. 'Mum tells everyone "smart casual", but that can mean anything. You look great.'

Sophie looked down at her best jeans, smart jumper and boots, which were admittedly a little muddy after the short walk. 'Thanks.' She could have said the same to Brody, who was in chunky boots, black jeans and a thick checked shirt, open to reveal a grey T-shirt.

'Shall we go into the sitting room? That's where the main action is. I'd be happy to hide out in the kitchen all evening, but I ought to do my duty and introduce you.'

Sophie was amused that Brody had at least three reception rooms to host parties in. He led the way down a corridor that had so many doors off it, Sophie lost count. At the end was a room where the volume of noise and music had swollen to a degree where she couldn't hear what he was saying to her. Her pulse beat faster. There was a Christmas mix-tape on, the same sort of thing she'd endured in supermarkets and shops for a month, and for a second it took her back to that moment when she'd opened the door to her stockroom.

She'd survived the lantern parade, but this party was a different proposition: a Christmas social occasion that she couldn't bail out of very easily. Part of her didn't care what people thought of her, but there were bound to be more questions about her unusual approach to Christmas. There was no way she was going to air her private life to a bunch of strangers, so she'd simply have to smile, make a joke of it and change the subject.

The sitting room was spacious enough for three enormous velvet sofas and an inglenook fireplace with a blackened beam. There also seemed to be numerous nooks and corners lit by lamps or decorated with copper jugs of holly and spruce. With the fire glowing and at least two dozen people chatting, guffawing and drinking, it was very warm. The ladies' sequinned outfits shimmered like Santa's grotto, and while several of the men sported garish Santa jumpers, most were in smart jackets and two were in black tie. Even the vicar wore a velvet jacket over his shirt and dog collar.

Sophie felt decidedly underdressed and hoped she wouldn't tread mud into the rugs that covered most of the oak floorboards, even though they were well worn and slightly tatty already.

'Sorry. I appreciate it's a bit full-on . . .' Brody said, perhaps sensing her nerves.

As soon as she walked in, Louise McKenna spotted them, like a lioness scenting game. Or was that being unkind? Sophie thought as Louise wiggled between the guests, clearly on a mission. She was tiny, five feet at most, with toned arms and a blow-dried honey-blonde bob. Sophie couldn't really see much resemblance to Brody. Perhaps he'd taken after his father, who she knew had died when Brody was a teenager.

'Sophie. What a lovely surprise. I wasn't sure you could make it.' She moved to kiss her on the cheek.

'I did mention I'd bumped into Sophie, who said she was coming, Mum,' Brody reminded her.

'Ah, of course you did.' She smiled at Sophie. 'Please make yourself at home. There's acres of food and gallons of fizz.'

'Louise!' A woman in a purple sari called out. Sophie recognised her from the doctor's, where she worked on reception. 'Sorry to interrupt, but have you any idea where the cocktail serviettes have gone?'

'Aren't they on the Welsh dresser in the kitchen? I'll come and look. It'll be quicker than you rooting through all the drawers. Help yourself to food and drinks, or get Brody to wait on you,' Louise said, with an apologetic grimace to Sophie before dashing out of the sitting room.

Sophie thought it must have been tough for Louise to jointly manage the family business – and support her son – on her own. No wonder she was used to multitasking and was such a whirlwind in the community.

'I *did* tell Mum you were coming,' Brody said with a sigh.

'She seems very busy. I expect she forgot, and this must have been a lot of work to plan.'

Before Brody could utter another word, a man and a woman bounded up, reminding Sophie of Harold when he'd snaffled her guests' breakfast.

'Are you Sophie from Sunnyside?'

The man, whose comb-over had worked loose and was flapping over his head, snorted with laughter. 'The one running the hotel for folk who hate Christmas?'

'Oh, Gerald, don't be so rude!' his wife cried in embarrassment.

'It's not for people who hate Christmas, as such,' Sophie protested.

Gerald chortled and patted Sophie on the arm, much to her horror. 'Brave of you to venture into the festive lair, my dear.'

Sophie's stomach tightened and she contemplated all kinds of action involving the launch of trifle and sausage rolls at his shiny pate.

Brody stepped in with a knowing smile. 'Gerald, how are you and, more importantly, how's Winston? I hope you've been keeping him off the steak and chips. You know we agreed it was contributing to his weight issues, and Labradors find it hard to resist a treat.'

His wife gasped. 'Gerald! You promised not to give Winston any more leftovers! No wonder he's not getting any slimmer and is costing us a fortune in vet's bills. Not that your prices are unfair – unlike some vets – Brody,' she added hastily.

Brody ushered Sophie away from the couple while Gerald's wife was still berating him, glad that his plan had done the trick. 'Come on,' he whispered to Sophie. 'I have an urgent need for you to help me with something completely unimportant.'

Chapter Nine

Unfortunately Brody was hijacked before they'd even reached the buffet table, and Sophie's next hour or so passed in a whirlwind of eating, drinking and making polite small talk with people whose names and roles she was now struggling to remember.

She recognised some faces from the village, though it was difficult to place them when they were dressed up and out of context. Nonetheless, she did her best, because it was a good opportunity to network and get to know the locals better. However, that wasn't the main reason she'd agreed to come. She'd hoped to be able to spend time with Brody, but by now she might have realised he'd be swept away on host duties. Tonight wasn't an occasion to spend quality time with him, and Sophie fully understood.

He was just a few people away now, currently trying to escape from a man in a greasy tweed jacket who had Brody virtually pinned against the inglenook. He caught Sophie's eye and shared a knowing look with her. Hopefully he'd be able to find an excuse to escape from Tweedy Man and come over.

Ping!

Everyone turned to see Louise in the centre of the room, holding up a fork and a wine glass.

'Ladies and gentlemen, can I please have your attention for a moment!'

The chatter in the room faded away as if someone had turned down the dial on a radio.

'Thank you, everyone!' Louise called. 'I promise this isn't a speech. I only want to thank you all for coming. It's a very busy time of year. This year has been tough for many of you, I know that . . .' She hesitated for a moment. 'We've lost people we love, and this time of year always makes us think about those who are no longer with us, no matter how many years have passed since they left us.'

A soft murmur of agreement rippled through the guests.

'So tonight we raise a glass to their memory, and we also look forward to the future. It's a testament to the strength of this wonderful community that so many of you gather here once again to celebrate our achievements and strengthen our connections. I'm so grateful to you all for your support through foot-and-mouth, fire . . . and floods.'

Groans rang out at the hardships they'd faced during the year.

'*Especially* floods, considering the damage done to many businesses at the start of the year,' she went on, reminding Sophie of the torrents that had caused such havoc in the January before she'd arrived at Sunnyside.

Sophie looked at Brody, arms folded, watching his mother tensely.

'Our business wasn't the only one inundated. For some, it was the last straw.' She paused again and there was a stillness in the room. 'But enough of the doom and gloom. We are all here and, thanks to us all pulling together, everyone is still going.'

'Just about still going, Louise!' the vicar quipped.

'You're the fittest of the lot of us,' Louise replied.

Laughter rang out and Louise raised her glass. 'To buggering on, despite everything, and a happy Christmas to us all!'

Glasses were raised and everyone toasted to that.

Brody held his drink high and as soon as his mum had finished her speech, he gave her a big hug.

Louise kissed his cheek and hastily wiped her eyes, before fixing her hostess smile back in place. Sophie felt a new-found sympathy and respect for her, even if she did think Louise was a little too protective of her son. Brody clearly cared for his mother and must have felt obliged to be the male support in the family from a very young age. No wonder they were close.

The music was turned back up and the chatter resumed.

Finally Brody carved a path over towards Sophie.

'Phew. Sorry I couldn't get away to talk to you earlier, and I'd no idea Mum was going to give a speech.' He gave a lopsided grimace.

'It was very heartfelt. I hadn't realised it had been such a hard time for her and the business.'

'It's been a difficult year,' he admitted. 'The premises were totally flooded and it's taken months to properly clear them out. It was before you got here, so how would you know? As for losing people, Mum probably means my auntie – Mum's younger sister – who died back in May.'

'I'm so sorry.'

'It was horrible for Mum. I have to be honest, I didn't expect her to get emotional this evening. It's normally her favourite night of the year.'

'Painful memories have a habit of surfacing when you least expect them. Your mum's been under a lot of pressure too.'

'We all need a break. Apart from you, of course,' he said, sounding brighter again. 'As this is your busiest time of year.'

'But after my guests leave, I plan to spend the twenty-seventh collapsed in a heap with the cats.'

'You never know, there might be something better to do . . .' he began, before adding hastily, 'I mean, we'll all need some fresh air by then, and some alone-time to recharge. Maybe we could take Harold for a walk. If we're both around, that is.'

'Maybe,' Sophie said, sensing Brody's reluctance even to commit to a walk, perhaps because he was wary of making plans that he couldn't keep at such a busy family time. 'Though you said you might have plans, or other people might have plans for you? Won't the surgery be open by then too?'

'My colleague's on duty after the holiday, so I'll have Boxing Day and the day after off. I volunteered to be on emergency call over Christmas Eve and Christmas Day.' He smiled. 'I'll need my own Christmas escape by then . . . and I bet you will?'

She told him briefly about her guests, but it was only a minute before Brody was called away. Almost immediately he was replaced by his mother brandishing a bottle of prosecco.

'Sophie!' Louise said brightly. 'I've been trying to talk to you all evening. Can I give you a top-up?'

'Er, yes, please.' She held out her glass, sensing that Louise's multitasking meant she never spent time with anyone without an ulterior motive, however well intended.

'Are you enjoying yourself?' Louise asked, expertly judging the level of fizz required to fill the glass, but not foam over the brim. 'Even if this isn't really your thing?'

Sophie's enthusiasm waned a little, but she had honed her own set of skills by dealing with difficult customers and guests.

'Thank you again for inviting me. It's been great to meet so many people from the local community,' she replied diplomatically. 'I've been made very welcome.'

'Oh?' Louise's eyebrows lifted.

'Yes, and the food is delicious.'

'The caterers are brilliant, and I have so many friends to help out with serving and clearing away . . . Brody tells me you'll be managing on your own over Christmas, you poor thing.'

'Vee's been helping me and we're well prepared. The guests don't arrive until three tomorrow and they leave on the twenty-seventh.'

'Still, that's a long time to manage alone.' Louise shuddered. 'Rather you than me.'

'It *will* be hard work, but I'm very ready for it,' Sophie said firmly.

'I'm sure you are. You're not having a traditional turkey and Christmas pud, I assume?'

'No. Actually I'm making a giant paella. With king prawns and chorizo and chicken.'

'*Paella*,' Louise echoed, as horrified as if Sophie had said she was serving mealworm curry.

'Yes, it's a Spanish theme,' Sophie went on, sensing other guests listening in and an undercurrent of unspoken pity and amazement. 'And afterwards we're having pavlova,' she continued, before Louise could comment further. 'Which is Australian, as you probably know. I absolutely *love* pavlova. Maybe a few of the guests will even make it into the hot tub. I've booked a flamenco group too.'

'A flamenco group?' The bottle wobbled in Louise's hand. 'And sangria and paella in the hot tub. Oh, well. That's very . . . different.' She smiled tightly.

'We won't be eating the paella in the hot tub. That could block the filters,' Sophie said in her best jokey tone. 'However, as for enjoying a different kind of Christmas, that's the whole idea. My guests are coming specifically to escape from the traditional festive celebrations.'

'Are there many of them?' Louise asked.

'Yes. I'm fully booked.'

'Wow! Good for you. Well, it takes all sorts, I suppose.'

'It does,' Sophie replied, as the wide-eyed guests listened

in. Anyone would think she was holding a naked foam party at Sunnyside, by the way some mouths gaped in shock.

'Makes our plans sound rather dull. Although there's a lot to be said for tradition.' Louise rolled her eyes. 'Brody would probably faint if I served up a paella instead of turkey and all the trimmings. He's a traditional sort of chap, as you've probably found out, even if he didn't follow in his father's footsteps.' With a wistful pause, she politely excused herself. 'Well, I must leave you to enjoy the party. I'm needed to help plate up the mini-puddings'. She scurried off, still with the bottle, leaving Sophie on her own again.

The other guests had turned their backs. Whether that was a coincidence or because they really did think Sophie and her guests would be enjoying more than paella in the hot tub, Sophie wasn't sure. However, she suddenly felt adrift in an ocean of sequin-clad strangers, with Louise's comments stuck in her mind.

She was amused by the idea of Brody being a 'traditional sort of chap'. That made him sound like some tweedy 1950s bore, when he was the complete opposite. Plus, being a vet was an important job – a vocation – and his mother ought to be proud of him.

Sophie took a glug of her prosecco and regretted it. It left a bitter taste in her mouth, and how hot the room had become in the past few minutes. She wanted to take off her jumper, but was too embarrassed to stand there in her old T-shirt.

The lights from the tree seemed to blind her and the fire felt very hot. Her throat was dry from talking, and her jaw ached from trying to keep forcing a smile to her face. Everything became loud and oppressive, and she felt a sense of claustrophobia in this room full of strangers.

The vicar's wife approached her, a young woman called Jo, not much older than Sophie. She was wearing black from head to toe, apart from gold sparkly Doc Martens. Sophie had actually first been introduced to her at the farm shop and had immediately liked Jo's humour and warmth.

'Are you OK?' Jo asked. 'These parties can be a bit of an ordeal, if I'm honest, and it's easy to get worn down by all the bonhomie. And,' she lowered her voice to barely above a whisper, 'you won't be the only person in Bannerdale who'll be secretly relieved when it's all over for another year. My husband is absolutely knackered already, from all the nativities and events he has to attend at this time of year. In fact we've booked a break to Tenerife straight after Epiphany to recover from it all.'

Sophie had to smile. 'You must both be desperate for a holiday,' she said, grateful to Jo for being the one person who seemed to understand how exhausting the season could be, for various reasons. 'And it's so hot in here – I think I'll go out for some fresh air for a bit.'

'Good idea,' Jo said, with a gleam in her eye. 'When you come back, find me. I can tell you all the wicked things I know about everyone here.'

'I'll do that.' Sophie laughed. As tempting as Jo's offer was, she thought this could be her moment to quietly leave and go home. It was silly of her, but she had to get out: into the cold, clear night to be on her own.

She slipped into the hall and through the kitchen, where Louise's friend was taking out a tray of mince pies from the Aga. Fortunately she didn't even notice Sophie dart through the door and into the boot-room.

Sophie's chest tightened as she breathed in the frosty air after the heat of the party. She walked further from the house, into the shadows beyond the pools of light spilling from the windows.

Safety. Solitude. Silence.

This hadn't been the best idea. She'd hardly spoken to Brody; he was in demand with his guests and was so busy topping up drinks and checking the fire. That was as it should be, and the last thing Sophie ever wanted was to be 'needy.'

Perhaps she should go home.

She heard a snuffle from the stable block and then jumped as something warm and wet nuzzled her.

'Harold!'

The security light clicked on, revealing the Labrador at her side, his tongue rough and warm against her fingers. She bent down to ruffle his ears, comforted by the warmth of his coat.

'How are you, handsome?' she asked, amused by his bow tie, which was now rather skew-whiff. That was Harold all over; Brody too. A bit dishevelled, but undoubtedly good-looking and a comforting presence. Sophie's deep sigh brought another wave of cool air into her lungs, but this time it freed the tension.

Harold padded ahead.

She halted, halfway between the house and the stable, unsure of which way to go: back to the warmth of the festivities inside or forward into the cold, silent night. Frozen between the past and the future: staying in her safe, lonely bubble or breaking out and taking a chance.

Chapter Ten

'Sophie?'

At the familiar deep voice, she turned to see Brody walking towards her with a glass of fizz in either hand. 'I've been looking for you. Are you OK?'

'Yes, I'm fine. I needed a breath of fresh air.' She fanned herself.

'It's too hot inside, isn't it?' he said with a lopsided grin that sent her hormones into overdrive. 'Mum kept going on about keeping the place warm, but she hadn't factored in fifty people all creating their own hot air!'

'They're enjoying themselves,' Sophie said. 'It is allowed.'

He laughed and she realised that, in seeking her out, Brody had made the decision for her: she would stay. Her skin tingled with excitement. Was it possible that this Christmas could be a fresh start when she cast away the bad memories of the past?

'I'm sorry I haven't had much time to spend with you. I should have realised how hectic it would be as host. Doh!'

'It's OK,' she replied, finding Brody's awkwardness endearing. 'Harold came out to find me.'

'He's a better host than I am. Aren't you, mate?'

Sophie patted the dog's head, silently thanking Harold

for keeping her in the stable yard just long enough for Brody to find her. A few minutes later and she might have been on her way back to the guest house.

'Um, I brought you a fresh glass of fizz. It's well chilled because I kept it in the outhouse. Don't tell anybody, but it's also real champagne from my secret stash. I'm giving you the good stuff.'

He held out the glass and Sophie took it, feeling the condensation against her fingers. 'Thank you.'

'Why don't we go and drink these somewhere quieter?' he suggested.

'Is that allowed?' Sophie joked, while privately admitting she couldn't think of anything she'd rather do.

'Probably not, but I'm past the point of caring. Everyone can get along fine without me. Most of them are stuffing their faces with sausage rolls and getting plastered on the free booze. I doubt they'll notice I'm gone.'

Sophie thought they definitely *would* notice, but Brody was already on his way to the stable block.

'Come on, I think we should check on the real VIP guests.'

Momentarily puzzled, Sophie followed him towards the stable block, where all became clear when Brody switched on the lights. They heard snorting and found Gabriel and the sheep peering over the top of a low door in his stall.

'Hi, Gabe!' Brody stroked the donkey's face and he made snuffling noises. 'Are you pissed off to be in here while everyone's partying? Or are you glad to be out of it?'

'Glad to be out of it,' Sophie answered for him.

'Come and say hello,' Brody said to her. 'If you want to. Gabe's a gentleman. The sheep might be a bit harder to win over.

Sophie had never said hello to a donkey before and was slightly wary, but she wasn't going to miss out on the chance.

'I'm still too warm. Running around and being nice to people is hard work,' he said, pulling off his thick overshirt.

Sophie took a sip of her champagne, noticing that the T-shirt Brody was wearing underneath showed off his toned arms and biceps. Clearly there were some advantages to manhandling livestock for a living.

Together they fed apples and carrots to the donkey. 'Early Christmas treats.'

'I'm sure Gabriel deserves it.'

Brody stroked Gabe's muzzle. 'I did keep trying to get to you and see if you were OK. I saw you pinned down by Brian from the Traders' Association, and then Uncle Trevor was making a beeline for you.'

'I was OK. I just needed some fresh air.'

'Phew! That's a relief, as I thought for a moment you'd bailed out early.'

For a second Sophie was ready with a fib, and yet there was an intensity to the way Brody looked at her that made her think he could see into her soul. Even if that was fanciful, she was sure he was far too good a judge of people not to know when someone was lying. Perhaps it was time to be honest.

'OK, I can't deny it, I *might* have been thinking about going home, when Harold intercepted me.'

'It would have been alright if you had bailed out.'

'Oh?' she said, disappointed.

'It would have been fine, if that's what you really needed to do, but I'd have missed you. A lot, actually.' He whistled. 'Well done, Harold.' He patted the dog, who trotted over. 'Extra helping of turkey for you on Christmas Day. Only a small one, mind, as we can't have you turning into a patient, can we?'

Sophie laughed and took another sip of her fizz, sensing the flame of optimism flicker into life again. 'Thanks again for asking me. I'm glad I came. Tonight, and to the Lakes.'

'You've done really well, if you don't mind me saying so. Upping sticks to a new area and starting a brand-new business among a load of dour northerners. That's an achievement.'

'You haven't been dour. Everyone – almost everyone – has been incredibly welcoming.'

'I'm glad to hear it.'

'And I *might* have seemed confident, but underneath I was a lot more nervous about embarking on a new venture than I may have looked. I thought running a guest house would help me make new friends.'

'Joking apart, though, you're a long way from home here.'

'Well . . . maybe that's because I wanted to be a long way from the past.'

'Oh?' Brody sat on a bale of hay, as if signalling that he was ready to listen.

It felt rude not to repay his attention and, besides, Sophie was in a mood for sharing. They were finally becoming something a little more than neighbours: friends and perhaps, one day, even closer than that?

She sat down next to him. 'I chose Sunnyside for all kinds of reasons. I won't say I was running away, because it was *my* decision to buy the guest house, although I was keen to make a completely new start after Ben and I split up.' She surprised herself by how good it felt to finally open up a little.

'Ben?'

'My ex. We, er – *he* decided to have an affair with my now ex-best friend, Naomi.'

Brody whistled. 'Bloody hell.'

'Yeah. I used to run a year-round Christmas shop in Stratford-upon-Avon.'

His eyes widened in amazement.

'Hard to believe, I'm sure, now that I'm helping people get away from all the clichés,' Sophie said.

'You are full of surprises. I knew you were in retail, but I thought you had a general gift shop?'

'That's what everyone assumed, so I didn't go out of my way to correct them,' Sophie said with a sigh, realising that even though she hadn't lied, perhaps she hadn't been quick enough to admit the truth. 'What no one up here knows, apart from Vee, is that I caught Ben and Naomi together in the stockroom on Christmas Eve. They weren't playing

"Santa", I can tell you. More like "Hide the Carrot" . . .'
Sophie surprised herself by the way she could joke about it
now. It was gallows humour, though.

Brody's glass wobbled and some fizz splashed out.
'My God!'

'Please can you be discreet about this? I haven't told
anyone but Vee about Ben's affair. I probably shouldn't be
telling you now. It's hardly appropriate at your party.'

'No, you should. That's shitty, it's awful.'

'It was a pretty dire time for me, I'll admit. So I came up
here to make a completely new start, because I lost more
than Ben when we split up. In the melee between running
the shop and being a couple, I managed to lose touch with
some of my old mates from university and from my jobs
before I went self-employed.'

Sophie regretted prioritising work and Ben, and losing
contact with some of her hobbies and friends, letting them
drip away slowly without her even realising it.

'I'd been too busy for stuff like Zumba and regular nights
out with the girls. I didn't realise quite how demanding the
relationship had become until it was almost too late . . .' She
heaved a sigh. Even Lyra had once hinted that Ben could be
needy, though she didn't phrase it like that. 'I've started to
put that right. I've had three friends to stay already, as well
as my family,' Sophie said, happy that she'd managed to
rebuild some of those relationships.

'Finding your ex and a close friend together must have
made life very complicated,' Brody said. 'Most of my
mates have four legs, apart from Carl. Though he is the

most loyal friend I've ever had, and one thing's for sure: I'm never going to find him writhing on the floor with . . . a girlfriend. Relationships are always complicated, that's for sure.'

Sophie laughed. 'I've worked that one out.' She also noted his use of 'a girlfriend'. She didn't know why, but she was sure Brody had hesitated a tiny bit before he used the words. Maybe she was being paranoid. She wondered if he was going to elaborate, but he didn't, so she continued. 'Our social life revolved around drinks and dinner at mutual friends' houses or in the pub. The trouble is that "mutual" meant our friends either took sides or wanted to stay mates with Ben as well as me.'

'That must have made for some awkward conversations,' Brody observed. Harold licked sticky fizz from his fingers. 'Harold, don't be a lush.'

Sophie laughed, partly at Harold's antics and because she was desperate to cover quite how hurt she'd been that most of Ben's mates – the couples as well as the men – had decided to switch loyalties to Ben and Naomi. Her own friends had stuck by her, particularly Lyra, and this had made it doubly hard to move so far away.

Brody shook his head. 'People can be weird. Why do you think I prefer animals? Present company excepted, of course.'

He smiled again, and Sophie warmed further to the empathy in his eyes. She was sure she wasn't imagining it and it wasn't just the fizz, but it felt like there was a definite spark between them: somehow she felt Brody must have gone through heartache himself. How else could he be single at thirty-five?

'I could have walled myself up with the cats,' she said, trying to keep everything light, despite feeling the hurt afresh as she told Brody, 'I could have coped with losing his connections if Ben hadn't gone off with one of *my* best mates. Because Naomi and I had mutual friends who also wanted to keep seeing us both.'

'Ouch,' Brody sympathised. 'That sounds like adding insult to injury.'

'It was painful, that's for sure. My own friends were shocked and sympathetic to start with, but then most of them carried on as if nothing had happened. Of course they had to arrange different times to see us, which was difficult when they were all busy. Anyway,' she went on, twirling her almost-empty glass in her fingers, 'I tried to understand their point of view, but it was just too hard. I felt too raw to be reasonable.'

'Why should you have to be reasonable? I'd have been so pissed off,' Brody declared.

'Oh, I was. Raging and hurt, but you have to get over it. I didn't feel like I belonged to my old life any more, so I decided to start a new one. I'd always had a yearning to run a guest house, but Ben wasn't keen. Now I had nothing to stop me – and so here I am.'

'I think you're brilliant. So does Harold.'

The Labrador nudged Sophie's leg to show her he agreed.

'It took real balls,' Brody said. 'Sorry. You know what I mean.'

She giggled. 'It's OK. It was mad in a way, really impulsive, and my parents and brother and his wife were so worried about me. They wanted me to wait and see how I felt, but it was too late. I sold the shop, saw Sunnyside and burned all my bridges. By spring, I knew it was the right decision to come here. You're the only person I've told, apart from Vee.'

'Well, I'm honoured you trusted me, and it goes without saying that this stays between us. As you can probably tell, I'm not one for village gossip – the main people I hang out with all day having fur and four legs.'

Sophie thought for a moment and then decided. 'Same. Though I've probably ruined the party mood with my personal woes.'

'You haven't ruined my evening. Far from it.'

Brody was giving her that look again. It made Sophie glow, as if she was sitting in front of the fire in the farmhouse. And how had she not noticed what a gorgeous voice he had? That Cumbrian accent was both soft and rugged, like the moss growing on the felltop rocks.

Wow, this fizz was strong . . . or could it be that, in sharing her past with him, this was the moment when she'd truly arrived in Bannerdale: the emotional moment as well as the physical?

Sophie took a large sip of her drink. Emboldened by Brody's reaction, and possibly too many glasses of champagne, she said, 'You should really reciprocate, you know? Share some of your secrets too.'

'My secrets?' He laughed, yet Sophie detected a hint of

wariness behind the amusement. 'I'm not sure I have any that you'd want to know.' He shrugged.

'But you do have some?' she pressed.

'You seem to forget, I'm a boring country vet.'

'That's not an answer.'

Again that wistful smile emerged, the one that revealed a glimmer of longing for some distant horizon. Sophie wasn't sure she was in the picture he was imagining, yet Brody put his empty glass on the hay bale and looked at her so intensely that a shiver ran down her spine.

The animals snuffled innocently in their stalls; the stable had an earthy comfort that felt like a safe space. *She* felt safe, and Brody knew everything about her now. She had nothing to lose.

'I'm not sure I should be doing this . . .' he said.

Sophie moved a little closer to him. 'Doing what? Talking to me? Listening? Telling me about yourself? We've lived next door to each other for the best part of the year. You can trust me.'

'I know that. If I trusted anyone, it would be you, but . . .'

'But what?' Sophie felt confused. Maybe she'd misread the signs, but she thought they had a special connection. She was longing to kiss Brody. Willing it.

For a few magical heartbeats she was certain he was going to lean in and kiss her. Instinctively she closed her eyes, anticipating the warmth of his lips on hers, ready to sink into a moment she'd been thinking about more and more since the lantern parade. The moment when she kissed a lovely, empathetic and divinely sexy man at a Christmas party.

'I'm sorry. I can't.'

Sophie opened her eyes to find that Brody had shuffled away from her, and now he couldn't even meet her eye. 'I'm sorry,' he mumbled again.

'*Brody! Where are you?'*

The shout was like a gunshot going off. 'Fuck, it's Mum!' He leapt up so quickly that he knocked Sophie's arm and her glass slipped from her grasp and shattered on the cobbles. Harold's barks echoed around the stable.

'Harold. Come here! He'll cut his pads,' Brody said.

Sophie crouched down, her heart hammering. 'I'll clear it up.'

'No!' he replied sharply, then more softly, 'No, I'll do it. You might hurt yourself.'

'What do you mean?' Sophie insisted, feeling like she'd been dumped in a tub of cold water. Surely Brody hadn't been too scared of his mother finding them together . . . If so, then he definitely wasn't the man she'd thought he was.

'Brody! Are you in there?' The voice was closer.

Before either of them could reply, Louise stepped out of the shadows into the stable, her sequin jumpsuit shimmering in the light.

When she saw Sophie, her jaw dropped momentarily.

'Oh. It's you,' she said tightly. 'I wondered where you'd both got to.' She dragged her gaze from Sophie to her son. 'Brody, there was a phone call for you.'

118

Brody pulled Harold tighter to him. 'Phone?' he said, as if he'd never heard of such a device. 'No one has called me, Mother. I've got my mobile here with me.'

'On the *house* phone.' Louise glared at them both. 'It was Tegan. She was in a taxi on her way from Windermere station.'

Now Brody's mouth gaped open. 'Tegan's at *Windermere*?' he said.

'She was,' Louise replied. 'She's now waiting for you in the drawing room.'

'Jesus Christ . . .' He ran a hand through his hair.

Louise's eyes narrowed in confusion, then she said smoothly, 'I expect she just wanted to surprise you, so I said I'd come and find you. I thought you'd be over the moon to see your fiancée. I'll see you back at the house.'

Sophie felt as if she'd been knocked to the floor by an invisible force; like in one of those dreams where you're paralysed and are helpless to stop a truck bowling towards you, or you're falling slowly but inevitably to Earth.

Disbelief, shock, numbness: all these feelings had landed on her at once. Almost exactly the same feelings that had crushed her when she'd caught Ben and Naomi together. And Brody was the last person she thought would make her feel like this.

'I – I didn't know you w-were engaged.' The words sputtered out.

Brody couldn't even look at her. 'Not many people do,' he murmured.

'And that makes it *better*?'

'No. I'm sorry for inviting you here. To the house. To the stable.'

'No. It's me who should be sorry, for letting things get this far. I would never, *ever* be part of cheating on a woman – on anyone in fact. I know how it feels!'

'Nor me. It's why I couldn't – can't – be anything more than your friend. I am so sorry, Sophie.'

This time, when Brody shoved both hands despairingly through his hair, Sophie didn't find it charming any longer. Every gesture, every self-deprecating look or comment was just one more thread in the web of deceit he'd spun her. She was such a fool for falling for it. Doubly foolish, after the last time, when she swore she wouldn't be so naive again.

Chapter Eleven

Brody's world fell away from under him. All his worst nightmares had come true and it was all his own fault.

'I can—' he began.

'Explain?' Sophie cut him off, her tone dripping in disdain, and curled her lip in disgust. She was looking at him as if he was a particularly revolting insect that she'd found in her bed.

'No. Not *explain* exactly. Not right now. Look, it's – complicated.'

'Oh, really? It looks pretty straightforward to me. Your fiancée, who you failed to mention during any of the conversations we've had, has travelled up here specially to surprise you.'

'I never wanted to hurt you or Tegan. Or anyone. I was enjoying your company. I really do value your friendship . . .'

Immediately Brody realised he'd flung fuel on a fire that was already out of control.

'I *valued* your friendship too,' Sophie said bitterly. 'But I think any connection between us has to end now. I need to leave.'

She marched off, but Brody caught up with her. 'Sophie, please,' he pleaded, reaching out for her arm to stop her.

She pushed his hand away. 'No, I'm going home. And I'm sorry, but I'll be finding another vet after Christmas.'

The sound of her boots ringing out on the cobbles made his head throb. Brody leaned against the stable wall. He wanted to bang his head against it, for how stupid he'd been. Even though he had feelings for Sophie, he thought he'd done well to hide them, so he wasn't leading her on. And now, after what she'd told him tonight, he felt like an even bigger idiot for breaking her trust and losing her friendship.

When he turned round, Gabriel was chewing a piece of hay and watching him from accusing eyes.

'Yeah, I know. I fucked up royally, Gabe!'

With that, Brody marched out of the stable, already knowing there'd no be sign of Sophie and that he'd have to face the music inside the house. He'd have to clear up the glass later.

Why was Tegan even here? Why now, of all times? Immediately he realised it really didn't matter when she turned up. He shouldn't have asked Sophie to the party, or for a drink in the stable. It had felt like an innocent gesture – the chance to know her better. He just hadn't expected that his feelings of friendship towards her would start turning into something else.

'Isn't this a wonderful surprise!' his mother gushed the moment he walked into the drawing room.

Tegan looked like a snow-queen, in a long cream coat,

white jeans and a fluffy sweater. Her hair was drawn back from her face in an updo that made her look otherworldly.

'And she looks beautiful!' Brody's Uncle Trevor declared. 'Fit for the top of the Christmas tree.'

'I hope not!' Tegan replied, stepping forward to greet Brody. 'I hope I haven't arrived at an inconvenient moment,' she murmured as he kissed her cheek.

'No. Of course not. It's a lovely surprise,' he said, grinning like an idiot, as everyone expected, while inside he was dying. All he could see was the expression on Sophie's face when she'd heard his mum say that his fiancée was waiting for him. Brody had known exactly what Sophie had been thinking, and it cut him like a knife.

Should he shout out the truth now to everyone in the room – to his family? 'Everything I do is a lie, everything you see is bullshit.' But he couldn't; he knew it would hurt even more people than he already had, so he was trapped.

'Shall we let these two lovebirds have some privacy to catch up?' his mother winked, with an emphasis that only Brody detected.

With a few murmurs and titters, the other guests went back to their drinks and conversations.

His mum spoke to Tegan, who was standing patiently by. 'I bet you're dying to be on your own together. You must be exhausted after such a long journey. How was it?'

'Not too bad. I managed to get a seat at the front of the plane. They upgraded me when I went to check in, so I've managed some sleep.'

'That's good, isn't it, Brody?' His mother patted Tegan's arm. 'So I'll leave you to it.'

To what? thought Brody, but gathered himself. The moment she'd moved away, he said, 'You must be knackered from the journey.'

Tegan huffed sharply. 'Are you saying I look it?'

'I didn't mean that you don't look nice.'

She sighed. 'I'm winding you up. Yeah, I'm tired. It's been one hell of a time and a long journey. You look a bit ragged too.'

'I've been on-call this week,' he said hastily. 'Do you want to go upstairs? Get changed and have a rest?'

'Yes, please, but my bags are still in the hallway.'

'I'll get them and take them up.'

'I can carry my own bags,' Tegan muttered, following him out of the room.

'It's no trouble.' He strode off into the hall, picking up her suitcase in one hand and her overnight bag in the other.

'Brody. Let me help, *please*. I can carry my own bags,' she called as he thumped up the stairs ahead of her.

He hadn't meant to snap, and he knew that guilt was making him want to take care of her. Guilt: towards Sophie, Tegan *and* his mother. The situation was complicated enough without him making it far worse.

Tegan closed the bedroom door behind them. 'Are you sure this is a lovely surprise?'

Brody put down the bags, unable to reply for a moment. Sophie's expression flew back to him: her utter disgust and disappointment.

'It's a surprise, definitely,' he said. 'I thought you couldn't come home until the twenty-ninth? That you had to stay in New York over Christmas . . .'

'So did I.' She sat on his bed and unzipped her shoes. 'I finished the project early or, rather, I'd done everything I could. There's a delay, and Wes, my boss,' she qualified, 'suggested I take the chance to come home in time for the big day. He's not a total ogre, you know.'

'I'm amazed you managed to get a flight.'

'So am I, but I called the airline and I'm a frequent flier by now, so they were pretty helpful. That's why they upgraded me at check-in, because Economy was full.' She curled her toes and let out a sigh.

'Sorry about the mess. I'd have tidied up, if I'd known,' he said, gathering up a pile of his clothes from the bed and searching for a place to dump them, but the nearby chair was also piled high with jeans and sports gear. He decided to add to it anyway.

'Brody. *Please* look at me. I know you're pissed off that I descended on you unannounced like this.'

He turned round, giving Tegan the chance to explain. It was wrong not to listen to her, just as it had been wrong to think he could be 'just good friends' with Sophie.

'I wish I'd warned you, but I was almost too scared to. I couldn't turn down the chance to come home. Not with my dad so poorly and waiting for his operation. What if something . . . happens and he doesn't make it? I wouldn't forgive myself for not having this Christmas together.'

Finally Brody allowed himself to take in Tegan's face. He

caught his breath. She was bound to be exhausted after a manic time at work and a transatlantic flight. Even so, there were dark smudges under her eyes, and her cheekbones seemed sharper with worry and sleepless nights, probably because of all the concern she was feeling about her dad. No matter what had happened between them, he still cared for her.

'How I feel doesn't matter now. Your dad does. Family is the most important thing.'

Tegan stepped forward and rested her fingers on his arms. Brody let his own hang limply by his sides.

'How you feel does matter,' she told him, finally letting go of Brody. 'It always has, and I'm so sorry things have turned out this way.'

He felt his throat tighten. There was so much he could say right now: so many hurtful, bitter words. But none of them would help Tegan or make him feel any better.

'Yeah, I'm sorry too, but the important thing is that we have to get through the next few weeks, or however long you're back for.'

'You're a lovely, good, kind man.'

A lovely, good, kind man. The words stung like salt in a wound. Being a lovely, good, kind man hadn't been enough for Tegan, and now it wouldn't be what Sophie thought of him, either.

'And any woman would be lucky to have me?' he said bitterly.

'You know they would. Don't start this again,' she begged.

Brody ignored the last part of the sentence. 'Are you staying here tonight?' he asked. 'Or do you want to go to your parents'? I can ask Mum to give you a lift. I'm sorry I've had too much to drink to be able to drive you.'

'I – thought I'd stay here. I think it's what everyone will expect. I called them on my way, and Mum even said I should stay with you tonight. She said you must have missed me and that she and Dad could wait until tomorrow.'

He felt sick at the charade they had to put on.

'So I came here first. I think your mother will expect me to stay too.'

'So many expectations,' Brody murmured.

'Yes. But it might not be for long.' Tegan let out a sniff and stifled a sob. 'I didn't mean that. I hope it's not for that reason.'

She started to cry, and Brody's tough shell cracked. He sat on the bed next to her and took her in his arms and let her cry into his shoulder. Only a cold-hearted bastard wouldn't want to comfort the woman he'd loved. The woman he'd thought he was going to marry, until Tegan had found someone else and slept with them. Maybe that's why he'd felt closer than he expected to Sophie tonight, because he understood exactly what she'd gone through, more than he could admit.

Now his engagement to Tegan was a sham, their relationship purely for the benefit of their families.

Tegan was convinced the stress of her brother's acrimonious divorce had been one of the contributory factors to her father's first heart attack. The Jamesons had had a difficult year, with Alan's continuing ill health forcing him to sell his construction business and take early retirement. Tegan's mum, Fiona, had had her own health scare, which had fortunately proved to be benign, but the family had been under continued stress for a good eighteen months now.

A week after Tegan's brother had announced that he and his wife were splitting up, Alan had had his heart attack. It had been touch and go whether he'd make it for a while, but he had pulled through. Now he was waiting for major heart surgery and had been warned to avoid stress, so that he was in the best possible shape for the operation; but with the time he'd had of things lately, this was easier said than done.

That's why Tegan had begged Brody not to reveal that they were breaking up until after the New Year, or when her father was stronger and had started to recover from the surgery, so that the news wouldn't impact his fragile health.

Brody soothed her.

Tegan wiped her eyes, and he held her closer to try and calm her.

'I won't let you down,' he promised.

'I know. Unlike me.' She sniffed. 'I know I'm asking a lot and I can't tell you how much I appreciate it. I think we need to set some ground rules, though, for the next few weeks, to try and make sure things aren't awkward.'

How could things be more awkward than they already were? Brody thought. 'What kind of ground rules?'

'Well, that we're sharing a room – whichever house we're staying in – so that our families don't suspect anything.'

'No one will know where we're sleeping while we're at Felltop,' Brody reasoned. 'And no, my mother does not come into my bedroom.'

'I never thought she would,' Tegan said. 'We do have to be convincing, though. I don't want Mum and Dad – or anyone – thinking something is amiss. You did agree to that, Brody, and I'm grateful. I would never forgive myself if Dad had another attack, especially now that the operation isn't so very far away. You know what happened when Harry told him he and Sarah were—'

'Yeah. I know . . .' He stared at the floor, not needing to be reminded why they were in this situation. 'Does Wes know about our arrangement?' he asked, though even saying the man's name left a sour taste in his mouth.

'He's aware that I don't want to cause trouble. He thinks I'm going to tell the family while I'm over here.'

'But you're not. Why haven't you told Wes the truth? You don't need to lie to him, do you? There are already so many lies.'

'He wants me to come clean.'

'Does he?' Brody raised his eyebrows. That was rich, coming from Wes, who had been quite happy to conduct an affair with Tegan behind Brody's back.

Tegan had met Wes six months previously, when she'd taken a secondment in New York from the Manchester advertising agency where she had been creative director.

She was thrilled at such a huge promotion, and Brody was incredibly proud of her. Tegan had assured him the secondment would only be for six months and would then lead to another promotion when she returned home.

'So you won't tell anyone what's happened, will you?'

'I promised I wouldn't.'

'It can't do any harm. Not until Dad's safely on the road to recovery. Because if ever my parents found out that we broke it off months ago and we've been lying to them, I dread to think what might happen. You know how gossip spreads around here. It's such a – claustrophobic place. Everyone thinks they're entitled to know other people's business. I hadn't noticed it quite so much until I started working in a big city.'

Perhaps that's because, in a small village, people might not be perfect, but they cared about each other, Brody thought. What he said was, 'I haven't breathed a word to anyone.'

'Thank you. You don't know what that means to me. I've been worried sick about them finding out, and Christmas would be horrendous if Dad took a turn for the worse.'

Christmas would be pretty dreary anyway, Brody thought, with both of them pretending everything was hunky-dory and wonderful – lying to themselves and to everyone else.

Tegan lay back on the pillows of his bed. 'Do people expect me to come down and join the party?' she asked. 'Only I've got a bit of a headache.'

Brody heard the sounds of cars moving on the gravel

drive of the farmhouse. He went to the window and drew the curtains aside.

'It sounds as if it's all breaking up, and it's getting late anyway. I'll say you're not feeling great, which is understandable after the journey.' He closed the curtains again, feeling totally despondent.

'Thank you.' She pulled the down throw over her. 'For everything.'

'I'll have to pop down and say goodbye to people. Will you be alright?'

'Yes.' She nodded.

'I'll bring up some tea, if you like.'

'You don't have to.'

'I don't have to do anything. I want to help.'

'Brody?' Tegan said. 'If it's easier for you, I'll sleep in the spare room. I'll move my bags out of here when everyone's gone.'

Brody was relieved, yet he still felt sad. He nodded. 'I need to put some heating on in there.'

'Don't do anything special for me. I mean it.'

'I'd put the heating on for anyone.'

She nodded. 'Sure.'

Briefly she sounded very American, which reminded him of how far apart they'd grown, in every way.

'What I meant is that I wouldn't punish you by making you sleep in a cold bedroom. I'm not that vindictive.'

He wasn't vindictive, but he was deeply hurt and so conflicted that he didn't know what to think. Were lies ever justified?

'Thank you. I do appreciate it,' she said softly.

Brody went downstairs, said goodnight to the last stragglers who were leaving and then went into the kitchen.

By the time he came back up with a mug of tea, Tegan was fast asleep under his quilt and he hadn't the heart to wake her. He left the tea by the bed and went back downstairs to start tidying up.

It was hard having Tegan back. The two of them had been having difficulties for ... at least three months now. Brody hadn't wanted to acknowledge their drifting apart at first, but it had started not that long after she'd arrived in New York in September. At first they'd been WhatsApping each other every night, then every few days. Tegan had said she was too tired or too busy, and the time difference hadn't helped.

They'd got engaged just before she'd left for New York, keeping it low-key among their close families and friends. Looking back, if he was being brutally honest, Brody hadn't been one hundred per cent ready to make the commitment, but he did love Tegan. Then he'd found out it wasn't them drifting apart, but Tegan drifting into another man's bed.

All of this he'd longed to be able to tell Sophie. Should he go to her tomorrow and explain. Would she trust him? Was it fair to Tegan? Did Tegan even deserve him to be fair?

She had done wrong, yet she was having a horrific time and he couldn't help but worry about her and feel sorry for her. Losing your father at any time was devastating. He never wanted anyone to go through the experience he had; but even if he couldn't prevent it happening, he had no intention of making things worse.

Chapter Twelve

Bloody Christmas. Bloody Brody.

If Sophie was brutally honest, the fact that Brody had turned out to be a lying git had nothing to do with Christmas. It wasn't Christmas's fault. She had to admit that much as she pulled up outside the farm shop the next morning.

It was only just starting to get light, but the car park was already almost full with Christmas Eve shoppers. Wispy snowflakes were falling and the coloured lights strung along the wooden porch shone through the gloom. The decking was piled high with bags of logs, fir wreaths and holly sprays. Carols were playing from the loudspeakers, and customers in Santa hats were greeting each other warmly.

Sophie felt like the love-child of Scrooge and the Grinch.

Last night had been humiliating and upsetting. She'd never forget the few seconds of silence that had hung between her and Brody after Louise had announced that his fiancée had arrived.

She'd hardly been able to speak. Louise only looked on, perhaps too shocked to say more. Sophie thought she saw the glint of tears in Louise's eyes, as if she was about to cry. Had she suspected that something more than feeding the donkey had been going on? Sophie had wondered why Louise had been so spiky, and now she knew exactly why.

The worst thing was that Sophie was beginning to think there was something wrong with her. She was having doubts about the 'Escape for Christmas' break. Could she handle it? Was she stupid for even thinking of it? Were she and her few guests the only people on Earth not to love Christmas? Was she . . . just bitter and flaky – or a bit *weird*?

'Good morning! Happy Christmas!' A man Sophie recognised from last night's party greeted her cheerfully.

'Morning,' Sophie ground out, before tagging on a smile.

It's not his fault, she reminded herself. It's no one's fault but your own, Sophie Cranford, for being far too naive and trusting. Only bad things happen to you at Christmas.

She collected her bags from the car and found a trolley. The handle, wet with melting sleet, chilled her fingers. Sophie entered the portal to Christmas mayhem and braced herself. From this moment on, she had to set aside her troubles and put on a brave face, whether that was in the farm shop with 'normal' people or when she got home to prepare for the arrival of her guests later that day.

The guests had come to get away from Christmas, not to have a miserable time with the host from hell. She imagined the reviews:

> *Stunning location: shame about the host.*
> *Host made me us feel like we were a hindrance. Won't be going back.*

Avoid at all costs. Hostess spent the time with a face like a slapped arse.

'Deck the halls with boughs of holly!' The volume on the speakers was even louder inside the shop, giving Sophie an instant headache, and the scent of the festive season was almost overpowering: cinnamon mixed with pine and cloves in a noxious Christmas pong that made her feel nauseous.

Gritting her teeth, she pushed her trolley past pyramids of dates and satsumas to the collections counter. She'd pre-ordered as much of the food that she'd need as she could, and checked off the receipt to make sure everything she'd requested was available. It contained local bacon, eggs, Cumberland sausage, bread, tomatoes and mushrooms for the breakfasts. She'd also ordered chicken thighs, fresh prawns and squid rings for the paella, along with a large bag of rice and some saffron.

She added a bottle of wine and large box of chocolates as a gift for Vee – who definitely didn't deserve a grouchy boss, after all she'd done – before heading to the deli section for her tapas ingredients. She'd already bought in some that should be simple to prepare from jars or packets – olives and anchovies – and now added chorizo and serrano ham. She sincerely hoped the cats didn't get into the kitchen or dining room; all that meat and fish would drive them insane.

The cats!

Phew. She'd almost forgotten they would need extra food while the shops were closed and Sophie was busy. The aisles were getting more crowded and she lost count of the times she said 'Sorry' in her quest to wheel her trolley to the pet-food section, where she added some kibble and several tins of cat food to her trolley. Not turkey or reindeer; tuna and quail. The cats deserved a treat, but it wouldn't be a festive one, that was for sure.

'Sophie!'

Brody emerged from behind the dog-food section with a Christmas stocking full of canine treats and a huge bag of carrots. Sophie tried to walk off in the opposite direction, but she was cornered by a display of cat selection boxes.

'Can I come past, please?' she said, her voice holding firm.

He looked washed out and hadn't shaved. But why should she care? Hopefully he felt as bad as he looked. Brody also didn't move out of the way. 'Please don't be like this,' he pleaded.

'I'd just like to take my cat food to the till,' she said haughtily, aware of how ridiculous she sounded.

He clutched the dog stocking to him. 'I'm not trying to stop you. I only wanted to explain . . .'

'I don't think you can explain being engaged and—' She paused while a woman plucked a pouch of reindeer cat food from the shelf. 'And what happened in the stable.'

As soon as the woman had gone, Brody grabbed the end of her trolley so that she couldn't move. 'Nothing happened.'

Sophie didn't correct him, wanting to put last night to the back of her mind.

'Sophie, I really do care about you,' Brody said. 'And believe me, I want to explain, but I just can't . . .'

'*Can't*?' Sophie hissed. 'What does that mean?'

'That I – can't give you an explanation for my behaviour. Yet.'

'"Yet?"' she scoffed. 'Brody, I don't think you'll ever be able to give me a good enough explanation as to why you didn't tell me you were engaged. Now please, I would *greatly* appreciate it if you could let go of my trolley, so that I don't have to reverse it back around the shelves. I need to get home to my guests and my cats.'

'You'll understand one day,' he murmured. 'I promise.' He decided to step aside and create a gap between the cat toys and the kitty litter, allowing Sophie to wheel her trolley past him.

'Thanks,' she said and kept her eyes firmly to the front.

The whole charade was so childish, yet she felt awful that he'd lied to her, after everything she told him she'd been through, and she couldn't help but wonder if something might have happened between them, if Tegan hadn't surprised him. If not last night, then at some point over Christmas maybe?

Hating the thought of what might have been, she pushed her trolley towards the tills. There were two operators, one with three people queuing and one with two. Sophie chose the shortest one, hoping to get out of there fast.

She soon realised she'd picked the short straw, because the person in front of her had a problem with their payment card, and their pigs-in-blankets were out of date. It all added to the delay and the tension, as her queue didn't move when she simply wanted to make a speedy exit.

Then, to her horror, she found herself standing right next to Brody as he joined the other queue beside her. She looked over her shoulder at him, but he was just staring at the floor, holding on to his dog stocking and a large bag of carrots for dear life.

'Next, please!' the assistant called. 'Oh, hello, Brody! What are you doing for Christmas? Not working, I hope?' The bells on her antler headdress tinkled merrily.

'I'm on-call,' Brody told her.

'But you'll be able to have Christmas lunch?'

'Yes, but I'll have to stay off the wine.'

'Poor you. Oh, is this stocking for Harold? I do love Harold. And are the carrots for Christmas dinner?'

'No, they're for the donkey.'

'Well, we can't forget our pets. They're part of the family, aren't they? Will you be spending the day at Felltop or at your mother's.'

'I'll be at . . .' Brody hesitated. 'We're going round to a friend's.'

Sophie let out a snort of disgust. He couldn't even say Tegan's name. Why was it such a secret? Why wasn't he proud to tell everyone about her. Sophie had an inkling . . .

Brody tapped his card on the terminal.

'Have a lovely time, and don't work too hard,' the assistant trilled, her antlers jingling.

Sophie watched him scurry away without a glance at her.

'Next, please!'

'Oh, sorry.' Distracted by Brody, Sophie hadn't noticed it was her turn when her own queue moved on.

Her till operator was the farm-shop owner, Hazel, who after nine months of serving Sophie knew her well enough to chat to. She wore an elf hat with a bell on top and had rosy cheeks painted on with lipstick.

'Stocking up for the guests, are we?' Hazel asked, scanning the bar code on the pre-order box. 'I bet they need a proper Cumbrian fry-up in this weather.'

It wasn't too painful to be cheery in response, as Hazel was a naturally sunny soul who had always been very helpful to Sophie. 'They do,' Sophie replied. 'I get lots of compliments for the breakfasts, and that's down to the ingredients. The guests love to know everything's local.'

Hazel glowed with pride. 'We do try to obtain everything in the Lakes and, as you know, the meat's from our own farm.'

She scanned the bar code on the bag of kibble. 'Not the cat food, though. That's from God knows where – unless you want to give your two fresh chicken?'

Sophie snorted. 'They wish!'

Hazel's bell tinkled as she laughed. 'Not even on Christmas Day? I bet they get some turkey leftovers as a treat.'

'We're not having turkey,' Sophie said as lightly as she could, having rehearsed her response a dozen times already.

Hazel's eyebrows twitched as she scanned the tins of cat food. 'Oh? It's duck then? Or goose. We stock both in the shop.'

'Er. No . . .'

Hazel paused. 'Oh, I *see*. You've got veggies for Christmas!' She grinned. 'So many people are now. We keep some lovely cranberry-and-mushroom bakes in the deli section. We even have a vegan nut-roulade. You have to cater for all tastes now. Still, it's a lot of work, having to cook two meals. My son-in-law's a vegan and his wife's a pescatarian. Lucky I run a farm shop, eh? Although they get what's left in the shop on Christmas Eve!'

'We're having a paella,' Sophie told her, sensing ears pricking up behind her.

'Paella. That's novel. Are your guests Spanish?'

'No, just having something different.' With her cheeriest grin, Sophie held out her card to pay the bill. 'But I ordered everything I needed in advance. It's in the box,' she said.

'Ah.' Hazel pushed the terminal closer. 'Actually I think I remember the team making up your order. Prawns and chorizo and rice . . . Did we have everything you need? Because we won't be open until New Year's Eve now. We're all having a nice rest!'

'I don't blame you,' said Sophie.

'Happy Christmas, and good luck with your paella!' Hazel trilled, her elf hat jingling madly.

Sophie pushed her trolley out of the shop, certain that she would be the topic of conversation within the queue for at least the next few minutes. She loaded up the car as quickly as she could, keen to get back to the guest house and start making the pavlova and tapas. She also wanted to catch Vee before she left for Christmas.

Her heart sank when she saw Brody jump out of his Defender and aim straight for her.

Turning her back, she opened the passenger door of her truck.

'Do you need a hand?' he asked.

'No, thanks.' She lifted the box into the passenger footwell.

'Sophie . . .'

'There's nothing to talk about.'

He put the jute bag containing her other purchases on the car seat. 'You're angry and upset. I can understand that.'

Sophie was stung into responding, against her better judgement. 'You couldn't even tell the assistant you were spending Christmas with Tegan. It's strange that you have a fiancée you never mention.'

'Because not many people know we're engaged.'

'Apart from everyone at the party.'

'They know she's my girlfriend, not about—'

'The wedding?' Sophie shot back.

'We haven't arranged a wedding yet,' Brody said wearily.

Sophie scoffed. 'I don't expect there will be one at all, if she finds out you're interested in other women.'

'I'm not. I mean, I am. Interested in you as a friend. Oh, shit,' he added.'

Sophie shook her head in disbelief.

'I can see this is only making things worse between us,' Brody said gloomily. 'I'm sorry about everything. I know you don't believe me, but I honestly mean it.' He touched her arm and Sophie froze, without flinching or moving away. 'I *do* care about you, Sophie. You may not believe it, but it's true and, one day, I hope you'll understand.'

There was such longing in his voice, and pain in his eyes, that she thawed a fraction of a degree.

'Let's not talk about this again,' Sophie said quietly. 'The most important thing is that it never happens again and you don't upset Tegan. I would never want anyone to be hurt, the way I was before.'

'Sophie, I can promise you I am nothing like your ex,' he said, almost angrily. 'I would never want you to think I was that much of a bastard,' he added in a softer tone.

She wasn't in the mood to let him off the hook any further than she already had. 'I have to go to Sunnyside. My guests will be here at three and I've still so much to do. Have a good Christmas.'

Without awaiting his answer, she jumped in the car and closed the door, waiting for Brody to pull away before she set off. Her heart rate slowed and she took a few deep breaths to calm down before driving off towards the steep lane that led up to Troutbeck hamlet and Sunnyside.

Last night – or the past couple of weeks – had only been a temporary blip in her fresh start at Sunnyside. The important thing was to put the whole affair behind her and concentrate on making her 'Escape for Christmas' weekend a massive success. Without Brody on her mind all the time, Sophie told herself, she really could focus on her guests.

With another sigh, she pulled into her driveway.

It was only 9 a.m., but there was a strange car parked next to Vee's car. It was a vintage Alfa Romeo, in a tomato-red that stood out against the frosty ground and grey slate walls of the guest house.

Could it be Nico Lombardi. At this hour?

Perhaps he wanted to park at the guest house while he went walking. That was OK, but he definitely could not have his room until 3 p.m. Sophie had way too much to do before she was ready to welcome guests.

Instead of a tall, dark Italian, a small woman with tight iron-grey curls climbed out of the Alfa.

Sophie hurried over. 'Hello, can I help you?'

The woman peered at her above pink-framed specs, as if Sophie was late for school. 'I sincerely hope so. I'm staying here for the next few days.'

'Oh, you must be Mrs Agatha Freeman.'

Her eyes narrowed. 'I am, but how on earth do you know that?'

'Um. You – er – mentioned that you drive an Alfa when you booked,' Sophie said, desperate not to let on that Agatha was exactly how she'd imagined her, apart from the flashy Italian sports car.

'Did I?' Agatha frowned. 'Oh, well. I suppose I'm far too early to check in, aren't I?'

'I'm afraid so. We're still busy preparing rooms. Check-in is at three p.m.'

'Thought so,' said Agatha, then shrugged. 'No matter. To be honest, I just thought I'd work out the lie of the land and do a drive-by, in case the place was a grotty hole and I still had time to bail out and go home.'

'I do hope you don't feel like that,' Sophie replied.

'It looks pretty promising from the outside, but you never know what you're going to find when you start turning over duvet covers and inspecting bathrooms, do you?' She glared at Sophie. 'I've found that appearances can be deceptive.'

Unable to disagree, Sophie simply smiled. 'Would you like to leave your luggage until you can check in?'

'No need. I don't have much. It's only a couple of days, and we won't be expected to doll ourselves up for dinner or get involved with any of that fancy-dress nonsense, will we?'

'No, you can wear exactly what you like,' Sophie reassured her.

'Hmm. Bloody good, because I worried that with the Spanish theme I might be expected to don a sombrero and shake my maracas.'

Sophie stifled a snort that she badly needed to let out. 'That's only the flamenco troupe. Guests don't have to join in with the actual performance.'

Agatha harrumphed. 'Thank God for that. Anyway, like I say, I only wanted to check the place wasn't a dilapidated wreck or, worse, non-existent. Now that I have, I'm quite happy to wait until the official time. I'm not one of those people who think rules don't apply to them. The whole country would fall apart if we all did exactly what we pleased, wouldn't it?' Not requiring an answer, Agatha ploughed on, 'No, I plan to head into town, do the waterfall walk and grab a bite to eat. Will anywhere decent be open for lunch?'

'Several of the cafés in Bannerdale should stay open until mid-afternoon and there are a number of pubs. They'll be open all day. Would you like a recommendation?'

Agatha wrinkled her nose. 'Hmm, I'll find a café, if I can. The pubs are sure to be full of revellers, and I want to save any revelling for later. I hope my fellow guests are civilised,' she said, knitting her bushy eyebrows together and glaring at Sophie.

'I hope so too,' Sophie agreed with perfect sincerity, while trying not to laugh. 'Have a nice lunch, and I look forward to seeing you later.'

Agatha jumped back into her car and sped off, the wheels spinning on the gravel. At the gate she tooted her horn loudly at a passing tractor before roaring off down the lane.

Wow! Sophie paused by the open car door, feeling as if she'd been steamrollered.

She was used to guests' quirky ways, but Agatha Freeman was something else. She both lived up to Sophie's expectation – a Miss Marple meets mid-century headmistress – and defied it, with her sports car and her talk of saving 'any revelling for later'.

Sophie had better get over her disappointment about Brody fast, because she was going to need every ounce of her energy to get through the next few days.

Chapter Thirteen

'Thank you, Ms Rice. I'm sure Ivy will be fine with these antibiotics, but don't hesitate to contact us if you're concerned,' Brody said.

The pets of Bannerdale clearly didn't know it was Christmas Eve. Since 9 a.m., when he'd returned from the farm shop, Brody had been dealing with all kinds of creatures, including a hamster with a urinary-tract infection, who was sent home with antibiotics and instructions to dip his carrot sticks in the meds.

Ivy, the British shorthair, was the last patient. She had ear mites and, while Brody was trying to examine her, she'd taken out her displeasure on him by clawing his arm. Her talons had drawn blood, though the owner had chortled as if it was hilarious.

'Ivy is such a character! Naughty puss!' Ms Rice declared, stroking Ivy's head. Ivy hissed at Brody.

'And a happy Christmas to you too, Ivy,' he grumbled, bleeding over the exam table.

'She's grateful really,' Ms Rice said. 'Aren't you, sweetheart?'

Ivy retreated into her carrier, snarling at Brody.

It was now after 2 p.m. and he'd stayed a full hour after opening time to see urgent cases, sending the staff home and managing the last appointments on his own.

After he bolted the door behind Ms Rice and Ivy, he flung off his Santa hat. He was so wrung out by the events of the past twenty-four hours that, if he'd been a cartoon character, he'd have sunk down against the door and melted in a puddle on the reception floor. He couldn't even relax with a pint, because he had to drive home, and he was on-call until the start of Boxing Day.

Then he reminded himself that however much his patients weren't impressed by him, it was nothing compared to Sophie's opinion of him.

Brody took off his scrubs, had a wash, got changed and put some Savlon on the nasty scratch on his arm. Now he was fifteen minutes late to meet Carl, whom he'd summoned for emergency moral support at the Red Lion. He desperately needed someone to talk to before he went back to Felltop that afternoon. Because he had slept in the spare room and left early for work, he hadn't seen Tegan since last night.

She was heading to her parents' house after breakfast to spend the day with them. Christmas Day itself was to be split between his mother's and Tegan's parents. She was staying at their house on Christmas night and, although Brody had been invited to stay too, he'd said he ought to be at Felltop in case he was called out and disturbed them in the night, which had been a good excuse.

The Red Lion had Slade blaring out of the speakers,

mulled wine on tap and hordes of locals who'd crowded in after finishing work early. It reminded Brody of breaking up from school, but with real ale, and without the scraps with the private-school kids up the road. *Yet*.

He weaved his way through the main bar to a small room at the rear of the pub, warmed by a roaring fire. Carl lounged in a corner of the snug, looking as annoyingly handsome as ever. Brody didn't know why Carl hadn't found a permanent partner yet, although he knew that, sadly, it wasn't for the want of trying. He grinned broadly when Brody walked over to his table, revealing a set of perfect teeth as white as mountain snow.

'Hello there. I thought you'd decided to stand me up.'

'Sorry, I got held up treating a last-minute patient.'

'Wow.' Carl winced when he saw Brody's hand. 'You're not as popular with the animals as with the owners then?'

'Not with a black-and-white cat called Ivy, who objected to me trying to treat her ear mites.'

'Ouch! "Ivy", though. Very seasonal.'

'I don't think she was feeling too festive.'

'You don't look in the Yuletide spirit, either. Don't take this the wrong way, but you look like you've not slept.'

'I haven't had a lot of kip, no.'

'Anything to do with the party last night?'

'Yes, you could say that. Tegan decided to turn up out of the blue.'

'Tegan?' Carl exhaled. 'I thought she was in New York until New Year?'

'So did I.'

'Well, that was a nice surprise. No wonder you didn't get much sleep,' Carl said with an eyebrow-raise.

Brody was lost for words. He stared miserably into his alcohol-free beer.

'Oh dear . . .' Carl murmured. 'She's not pregnant, is she? I mean I know it might not be how you'd planned things, but a baby will be wonderful. Can I be a godfather? Not in the Mafia sense, but in the "renouncing Satan and all his works" sense. Although I can't promise to renounce *all* his works, to be fair, as some of them are rather a lot of fun.'

Brody allowed himself a smile before letting it subside again. 'Tegan's not pregnant.'

'Oh, shame. I was rather looking forward to there being a baby at your wedding. You do still want me to be best man? I mean, I know you haven't made any plans and haven't actually asked me yet, but I'd kind of assumed. I promise I won't speak to you ever again if you don't ask me.'

Brody felt his mouth tilt momentarily upwards in a smile, before it quickly disappeared. 'Believe me, if I was getting married, I would never dream of asking anyone but you.'

'*If* you were getting married. Shouldn't that be *when*?'

Brody would have taken a large gulp of his beer if he thought it would have done any good, but it was zero-alcohol and therefore of no use whatsoever to dull the pain from the mess he found himself in.

'Now you're worrying me, buddy. Would you care to share with Uncle Carl? You know what they say: a problem shared is a problem doubled?'

'There won't be a wedding, Carl.'

With delicate precision, Carl replaced his pint on the table. 'Ah. I see.'

'I've got myself into a bit of trouble,' Brody went on, glancing looked around to see if anyone he knew might be close enough to overhear their conversation.

'What kind of trouble? Does it involve Sophie from Sunnyside by any chance?'

'Why would you think that?' Brody asked defensively.

'A hunch and, judging by your face, I'm not far wrong. What happened? My favourite village vet hasn't gone and done anything silly, have you?'

'Probably, though not in the way you're thinking.'

Carl rested his head on his chin. 'What am I thinking?'

'That I – we – got involved with someone else.'

'Well, did you?'

'Yes and no. It's complicated.'

Carl rolled his eyes and sat back against the banquette. 'It always is, where love's concerned.'

'It's not love. It was, but it isn't now.'

Carl sputtered in exasperation. 'Can you please stop talking in riddles or we'll be here until next Christmas. Spit it out, man!'

Brody took a mental deep breath. 'Tegan and I were engaged, as you and a very select group of other people know. Just because we didn't want a fuss, and you know I'm a private person.'

'And I'm honoured I was one of those people.'

'Well, you're also the only person – apart from the two of us – who knows that we aren't engaged now.'

Carl let out a long breath. 'I'm so sorry to hear that, my friend. I thought you and Tegan were crazy about each other. I know you've known each other for years, with your dad and hers being mates, so I wasn't surprised when you finally got together, or when you told me you were engaged. I thought you'd done the whole getting-down-on-one-knee thing and proposed.'

'Actually I didn't. And neither did she. It was last September, when we were watching some daft show on TV about brides from hell, and we were about to turn it over when Tegan said we should do that. And I said, "What? Have a wedding from hell?" and laughed.

'And she said, "No, Brody, we could have a lovely wedding. A small ceremony, keep it to a few dozen friends and family, and an evening party for the rest. Not right now, but at some point when – fingers crossed – when dad's feeling better."'

Carl listened intently.

'And I realised what was happening, and I was . . . well, I was shocked that she felt that way, but I *was* in love and so I said, "Why not?"'

'As you do,' Carl said.

'Don't be so cynical. I felt so happy and it seemed right in that moment. We'd no plans to set a date, but it seemed natural to make the commitment, especially with Tegan about to go to New York. Finally, after a couple of failed relationships and a lot of lonely nights, this beautiful, gorgeous woman wanted to marry me, and I felt the same.'

'And you'd have done anything to make her happy,' Carl

said wearily, as if he fully understood where Brody was coming from. Which he probably did, having not been the luckiest person in love himself.

'Yes.' Except that now Brody knew better. 'What I should have done was the thing that would have made us both truly happy. And that would have been to say: "Well, maybe let's wait. Let's wait until we're totally sure. Let's take a bit more time, because there's no need to rush."'

'Yet you didn't.'

'I was afraid of losing Tegan and, at the time, I really did convince myself I was ready for the commitment. As you say, we'd known each other for years as friends and had been together properly for three months. Plus, Tegan was ecstatic and was saying, "My parents are going to be over the moon, and Dad will have something to look forward too. I can't wait to tell them. Won't your mum be pleased too?"'

'So I'm guessing you *have* now told Tegan that the engagement is off? Last night was it? When she turned up?' Carl winced. 'Poor love. I bet she's devastated.'

'No, she's not devastated. She knew it was off before she arrived.'

Carl almost coughed up his beer in astonishment.

'I broke it off a few months ago, when she told me she'd been sleeping with her boss in New York. So we're no longer a couple, but no one else knows, and Tegan – neither of us – wants anyone else to know. Not yet.'

'Jesus, Brody. Why not?'

'Because we don't want to ruin Christmas. And before you roll your eyes and laugh, it's not a simple matter of standing by the tree after we've opened the presents and telling everyone: "Oh, by the way, we won't need the couples massage voucher, we're splitting up. Happy bloody Christmas to you all!"'

'No, perhaps that wouldn't be the best timing.'

'In fact it's a totally shitty situation. Tegan's brother and his wife decided to tell her parents they were getting a divorce at the end of November, and you know her father's not been well. He's waiting for a triple bypass in the New Year and there's a chance he might not make it, as it is. Tegan told me the doctors warned him to avoid any stress, so she's understandably petrified that any further shocks could make him even worse. What if he deteriorates and he's not fit for the surgery?'

'Brody, mate . . .' Carl patted his back. 'This is genuinely awful.'

'Yeah. So we decided to wait until after her dad's op, and tell him when he's stronger in a couple of months' time. It's not ideal, but after what happened with my dad, I wouldn't feel right it I did anything to make hers worse.'

'I can totally understand that, but it will be tough to pretend and lie all over Christmas and beyond.'

'We'll cope,' Brody said grimly. 'It's not for long and if it helps her dad's recovery, it's worth it.'

'OK. I don't envy you putting on a front, but I can buy that.'

'Thanks.' He heaved a sigh of relief at having shared the truth with someone he trusted. But then he remembered the other dilemma. 'Problem is there's something else.'

Carl groaned. 'Oh God. What now?'

'I – um – have liked Sophie for a long time now, but obviously I didn't do anything while Tegan and I were together. I wouldn't dream of doing anything about it and dragging her into this mess.'

'Being a noble knight in shining armour, you mean?'

'Don't joke. I have been tempted. Things hadn't been great with Tegan for a while. Even before she went to New York last summer I worried that living far apart would put a strain on our relationship, but I thought it was short-term and we could get through it. We didn't. We grew away from each other, and then she started seeing bloody Wes.'

'Were you pleased? Relieved?'

'Of course at first I was deeply hurt and betrayed. More than I'd ever expected to be. The relief came afterwards and sooner than I'd thought, which is telling in itself. It was just about bearable pretending to be engaged while Tegan was going to be in New York for Christmas, but then she turned up here last night. She said her boss had let her come home. Playing the caring new boyfriend, making sure she was able to spend time with her sick father.'

'What a generous guy!' Carl scoffed.

'Yeah. Isn't he?' Brody said, recalling how sick to his stomach he'd felt when Tegan had confessed to him about Wes. 'It's a whole different thing, now she's actually *here* and—' He paused. 'This is where it gets really complicated.'

Carl sat up straight in his seat. 'Oh dear. I think I need another drink before I hear the rest of this.'

Chapter Fourteen

Mrs Agatha Freeman was at the Sunnyside reception on the dot of three, and Sophie would not have expected less.

'Hello. Did you have a nice walk and lunch?' she asked. 'Did you avoid the revellers?'

'Yes, to the first two. Not wholly to the third. Never mind, I found a quiet corner of a café where I could read my book in peace. Now I can leave all that tinsel and tat behind and properly relax.'

Sophie wondered what her reasons were for avoiding Christmas, but had no intention of prying. She had a feeling Agatha wasn't one for baring her soul.

Aware that her other guests might arrive at any moment, Sophie gave her a whistle-stop tour of the dining room, guest lounge and veranda. The sun had come out and there was snow on the distant fells, with the lake shining in the valley. The view was at its tip-top best. However, Agatha didn't comment, simply nodding and hmm-ing.

'That's the hot tub,' Sophie said, pointing out the area on the terrace with the view over the fells.

'Oh, I won't be using the hot tub.' She shuddered. 'I've stayed at holiday cottages where they have one. Never got in, though! They don't change the water between guests, just lob in a load of chemicals. Might as well bathe in the toilet!'

Sophie stayed in polite-hostess mode. 'That's obviously your choice, Mrs Freeman, though I can assure you that the hot tub is completely sanitary.'

'My dear, I know a few things about germs.' Agatha finally managed a smile. 'Please call me "Agatha". Let's not stand on ceremony, as we're going to be seeing a lot of each other over the next few days. Now I'm looking forward to a rest and a cuppa in my room. I presume there are tea- and coffee-making facilities?'

'Of course,' said Sophie, hoping Agatha wouldn't think home-made shortbread was unsanitary.

'I'm very pleased to hear it. Can't bear those horrid things in plastic packets.'

Sophie wondered what Agatha would make of the *turrón* nougat that she'd left as a gift too. Would she consider it too exotic? What about the paella?

She put on a sunny smile, even though she was now second-guessing all of her carefully made plans. 'There's an information pack in your room, including the format for the evening. Supper is tapas and the flamenco display. Tomorrow,' she almost said 'Christmas Day', but checked herself, 'is a paella, and you can join in the quiz, although some of the guests might decide to use the hot tub.'

Agatha shuddered. 'The quiz sounds infinitely preferable.'

'I hope it will be fun.' Sophie smiled warmly.

Agatha rubbed her hands together. 'I was on an episode

of *The Chase*, you know? And I won three rounds of *Fifteen to One*, but I expect you don't remember that one?'

'Er, I'm afraid not.'

'Just as long as this quiz of yours has proper questions about capital cities and history. None of that rap music and celebrities that no one's ever heard of.'

'Like I say, it should be fun . . .' Sophie inwardly shuddered at the Pop and Celeb rounds she'd spent ages devising. 'Erm, there are cocktails from seven, followed by the tapas and the flamenco. I've got in plenty of soft drinks. If you don't like cocktails.'

'Soft drinks?' Agatha snorted. 'On Christmas Eve. Sorry, *not* Christmas Eve. Good grief, whatever gave you that idea? My dear, I shall be the first to sample the Pornstar Martinis.'

Agatha was one of those guests who was totally unpredictable. Miss Marple one minute, and party animal the next. Sophie sensed trouble . . .

She hadn't even reached the foot of the stairs when the door opened and a young woman with a large rucksack walked in. She was barely five feet and petite, like a long-distance runner, with black hair caught up in a ponytail. She reminded Sophie of one of her best customers at the Christmas shop: a lawyer from Hong Kong who owned a huge house in Stratford that she decorated with a different theme every year.

'Hello!' Sophie called, hurrying to greet her new guest. By default, this must be Suzanne. 'Welcome to Sunnyside. I'm Sophie, the owner.'

The woman shrugged the rucksack off her shoulders. 'Hello. Thank goodness I'm here. The traffic's been terrible.'

'Have you come all the way from Cornwall in one day?'

She looked puzzled. 'Cornwall? Why would I drive up from Cornwall? No, I've come from Edinburgh.'

'Ah, of course. Sorry. One of our other guests is from Cornwall. Apologies, my mistake. You must be Amber.' Sophie could have kicked herself. With all the disruption and drama, her head wasn't in the right place. Of course this woman could also have been Amber.

'I am.' Finally Amber smiled and the tension ebbed from her strained features. 'It is gorgeous here. It's such a relief to find a place that looks as nice it does on the website.'

'Thanks. We'd never want anyone to be disappointed and, actually, I think the photos don't quite do it justice. Now would you like to leave your bags here and check in and have a very quick tour, so you can relax? There's tea and coffee in your room or you can bring drinks down into the guest lounge.'

'That sounds great. I think I'll make a mint tea and chill out for a bit, before the tapas and cocktails. You do have mint tea?'

'Not in the rooms, but I have a wide selection of teas in the kitchen. I'll bring some sachets up to you.'

'Great. Thanks.'

Despite being in welcoming host mode, Sophie's stomach was knotting at the thought of all the work she had to do. Thank goodness Vee had persuaded her to ask Ricky in for a few hours on Christmas morning to help with the washing up and laying out breakfast. It would be worth every penny, and he said he'd be glad to get away from 'doing cringe family stuff' at home for a few hours. She'd have him home by Christmas dinner, though.

Having established that they were on first-name terms, Sophie collected some tea sachets from the kitchen and showed Amber to her room. She kept her run-through brisk, as she could already hear the arrival of another guest downstairs.

But it soon became clear there was more than one guest, when she heard conversations and laughter.

Three people stood in reception. Two had to be Una and Hugo Hartley-Brewer, judging by their Midlands accents. Even if they hadn't spoken, Sophie would have guessed by the matching Berghaus puffer jackets and walking shoes. Una was short with curly ginger hair, while her husband was well over six feet and obviously still self-conscious about the fact, even though he looked around sixty. He slouched and hunched like a teenage boy who didn't want to be noticed by *anyone ever*.

By default, the smiling woman in a sunflower-yellow mac must be Suzanne Smith, a fact confirmed by her accent, which was straight out of *Poldark*.

They all looked at Sophie as she trotted down the stairs.

'Hello, everyone! Sorry I wasn't here when you arrived. I've been showing another guest to her room.'

Relieved to hear they'd all been chatting away, Sophie gave them a joint tour and showed them to their rooms. That left only Nico Lombardi. She checked her phone and emails, but he hadn't sent her any messages to say he'd be late. Still, he obviously ran to his own schedule and he'd turn up sometime. She had enough to stress about without worrying about him and, if the worst happened and he didn't materialise, he'd paid up front for the room anyway.

As she prepared the tapas, Sophie hoped Nico didn't leave things too late, because it was now almost sunset outside and the skies seemed very heavy. Vee had told her that Kev had checked the official National Park forecast and hoped he wouldn't be called out over Christmas. It was likely to snow above 1,600 feet, with a distinct possibility of sleet or rain for the lower levels. That might put paid to any frolics in the hot tub this evening . . .

Sophie had, however, received a message from the flamenco troupe confirming the details for tonight. The six members of the group were on schedule to arrive at 8 p.m. and would require somewhere to change. Sophie only had one spare place, her own flat, but that was OK. No, they didn't need food (thank goodness for that) and they'd be leaving at nine-thirty.

It was rapidly turning dark when she went outside to the bins, and to switch on all the lighting around the garden and hot-tub area. She pulled her fleece's zip up to her chin and shivered. Even with sleet in the air, it looked very magical: perhaps a little *too* festive, but too late for that now.

Over the field, she noticed the lights were on in Brody's yard and at the back of the house. Her brief glow of pride turned to a sharp pang of regret – and loss.

Was he there now with Tegan, cosied up in front of the fire? Were they in bed together?

Cursing under her breath, Sophie stomped back towards the door to the kitchen. She absolutely mustn't be distracted by Brody-bloody-McKenna. Not now. Not—

'Oh my God!' she shouted.

A dark figure stepped into her path outside the back door.

'Who are you? What do you want?'

'I rather hoped you had a bed for the night.' The voice was laced with amusement, though Sophie didn't feel like laughing.

The man stepped into the light spilling out of the kitchen window. 'I'm Nico – Nico Lombardi? I couldn't see anyone in reception, then I noticed all the garden lights go on, so I came round the back. I hope I haven't scared you?'

'No,' replied Sophie, her heart rate still leaping around like popcorn in a pan. 'Well, yes, a bit, but it's OK. Sorry I wasn't manning reception. I'll show you in through the front door, if you'll come with me.'

Gesturing for Nico to walk ahead, Sophie followed him to the front door, asking him if he'd had a good journey, while she tamed her pulse rate. She showed him into the reception area, where Una, Suzanne and Agatha were helping themselves to the honesty bar earlier than planned. They all glanced up, then did exactly the same as Sophie had done when she'd first got a look at Nico. Three jaws unhinged in unison, and no wonder.

Nico might have stepped straight off the cover of a romance novel about titled Italian billionaire surgeons. Tall, dark-haired, handsome and chiselled, he was possibly the most beautiful man Sophie – and her guests – had ever seen.

Chapter Fifteen

Brody picked up Carl's empty glass. 'I'll get this round. It's the least I can do, for bending your ear for the past half an hour.'

'Do you mind making it a G&T this time?' Carl asked.

The queue for the bar gave Brody time to reflect on the situation he'd got himself into. A couple of years ago he'd been beginning to wonder if he'd ever find 'The One'. He'd wanted to meet someone to settle down with and have a family with one day, though his demanding job with its unsociable hours made that difficult.

He found that other vets understood, so he'd dated a couple of veterinary associates who lived locally, but then they'd moved to other practices or the relationships had simply petered out. Or perhaps it had been his fault and he hadn't put in enough effort ... He wondered if he'd been using his job as an excuse not to get too involved. Being too busy was easier to accept than the truth: that he was afraid of being hurt and ending up lonely.

Tegan seemed to have walked back into his life at exactly the right time and they'd soon started a relationship, much to the delight of their families. They'd known each other for most of their lives, although they'd lost touch a bit when they'd gone to different schools, and Tegan had done a marketing degree at UCL while Brody had done his vet's training. Tegan had stayed in London for a couple of years before she'd moved back to Manchester. Naturally, on her visits to Bannerdale, their paths had crossed again and slowly their friendship had developed into something more romantic.

In Tegan, Brody found someone who was also ambitious and career-minded and who understood how important his work was to him. Tegan's agency was landing some seriously prestigious clients, for its size, and was gaining an enviable reputation. She'd told Brody that she was feeling like a 'big fish in a small pond' and he supposed he should have recognised her signs of restlessness, but he fully supported her ambition when the opportunity to go to New York came up.

'Here you go,' he said, after finally getting served and placing a large gin and tonic in front of Carl.

'Thank you.' Carl sipped with an appreciative sigh and let Brody settle into his seat. 'So, you were saying . . .'

'I was with Sophie in the stable and—'

'You were visited by angels?' Carl offered.

'Not exactly, though Gabe and the sheep were there. The thing was, we'd both had enough of the party. We got talking, and it turns out we've been through similar experiences and have even more in common than we first thought.'

'I don't know her that well, but whenever I've bumped into Sophie she always seems lovely. And I did think, when I saw you on the way to the lantern parade, that you looked to be getting along well.' Carl smirked as he took a larger sip of his gin.

'Yes, I think that brought us closer, and then she came to the party. I found myself wanting to kiss her; it was all I was thinking about, and she must have felt the same, but I pulled back before things went any further. That was excruciating enough, but then Tegan arrived.'

'What? In the stable?' Carl let out a gasp.

'No, thank goodness, but my mother almost walked in on us when she came to find me.'

'But nothing *actually* happened?' Carl checked.

'No, but even though *nothing* happened, I suspect Mum would have to be blind not to have sensed there was a connection between Sophie and me. The thing is Sophie didn't even know I was engaged. I guess when she first arrived she wasn't close enough to be one of the people I shared that with—' Brody broke off, realising what a mess he'd got into.

'And then, by the time we were friends, I'd found out that Tegan had cheated on me, so I wanted to talk about it even less,' he went on. 'But now – because Sophie just heard "engaged" and doesn't know the real story – she's absolutely furious with me, and rightly so. I bumped into her this morning and she wouldn't even look at me; she thinks I'm the spawn of the Devil and a right bastard.'

Carl pondered for a moment, then shrugged. 'Well, you can't really blame her, can you?'

'No.' Once again Brody was confronted by the memory of Sophie's face: her disappointment, hurt and disgust.

'Oh my, *what* a tangled web you weave.'

'I honestly didn't mean to.'

'Look, I hope you don't mind me saying this, but ... Have you ever thought that you're tying yourself in knots trying to keep everyone else around you happy, at the expense of your own happiness?'

'I can't let people down,' Brody replied softly.

'Buddy, sometimes you have to let them down or go under yourself. I know you hate disappointing anyone, but I think maybe you've gone too far the other way, and now you're over-compensating when it comes to family.'

Carl's comment cut through him. Brody did feel guilty about putting his vocation as a vet first; and maybe, because of the similarities between what had happened to his dad and Tegan's, he wanted to do everything he could to make sure things turned out differently this time.

'Or perhaps – and forgive the cliché – maybe you simply haven't found the right girl yet. And yes, I am including Tegan in that list ... But what about Sophie? Do you think once you're able to explain, she'll understand?'

'I've liked her since she first trod in donkey dung in my stable yard.' Brody smiled. 'She came round to introduce herself shortly after she moved in, and Gabriel had left a present in the yard. She was so eager to say hello that she stepped right in it.' He winced, but felt happy inside. 'I spent ages scrubbing her boot while she sat on a hay bale.'

'Sounds like a match made in heaven.' Carl chuckled.

'It sounds silly, but I found myself looking forward to seeing Sophie or hoping to bump into her. When I saw her name on the appointment list at the surgery, I couldn't wait for her to bring the cats in.'

'And it sounds like she's clearly fallen for your rugged charms, otherwise she wouldn't be so upset now, would she?' Carl went on.

Brody snorted. 'I hope you're right about Sophie, although I don't have rugged charms.'

'Now you're fishing! You know very well that half the village fancies the scrubs off your handsome arse.'

'You don't,' Brody said, his toes curling in embarrassment.

Carl rolled his eyes. 'That's because: A, you're not my type; and B, I know where your hands have been.'

Brody finally erupted in laughter. 'God, Carl, I'm sorry. You invite me for a Christmas drink and all I do is bring along my own personal raincloud and unleash a deluge on you. I haven't asked you how you are, or how you're spending Christmas? Still going to your sister's?'

'Don't worry – it's what mates are for. I'm going to my sister's later today, and my parents are coming too.'

'That will be nice. Some family time,' Brody said, knowing that Carl was part of a close-knit unit.

'It should be, though I doubt I'll have much time to relax. I'm the only one who knows how to deal with the turkey. Or the whole dinner, to be honest.'

'You love cooking, though?'

'I do, and I shall probably have to go all Gordon Ramsay and start barking at people.' He grinned. 'It's the one day when I can be as bossy as I like and no one in my family minds a bit.'

'You'll be in your element,' Brody replied, finally smiling and feeling better, after having Carl to chat to. At least there would be one household experiencing uncomplicated peace, joy and harmony – up to a point.

'If you need me, though, you only have to call; and I'm around on Boxing Day – ish.'

' "*Ish*?" ' Brody queried, intrigued.

'Someone from mountain rescue asked me if I wanted to go for a Boxing Day hike on the fells with him.'

'Mountain rescue?' Brody couldn't believe what he was hearing. 'You're not in the mountain-rescue team.'

'Not at the moment,' Carl said. 'You never know, I might volunteer after Boxing Day. They're *always* looking for people to hand out flapjacks and hot soup in the middle of the night.'

Brody laughed, before jokily winding up Carl about the man he was meeting up with. They stayed and talked for another half-hour before they both headed home, Carl on foot to his cottage in the village and Brody to his car at the surgery. With every step, his happier mood ebbed away. He was due to spend the evening with Tegan when she came back from her parents', and they were going back there with his mother on Christmas Day to spend it together with the families.

He thought of Carl and his family, laughing and getting under each other's feet in the kitchen. He thought of Sophie, trying to entertain her guests, and hoped they'd both be having a better time of it.

He turned on the windscreen wipers to clear the icy sleet that was falling from the skies. As he passed the last of the Christmas lights decorating the ferry houses by the lake, he thought about his dad and what he might have said about the 'right old pickle' Brody was in.

Brody hoped he would have approved of lying to spare someone's feelings and to protect their health, but he wasn't sure. His dad was always such a straight talker, and Brody worried that he wouldn't be proud of him, for this or the way his life had turned out.

No answers came and he drove on up the fells, his head-lamps highlighting the snow settling on the stone walls and fields. The wheel wobbled and he found his eyes wet with tears. Suddenly he missed his father as much as the day he'd lost him. He dreaded the sham that awaited him at home and had never felt less festive in his life. Even though it had been years since his dad passed, this time of year always made him miss the loved ones who weren't there.

Chapter Sixteen

Five of Sophie's guests were now in the lounge, chattering away while sipping cocktails and tucking into bowls of nibbles. Someone had told the smart speaker to play Abba's *Greatest Hits* and as yet no one was complaining, so Sophie decided not to interfere, glad to see it going well so far.

After the initial shock of finding that Nico Lombardi was the living embodiment of your typical Titled Italian Billionaire cover model, Sophie had given herself a stern talking-to to pull herself together and keep things professional.

Nico proved an expert at mixing Aperol Spritzes. Agatha, Suzanne, Una and Hugo had all either tried the drink before or been persuaded to try one now. Hugo was already on his second. No one had ventured out to the hot tub yet, which was fine with Sophie, as it saved on the heating costs. She could hardly blame them, as it looked like the sleet could be turning into snow and settling.

She had been worried about the flamenco troupe, but they'd messaged half an hour earlier saying they had a four-wheel-drive van and, being local, were used to the weather. She flitted between the guest lounge and the kitchen, checking the guests had everything they needed while preparing the tapas, which would be followed by her tropical pavlova after the dancing.

There was no sign of Amber, which seemed a bit odd. Sophie had been up to her room and heard the TV on, but she knew better than to disturb guests. Her only dilemma was whether to alert Amber to the fact that the tapas were being served. Tapas were on the agenda for the evening after all, and she'd assumed everyone would come down for meals, rather than having to serve people in their rooms. Perhaps Amber had fallen asleep after her nightmare journey or simply not felt like company.

Sophie busied herself with laying out the Spanish meat and cheese on platters and took them through to the others.

Hugo and Una were in the middle of telling Nico about their walking holiday in Sicily. Sophie's arrival was greeted with appreciative sounds, though the guests carried on talking. Sophie didn't mind being politely ignored. It suited her current mood and she didn't want to engage too deeply in conversation about her own circumstances, if possible. She placed the plates on the sideboard for guests to help themselves, but lingered to listen.

'Sicily was our first proper holiday without one of our grown-up children,' Una said sadly. Sophie noticed that she'd changed into a sparkly jumper, while Hugo was still comfortable in his fleece. 'That's why we're here now, really. Both our children aren't spending Christmas with us this year. Our daughter's going to stay with her new partner's parents in Norfolk.'

'And our son is a doctor in London, so he's on duty over the holiday,' Hugo added gloomily.

'*And* we lost our dog in November. He was a yellow Lab and thirteen,' Una sniffled.

The other guests offered their condolences, and Sophie's own heart went out to the couple. Christmas must have felt very desolate to them this year, after being used to having the family and their beloved dog there.

'We couldn't face Christmas on our own,' Hugo explained. 'I know it sounds silly, but there doesn't seem much point, now the kids have flown the nest and there's no Archie to beg for turkey at the dinner table, so we thought we'd get away from it altogether. Do something different, rather than even trying to make it the same.'

'Plus, we love walking, it's a great location and Sophie's plans sounded like fun,' Una added.

There were more sympathetic murmurs. 'It's a lot more fun than spending another Christmas at my cousin's!' Agatha declared. 'I lost my dear husband just over a year ago, and my cousin insisted I must spend Christmas with her and her partner. They're good souls, but they told me I couldn't spend the season moping around. They wanted me to watch the King's speech and stand up for the national anthem!'

'I don't mind watching it, but that sounds a bit much,' agreed Una.

Nico caught Sophie's eye and winked. She smiled back and hung around, listening to Agatha.

'It is, on top of all that bloody turkey. I'd rather fall asleep over my book or some trash on TV. Ron – my late husband – and I used to take the opportunity to watch rubbish on the telly and eat our own weight in cheese. We never had turkey. Ron was a great cook and he'd rustle up something like a moussaka or risotto. We loved our holidays in the Med, doing a bit of sightseeing and eating out by the harbours together . . .'

Sophie smiled, understanding now why Agatha had been so attracted to the Spanish theme and to not spending Christmas with her rather patronising cousin, however well-meaning she was.

'I'm sorry for your loss,' Suzanne said from the leather armchair, where she'd pulled a blanket over her legs. Sophie winced inwardly. It was Jingle's blanket. How could it have got into the guest lounge? Suzanne's black sweater-dress had already attracted white cat hairs, but luckily she didn't seem to have noticed.

'How long were you married?' Suzanne asked Agatha.

'Forty-nine years, give or take. We met at a bus stop in the pouring rain when we were both on our way to job interviews. We looked like drowned rats, but it didn't seem to put either of us off. I had to give him the number of my landlady; not that she would allow a man in my digs. Things were so different back in those days.'

Nico laughed deeply and his warm brown eyes crinkled at the corners. 'Sounds like love at first sight, Agatha.'

'I suppose it was,' she agreed, gazing momentarily at the fire. 'Hmm, well, enough of me boring you. I suppose you must all be escaping Christmas for some reason. What about you, young man? I'd have thought you'd have had a string of young women begging you to fill their stocking?'

Instantly, the room went silent. Sophie sprang into action. 'I think it's time for the sangria! I'll be back in a moment.'

'Want a hand?' Nico offered with a look that said: *please help me escape*.

'I didn't mean to embarrass you,' Agatha said.

'Not at all. I'm finding it all hugely entertaining.'

'And you'll tell us all why you're escaping when you come back?' Agatha commented.

Nico gave an enigmatic smile and followed Sophie to the kitchen.

Once in the fragrant warmth of the room, he sniffed the air with a happy sigh. 'That smells good,' he said.

'It's the *croquetas*,' Sophie replied, happy that her food was being appreciated. 'They've been warming in the oven.'

'Sounds delicious.'

'Please ignore the mess. It is clean, though!' she added, feeling Nico occupying every inch of space in her modest but well-equipped kitchen. 'This is normally out of bounds to guests, but I thought you might need a break.'

He smiled at her, flashing his perfect teeth. Perhaps he *was* a model. 'It's fine, honestly. It's fun and you're a great host.'

'Are you – er – in publishing by any chance?' Sophie asked him.

'Publishing?' He frowned. 'Whatever gave you that idea?'

'Just a hunch. Guesswork. I sometimes try to work out what my guests do for a living. Which sounds weird, now I've said it out loud. It's simply that you get to meet so many people, running a guest house, which I love. But forget I said anything. Honestly, it's not my business. Or anyone's . . .' She was digging a deeper hole by the second, although being in such close proximity to Nico was enough to make anyone flustered.

'It's a B&B – I expected to be asked questions. But I thought it might be much later on in the evening.'

'If you will make such strong Aperol Spritzes,' she joked with him.

'You haven't tried one yet.' His deep-brown eyes twinkled.

'Oh, that's kind of you to offer, but I don't think I should drink on the job.'

'Pity. I was hoping I'd get to know you better. I'm intrigued to know how a beautiful woman ends up here and running an "Escape for Christmas"?'

Sophie's cheeks heated up. 'It's far too early in the evening to talk about that. Let's just say that I used to love this time of year, but I've gone off it recently.' She handed a bottle of red wine to Nico. 'Now because you did such a great job with the Aperols, would you like to make this sangria? Maybe with more lemonade than originally planned?'

'Excellent idea.'

A few minutes later Nico carried two large jugs of sangria into the guest lounge, while Sophie brought out a platter with the warm ham-and-cheese *croquetas* and some other hot dishes. They weren't home-made; she'd found them in a deli in the village and had stored them in her freezer.

'Please tuck in,' she said. 'There will be more tapas later, and then dessert after the flamenco, so there's plenty for everyone.'

But where was Amber? Perhaps now was the time to pay a visit to her room and gently suggest that the food was being served.

Leaving everyone to enjoy the sangria and tapas, Sophie hurried upstairs, checking her phone as she went. The flamenco troupe was due in an hour, but she worried it might take them longer in this weather. It was properly snowing now, and the fields and garden were white all over. She'd check on Amber and then, if she'd not heard back, she'd call them again.

As she reached Amber's door, she heard sounds of someone moving in the room. Sophie knocked softly and said, 'I'm sorry to disturb you, but I wanted you to know that drinks and tapas are being served in the guest lounge, if you'd like to join us all.'

After a few seconds Amber opened it. 'Sorry, yes, I'm coming down. I fell asleep and I'm just changing. I'll see you all very soon.'

Relieved to hear her guest sounding perkier, Sophie went back down into the office and called the flamenco people. Jingle and Belle were squashed together on one radiator cradle for warmth. Sophie lifted the curtain of the office window while listening to the ringing tone.

Oh God, in the light spilling from the house, she could

177

see how much the snow had settled. There were a couple of inches lying on the hedge and the garden statues, while large flakes swirled and danced in the wind. There was still no reply from the flamenco troupe and Sophie started to panic a little. What if they didn't turn up? How would she entertain her guests? How would the troupe get home, if they did make it?

Setting her fears aside, she went back to the guest lounge, where the chatter was louder and more convivial than before. Nico was topping up Una and Agatha's glasses, Hugo and Suzanne were laughing at something hilarious, and the tapas were clearly vanishing at a rapid rate.

'Una Paloma Blanca' was blasting out of the smart speaker. Sophie hadn't heard the cheesy Spanish pop song since she was little, when her parents used to play it. She thought of her parents, at home with her brother and his family. Would they be worrying about her? She must find time to call them. Actually she missed them . . . For a few seconds, she felt horribly alone.

After ten months of running Sunnyside, she was aware that the guests' safety, comfort and happiness all depended on her – and at such an emotionally charged time of year too. However, glancing round at them all, having a whale of a time, she could relax on that score. Her main worry now was how soon the flamenco people would turn up.

'Hello! Sorry I'm late. Fell asleep.' Amber appeared in the doorway, dressed in a purple sequinned jumpsuit. 'You look like you're all—' She stopped mid-sentence and her face drained of colour.

Her eyes had locked with those of Suzanne, who was clutching her glass tightly. Everyone stared at them and then they both said in perfect unison: *'What the bloody hell are* you *doing here?'*

Chapter Seventeen

'That fire must be interesting.'

Brody glanced up to find Tegan standing by him with a tray of food. 'What do you mean?' he said, startled.

'You must have been staring at it for at least a minute. Probably longer. You didn't even notice me come in.'

'Didn't I?' He grimaced, feeling guilty that he had been in a world of his own. Tegan had left the snug some time ago to make a drink. 'Sorry, I was well away,' he said. 'Maybe I fell asleep. It's been a busy week at work.'

She put the tray on the coffee table. 'I grabbed some food from the supermarket on my way up from Mum and Dad's earlier. It's only bits that we can graze on, but I thought you wouldn't want a full meal before the big blow-out tomorrow.'

'This looks good to me,' Brody said, his stomach rumbling to prove the point. The cheese and crackers, pickles and sausage rolls piled onto plates did look appetising. 'Thanks for getting this. I should have done some shopping myself, but I didn't think. I had to pop back into the surgery after I'd been to the pub with Carl, and then I wanted to come straight home.'

'You're still friends with Carl then?' Tegan joined him on the sofa.

'Well, yes,' Brody replied, puzzled as to why Tegan would think he'd suddenly fallen out with Carl.

She had been waiting for him once she arrived after visiting her parents. Since then she'd had a long nap upstairs, still suffering from jet lag, so this was the first time they'd really seen each other to chat properly since she got here.

She smiled and Brody was reminded once again of how pretty she was, with her blonde hair and blue eyes. She was wearing one of his sweaters and it swamped her slender frame, which was even slimmer since she'd been in New York. Probably from working hard and the stress she was under, with her dad's poor health.

Brody sliced into a wedge of Cheddar. 'How are your mum and dad?' he asked, because they hadn't really talked about it, with Tegan going to bed for a rest.

She sighed. 'Dad's as well as he can be, considering that he's been waiting so long for the operation. He's so looking forward to Christmas.' She paused. 'Thank you for doing this – pretending. I know it can't be easy. You're a straight kind of guy. Lying isn't in your DNA.'

Brody avoided the obvious retort, because it was point-less to bring up her betrayal again. They were beyond that, and they simply had to be cordial enough to get through the next few days before Tegan returned to New York. Lately he'd dared to glimpse a future beyond their sham relationship, in which Sophie figured: a fresh start for all of them. But look how that had ended.

He popped a nugget of cheese into his mouth, so they could hopefully change the subject. He also thought about what Carl had said earlier and hoped he was right: Sophie must care about him too, to have got so upset. His heart sank a little more, but he reminded himself that this was only for a few more weeks, perhaps a month or a bit longer until – he sincerely hoped – Tegan's father was out of danger. At what point, however, did he and Tegan announce they were splitting up?

She certainly hadn't given him a timeline, so it made it difficult to ask when they could break the news to their families.

They finished their supper and Harold sauntered in and sniffed at Tegan, before settling down in front of the fire. A gust of wind blew the flames out suddenly, making Harold bark.

'Come here, boy,' Brody said, beckoning Harold to him. The dog grumbled and shifted a few inches back from the hearth.

Tegan went to the window and lifted the curtain. 'It sounds rough out there and it's *still* snowing.'

When Brody got up to join her by the window, even he was surprised. Several inches of snow had settled on the bonnet of the Defender and on Tegan's car. Thick flakes were still swirling around in the wind.

'It wasn't forecast to come down like this, was it?' she

said. 'There was barely a sprinkling when I left Mum and Dad's house, so I thought it would blow over.'

'I didn't expect this much snow, either, but I'm not surprised. You know what it's like up here on the fells. We're eight hundred feet above sea level. Your parents live at the southern end of the lake. It's a totally different climate down there.'

Tegan let the curtain fall and faced Brody, hugging herself. 'I'm worried we won't make it down there tomorrow for Christmas dinner. It looks pretty bad out there.'

Having thought the same thing for the past hour, Brody decided it was best to be honest, so that Tegan didn't get her hopes up too much. 'It might be tricky, if not impossible. The Defender's good, but even it will struggle in these deep, fresh drifts. It's just not worth the risk.'

Tegan didn't answer, but then sighed heavily. 'I really wanted this Christmas to be perfect. I can't help thinking . . . what if it's my dad's last?'

Tears trickled down her face, and Brody would have to have a heart of stone not to want to comfort her as she cried, wetting his sweater with her tears. She'd had a huge amount of worry, working abroad while her father was so ill. No matter how much she'd hurt him, he had to remember that, and he couldn't bear seeing Tegan in this state.

'I can't tell you not to worry. I know it's a major operation, but also one that surgeons do successfully every day. I'm *sure* he'll be fine.' He looked into her tear-stained face. 'Honestly.'

Tegan nodded. 'You're right. I'm probably worrying too much.'

'He's your dad,' Brody said gently. 'It's natural to be concerned about him.' He might also have added that he knew what it was like to lose a father and how high the stakes were, but that would definitely not have helped.

'Yes, it is—' Without warning she broke free, looking embarrassed. 'Sorry. I'm a bit all over the place. I'm still jet-lagged, and it's an emotional time of year for me. I can't bear the thought of travelling all this way – and all this pretence – and then missing the big day itself. I should have stayed there tonight, which would have been easier anyway.'

'It's only one day, Tegan. There's a thaw forecast later tomorrow and rain after that, so we can go on Boxing Day. I wish I could do something about the snow, but I've a nasty feeling we're going to be stuck here for a while.'

'But Mum's got in all the food . . .'

'Which will keep,' Brody said gently. 'It might be a good idea to have a chat with them. Warn them? I'm sure they'd want to be prepared, if the celebrations need to be postponed.'

Tegan wiped her eyes with a tissue. 'You're right, of course. Always so sensible. I don't want to call them, but I suppose I must. I'll just hang on a little while longer in case it stops snowing.'

It wouldn't, thought Brody, who had lived long enough at Felltop Farm to know that the roads would be impassable until at least the same time the next evening, and probably even longer. He and Tegan were going to have to spend

Christmas Day together by themselves. Plus, it only put off the moment when he'd have to take part in the jollities at her parents' while feeling hollow inside. Any second he might be ready to blurt out the truth, so great was the pressure lying on him. He could only pray that he wouldn't get a call-out to a sick animal, because he knew he probably wouldn't make it.

He cleared away the supper tray while Tegan went to wash her face, when a WhatsApp call came through. Brody leaned against the kitchen worktop to take the call, smiling at his mother, who was wearing a tinsel headband.

'Hi, Mum. You look festive.'

'I must admit I am feeling jolly. I've just come back from the neighbour's drinks party. Talk is that you have quite a lot of snow up at Felltop. I was phoning to see if Tegan made it up there safely.'

'Yes, she was waiting for me when I got home.'

'That's a relief.' His mother wrinkled her nose. 'Although is it going to spoil the plans for tomorrow?'

'I suspect it will. In fact I'm pretty certain of it. We must have had three inches of snow here; it's still coming down fast and there are drifts lying around.'

'Poor Tegan. She must be so disappointed.'

'Well, let's wait and see, but if need be, we can postpone everything until Boxing Day.'

'What am I disappointed about?' Tegan asked, walking into the kitchen.

Brody braced himself. 'It's Mum,' he said, holding up the phone. 'She was asking how you are.'

Tegan nestled next to Brody, so that she could squeeze into the shot. She waved and went straight into acting the perfect daughter-in-law-to-be. 'Hello, Louise. It looks like we're going to be stuck here tomorrow. It's getting bad out there.'

'I'm sorry to hear you'll miss the big day, but can you postpone?'

'I just called Mum and Dad. They're gutted of course, but they don't want us making any dangerous journeys. Hopefully there will be a thaw by tomorrow night, so we can do everything on Boxing Day.'

'Oh no, I'm sorry your plans have had to change,' Louise said sympathetically. 'I guess the only consolation is that you two lovebirds get to spend a cosy Christmas Day together.'

Brody felt queasy, but Tegan played her part, without missing a beat. 'There is that,' she said brightly, threading her arm through Brody's. 'What will you do tomorrow, now we can't all go to my parents'?'

'I'll be fine,' Louise said. 'To be honest, we've all been talking about the weather at the neighbour's and they've invited me round, as Plan B. So I might join them for lunch and then crash out here in front of the *Strictly* Christmas Special.'

'I'm sorry we won't see you,' Tegan said.

Brody could tell his mother was putting on a brave face and would probably much miss seeing him and Tegan. She was a very practical mum, he thought, and was pretending she was fine, for their sakes. Once again he thought of how she must have coped in those first Christmases after his father had died. They'd gone to his auntie's in Norfolk, and he'd spent most of it walking their dog or hiding in his room with a Game Boy. He wondered quite how many people actually had a 'perfect' Christmas?

After a few more minutes of conversation about Louise's plans, the call ended.

'That wasn't too bad, was it?' Tegan said. 'And your mum's right. We do get to spend time together – and not just for appearance's sake. Perhaps it will do us both good to have some time to talk.'

'What about?' Brody asked, more briskly than he meant to sound. 'Sorry. I mean, there's nothing to discuss, as far as "us" is concerned. We've both accepted it's over, haven't we?'

Tegan looked shocked. 'I guess we have,' she muttered, then added, 'I think I'm going to have an early night. I'm sorry I haven't got your presents to give you in the morning. They're at my parents' house.'

'I didn't think we were giving presents . . .'

'Well, we *have* to, Brody. What would everyone think if we didn't?'

He nodded.

'Did you think of that yourself?' she said. 'Please tell me you did.'

'I – er – wasn't sure,' Brody said. 'So I got you something, just in case. I didn't want to admit it, in case you hadn't.' It was true. He'd agonised over a gift that he didn't have the heart to buy. Jewellery was far too personal; books felt too impersonal. In the end he'd bought a hand-made and very beautiful cosmetic bag from Carl's shop and had filled it with luxurious organic potions from the posh cosmetics shop next door.

Tegan picked up his hand and looked into his eyes. 'Brody, remember that, in the eyes of the world, everything is the same as it was.'

Brody heard her walking up the stairs, which creaked as they had for as long as he could remember.

But nothing was the same as it always was.

Chapter Eighteen

Amber glared at Suzanne, who seemed to shrink back under the cat blanket for protection. 'Well, what *are* you doing here?' she demanded.

Suzanne finally snapped into action. 'I could say the same about you. Are you stalking me?'

'Stalking you?' Amber sneered. 'As if I'd want anything to do with your family.'

Suzanne got up, the cat blanket falling onto the floor. In her knee-high boots she was almost a foot taller than her adversary.

Sophie stepped in. Which was a mistake, because she then seemed to take the brunt of their anger.

'Did you know about this?' Suzanne asked.

'About "what?"' Sophie said. 'If you mean, did I know that you were – acquainted – then absolutely not. I saw you had similar surnames, but "Smith" is a very common one. I mean, it's not unusual,' she added in case her words were misconstrued.

'We're not "acquainted",' Amber said haughtily.

Suzanne groaned. 'It's worse than that. We're related.'

'*Related?*' Sophie repeated.

'We're sisters,' Amber explained. '*Half*-sisters, to be accurate.'

'If we're being accurate,' Amber said smoothly, 'we're only related because my father decided to have an affair with Suzanne's mother. It was years ago obviously, but we've only recently found out that he had another family. It seems he was doing more than working on the oil rigs while he was up in Scotland.'

'To be fair, we'd no idea *you* even existed,' Suzanne shot back. 'And it wasn't an affair, because *my* mum didn't even know he had another family.'

'*My* mum was actually married to him,' Amber retorted sharply.

'Um, would you both like to talk about this somewhere more private?' Sophie suggested, aware that the other guests were gripped by the drama unfolding in front of them.

Suzanne glanced around her, shame-faced, as if she'd only just realised they had an audience. 'I think it's better if we don't talk about it all. I apologise for the trouble,' she said spikily.

Amber folded her arms. 'I think I'll go back up to my room and have my tapas there. If you don't mind,' she directed this at Sophie. 'I'm sorry for causing a scene too, but of course I'd never have dreamed of coming if I'd known Suzanne was going to be here. I came here to *avoid* any family drama.' She walked off and thumped up the stairs.

Suzanne shrugged apologetically as Amber left.

'Why don't you come into the office and we'll have a chat

about how to – er – manage the situation,' Sophie said, although she was at a loss as to what she could possibly do, now that the two warring siblings were stuck under the same roof.

Suzanne nodded. 'Thank you. I'll just pop to my room and then I'll be straight back,' she said, emphasising the last few words as if to show she wouldn't be petty enough to flounce off upstairs.

'I'll be in the office whenever you want to talk.'

As Suzanne also went upstairs, Sophie finally turned her attention to the watching audience.

Nico lounged in a chair, one leg crossed over the other as if he owned the place. 'Should I fetch some popcorn?' he said.

Una giggled. Hugo smirked.

Agatha wagged her finger at him. 'Nico Lombardi. You are a very, *very* wicked man.'

While Suzanne was upstairs, Sophie collapsed into her office chair to compose herself. There was nothing she could – or should – do about her guests' personal lives, unless their behaviour impacted on the comfort of the other visitors, who were clearly intrigued and entertained, but she wouldn't allow a full-on war to break out.

Amber was out of the way – for now – and maybe Sophie could find out a little more information about the situation from Suzanne; maybe enough insight to keep the peace until morning. If either or both of them wanted to leave, that was their decision.

It was a mystery to her how the two sisters had both ended up at Sunnyside ... perhaps they had more in common than they liked to admit, because they'd chosen the same guest house for a getaway. Hopefully, once they'd calmed down, they'd feel better tomorrow and wouldn't want to leave, but if they did, she couldn't stop them. One thing was for sure: the drama unfolding at Sunnyside had taken her mind off what might be going on at Felltop Farm.

A few minutes later Suzanne poked her head around the office door, with a slightly sheepish expression that might have been embarrassment.

'Erm, sorry to bother you, but I've just heard someone at the door,' she said.

Sophie nodded. Counselling Suzanne would have to wait for a while, and the little scene in the guest lounge had made her forget that the entertainment was due to arrive.

'Thanks for letting me know. It's probably the flamenco troupe. I'm so glad they could make it, though I suspect we're going to have to put them up for the night. Can we talk a bit later? I want to do what I can to make your stay as comfortable as possible.'

'Maybe tomorrow. I'm sure you've enough to worry about now. I'm going back to the lounge. Now that I'm here, I don't intend to miss out on the fun, so it's best to put it to one side for the time being—'

'If you're sure,' Sophie said, wondering what Suzanne would have to say to the others.

Suzanne had stopped mid-sentence, fumbled for a tissue

from her pocket and sneezed violently. 'Oh God. Sorry, I didn't think I had a cold, but my eyes are so itchy and I keep sniffling.'

Sophie watched her go, seeing her trousers covered in fur. Somehow she had to retrieve Jingle's blanket and make sure the cats stayed in her flat. First, however, she had to deal with the dancers, who were probably half frozen and traumatised by their horrendous journey.

She opened the front door to a blast of icy air.

A red-faced muscular man stood in the porch, snow melting on his bald head. He looked more like an Olympic wrestler than a snake-hipped flamenco dancer. Perhaps he played the guitar, Sophie thought, spotting a people carrier on the drive through the swirling snow.

'Thank goodness you're here,' she said warmly.

The man frowned. 'You've been expecting us?'

'Of course, though I'm amazed you got through the snow. I suppose the dancing will soon warm you all up.'

'*Dancing?* I think there's been a mistake,' he said, brushing melting snow from his head.

'So you're not the flamenco troupe?'

'No, sorry. It's just me, my wife and our two kids. Or should that be two and a half,' he said anxiously. 'My wife is thirty-eight weeks pregnant.'

'Oh, erm – congratulations.' Sophie didn't know what else to say, or why this harassed man was at her door in a snowstorm.

'We were trying to get to my mother-in-law's in the next village. We managed OK in the Jeep until about half a mile away, but since then it's been a nightmare. It wasn't snowing further down in the valley and we wouldn't have set off, if we'd known. I finally got the car moving again, but there's a tree blocking the road past your gate. We saw this is a guest house, so I turned in . . .' He paused for breath. 'We were really hoping you could put us up for the night. Actually I don't know what we'll do if you can't.'

'I'm so sorry, but we're fully booked,' Sophie said. But, seeing the man's crestfallen expression, she knew there was no alternative and she couldn't simply leave them outside. 'Don't worry. Come inside out of the cold, get warm and comfortable and we'll work something out.'

His shoulders slumped in relief. 'Thank God for that. I'll help my wife and the kids out of the car. This wasn't how they were meant to spend Christmas, and I'm sure you weren't, either. I'm Piotr Nowak, by the way.'

Sophie smiled. 'It's no problem at all, Mr Nowak. Please come inside and warm up.'

'Call me Pete,' he said. 'Thanks for taking us in.'

While he returned to the people carrier, a series of calculations ran through Sophie's mind. Did she have enough food? Yes, because she'd stocked the fridge and the freezer well. Where would the Nowaks sleep? They would have to have her bedroom. She'd have to kip on the sofa in her sitting room and shut the cats in the office.

How would they get out in the morning? If the snow continued and the temperature dropped overnight, the roads could turn to hard-packed ice. She'd heard several tales of Troutbeck being cut off for days, with not even a snowplough or gritter able to get through.

With extra mouths to feed, she definitely didn't have enough food to last beyond Boxing Day. But what happened beyond tomorrow had to be set aside, because Piotr was helping his wife up the step to the porch. Mrs Nowak – Anna – didn't look much older than Sophie herself.

'Thank God you let us in,' she said, looking close to tears. 'It's been a nightmare, but I'm just so glad we're safe.'

The children, who were about three and five, stuck like glue to their parents. This must be very strange for them.

'Mummy?' the little boy whimpered. 'How will Santa find us here?'

'He'll leave your presents at Nanny's,' Anna said. 'They'll be waiting for you tomorrow when we get there, I promise.'

'I hope so.'

The little girl started to cry.

'She's worn out,' Pete said, picking up the toddler. 'Aren't you, Maria?'

Maria buried her face in his father's shoulder while the boy, Baxter, stared at Sophie as if she was Peppa Pig come to life.

'Well, would you all like to come through to the flat. I'm afraid the only room I have available is my bedroom.'

Anna cried in horror. 'Oh no! We couldn't turn you out of your own bed. That's not fair.'

'We'll be very happy on the floor in one of your guest spaces – like a breakfast room?' Pete offered.

'Well, we do have a guest lounge and dining room, but the guests are in there now and we're actually expecting a flamenco troupe to turn up.'

'Flamenco?' Pete echoed. 'That's random for Christmas Eve.'

'Yes, we're having an alternative Christmas here. All of the guests have come here to escape from the traditional arrangements.'

Pete exchanged a glance with his wife. 'Oh.'

'I know it sounds weird, but you'd be surprised how many people want to avoid the traditional festive season, for all kinds of reasons. Now would you like to come through to my flat? I have to warn you that I do have two cats, but I'll move them into the office. I'll need to change the bed too, but get yourselves warm.'

'We can do that, if you can give us some linen,' Pete said.

'I won't hear of you doing it. We don't mind cats.'

'OK,' Sophie replied, not being in a position to refuse help, with the paying guests to look after. 'I'll show you my kitchen too, so you can make yourselves a hot drink. There's toast and hot chocolate, or you can join the other guests.'

'This is incredibly kind of you and we'll pay the going rate,' Anna said, wincing. 'I'm ready to have a lie-down myself. My bump has been kicking off like Lionel Messi.'

Sophie walked through the office into her sitting room, where Jingle and Belle had taken up residence on the window seat.

'Cats!' Maria cried. 'What are they called?'

Sophie prepared herself. 'The black-and-white boy

with the tuxedo is Jingle and the little tortie is Belle,' she said softly.

'Jingle Bells! I sang that in the play at school,' Baxter said proudly.

'You did, and beautifully,' Anna agreed.

'Can I play with the cats?'

'They're quite shy,' Sophie said, always nervous when strangers – especially children – wanted to stroke her cats. 'We'll meet them tomorrow. You can help me give them treats.'

'Thank you,' Anna mouthed over the children's heads.

'Let's have a hot drink and you two can go to bed,' Pete added.

'There's only a double,' Sophie said. 'I'll take the sofa in my sitting room. Look, I haven't tidied up at all. It's a real mess, I'm afraid. All the effort goes into the guest areas.'

'Please don't worry. We're just incredibly grateful to be safe and warm,' Anna replied as Sophie cringed at the state of her room. Her bed hadn't been made, there were clothes piled all over the place, and a bra and some knickers were drying on the radiator.

'It's so generous of you,' Pete said. 'I'll sleep on the floor and the kids can share with Anna, though I still feel bad about you sleeping on a sofa.'

'I'll be fine,' Sophie commented. 'So I'll fetch the linen and some towels. You'll find a little shower room off the bedroom.'

Anna held out her arms. 'I'd hug you, if my bump wouldn't get in the way,' she said, adding in a whisper, 'I

197

didn't tell the kids of course, but I seriously thought we might be stuck in the car all night and found frozen in the morning.'

'I'm glad you knocked on the door!' Sophie replied, horrified at the very idea of the family spending a night in their car. 'I'll fetch the spare linen and let you settle in.'

Jingle and Belle stayed on the window seat, keeping a wary distance from the strange and noisy visitors. As long as the bedroom door was kept closed, they wouldn't be able to get inside and lie on her bed, as they sometimes did in cold weather. Sophie didn't want any of the Nowaks to wake up with a mog on their faces.

After delivering the linen, she went back to the kitchen and started to heat up a fresh batch of tapas. Now she didn't even have a private haven to retreat to in her own home. She returned her attention to whipping the mascarpone and cream for the pavlova. Midway to dolloping it on the meringue base, a call came through on her phone.

Of course it was the flamenco troupe. They'd tried their very best to make it, but it had taken an hour to get two miles from their base near Kendal. The snow wasn't abating and so, reluctantly, they'd had to return. They'd tried to call earlier, but the signal had been poor because of the weather and the hills.

Sophie wasn't surprised and didn't want anyone to risk themselves in this weather. Plus, on a practical level, if they had turned up and – very likely – became stuck, she was running out of room and didn't have a stable in which to put up any more unexpected guests.

She only hoped her paying guests would be under-standing, and not too disappointed. She couldn't help but feel she'd been a bad host tonight and had let everyone down. Hopefully Nico had carried on making the extra-strength cocktails for everyone to share. And after the way her evening had panned out, she wished she could have one too.

She returned to the guest lounge with a large platter of spinach tortilla and Padrón peppers. Suzanne was sitting in the window seat and the cat blanket had slipped down the side of the chair, so this was Sophie's chance to move it dis-creetly out of the way.

'Hello, everyone!' she said in her cheeriest voice. 'I'm afraid you won't be surprised to hear that the flamenco group can't make it. Hardly a surprise, given the weather, but still, I'm sorry to disappoint.'

'Probably for the best. It looks as if we're snowed in,' Nico replied and there were other murmurs of agreement.

'How is the family doing?' Agatha asked.

Word had obviously got round.

'They're fine. I've given them my room.'

'That's very generous of you,' Nico said, looking intensely at her.

'It's fine – I have a very comfortable sofa. Now I was saving the quiz for tomorrow, but perhaps we can do it now?'

She was met with less enthusiasm than she'd expected.

'We could . . .' Una said quietly, 'though I was rather looking forward to watching the dancing. It's such a shame the troupe couldn't get through.'

'Can't be helped,' Agatha replied. 'But I know what you mean. A quiz feels rather a comedown, compared to the allure of a handsome Spaniard in Cuban heels shaking his maracas.'

Sophie slid a suspicious glance at Nico, wondering what on earth he'd put in the sangria while she wasn't looking.

'Well . . .' Hugo began, exchanging a knowing look with his wife, 'we could suggest an alternative.'

'As long as it doesn't involve us all throwing our car keys in a fruit bowl.'

Everyone under fifty looked nonplussed, apart from Una, who turned bright red and squeaked, 'Certainly not! I was thinking that Hugo and I could teach you all a bit of dancing. We can't flamenco, but we did win the Stratford Stompers Veterans' Salsa contest last year.'

'Salsa?' Nico grinned. 'That sounds very . . . exotic. I'm happy to partner up,' he said, looking at Sophie again.

'It's divine! Do any of you have dance experience?' Una asked.

'Not of the salsa. Ron and I used to enjoy a bit of disco in our youth,' Agatha piped up.

'How about you, Suzanne?' Hugo asked. 'Can you dance?'

'Mum made me and my sister go to ballet lessons, but I wasn't keen,' Suzanne said disdainfully. 'I wanted to do street instead, but she wouldn't let me.'

'You'd still have a sense of musicality, though,' Una said reassuringly. 'Amber?'

Everyone looked towards the doorway, where Amber

had materialised. She didn't answer for a moment, then she murmured, 'I did ballet lessons too.' She shot a glance at Suzanne. '*I* loved it . . .'

Sophie realised that Amber must have been there long enough to overhear and now shot her own barb at her half-sister.

'That's excellent!' Hugo declared and turned to Nico, 'Nico? What about you?'

He jokingly held up his hands in surrender. 'I have two left feet.'

'I'm sure you'd be brilliant,' Una encouraged him. 'We can teach everyone the basics.'

All eyes turned to Sophie, like a pack of dogs about to be fed. 'What about you?' Nico asked.

'M-me?' she hesitated. 'I can't dance, either. Last time I did anything to music was in a club years ago, before I met . . .' she was about to say 'Ben', but stopped, 'when I was younger. I don't think that counts as dancing.

'Everything counts,' Hugo said. 'Now, all we need is some music. Let's create a space in here and we'll show you some easy steps.'

Half an hour later everyone was hot, sweaty and in fits of giggles. The Gipsy Kings were blasting out, and all of them got to know each other better as they kept changing partners, although Suzanne and Amber had managed to avoid dancing with each other.

Una beckoned Sophie. 'Do come and join in.'

She shook her head. 'I can't dance. I definitely can't do a salsa,' she went on, trying to sound breezy about it, but dreading the thought of having to join in. 'And I need to look after my guests – fetch the drinks and more tapas.'

'Pssht!' Agatha said. 'We can do that. I'll look after the bar.'

'*I'll* look after the bar,' Amber said from the corner. 'I did bar work when I was a student. I needed the money,' she continued pointedly.

'I had a part-time job too. In a newsagent's,' Suzanne shot back. 'We weren't well off, either.'

'It's lovely to see you came down,' Sophie said, cutting off a potential source of conflict.

'Well, I heard the music and smelled the delicious food,' Amber replied. 'And I wanted to do my bit and help.'

'Thank you, Amber,' Sophie said gratefully. 'Thank you both, but I couldn't possibly allow my guests to do all the work while I make an idiot of myself.'

'Why not?' responded Nico, sweeping Sophie into his arms without warning. She was so surprised that her breath was taken away. 'You're our host!' He twirled her round so fast she let out a gasp of shock. 'It's your job to entertain us!'

Sophie found herself bent over backwards, supported by his strong arms. She thought she was going to fall over and let out a little shriek, but Nico pulled her upright just in time.

'Bravo!'

'Encore!' Una whooped.

Applause and delighted laughter broke out from the other guests. Even Amber seemed to be smiling.

'So you don't have two left feet then . . .' Suzanne observed to Nico.

'My mother made me go to Latin classes for a while when I was a teenager. If I'd mentioned that, I'm afraid you'd all have had inflated expectations of my ability. I couldn't handle the pressure.' Nico's eyes twinkled.

'You're a dark horse, that's for sure,' Agatha remarked, scrutinising him while Sophie caught her breath after literally being swept off her feet.

'That really *was* wicked of me,' Nico said to her. 'I suppose I should apologise.'

Sophie felt herself blush. 'There's no need. Everyone seems to have enjoyed it.'

'But did *you* enjoy it?' Somehow he made a simple question sound quite indecent.

'It was – er – exhilarating.'

'That's a word for it!' Agatha declared, chortling.

'You *must* at least have a go at learning the salsa,' Una said to Sophie. 'You've been working so hard to look after us.'

'You're paying me to do that,' Sophie said, only half joking.

'Oh, let your hair down for once!' Agatha declared. 'We'll muck in with the food and booze. Now let's get the real party started.'

Sophie laughed and decided that Agatha was right. They should all let loose and celebrate in their own way. Somehow her guests had also become co-hosts and were taking matters out of her hands.

She was partnered up with Hugo for her first lesson.

Nico was with Suzanne. Una with Agatha. Amber had gone to the bar to mix another jug of sangria. The music had been turned up louder, the beat of the salsa drowning out the wind howling outside.

Somehow, despite nothing really going to plan, Sophie had got exactly what she wanted: laughter and dancing, a family rescued from the snow and guests getting on like a house on fire (apart from the minor glitch of two warring siblings).

That was way more than she could have hoped for when she'd first posted the ad a few months ago, or when her year had started. She might be hurt over what had happened with Brody, but she knew she needed to remember quite how far she'd come this year.

Chapter Nineteen

'No. Please – no more. I'm absolutely done for!' Agatha collapsed into the armchair, very red in the face. 'And no more
sangria for me. I feel quite discombobulated.'

'Discombobulated?' Nico echoed. 'That sounds like fun.'

Everyone was having fun, Sophie thought, even Amber
and Suzanne, although they were pointedly seated at opposite sides of the guest lounge.

Hugo and Una were both glowing, their secret salsa
experience really saving the day and making it such a fun
first night. Hugo had already been upstairs to exchange his
checked shirt for something 'more appropriate', which
turned out to be a racy pale-blue one. Neither of them
seemed the slightest bit fatigued, despite Suzanne mopping
her brow and Sophie feeling like she'd climbed to the top of
Helvellyn. Who knew that wiggling your hips and twirling
around could be so knackering?

Amber had been persuaded to try out a few steps with
Nico, in between mixing more cocktails behind the safety of
the bar. 'Shall I fetch some cold drinks. Soft ones?' she
suggested.

'And if we've finished dancing, I could bring in the pavlova . . .' Sophie offered, keen to have a break.

'What a jolly good idea!' Agatha declared.

By the time Sophie returned with the pavlova, Agatha was snoring, despite the music still being on.

Una joined Sophie in dishing up the pavlova. 'You know, we were both so worried about spending Christmas away from home. Even though it felt right when we booked it, we've both had misgivings ever since, but you've gone to such an effort and made us feel so welcome.'

'I'm thrilled to hear it,' said Sophie, boosted by the compliment. By making people's stay special, she hoped to build up repeat visitors, who were the mainstay of a guest house's business.

Una beamed. Her hair had come loose from its bun and her skin was glowing. 'And in fact, although I wouldn't dare tell the children, it's been one of the best Christmas Eves we've ever spent.'

'I'm delighted about that.'

Agatha let out a loud snore. Nico, Hugo and Una all burst out laughing.

'I suspect Agatha would concur,' Hugo said, in a passable imitation of her voice.

Una giggled. 'You are naughty, Hugo.'

He raised his eyebrows. 'Am I? I do hope so.'

Nico simply smiled as he accepted a generous bowl of pavlova from Sophie.

Agatha woke up and Sophie served everyone else, wondering what had happened to Amber and Suzanne. She got her answer a moment later when she heard raised voices from upstairs. When she opened the door, she immediately heard the two women having a heated debate on the landing.

'Oh dear,' Sophie exclaimed. 'I'd better go up and referee.'

'Chill out! It won't get that bad,' Nico said with a smile. 'Probably.'

'It's OK for you to joke, but I need to think of the other guests. The Nowak family are trying to get some rest.'

'If they slept through the salsa party, I'm sure they won't be bothered by a couple of people rowing upstairs.'

'I'm concerned about someone getting hurt. I have to try.'

'You're an angel,' Nico said. 'And a great cook. This pavlova is more-ish. Shall I dish out second helpings while you try to act as peace envoy? Tricky family situations aren't my forte.'

'Yes, please,' she said.

A loud thud came from upstairs. Possibly a door slamming. Hopefully not an object being thrown . . .

Sophie went up to the landing, where Amber was standing outside Suzanne's room, with her hands on her hips. 'Look, this is silly. I only said it would be grown-up if we actually talked to each other about the situation. I didn't know you'd be here, but we should just make the best of it.'

'There's nothing more to be said. I'm going to bed.' Suzanne's muffled voice came through the door.

Amber turned away and walked down the landing towards Sophie. 'You see if you can do anything. I have tried, but it's no use.'

'It's late and you've both had very tiring journeys. Maybe it's better to leave it for tonight?' Sophie offered.

'Probably a good idea,' Amber agreed with a resigned sigh. 'The sad thing is that we're arguing over something that's not our fault at all. It's our families that are in dispute or, more accurately, my mum and Suzanne's mother and our respective siblings. They're even more upset than we are, and I can't help feeling that our father has left us a legacy of bitterness and hurt.'

'That sounds very tough to deal with,' Sophie replied. 'Especially at this time of year. Could I ask one thing? Did you both simply end up here from opposite ends of the country? Is it a coincidence?'

'Not really. My dad – *our* dad – used to stay here years ago, way before you took over. He passed away earlier this year, but I remember him sending postcards from this guest house when he was away working, and I guess he must have sent both of us cards from here.' She sighed. 'Dad was a maintenance engineer and he worked on wind turbines as well as oil rigs. We only realised, when we found out about each other, that he'd been staying here on his way between Scotland and the South-West.'

'Oh, I see. And that's why you decided to come here at Christmas?'

'I can't speak for Suzanne,' Amber said, 'though I'm guessing she wanted to make some kind of pilgrimage, like me. I'm on my own, since my divorce. My mother is spending Christmas with my brother and his family, but I couldn't face the recriminations and arguments.' She heaved a sigh. 'I haven't been feeling very festive since I found out that my perfect dad led a double life, so I decided to book in here to see if I could find some closure and forgiveness. I looked up your website and it resonated with me.'

'I'm sorry for your loss. I can see why you both wanted to get away and were drawn to a place that had special meaning for you.'

'I also hoped to gain some insight into why Dad led a double life all this time. Now I'm not sure.'

'I do understand. Honestly,' Sophie replied, having wondered why Ben and Naomi had also been OK with lying to their nearest and dearest.

Amber looked back at her half-sister's closed door. 'I apologise for the trouble we've caused. It's not your problem to sort out. It's ours, though I doubt if we're going to make any progress through a locked door. I'm coming back downstairs now. I don't feel like being alone in my room, even if Suzanne does.'

'Good idea. You can always make a fresh start tomorrow.'

Amber gave a brief smile. 'I shall probably go out for a very long walk.'

Sophie nodded, thinking that no one would be moving very far the next morning, judging by the drifts of snow piling up around the guest house. She'd checked the forecast, which had said that a thaw wasn't likely until late afternoon on Christmas Day. She'd still no idea how the Nowaks would reach their family.

With Suzanne's door still firmly shut and the tension

diffused for now, Sophie went back downstairs to find her other guests tucking into their second helping of pavlova and sharing holiday stories.

Agatha had woken and was regaling everyone with a tale about being stranded in a remote jungle area of Papua New Guinea, where 'the spiders were the size of dinner plates'.

Sophie shuddered.

Nico offered a bowl of dessert to Sophie. 'Here you go. We all thought you needed it.'

'Thank you,' Sophie replied, realising that she suddenly felt completely knackered. The only spare seat was on the sofa next to Nico, so she perched beside him. It was now after ten and too late to deploy the quiz. Sophie allowed herself to relax and enjoy the pavlova, wondering how late her guests would stay up. Normally most would probably want to see Christmas Day arrive, but on this occasion she rather hoped they'd decide to have an early night.

Refreshed by her power nap, Agatha pointed her spoon in the direction of Sophie and Nico. 'So,' she said, encompassing them both in one gaze, 'how about you two youngsters? Nico, what is a handsome young chap like you doing at a party-poopers' Christmas break? And, Sophie, what on earth is a lovely young woman like you doing hosting such a mad affair?'

It couldn't last long, could it? Sophie thought, filling with dread. Sooner or later she'd have been put on the spot. Did she owe it to her guests to explain? Or was it her private business? Her guests had been open and generous in sharing their stories and yet, as hostess, it was her duty to keep her personal problems to herself.

Nico saved her. 'My answer is simple. I was meant to go home to Italy for Christmas, but a few weeks ago I found out my passport had expired.'

'Couldn't you get a new one in time?' Agatha asked.

'Yes, I thought there were passport offices where you can go and get ones on shorter notice,' Una piped up.

'You're joking. Not these days.' Nico shook his head. 'I did try and was told I'd no chance whatsoever, so I gave it up as a bad job.'

'Why didn't you stay at home?' Agatha said. 'Or go to a friend's? I'm sure they were lining up to look after you.'

Sophie thought this was going way beyond polite curiosity. She was about to try to change the subject when Nico said cheerily, 'Because I'd promised a colleague that his sister and her family could have my place. They're visiting from Australia, and it was too late to find a hotel or an Airbnb. Not that they could ever afford one. I decided it was easier to move out and find something for one person, not wanting to let them down after they were travelling all the way here.'

Sophie said nothing, yet she was still unconvinced.

'So you found this gem?' Hugo said, dropping his spoon in his now-empty bowl.

'I love the Lakes, and Sunnyside's "Escape for Christmas" came up when I was searching for short breaks in the UK.

To be honest, it sounded a blast. I wouldn't have to spend the day at a friend's or with some distant, boring relative – which I'm sure you, Agatha, can completely understand.'

Agatha nodded.

'I decided I could come up here. Join in with the party if I wanted to or go off walking . . .' He grinned. 'Or skiing. I wish I'd brought my skis.'

Una laughed. Sophie could have guessed that he skied. Of course he did, and probably very well.

'You know what,' Nico continued smoothly, 'I think Sophie could do with a break from hosting duties. I think it's time she relaxed. Why don't have you a glass of wine?' he said. 'It won't do any harm, and it is a special evening.'

'I shouldn't . . .' Sophie shook her head.

'Go on,' Una urged. 'A little one won't hurt.'

Hugo smiled. 'You deserve it, after what you've had to deal with, my dear.'

'I second that,' said Nico.

'Maybe a *very* small white wine then,' agreed Sophie, touched by her guests' concern for her own enjoyment.

'I'm on it.' Magician-like, Nico produced a bottle from the side of Agatha's chair, while Hugo grabbed a clean glass from the sideboard.

'Oh no, please stop. That's enough, thanks.' Sophie put her hand over her glass, preventing Nico from filling it to the top. Unlike her guests, she had to be up early to lay out breakfast.

Agatha pushed herself, rather wobbly, to her feet. 'Let us raise a toast to our hostess: the indefatigable and lovely Sophie. And wish ourselves all a very merry un-Christmas!'

'To Sophie!' the guests echoed. 'And a very merry un-Christmas!'

Sophie took a sip of the wine. She had to admit it was delicious and she felt her tense limbs relax a fraction. A tiny glass surely wouldn't do any harm . . .

'Help!'

Piotr Nowak dashed into the lounge, white as a sheet. 'Someone help! It's Anna. Her waters have broken. I think the baby's coming now!'

A second of stunned silence was followed by Sophie's heart rate shooting up. She almost dropped her glass.

'I, er – I'll call an ambulance now.' After the initial shock, she sprang into action.

'I fear you'll be waiting a long time,' said Agatha. 'Have you seen the snow?'

'You're right, but we *must* call them,' Sophie insisted. 'They can send an air ambulance.'

'If it can fly . . .' Hugo muttered.

Pete clutched the back of sofa for support. 'Oh my God, I hadn't thought of that. This can't be happening.'

'How many weeks is your wife?' Agatha asked.

'Thirty-eight.'

'That's good,' Agatha muttered, although Sophie failed to see anything remotely positive in a woman going into labour in her bed in a blizzard.

'I'm sure everything will be fine,' Una soothed, patting Pete's arm.

Nico was frozen in his chair. 'Oh dear . . .' he murmured.

Sophie snapped into action. 'I'll come with you to check on Anna now. Una, would you mind calling for an ambulance?'

'Of course. I'll use your landline.' She hurried out of the lounge to the office and Sophie followed, shepherding the shell-shocked Pete out of the room.

'Please try not to worry,' she soothed, with a confidence she didn't feel. 'The mountain rescue and coastguard deal with emergencies all the time.'

'I hope to God they do. I wish we'd never set out, but we didn't know the weather was so bad up here, and Anna just wanted to be with her mum.' Pete stopped outside the door to Sophie's flat. 'She's on her own, you see, and Anna was determined to keep her company.'

'I understand. It'll be OK.'

Sophie heard Una giving their details to the emergency operator.

'What about the children?' she asked.

'They're scared too, as you can imagine, with all the racket Anna's making – understandably. They're in your sitting room at the moment. With the cats,' he added.

'That's probably the best place for them,' Sophie said.

She opened the door to the sitting room. 'It's OK,' she said, seeing the two children curled up on her sofa under a blanket, wide-eyed in shock.

Pete knelt beside the sofa. 'Mummy will be fine. Everyone's going to help her and the baby. You'll have a new little sister soon.'

A loud wail cut through the crack in the bedroom door. 'Pete! Please do something. I'm not sure baby's going to wait around!'

'She had these two pretty quickly,' Pete murmured to Sophie. 'We thought that was a good thing, but now . . .' His colour seemed to drain from him before her eyes.

Sophie opened the door, to see Anna on all fours on the bed, and felt a bit sick. She clenched her hand tightly by her side to try and stop her fingers from trembling and attempted to take a deep breath.

What if the baby was born in her bed? How would they cope with delivering it? Weren't there cords to be cut – and *stuff* to be dealt with? Having wanted a family herself, Sophie still had no knowledge of precisely what went on during or after the birth. She'd parked the messier details for a later date, like leaving your tax return until an hour before the deadline.

Didn't labour go on for ages anyway? She prayed that the ambulance would arrive before any of them had to deal with it. She might have to multitask in running a guest house, but delivering a baby was one job she'd never planned for.

Pete rushed to Anna's side and rubbed her back. 'Help's on the way, sweetheart,' he promised. 'Try not to worry.'

'I'll go and see what's happening with the emergency services,' Sophie said. 'And explain the urgency.' She hurried into the hallway, feeling as scared as the kids had looked. No amount of planning could ever have prepared her for the emergency unfolding in front of her.

Amber was on the stairs. 'What's going on?' she said, looking worried.

Nico appeared in the door to the guest lounge, glass in hand. 'Apparently someone's about to give birth.'

Before Sophie could reply, Anna let out another scream and everything went black.

Chapter Twenty

'Hello, my friends. At least I'm not the spawn of the Devil, with you lot.'

Brody sighed, paying his second visit of the evening to the stable. He'd fed the donkey and sheep earlier and all were munching together happily in their pen. It was bloody freezing. Despite his Barbour, woolly scarf and beanie hat, he was chilled to the bone. The icy wind cut into his face, chilled by the snow that lay a foot high where it had drifted into corners of the yard. He pitied anyone who was out in such conditions. Only the hardy Herdwicks could withstand this weather, and he feared for a few of those.

As he looked over towards the farmhouse, he noted there was a light on in the bedroom. Tegan was clearly still awake. Well, it was only just past 10 p.m.

'What a bloody mess,' he muttered, stroking Gabe's neck. 'Sometimes I wish I was a donkey.'

Gabe carried on eating, oblivious to Brody's dilemma.

'You're a man of few words, aren't you, buddy?' Brody said. 'And you know what? In this situation it's probably best to say as little as possible.' He talked to the animals a while longer, making sure they were comfortable, then closed the stable doors.

While he'd been inside, the snow had started to fall a little less heavily and the wind had dropped a bit, at least temporarily. The skies had cleared and a full moon illuminated a vast expanse of glittering white, stretching as far as he could see.

When he'd last dared to look at it, Sunnyside resembled a storybook gingerbread house, its roof and gables thickly iced with white. Lights illuminated the windows and fairy lanterns glimmered in the garden. Was anyone crazy enough to be in the hot tub? Was that a snatch of music he could hear, when the wind dropped?

How he wished he was there, eating tapas and watching the flamenco dancers with Sophie. Maybe she was twirling around the floor now, laughing and out of breath. He hoped so, and that she was having fun. The last thing he wanted was for her to spend another Christmas feeling hurt.

Back inside, he hung up his coat, intending to warm himself by the fire, but raised voices from upstairs made him linger in the hallway. One was Tegan's and the other was that of a man on speakerphone. Brody could only hear snatches, but Tegan sounded agitated and upset. Was it her father on the other end, or had something happened? Brody's stomach knotted. He hoped her dad was OK. He really liked Alan and Fiona, Tegan's parents. He'd known them for ever because of them being friends with his parents, which was yet another reason why he'd gone along with the whole charade, and he desperately wanted Alan to recover.

Standing at the bottom of the stairs, Brody strained his

ears. Tegan's room was the first off the landing and her door must be ajar for the sound to carry.

'Why are you being like this?' Tegan's voice ramped up in volume. That didn't sound like a reply to a father. She was definitely worked up about something.

Brody crept further up the stairs. Their creaking would have given him away, had Tegan made any effort to keep her voice down. He could now hear her every word and most of those from her male caller, who had an American accent.

'No, he can't hear me. He's gone out to feed the animals.'

Brody didn't quite catch the reply but he did hear Tegan's response.

'Don't be sarcastic, Wes. Brody's a lovely man and he's a veterinarian. Of course he loves his animals.'

Brody's stomach turned over. It was all he could do not to break into the bedroom and tell that bastard, Wes, what he thought of him. He also felt ashamed to hear Tegan defending him. He'd rather defend himself, preferably by punching Wes on the nose.

'This isn't helping. Why have you decided to pick a fight on Christmas Eve?' Tegan said, with an edge of desperation. 'You know my dad's sick, and you're being snarky.'

'I'm being realistic, honey,' Wes said.

Brody balled his fist. How dare that slimy creep call Tegan 'honey'? Then he remembered that it was none of his business. But he still cared about Tegan and wished her well, even if anything resembling love had become purely the feelings of a concerned friend, which had been painful to acknowledge – as painful as the initial betrayal. Sadness crept over him when he realised that perhaps he'd never felt the deep love for Tegan that was necessary to make a lifelong commitment.

'I'm not speaking to you while you're in this mood. I don't know what's got into you!' Tegan cried and the call was ended abruptly.

Brody held his breath, pausing on the stairs, not daring to move in case a creak gave him away. He *shouldn't* have listened . . . And then he heard muffled sobs, a sound that cut him to the quick. He walked to the door of Tegan's room, making as much noise as he could with his boots and – ridiculously – humming 'Jingle Bells' loudly.

'Hi,' he called, pausing outside her door. 'I'm making hot chocolate and wondered if you wanted one. If you're not asleep,' he added. 'Obviously you might not be asleep now, with me making all this racket.'

A few seconds later he heard her call, 'Come in.'

She was propped up in bed, with her phone lying on the quilt beside her. She was smiling, but her eyes were a little red.

'Would you like a drink? I was making one before I went to bed to try and get some sleep, just in case I'm called out later.'

'In this weather? On Christmas Eve?'

'It's not likely and I hope it doesn't happen, because I'm not sure how I'd ever be able to attend. Would you like one too?' he tried again.

'No. Thanks for the offer, but I am going to sleep now. I was listening to a podcast . . .'

'OK. I'll leave you be.' He turned away, torn between whether to ask her if she really was alright or leave her alone.

'Brody . . .' she began.

'Yes?' He turned round.

'Nothing. Only thanks for being so—'

'Nice?' he said bitterly.

'Accommodating. Honourable.'

'Oh yeah. That's me. The honourable, animal-loving, kind . . .'

'What do you mean?' she said sharply.

Brody could have kicked himself. 'Nothing,' he muttered. 'Ignore me. I'm just being grumpy.'

'Not grumpy. I'm not happy about this – any of it – either,' Tegan said, hugging her knees. 'It's a crap situation, and I so wish things were different.

'Different how?' Brody asked. 'You're with who you want to be and, for everyone's sake, I'm willing to go along with the pretence until your dad's better. Things can't be different. They're already the best they can be, in the circumstances.'

'I suppose so,' she replied quietly, picking at a thread on the quilt.

'This is what you wanted, isn't it?'

'Yes, I guess it is. I only wish it wasn't so . . . hard. So painful. I've hurt you badly and I wish I could put it right.' She reached out a hand and rested her fingers on his wrist.

Brody froze. 'I'm over it,' he said.

There was a loud banging on the door downstairs. Someone was giving the iron knocker one hell of a bashing. Harold added to the din, barking loudly.

'Who's that?' Tegan looked panicky.

'God knows,' Brody muttered. 'Could be a local farmer or someone in the village, I suppose – though why they haven't phoned, I'm not sure.'

Her eyes widened. 'You're not going out in this weather?'

'If I can help, of course I will. I have to see who it is and what they want.' He left her and jogged downstairs. 'Harold! Quiet!'

Harold gave a final woof before lying down in front of the door, ready to repel intruders. The door almost shook with the force of the banging and a familiar voice was shouting, but surely it couldn't be . . .

'Brody! Open up! Brody!'

'Coming.' He opened the door to find Sophie standing in the porch, a coat clutched around her and her hair dripping with wet snow. She blinked in the light from the porch.

'Sophie? What's the matter?'

'I need you. Urgently.'

'Is there something wrong with the cats?'

'No! It's one of the guests. She's gone into labour and we need your help now!'

Chapter Twenty-One

'Come in,' Brody said as Sophie stumbled inside Felltop on wobbly legs, clearly shaken by what was happening. She'd run to the farm – as much as anyone could run through deep snow – slipping several times and actually falling into a drift at one point.

Brody put his hand on her shoulder. 'Take a breath,' he said calmly. 'And tell me exactly what's happened.'

'It's not happened. It's happening right now! A family was stuck in the snow, so I took them in. The woman's thirty-eight weeks pregnant and now she's in labour. We've tried calling for an ambulance, but they say they can't get through.'

Maybe coming here to ask for help was a mistake, but Sophie felt like it was her only option. Suddenly she realised that all the lights were on in the farmhouse

'What about the coastguard helicopter?' he asked. 'The emergency services should ask them.'

'They say they'll try to get someone to us, but it could be hours. And I don't think Anna's baby is going to wait that long. Can you do anything?'

'I . . .' For a horrible moment, Sophie thought Brody was going to say it was nothing to do with him. Then he nodded firmly. 'Of course, I'll do my very best to help.'

'There's something else,' she said. 'There's a power cut at Sunnyside. I thought it was everyone in the area, but how come all your normal lights are on?'

'A power cut at Sunnyside?' He grimaced and Sophie realised he was more worried than he was letting on. 'I've got a diesel generator as back-up. It comes on automatically if there's a power cut. I noticed the lights flicker, but didn't think anything because I was – busy,' he said. 'Are you sure the power's completely off and it isn't the fuses?'

'I've checked,' Sophie replied tersely.

'OK,' he soothed. 'I only wanted to make sure, because we're going to need all the light we can get. In the circumstances,' he added.

'Don't I know it!' Sophie yelled, then said, 'Sorry, this is – a bit overwhelming. We do have low-level emergency lighting that kicked in after the power went off. But it's only meant to help guide guests out of the building, in case they need to be evacuated. And it only stays on for three hours.'

'I'm sure the emergency services will be here before then,' Brody said.

Sophie wished she shared his confidence. 'I hope so, but ... what if the baby's born and something goes wrong?'

'I doubt it will come to that. You said Anna was part of a family, so I'm assuming she has other children?'

'Two,' Sophie confirmed.

'And do you know if she's had any complications with the previous births?'

'Not as far as I know. In fact her husband, Pete, said the others had arrived pretty quickly.'

Brody let out a short breath. 'That's something, but I can also see the urgency. Let me fetch my kit and I'll walk back with you.' He stopped, asking her, 'I don't suppose the family had a birth pack with them?'

'Yes. Yes, Anna mentioned it. They were sent one by the midwives because she was planning a home birth. It's in their car.'

Sophie was pleased to see him look slightly less concerned. 'That's good too and if she was planning a home birth, they must be expecting everything to be straightforward. Wait here a sec. At least I can be with her to reassure her, but hopefully the baby will hang on for the professionals.'

Relief flooded through Sophie and she realised she was shaking. 'Thanks. I don't know what I was going to do if you'd said no.'

'I would never have done that,' he said and put his arm around her. 'We'll manage somehow. And, Sophie, breathe . . .'

She nodded.

Tegan hurried downstairs then, pulling her fluffy robe tightly around her, aghast at the sight of Sophie dripping melted snow over the hall tiles. 'What's happened?'

'There's a medical emergency at the guest house next door,' Brody explained. 'I'm going to lend a hand.'

Tegan gasped. 'But, but you're only a *vet*. What can you possibly do?'

'One of my guests has gone into premature labour,' Sophie explained.

Tegan's eyebrows shot up. 'Wow! Haven't you called an ambulance?'

'Of course,' Sophie replied, unable to disguise her irritation at Brody's fiancée's patronising tone. 'But even a helicopter may not get here in time. I didn't know who else to call.'

Tegan clutched his elbow. 'Be careful, Brody. Don't get sued!'

'Thank you, Tegan,' Brody growled. 'I will be careful and I may only be a vet, but I'm going to do my best to help.'

Not long after, Sophie ushered Brody through the front door of Sunnyside into an unnerving scene. Although the low-level lights gave enough illumination to make out a path down the stairs and into the hall, their shadows cast eerie patterns on the walls.

'Anna's in my flat,' she said. 'And the lights aren't on in there at all. We're relying on torches and mobile phones, plus a couple of lanterns in there.'

The guests appeared in the doorway from the lounge. Nico, Una, Hugo, Suzanne and – amazingly – Amber were all waiting for news. There was no sign of Agatha. Sophie hoped she hadn't fallen over in the dark and added to the casualty list. 'Pete brought the children into the lounge with us,' Una told Sophie. 'He thought they'd be happier in here.'

Ignoring everyone, Sophie ushered Brody through to her flat. Anna let out a wail. Pete was waiting in the sitting room.

'Thank God!' he said with a huge sigh of relief. 'Is this the doctor?'

'Not quite,' Sophie replied. 'He's the local vet.'

Agatha emerged from the bedroom. 'A *vet*?'

'I'm here to help,' Brody retorted sharply. 'So if we could just see the mother, there's no time to waste.'

Agatha nodded. 'I'm sorry. Thanks for coming and, between us, we should manage. I'm Agatha, and I'm a nurse. Retired nurse actually, but I have assisted at many births. I'm afraid I've also had several cocktails, though frankly I'm sobering up rapidly now. I've been helping to look after Anna, keep her calm and do her breathing exercises. I've timed the contractions. They're three minutes apart.'

'That doesn't sound very far apart . . .' Sophie murmured.

'It isn't,' said Agatha. 'You look quite pale, my dear.'

'I'm – er – don't worry about me.'

'Thanks, Agatha,' Brody cut in firmly. 'With both of us, I'm sure we can help deliver a baby. If we have to,' he added hastily. 'Which I'm sure we won't.'

Pete let out a groan.

Suddenly Amber popped her head around the door of Sophie's sitting room. 'Hello,' she said. 'Can I help?'

Sophie nodded. 'Yes, please! Would you mind finding as many torches or sources of light as you can. There are more battery tea lights in the store cupboard in the kitchen. Can you please bring them here?'

'No problem.'

'How are Baxter and Maria?' Sophie asked.

'They're fine. I made them banana smoothies and we

told them they're going to have a sleepover until the baby arrives.'

'Thanks. I do hope Anna hangs on until the emergency services arrive,' Sophie replied. Beam me up, she pleaded silently; please let me wake up, because this cannot be happening. I cannot be trapped in a snowdrift in the dark with a woman in labour in my bed and only a retired nurse, who's been on the cocktails all night, and a vet to help.

Anna cried out again and swore ripely when Sophie and Brody went back inside with Agatha, while Pete went to the lounge to reassure the children. Sophie closed the door behind her.

'Is this the doctor?' Anna asked hopefully, lying back on the bed between contractions.

Brody sat down. 'I'm afraid not. I'm a vet,' he said.

Anna gasped. 'This is meant to be *Call the Midwife*, not *All Creatures Great and Bloody Small*! Arghhh!'

'I can help you until the ambulance arrives,' Brody said calmly.

'Great! Shame I'm not having bloody kittens!' Anna shouted. 'Sorry, but a vet?'

'Brody's very experienced,' Sophie assured her, thinking it was the best she could do and that Anna was lucky he lived so close by.

'With cows!'

'Yeah, with cows, puppies, kittens . . . I delivered a foal last week,' Brody said.

'Oh my God!'

'But if I can ask you a few questions, it will help me update the emergency services. They'll get a medic on the phone to advise us too,' he said, taking charge of the situation.

'Just do whatever you need to, if it'll help the baby,' Anna pleaded.

'I think it's a good idea, my dear,' Agatha soothed, patting Anna's hand.

'Would it be OK if I examined your – er – bump?' Brody said awkwardly. 'To see what position he or she's in? '

'She,' Anna grunted. 'And yes, it's fine. Anything that will help is fi-i-i-ne!'

'Shall we leave?' Sophie asked.

'No! I think at least one of you should stay, if Anna agrees,' Brody said. 'It won't take me long.'

'I'll stay,' Agatha offered.

'Thank you. Oh God, another one . . .' Anna grasped Agatha's hand as a powerful contraction bore down on her.

'I might need to use the landline phone,' Brody called back to Sophie. 'I don't think the mobile signal's working.'

'OK. I'll bring the cordless in here.'

After returning to the bedroom with the cordless phone, Sophie decided to check how everyone was doing in the guest lounge. To her relief, Suzanne was showing Maria a *Peppa Pig* video on her mobile, while Baxter bashed Nico and Hugo with the inflatable flamingo. Una was soothing Pete.

Amber walked in. 'I found some battery tealights in a kitchen cupboard,' she said, handing a box to Sophie.

'Thanks, that's a big help,' Sophie said before asking Pete. 'Do you want to come to see how Anna's getting on?'

He nodded and turned to the children.

'I'll be back in a little while. Just going to look after Mummy,' he said, though the kids were too engrossed to worry. Once out of earshot, his brave face crumbled. 'How's Anna?' he asked on the way back to the bedroom.

'Doing well,' Sophie replied, more hopefully than anything. 'Brody's checking on her now. If you want to go in?'

In the sitting room, two pairs of yellow eyes watched them from the window seat, as if the unfolding drama was part of a normal day at Sunnyside. Sophie had never wished she was a cat as much as she did at this moment.

Brody emerged from the bedroom.

'How is she?' Sophie and Pete asked, almost in unison.

'The good news is that, from what I can tell, the baby is in the right position. It isn't breech or anything tricky like that. Agatha agrees with me. I've also been able to check its heartbeat with my stethoscope and that seems normal. For a human baby,' he added.

'Thank goodness for that. Any idea when it might arrive?'

'I can't tell that . . . it could be a couple of hours, though.' He heaved a sigh. 'You know it would have been much better if we could have moved Anna to the farm, where it's light and warmer.'

'Do you think it's still possible?' Sophie said. 'Though it would mean going out in the snow and cold.'

'I don't think it's an option anymore. She needs to stay here for now. I'm going to phone again to check where the emergency services are and, hopefully, they'll make it in time.'

Sophie suppressed a shudder of fear. Brody spoke to the call handler before relaying the message to Sophie.

'OK, they have tasked a helicopter, but they can't give an ETA yet. They are also attending a serious road traffic accident in Keswick.'

'Is there nothing else we can do?'

'They've already alerted the mountain-rescue team, who should be walking up here from the Bannerdale base right now. They have a doctor on the team and should be with us within an hour or so.'

'What a relief,' Sophie sighed. 'Not that I don't trust you to deliver the baby – I know you'd be brilliant.'

'I don't want to be brilliant,' Brody said. 'I just want Anna and her baby to be safe.'

'I know she will be, with you here,' Sophie replied gratefully. 'Thanks for not abandoning us.'

'Like I said, I'd never do that.' He took her hand. 'Sophie, there's something I ought to tell you. Not now, but when . . . this is all over. About Tegan. I hope you'll hear me out.'

'You're right. Not now,' Sophie shook her head. 'Or ever. I simply want to forget what happened between us and move on.' She was grateful Brody was here to help, but it didn't change anything between them.

'You mean as friends?' he said, with a sharp edge that took her aback. He was the one who'd tried it on while he was engaged.

'I don't think we can go back to being friends,' Sophie replied. 'But that doesn't mean I'm not grateful for this – for your help now. Come on, you go back to Anna while I make sure my guests and the children are OK.'

Chapter Twenty-Two

An hour later Sophie had forgotten that anything bad – or good – had ever passed between her and Brody. The only thing she cared about was Anna, and her baby, who had decided not to wait for the professionals to arrive after all. The little one was ready to make her entrance imminently.

Sophie had propped the phone up on the bedside table and put it on speaker. Every tea light in the house had been deployed in the 'delivery room', and the floor and bed were covered in bin bags.

The kids were sleeping in the guest lounge, after finally nodding off to stories read to them by Amber and Suzanne by the light of a torch. Nico and the Hartley-Brewers had gone to find clean towels.

Pete was holding Anna's hand and mopping her brow.

All dignity had gone out of the window, because Brody and Agatha now had no choice but to deliver the baby. Thank goodness the birth pack had been to hand, so Brody at least had the right equipment to make it easier.

'Right, I need a hand,' he said.

'Me?' Sophie squeaked.

'Yup. You and Agatha. Baby's on the way. There's a

sterile gown in the pack. Someone needs to tie me into it. And get plenty of towels in here, please!'

After a moment of feeling frozen with fear, Sophie got to work, helping Brody into the gown and slipping the sterile sheets from the pack underneath Anna, who was panting and grunting. More towels had arrived. She had to look away while Brody declared to the emergency operator that the baby's head was emerging, suddenly feeling a little faint herself.

Anna was grunting and squeezing Pete's hand tightly.

'Can you pant for us, Anna?' Agatha asked. 'Just while we check the cord?'

'It's OK,' Brody said, 'I think we're ready. You can push the baby out now, Anna. Big, big push!' He needed his brow mopping too, his forehead glistening with perspiration.

Pete kept saying, 'You're doing brilliantly,' over and over again, and Anna kept swearing at him for putting her through this.

'One more push,' Brody urged.

Then suddenly Anna let out a huge groan and the baby was born, a writhing pink bundle.

'One little girl, as ordered!' Brody declared, wrapping the baby in a waiting towel. She didn't yell, and Sophie's skin went cold. Why wasn't she crying? Weren't newborns supposed to scream the house down?

'What's wrong?' Pete panicked.

'Is she OK?' Anna asked anxiously.

Sophie heard the operator asking for an Apgar score, which seemed to be some way of assessing the baby's condition. She heard Brody give the baby an eight and mention that she was a bit blue and slow to respond.

The baby sputtered and coughed. Sophie held her breath. Then the baby let out a huge yell and Sophie said a silent prayer of thanks, tears pouring down her cheeks. Mostly they were tears of relief, but seeing new human life being brought into the world in front of her eyes had reminded her of Ben and Naomi. They were going to be parents too, and she couldn't help but think of what might have been: of what she'd lost.

Immediately she checked herself. Having a baby was the greatest commitment anyone could make, and when she did do it – if she did – she wanted it to be with a man she could rely on and respect . . . and love.

'I'll cut and clamp the cord, then you can hold her properly,' Brody said, taking the sterile scissors from the pack and then handing the wrapped baby to Anna. 'There you go! Congratulations!'

Pete burst into tears as he and Anna cuddled their newborn daughter.

The emergency controller was talking about placentas, and things Sophie didn't want to know about. All she cared about was that baby Nowak had arrived safe and well and that miraculously Anna – so far –was OK.

Someone banged on the bedroom door and Sophie opened it a crack.

It was Nico. 'Don't worry, I'm not coming in. But the mountain-rescue team is here.'

'Thank God for that!' said Sophie.

Brody heaved a sigh of relief. 'They can deliver the placenta and take care of you now, Anna.'

'Well done,' Sophie said. 'To you all. I'll go and show the rescue team in.

'Is it a girl or a boy?' Nico asked as she hurried through the sitting room. 'We're all on tenterhooks!'

'A lovely, gorgeous little girl,' Sophie replied, feeling elated now that the baby was safely here.

Nico flung his arms around her and kissed her on the lips. 'Well done! Congratulations!'

Sophie blushed, taken aback by what had just happened. 'Thanks, but I didn't actually do the work.'

The hall was suddenly filled with people in red jackets and boots, brushing snow off their faces and shining powerful torches, whose light hurt her eyes.

'Hi, I'm Dr Kumar. Can you update me on the situation?'

Sophie almost fainted with relief. 'Oh yes, the baby girl seems fine, and I think we're all about to have a total meltdown.'

The doctor patted her shoulder. 'It sounds like you've done an amazing job. Where are they then?'

Sophie showed them through to the bedroom, where Brody, Agatha and Pete were looking after Anna and the little one.

'Boy, am I glad to see you!' Brody murmured.

'Are you trying to take over my job?' the doctor asked, jokingly. 'Not content with foals and lambs.'

'Believe me, I never want to do this again,' Brody declared, before the doctor spoke to Anna and checked the baby.

Pete slapped him on the back and hugged him. 'But I'm glad you did. Thank you so much – you and Agatha and Sophie. Thank you.'

'The priority now is to keep mum and baby warm, and once I've checked them over, we can get them to hospital,' Dr Kumar declared.

'Thank you,' said Sophie, feeling tears welling up again. 'I'm going to see how the guests are and make some tea, which we all need.' She went out to the hallway, where a powerful light had been set up in the hall, and spotted a face she recognised: Kev, Vee's husband. The adrenaline began to ebb away and she found she was shaking.

'Hey, you OK?' Kev asked, putting an arm around her.

'I think so. Yes, but I've never been so terrified in my life.'

'No wonder. You did amazingly well.'

'Brody did the hard part, helped by one of the guests who used to be a nurse. We're so lucky they were both here.'

'You played a huge role, organising everyone. No wonder you're in shock at what's just happened.'

'I need to make sure everyone's alright.'

'You sit down,' Amber ordered with surprising firmness. 'We're going to a look after you, for a change. All of us.'

'Good idea,' Suzanne agreed. 'I'll help make drinks for

everyone. The Mountain Rescue Team have brought some camping stoves for us to use.'

Una and Hugo appeared from the kitchen. 'We've got tea and coffee here, and I hope it's OK, but we all put our welcome biscuits and treats together.'

'And we brought our Christmas presents for each other,' Hugo said sheepishly.

Una gazed up at him. 'Know we shouldn't, but we did. Hugo loves a luxury biscuit, don't you?'

'I do, and Una can't resist dark chocolate. I bought a giant box.'

'You don't have to give us your Christmas presents,' Sophie said, touched by their thoughtfulness.

'I can't think of a better use for them.'

A short time later the guests were handing around steaming mugs of tea, snacks and hot chocolate for everyone. Never had Sophie seen the house more crowded, but it felt good to be surrounded by people.

She needed some fresh air to collect herself, so she grabbed her coat and went into the garden. Her hands had stopped shaking and it was bitterly cold, but she needed the jolt of fresh air and silence after the chaos that had unfolded. The snow had stopped and the night sky was clear. Torchlight and voices spilled out, along with laughter.

Sophie allowed her breathing to return to normal. Disaster had been averted, thanks to Brody's help. And what a woman Anna Nowak was . . . And her guests had rallied together to help.

'There you are, you star.'

Nico's voice startled her. He held out a large mug, steaming madly in the crisp air. 'I brought tea, with lots of sugar. You look like you need it.'

'Thank you,' Sophie said, taking it. She sipped and rested it on the stone wall. 'I'm not a star. Anna is.'

'Of course,' agreed Nico. 'But you organised us. I must admit, when I booked this, I'd no idea I was going to become part of a real-life nativity with a Christmas baby.'

'Believe me, neither did I. If I'd known this was going to happen, I'd never have organised this weekend.'

Nico laughed and, once again, Sophie couldn't help but wonder why he was really here, not buying the story he'd told them all earlier.

'Can I be honest?' she said, feeling that what they'd been through together had broken down the usual host–guest barriers.

'Of course. I always think it's best.'

'I've been wondering why you booked in here at all? I mean, Agatha, Una and Hugo are lovely people but, like a lot of my guests, they are on the more mature side.'

'OK, I'll be honest. I couldn't find anything else at the last minute.'

'Anything *better*?' she said, watching him through the steam from her mug.

'No, actually. It was the quirkiness of the offer that attracted me. There were a couple of options promising turkey, tinsel and carols, but they appealed about as much as a limp lettuce. Your escape, on the other hand, leapt out at me . . . For all kinds of reasons,' he added cryptically and with a touch of sadness, Sophie thought.

She smiled. 'It's not turned out quite how I expected.'

'On the contrary, it's greatly exceeded my expectations.'

The moon came out. Was that a twinkle in Nico's eyes?

'Particularly the hostess,' he added smoothly. 'You're a remarkable woman, Sophie.'

Even in the chilly air, she felt warmth rise to her cheeks at the compliment from this handsome man. Then she reminded herself that, so far, the previous two good-looking and charming men she'd allowed into her life had let her down badly. Of all her 'escapees', Nico struck her as the one with the biggest reason for running away and hiding from something.

'I'm just an ordinary person trying to do my best,' she replied firmly.

'Sophie?' Brody appeared on the terrace, still in shirt sleeves, with damp hair.

'Ah, the hero of the evening,' Nico murmured.

'Sorry?' Brody said brusquely. 'Sophie, the rescue team is preparing to move Anna and the baby to the helicopter. It's almost here. I wondered if you might like to come to the sports field with me and see them off? They won't be long, because the biggest danger now is the baby getting cold. The helicopter has the proper equipment to keep them warm.'

'Oh yes!' Sophie declared. 'Would you mind making sure everything's OK here?' she asked Nico. 'Especially Pete and the children, and Agatha. She was amazing, but she needs looking after now. I'll be back soon, but I feel I want to see Anna and the baby safely onto the helicopter.'

'Of course, I'll hold the fort.' Nico smiled 'By the way, well done, mate,' he said to Brody.

Brody grunted something vaguely resembling a 'Thank you' before striding off towards the front of the building. Sophie followed, drinking her tea on the move.

By the time she was inside the house, Brody was back in his coat, holding a torch. The mountain-rescue team was carrying Anna and the baby out in a stretcher chair, both swaddled like mummies against the cold. Pete saw her off to the gate. The Nowak children couldn't all go on the helicopter and Pete didn't want to leave them, so he had to stay behind.

The doctor comforted him just before they left the house. 'I promise we'll let you know how they are as soon as we can. Anna's got her phone too.'

With that, Pete went back inside. Without the team, it was darker inside Sunnyside and the tea lights and phone batteries wouldn't last for ever. It was going to be a very long night. Sophie grabbed a torch and hurried out after the team. Even in wellies, it was hard going, the snow coming almost to the top of her boots in places.

Felltop Farm had lights on downstairs, but the rest of the village was mostly in darkness. She and Brody walked past the fallen tree that had allowed a stretcher party, but not a vehicle, to pass.

'We'll get that cleared in the morning by one of the local farmers,' Brody suggested.

'The snow still has to thaw before anyone can leave, though,' Sophie said. 'So it'll be Boxing Day before we can get out.' Ironic, she thought, that her guests had come to escape and now they were trapped.

The roar of rotors grew louder as they trudged towards the sports field where the helicopter was waiting. The crew was hurrying towards the stretcher and, within a minute, both Anna and the baby were safely aboard. The mountain-rescue team moved away and the helicopter took off, snow spiralling into the air from the downdraught.

The thought of them soaring high in the sky to safety brought a lump to Sophie's throat. The rotors died away and she felt herself choking back tears. She found Brody's hand in the small of her back briefly – before it was hastily withdrawn, as if he'd suddenly remembered the tension between them.

She looked at him, his face uplit by torchlight. He looked completely shell-shocked.

'They'll be fine now,' Brody said. 'You did incredibly well.'

'I only watched. Anyone would think you'd done it before.'

'I was terrified of hurting the baby or Anna. I have never been so happy to see anyone as I was when the rescue doc turned up.'

'Me too, but not because I didn't have total faith in you,' Sophie said, adding quickly, 'in your abilities.'

'I'm glad you did. Even though I've attended hundreds of animal births, that was something else.'

She stopped and listened. A distant clanging cut through the still night.

'It's the church bells up in the village,' said Brody. 'It's Christmas Day.'

'Christmas Day . . .' She thought of all her plans to avoid it, and how they'd paled into insignificance compared to the situation they'd had to deal with. 'I'd forgotten about that.'

'Me too, but it's here, and I have a suggestion for you. I'll tell you on the way back to Sunnyside. I don't know about you, but I'm freezing my bits off.'

When Sophie heard his plan, she was dumbfounded. 'Move everyone into your house until the thaw? We couldn't possibly do that – apart from Pete and the kids coming to yours. They can be cosy and have a proper bed, in their own room. We can't all troop over to you, though. We can't invade your home.'

'I'm not suggesting you all sleep at the farm, only that you come over in the morning. You'll need to charge your phones and torch batteries. Why don't you all go back to bed for now, then come over for breakfast and stay until bedtime, so you're not spending the day with no power.'

Everything he said made perfect sense. It would be so much more comfortable for her guests – and, Sophie had to admit, for her too. However, there was one big problem.

'What about Tegan?' she said.

'She won't mind.'

'Have you asked her?'

'No, it will be fine.'

'She might not be fine when she finds ten strangers

invading her space, when she'd planned a quiet Christmas Day.'

'We were meant to go to her parents', not stay at the farm. She'll cope,' he said. 'Plans have had to change and we need to deal with it, same as we did tonight.'

They'd reached Sunnyside, which still looked strange, with its low lights and all the top floor in darkness.

'I think . . .' Sophie said, realising that she would be silly not to accept Brody's invitation. Her guests came first, and not her pride. 'You should take Pete and the children back with you, so they can have a proper night's rest. I'll tell the guests about the plan for tomorrow.'

They went inside to give everyone the news.

Sophie had to admit Brody was right about one thing: her guests would definitely not mind moving into his house. Tegan, however, might be a very different story.

Chapter Twenty-Three

In the end Brody returned to the farm alone because the Nowak children were fast asleep on the sofas in the guest lounge. After so much disruption and excitement, Pete decided to leave it until morning to bring them over to Felltop.

In one way Brody was a bit relieved, because it meant he had time to prepare Tegan for the fact that ten extra people would be arriving for lunch that day.

Harold bounded up to him, barking for joy, and licked his face.

'OK, boy! I haven't been to the North Pole.' Brody fussed him, crouching down to stroke the dog in the hall. 'At least you love me, Harold,' he joked, soothed by the normality of being back in his own home, with the usual Harold response.

A moment later Brody was reminded of how un-normal his life was, when Tegan walked into the hall from the snug. 'Brody!' she called.

He got up.

'What's happened?' she asked.' Is everyone OK? I heard the helicopter.'

'Mother and baby are doing well,' Brody said. 'Thank goodness.'

She gasped. 'Oh. My. God. You didn't have actually have to . . .'

'I had no choice. The baby wasn't going to wait for anyone. I had the emergency services on the phone and a retired nurse and Sophie to help, but really Anna – the mother – obviously did all the hard graft.'

'B-but you actually delivered a *baby*?'

'Well, yes. A little girl. The mountain-rescue medics arrived straight after she was born, and mum and baby are now on their way to hospital to be checked over.'

She flew to him and hugged him tightly. 'You are a hero. You really are.'

Brody cringed.

'Come and sit down,' she said, leading him by the hand to the armchair. 'I'll make you a drink and find some food. No wonder you look shell-shocked.'

'Thanks, but I'm OK, really,' Brody insisted, desperate to downplay his part in the proceedings. He'd already begged Kev not to mention his name in the incident report they'd be sure to post on the rescue team's website. The fewer people who knew about it, the better. He just wanted a hot drink, dry clothes and to go to bed. However, he had some news to break to Tegan first and he was pretty sure she wasn't going to like it.

He sat down heavily in his dad's chair, soothed by the hollow that both father and son had created. Very softly he murmured, 'Between us, that was a close one, Dad.' He seriously needed a shower and longed simply to close his eyes and decompress after the past few tense hours, but he owed Tegan some time first.

She came back in, with a tray of hot drinks and mince pies. Even though it was half-past midnight, Brody was starving and very grateful.

'Thanks,' he said, devouring two pies while he answered Tegan's many questions about what had happened.

'You've earned a break tomorrow. You can sleep in late, and then it'll be just the two of us together. I'll cook dinner. It might not be turkey, but I noticed that your fridge and freezer are well stocked.'

'Thank God for mum's over-ordering, plus all the leftovers from the party we had the other night,' he said. A well-stocked freezer was a tradition going back to his parents' time. They'd had too many times when storms and snow had cut off the house. Now he thanked his lucky stars that his mother had badgered him into topping up the diesel to the generator the other day too.

Tegan tucked her knees under her on the sofa and pulled a blanket over her. 'I'll miss Mum and Dad, but it's going to be quite cosy here with only the two of us.'

Brody put down his plate to broach the subject.

'Well, it actually isn't going to be only us for Christmas Day. The power in the village isn't likely to be on until Boxing Day, so I invited Sophie and her guests to come here. It seemed wrong to make them stay in a dark house when I've got so much space.'

Tegan's mouth fell open. 'What? All of them?

'Yes, plus the rest of the Nowaks – Pete and the two children.

'B-but so many of them?' Tegan spluttered. 'Can't they go to the pub or something?'

'It will be closed on Christmas Day. It'll be a difficult Christmas for all the villagers after this heavy snow has knocked out the power and blocked the roads.'

'Oh, why don't you ask the whole village then!' Tegan said, flopping back against the sofa in a huff.

'I'm not leaving Sophie and her guests to freeze, when we have power and light. I'd invited the Nowaks to stay with us tonight, but the kids were already asleep, so we decided not to disturb them and bring them out in the cold. They'll be here in the morning, however,' Brody said firmly, surprised to see that Tegan was being so selfish about this.

'Right. Well, I suppose we've no choice.'

'I *do* have a choice. And I've made it.'

It was, he thought, the first time he'd seen her taken aback by something he'd said. Perhaps the first time he'd truly surprised her because he'd not let her have her own way.

Tegan looked very annoyed and he half expected her to flounce off to her room in disgust, but instead her frown melted into a smile.

'Wow! Is this the new Brody? Decisive, determined, stubborn.'

'I'm only interested in doing the right thing by people. The practical thing.'

She shook her head and sighed, with another smile. 'You know your problem, Brody McKenna? You're too damn nice.' She pushed off the blanket, came over to his chair and planted a kiss on his cheek. Then she yawned and stretched her arms above her head. 'I suppose I'd better go and get some sleep if I'm going to have to play hostess.'

Brody watched her go, but her words chimed in his head like the midnight church bells: '*Too damn nice.*'

He didn't think of himself as 'nice', just an ordinary man doing his best. A best that hadn't been good enough for Tegan, and certainly not for Sophie. While he cared about the children and the guests, he had to admit he'd mainly invited them for Sophie's sake. He was determined to make amends to her, in any way he could.

Chapter Twenty-Four

Sophie woke with a crick in her neck the next morning, a cat kneading her stomach and total disorientation. Why was she in her tracksuit on her sofa under a spare duvet? Why was it already light? She should have been up in the darkness, preparing breakfast . . . now it was almost 9 a.m.!

Belle licked her toes, which were poking out of the duvet. Slowly the events of last night came back to her, along with snatches of children's voices from the hallway.

Miaow!

'OK, OK, I know you want your breakfast too.'

To say she hadn't had the greatest night's sleep on the sofa was an understatement. Although Agatha and the Hartley-Brewers had kindly helped to clear up her bedroom, she'd need to give it a deep clean before she felt comfortable being back in there. Memories of what she'd seen in her bed kept coming back to Sophie and making her shudder, even though the outcome had been joyful.

She got up, fed the cats and showered hastily in water that was barely tepid. The other guests would be enduring similar privations and she suspected they might all have left if they hadn't been cut off by the snow. She certainly wouldn't have blamed them, after the disaster their stay was turning out to be – a world away from what they'd signed up for.

At least the weather had decided to behave for Christmas morning. Winter sunlight, made dazzling by the snow, shone into the dining room as everyone enjoyed a makeshift breakfast. The boundaries between guests and landlady had long gone, with everyone lending a hand and making the best of things. Nico had brewed up coffee on the camping stove, while Una put the croissants in the oven, which was still slightly warm. Agatha and the Hartley-Brewers had laid the tables in the dining room.

A horrified Jingle and Belle had vanished into the snow to get away from the invaders, but soon returned to dry their soggy fur against the warm oven.

The children had changed into clean clothes in Sophie's flat, and Pete had called Anna. The children's delighted reactions as they spoke to their mum and heard their new little sister yelling in the background told Sophie everything she needed to know.

'She's doing fine. As is the baby,' Pete announced. 'I feel so bad about not being with her, but we'll just have to be patient.'

Sophie had had to lend Amber some wellies and they were two sizes too big, but she seemed excited about their adventure. 'It's very kind of your neighbour to host us all,' she said gratefully.

Agatha took Suzanne's arm. 'You'll be much cosier at Brody's place, my dear. He isn't exactly a stranger now, is he? He's a rather marvellous chap. If you could have seen what he had to do last night, you'd think so too. Imagine taking on responsibility for a mother and her newborn . . .'

Suzanne pursed her lips, then gave a brief smile. 'You're right. Especially after everything he did last night,' she agreed, and Sophie was glad that there had been no more public arguments between the half-sisters – so far.

'It'll be much warmer at this farmhouse too,' Agatha added, winding a woolly scarf around her neck.

'That's true. There's heating, and Brody makes a wonderful fire. I promise you the farmhouse is a far better proposition than Sunnyside today,' Sophie declared. 'Shall we go?' she added cheerily, rounding everyone up.

Suzanne nodded and pulled a beanie hat over her ears, but made no further comment.

Shortly afterwards, Sophie led her motley crew of escapees across the field towards the farmhouse, with each guest carrying food and drink as a contribution to the day's feasting. The sun was out, showing the landscape cosseted in a duvet of white, from the tops of the high fells down to the lake shore. Water was already dripping from the trees and hedgerows, although the thaw brought by heavy rain wouldn't arrive until the early hours of Boxing Day.

Nico walked beside her. 'I don't think I'd let strangers invade my home on Christmas Day,' he said. 'And after being up half the night, delivering a baby, too. Is Brody some kind of saint?'

'Hardly,' Sophie muttered. 'I think he just wants to help.'

The kids were chattering away, the little one in Pete's arms and the older one kicking up snow and throwing snowballs. 'Can we make a snowman?' Baxter asked his dad excitedly, forging ahead into drifts that came up to his waist. Luckily he was in a waterproof onesie.

'We can, later,' Pete promised, with a smile that was becoming frazzled.

By contrast, Agatha was remarkably chipper after her night of partying and playing midwife. 'Gosh, have I woken up and found myself in the Swiss Alps?' she declared, stopping to take in the panorama of snowy peaks and glittering lake. 'Now if only those church bells were cow bells.'

Everyone laughed and Sophie was glad to see them all in good spirits. The Hartley-Brewers and Amber whipped out their phones to take pictures of the stunning scene.

'Is that it?' Amber said, pointing to Felltop Farm. 'It looks very old.'

'It's well over two hundred years old,' Sophie said. 'And apparently there are parts that date back a lot further.'

With its snow-covered roof and whitewashed walls, the farmhouse seemed to grow out of the landscape. The squat chimneys had smoke spiralling out of them, and Sophie imagined the fire blazing inside the snug. Apart from her brief emergency visit last night, the last time she'd been in the house she'd been so full of hopes – only to have them overturned.

'Are you OK, my dear?' Agatha was by her side. 'Only you seem a little distracted.'

'Do I?' Sophie smiled, determined to be lively and

cheerful, for her guests' sake. 'I think it's sleep deprivation, and I'm sure everyone is tired after last night. Worth it, though.'

'I know what you mean, although once I did turn in, I went out like a light. Do you know, last night was the first time I felt I truly had a purpose since I lost my dear Ron.'

Sophie squeezed Agatha's arm. 'You were fantastic. I don't know what we'd have done without you.'

'Thank you for saying that. It's surprising how everything came back to me. I suppose you never forget a lifetime of caring for people . . .'

'I'm sure you don't,' Sophie replied kindly, realising how very much Agatha must miss the two pillars of her life: her husband and her career.

Trudging through the fresh snow was hard going, but they were soon almost at the farm.

'This is gorgeous,' Amber enthused as they neared the house. There was a covered balcony along the upper floor, accessed by a set of stone steps.

Even Suzanne stopped to look at the house with admiration. 'It definitely looks seventeenth century to me,' she said.

'The balcony was a spinning gallery, where the women used to spin wool outside in the old days,' Sophie said, remembering what Brody had told her. 'There are still a few left on farmhouses in the Lake District.'

'Have we woken up in a costume drama?' Una asked, holding hands with Hugo.

'Last night was surreal, that's for sure,' Sophie replied,

thinking that spending Christmas Day with Brody and his fiancée was going to be very strange, but she'd put on a brave face in front of the guests.

'Morning. Happy Christmas!'

Brody opened the door, wearing a reindeer sweater and a Santa hat. Harold dashed out, barking excitedly, before running back inside and skidding on the hall flagstones.

The scent of wood-smoke mingled with what Sophie recognised as mulled-wine spices and baking. She steeled herself to face not only Tegan, but the typical Christmas celebrations she'd been trying to avoid.

Pete Nowak was the first to respond with a 'Happy Christmas!' and shake Brody's hand.

The hall was soon filled with barking and greetings.

Amber looked around her in awe at the carved panels, flagged floors and oak staircase.

'It reminds me of a National Trust house we used to visit,' Suzanne remarked. 'An old farmhouse, hundreds of years old, that hadn't been altered for centuries. My dad used to go on about how beautiful it was . . .'

Sophie noticed Amber watching her half-sibling closely. Had the farmhouse triggered memories for her too? If it had, Amber didn't say anything.

'I'm afraid Felltop has had many alterations,' Brody said. 'There's Wi-Fi, by the way, as I'm sure some of you are desperate for it. You can charge your phones too.'

Harold ran up to Sophie, greeting her like an old friend, which involved hand-licks and rolling over to have his tummy rubbed. Brody avoided her eye. Sophie wondered how Tegan had reacted to his invitation and if he was already regretting the offer, in the cold light of day.

'I hope everyone is OK with dogs,' Brody said to the escapees. 'This is Harold, who's a big softy.'

'He really is,' Sophie agreed, as Harold turned his attention to the Hartley-Brewers.

'Oh!' Una cried, being greeted by Harold thumping his tail against her legs and jumping up at Hugo.

'Harold! Leave people alone!' A fresh voice with a transatlantic twang heralded the arrival of Tegan from the kitchen. Dressed in a sparkly jumper and a silver leather skirt, she reminded Sophie of a hip snow-queen. The children were wide-eyed.

'It's Elsa!' the little one said, pointing at Tegan, who smiled.

'Look at that tree, Daddy!'

'I'm *so-o-o* sorry,' Tegan trilled. 'Brody, can you please shut Harold up somewhere!'

'Don't worry, we love dogs,' Hugo said. 'Ours passed away in the autumn.'

'So it's seemed very quiet at home, with the kids away and no dog,' Una added, stroking Harold's back.

'I bet,' Brody sympathised. 'But Harold is very overexcited,' he said, grabbing his collar. 'I think you should settle down, boy. Why don't you go into the kitchen and have a treat?'

Harold seemed in two minds about this, enjoying all the new people fussing over him, but Brody kept hold of him firmly.

A beaming Tegan spoke. 'Now, shall I take your coats and you can all warm up in the snug?'

'Can I plug my phone in first?' Pete asked. 'Mine's about to give up the ghost!'

A chorus of 'Mine too' followed.

'Of course,' Tegan replied, beaming. 'There are plenty of sockets. It's such a huge place! Far too big for the two of us, isn't it, Brody?' She linked arms with him.

'It used to be my parents' house,' Brody explained, before moving away towards the hall coat-rack. 'Please everyone, make yourself at home.'

Sophie made a meal of searching her bag for her phone charger. It was excruciating watching Tegan play lady of the manor with Brody. Any 'bonding' between her and Brody during the crisis of the previous evening had completely evaporated now. They'd only been at Felltop five minutes and she wasn't sure she was going to last the day.

While Brody found charging spots for the phones, Tegan helped Sophie unwrap the food that the guests had carried over. She'd donned an apron over her sparkly outfit and was almost overflowing with bonhomie. Sophie told herself to be grateful. Without her neighbours, Christmas Day would have been miserable and cold.

The two of them unloaded cheeses, salamis and salads into Brody's fridge, which was already pretty full.

'I'm sorry that our contribution is such a mixture,' Sophie said. 'We were having paella, but the fridges have gone off. The house is freezing, but I didn't want to risk the chicken and seafood now, just in case. The last thing I want – on top of everything else – is to give people food poisoning.'

'*Paella?*' Tegan's eyebrows shot up, before she arranged her face into a sympathetic smile. 'Oh yes, Brody did mention you were all having an anti-Christmas break.'

'I'm not against Christmas . . .' Sophie began. 'We were planning an *alternative* celebration where people could escape the traditional festivities, if they wanted to. And,' she added as lightly as she could, 'that's certainly how it's turned out, though not quite in the way I'd expected.'

'No, what a night, eh? Brody's been downplaying the whole thing, but it sounds like he was quite the hero. I genuinely think he saved Anna and her baby.'

'Well . . . I wouldn't quite go that far,' Sophie said, guessing Brody would be mortified to hear such praise. 'But we're all very glad he was on hand to help.'

'He doesn't like the limelight,' Tegan went on, closing the fridge door. 'He's a quiet man, the strong and silent type. You have to know him *very* well indeed to see the real Brody.' With a smile, she handed Sophie a platter of cheese straws. 'Would you mind taking these nibbles through to the snug? I thought we'd lay everything out in there, so people can help themselves.' She frowned. 'I wonder where Brody's got to?'

Probably escaped the awkward atmosphere, Sophie thought, taking through the nibbles as requested, eager to get some breathing space from Tegan.

So many conflicted thoughts swirled around her head.

She couldn't warm to Tegan – and she was trying to – who was clearly besotted with Brody, which made it even sadder that she'd no idea there was another side to the man she was hero-worshipping.

On a more trivial note, Sophie also wasn't enjoying her relegation from host to guest. She had to keep reminding herself how grateful she was that her neighbours had invited them all to share their home. Gritting her teeth, she handed around the snacks, before returning to the kitchen for more nibbles.

Tegan had already prepared a platter of olives and some of the leftover tapas from the previous evening.

'Thanks. I think everyone's enjoying themselves. I won't put the Christmas mix-tape on,' Tegan said when they were out of the guests' hearing again. 'I don't want to offend anyone, though it's a shame for the kids.'

'Please put on any music you like,' Sophie said, not wanting to make a fuss or be the target of any more pointed comments. 'As long as it's not Ed Sheeran, of course.'

Tegan's eyes widened in horror. 'Ed? Why not? I love him!'

'I was joking,' Sophie said, now feeling awkward that her attempt to lighten the mood had backfired. 'He's – er – great. Honestly. Please. This is your home. Brody's home, I mean. Your home and Brody's.' Realising that she was digging a deeper and deeper hole, she grabbed the platter. 'I'll take these through!'

Tegan followed her with more plates, and then regaled the company with the history of Felltop Farm.

With everyone distracted, Sophie tugged on her boots

and coat and trudged into the stable yard for some fresh air. The sky was blue and she was sorely tempted to take off onto the fells and not come back until dark. They hadn't even had lunch yet . . . and there was still the afternoon and evening to get through.

It was very cold in the yard but, with the sun shining, there were also tentative indications of a thaw. Snow dripped off the guttering around the outbuildings, and parts of the courtyard were slushy now. However, there were other signs that stopped her in her tracks.

Was *that* . . . ? Could that be a trail of hoof-prints leading from the fields to the stable? Just as she was wondering, Brody, Pete and the children walked round the corner from the front of the house.

'Oh, look at those mysterious marks in the snow!' Pete said, coming to a dramatic halt a few yards away from the kitchen door. 'They look like animal prints to me.'

He led the little one, Maria, by the hand. Baxter ran up to the prints, crouched down and began examining them.

He looked up at his father. 'Is it a donkey, Daddy?'

'Hmm, I'm not sure. Shall we ask Brody?'

Sophie smiled, as it began to dawn on her what had happened.

Brody arrived and crouched down next to the prints. Scratching his chin, he let out a loud 'Hmm', then dug his finger into the centre of the print and sighed again.

'What is it?' Baxter asked impatiently.

'A tiger!' Maria said and held up her hands to be carried again.

Pete scooped her up in his arms. 'I don't think it's a tiger. Tigers have big paws.'

'I should hope not,' Brody said and straightened up. 'In my professional opinion, it looks very much like a reindeer.'

Sophie longed to capture the expression on Baxter's face. His little mouth opened and his eyes widened in awe.

'A reindeer?' he murmured.

'I think it must be,' Brody said. 'What do you reckon, Pete?'

'Looks like it to me too, and if Brody says it is, then it is.'

'A *Rudolph* reindeer?' Baxter said hopefully.

'Maybe.'

Pete nodded sagely. 'The tracks lead to the stable. Shall we go and see what we can find?'

'What if he's still in there?' Baxter said, moving closer to his father.

'I think it will be perfectly safe,' Brody promised. 'But we won't know until we go inside.'

He caught Sophie's eye. She smiled briefly.

Brody scratched his chin. 'You know, I *thought* I heard hooves on the roof last night, but decided I was dreaming . . . Let's go and see. Sophie, would you like to come with us?'

This was a direct invitation that Sophie couldn't refuse. She'd no idea what surprise Brody might have left in the stable, but there was no way she was going to miss the children's reactions to whatever he'd planned.

'Do you want to open the door?' Brody asked Baxter. 'We

must be very quiet. We don't want to scare any creature who might be in there.'

'Go on,' Pete urged, still holding Maria.

After a moment's hesitation, Baxter pushed at the door. The others followed, with Sophie at the rear. The stable was warm with the scent of hay and animals.

Baxter let out a squeal, then shushed himself.

There were no reindeer, but Gabe was in his stall, and the two sheep were in their pen. On the floor were two small baskets, one filled with carrots and parsnips and the other with hay. The donkey snuffled when he saw the visitors.

'A donkey!' Baxter cried and then, 'Where's Rudolph?' He looked a little crestfallen.

'And sheep. Baa!' Maria started making sheep noises.

'I think Rudolph must have been and gone,' Sophie said, playing along. 'He seems to have left some presents, though.'

'Dog!' Maria shouted.

Two fluffy dog toys with red ribbons sat on the hay bales. They had tags around their necks with names on.

Brody walked over to them. 'I wonder who these are for?' He checked the labels. 'This one says "Maria", so it must be for you.'

Pete lowered Maria to her feet and she grabbed her toy, hugging it against her.

'What do you think about that?' Pete said. 'Rudolph must have left gifts for you and the animals.'

Baxter picked his dog up. 'Santa did know I was here . . .' he said in wonder.

The amazement in the little boy's eyes made Sophie's eyes fill with tears. Brody gave a cough.

'Of course he did,' Brody said. 'Now, shall we – er – give the animals their presents? Sophie, can you help us?'

'I'd love to,' Sophie replied, picking up the baskets with a mixture of bittersweet feelings at her remembrance of the last time she'd been in the stable with Brody.

While they helped the children feed the animals, Brody had another surprise to share.

'I've got some news. I had a word with a local farmer, and he says he can meet you on the other side of the fallen tree and transport you in his tractor to your mother-in-law's in the next village, if you want.'

'So you and the kids can have Christmas lunch with your family after all,' Sophie said, feeling thrilled for Pete.

'That's fantastic. Thanks, Brody. And you too, Sophie. For everything.' Pete beamed.

Brody looked embarrassed, and Sophie felt the same way. 'Don't mention it. It was scary at the time, but I'm so happy we could help, even in a small way. The kids have been a delight.'

'They've absolutely loved this surprise,' Pete said, holding out a carrot for Gabriel on behalf of Maria. 'Though now they're going to want donkeys as pets.' He chuckled.

'When are they letting Anna and the baby out?' Sophie asked, patting Gabe's side.

'Tomorrow. It would have been nice to be all together today, but I'd rather she and the baby are properly checked over before they come home.'

'If you want, I could take you to collect Anna from the hospital and bring you to your mum-in-law's?' Brody offered.

'You could pick up your car from Sunnyside when the thaw happens,' Sophie suggested.

'That would be fantastic. Again, I can't thank you enough.'

Maria was playing with her dog. Pete shook Brody's hand and hugged Sophie. 'Happy Christmas. From me, Anna and the kids. *All* of the kids.'

'You too,' Sophie said. 'Happy Christmas.'

With the animals fed, Pete took the kids inside to pack up their stuff, ready to meet the tractor driver.

Brody closed the stable door, but Sophie lingered. 'Where did the gifts come from?' she asked him, impressed at what he'd done to make the morning festive.

'They were promotional items from a worming-treatment supplier. They were in the spare room, but when I saw them this morning I knew I had the perfect home for them.'

'The hoof-prints were a great touch too.'

Brody's weary expression was lit up by smiles. Sophie's stomach did a little flip, of desire – and regret.

'I enjoyed it. Dad used to do it when I was very small. Even after I stopped believing in Santa, he carried on doing it. When we had younger cousins visiting, I used to help. It was our secret tradition.' His smile became sadder and his wistful gaze alighted on the farmhouse as if he was remembering happier times.

'You must miss him on a day like this,' she said, feeling sorry for him.

'I do,' he said simply, and then, 'I did hesitate about the reindeer-prints and gifts, in case it was too much, but the kids have had a rough time, so I thought they deserved a bit of festive magic.'

'It is Christmas after all,' Sophie said. 'Pretending Santa is real is OK.' She almost said, 'Some little lies are alright . . .'

'Yeah, but you were trying to avoid Christmas and it's kind of bitten you on the bum. If you know what I mean.'

'It doesn't matter about me. I'm grateful to you – and Tegan – for taking us in. I appreciate all you've done for the Nowaks and my guests. It's just awkward being around Tegan. I'd never want to hurt her.'

'Neither would I,' Brody shot back. 'I'm sure you don't believe me, but I really want you to be here. And there's so much more you don't know . . .' He looked and sounded desperate.

Holding her breath, Sophie waited for him to say more, prepared to give him chance to explain.

'Brody!'

Tegan trudged towards them across the yard, an old pair of Brody's wellies on her feet, a pink teddy-coat around her shoulders.

'Aha!' she cried. 'I wondered where you'd got to.'

Sophie wasn't sure if she was included in the 'you'.

'I – er – arranged a surprise for the children,' Brody said. 'And some transport for the whole family. One of the local farmers is going to take them to Pete's in-laws in the next village.'

'So they won't be here for lunch?' Tegan asked.

'That should make things a bit less complicated,' Sophie offered, feeling like a spare part. 'I needed some fresh air,' she added, feeling as if she'd been caught out, 'but I'm coming in now to help with lunch.'

'Thank you,' Tegan said with a winning smile. She linked arms with Brody. 'Now, tell me about what you've been doing for the children. He's full of surprises,' she said.

'Well, it seems that Christmas has been thrust upon us, despite our best efforts,' Agatha remarked as they headed into the dining room.

The table was groaning with a buffet, made up of Sophie's food and the Felltop leftovers. Tegan had added a centrepiece with a candle and had piled festive serviettes on the plates. Candles glowed in the deep-set windows, which were filled with holly and ivy. It couldn't have looked more Christmassy if it had tried. A greatest festive-hits mix now played from the speakers.

'Well, well, this is all very – jolly,' Nico smirked.

'That spread looks marvellous, I will say,' Una added.

The others made appreciative noises.

'Harold! Stop!' Brody shouted, spotting a very waggy tail under the table. He caught hold of the dog's collar. 'I'd better keep him in the sitting room, before he eats his own weight in mini-quiche.'

Harold's tail stopped waving as he was led away by Brody.

'Should we help ourselves then?' Amber asked.

'I think so . . .' Sophie said, painfully aware that they were still her guests – yet this wasn't her home.

Hugo rubbed his hands together. 'Well, I'm not proud – I'm going to be the greedy one who goes first.'

'Wait!'

Tegan's shriek stopped Hugo dead in his tracks.

She walked in with a cardboard box. 'I forgot the crackers!' She opened the lid. 'Nobody minds a cracker, do they? Only it *is* Christmas Day, and I found these in the pantry. It seems such a shame not to use them.' Her eyes lasered in on Sophie. 'Unless it's too triggering for you all?'

Sophie felt like the Wicked Witch of the West. 'I've nothing against crackers . . .'

'I think I can cope too,' Agatha said archly.

'We never had crackers at home when I was little,' Suzanne commented. 'Dad said they were a waste of money.'

Amber exchanged a look with her. There was pain in her eyes, and empathy. 'I'll pull one with you,' she offered.

Sophie almost fainted in shock. The others were dumbstruck, apart from Nico, who was sniggering with delight at the reaction a humble box of crackers had caused.

'Well, if we're having crackers thrust upon us, let's go for it, I say. We can wear the hats while we eat the buffet!' He held one out to Agatha. 'Will you pull my cracker, Agatha?'

'Any time,' she replied with a wink. She almost toppled backwards as the two ends parted with a loud snap.

'Well done!' Nico said, donning his hat with a grin. 'Come on then. Get pulling!'

The others paired up to open the crackers and put the hats on, with varying degrees of enthusiasm. Slipping hers over her head, Sophie fixed a smile on her face.

Agatha stuffed hers in her pocket. 'I don't mind a cracker, but I've never worn a party hat in my life and I don't intend to start now.'

Brody walked back in. 'OK, Harold and the food are safe now. Shall we all get some lunch?'

Tegan handed him a paper crown. 'Don't forget your hat,' she said. 'There's no escape.'

Brody put it on and Tegan hugged him, before looking around the room with a happy sigh and declaring, 'Oh, I *do* love Christmas!'

Chapter Twenty-Five

His mother would be proud of him, Brody thought, as stepping in to entertain a houseful of strangers during an emergency was surely her idea of heaven.

While it hadn't exactly been hell, Brody had found it exhausting to keep up the bonhomie and the pretence of being the happy couple, in front of Sophie and the others. He'd tried to stay out of her way for a bit, keeping himself busy, loading and emptying the dishwasher, refilling glasses and trying to smooth over any tense moments with Sophie.

She had led her guests on a snowy walk into the village after lunch. Brody knew she'd done it to give him and Tegan some space and he was grateful. At first he'd felt guilty at landing so much work on Tegan, but she'd seemed to be in her element, acting as hostess.

It was now late afternoon and all the lamps had been lit in the farmhouse. Nico and Agatha had returned to the snug with glasses of mulled wine and mince pies. Nico was reclining in Brody's father's armchair, with his feet up on a tapestry footstool, and Agatha was relaxing on the sofa with one of Brody's father's Dick Francis novels.

The other escapees must still be outside, along with Sophie. Brody had detected a slight undercurrent of tension between Amber and Suzanne. Agatha, Una and Hugo seemed like decent people, but there was something about Nico that he didn't like, although he couldn't put his finger on what exactly. He'd no idea how Sophie handled the stream of guests flowing in and out of Sunnyside every week. He took his party hat off to her, for her skills and diplomacy. Then again, he had to deal with anxious animals and their owners. Sophie, however, couldn't lock her charges in a pet carrier if they turned feisty.

The back door opened and Sophie walked into the snug, bright-eyed from the snowy outing.

'Nice walk?' Brody asked, noticing how naturally pretty she was, uncaring about her messy hair or pink cheeks from the cold.

'Yes, and I popped home to check in on the cats and feed them. They've wormed their way under a duvet on the sofa.'

Brody smiled. 'Sensible creatures.'

Nico glanced up from his phone. 'Where are the others?'

'Una and Hugo are in the hall, being entertained by Harold,' Sophie said. 'Amber and Suzanne are still outside.'

Nico raised an eyebrow. 'Let's hope they're not having a snowball fight.'

'No ... I think they were taking photographs,' Sophie said, holding up crossed fingers.

'*They?*' Agatha said with raised eyebrows.

'Is there – er – some kind of problem between them?' Brody took his chance to find out what was going on.

Nico snorted. 'You could say that! It was like *EastEnders* at the guest house last night.'

'Thankfully it wasn't quite that bad,' Sophie jumped in, turning to Brody. 'They – er – are half-sisters and only recently discovered they had the same father. It's very, *very* complicated.'

'Right. I see. How did they end up at the same guest house for Christmas?'

'Let's say they have more in common than they'd like to admit,' Sophie said.

Nico sank back into Brody's armchair and tucked his hands behind his head. 'I'm thinking of writing a novel about it all, but I haven't decided if it's family drama, crime or horror. Ouch!' he winced and jumped out of the chair. 'Something just dug into my arse!'

Agatha tittered. 'I should have warned you that chair's on its last legs. I tried it but the springs are gone. It might be more comfortable to sit somewhere else.'

Nico glared at the chair and rubbed his backside. 'Yeah. I will.'

Tegan walked into the snug and put her hands on her hips. 'Well, you're all very quiet! I think we should play charades!'

'Good grief,' Agatha muttered.

'Um, I'm always rubbish at that,' Una protested, walking into the snug with Hugo and Amber.

'I'm quite good at it,' Amber piped up.

'Mum would never let me play,' Suzanne said, following behind.

'You could team up,' Tegan suggested.

Sophie stepped in. 'I don't want to be a party-pooper,' she said, obviously trying to be diplomatic. 'But . . .'

'OK, I wouldn't want to force anyone,' Tegan replied, deflated. 'We could always watch *It's a Wonderful Life* instead.'

Nico smirked. Brody had an irresistible urge to punch him on the nose.

Tegan's face lit up. '*Or* I could give you all a tour of Felltop!'

Brody gave an audible gasp. 'Erm, the place is a bit of a mess.'

'Oh, we don't care about that,' Agatha said, clearly delighted for any escape from party games and movies. 'I'd love a tour. This is a gorgeous old place, Brody.'

'It *is* gorgeous. Is it listed?' Una asked.

'No,' Brody replied.

'Are there any ghosts?' Amber's voice had a hopeful uplift. Suzanne looked petrified.

'I do hope so!' Agatha declared, putting her book aside.

Nico glanced up from his phone with a smug grin. 'Brody might not want us snooping around his house . . .'

Brody didn't think he'd been listening. Nico was correct, but Brody didn't want him to know that he agreed.

'Oh, he doesn't mind!' Tegan said airily. 'And there used to be a rumour about a ghost in one of the attic rooms. One of the maids from way back, wasn't it, Brody?'

'It's only a daft rumour,' Brody murmured. 'I've never seen it – her.'

Agatha was on her feet, clapping her hands. 'Ah, but attic rooms and ghostly maids! How *delicious*. We *must* have a tour.'

'That's settled. Is everyone coming?' Tegan asked.

Una dug Hugo in the ribs. 'Wake up! We're going on a ghost tour?'

'What?' Hugo's eyelids fluttered and he tried to come round.

'It's not compulsory,' Tegan said, looking at Sophie again. 'I wouldn't want you to be bored if you've already been around Felltop.'

'I haven't,' Sophie said firmly. 'And I really don't mind a tour.'

'Can we play "Sardines"?' Amber asked hopefully. 'Or "Murder in the Dark"? I'm sure it's going to be that kind of house.' Suddenly she smiled. 'I *am* joking, though I did love "Sardines" when I was little.'

From the rear of the group Suzanne let out a tiny gasp. 'I loved that game too.'

'And me . . .' that was Agatha, grinning wickedly at Brody.

Before anyone else could comment, Tegan jumped in. 'I think a tour will be *quite* enough excitement. Felltop is a *big* property. We wouldn't want anyone to get lost. Are you coming, Brody?'

No matter how painful it was, there was no way Brody was going to let Tegan – or anyone else – give strangers a tour of his home without him being there. To his dismay, everyone suddenly sprang into life at the prospect, with even Amber and Suzanne in unison about exploring every nook and cranny.

Only Sophie showed less enthusiasm, which was hardly surprising, given the circumstances. Brody felt for her. She could hardly refuse and seem to be a misery.

They toured the ground floor first, Tegan regaling everyone with the house's history and encouraging Brody to fill in any gaps.

'I'm no real expert,' he said. 'My family has only lived here since the war, and I can only tell you what my grandparents and parents told me.'

Despite Brody feeling like a fish out of water, the guests seemed impressed by his anecdotes, marvelling at the old beams, the bread oven tucked away in the diningroom wall and the small piece of oak panelling dating back to 1714. There had actually been a farmhouse on the site since the fifteenth century, a fact that seemed to impress everyone.

'You're practically landed gentry,' Nico observed.

Brody let out a snort.

'Shall we go upstairs?' Tegan said brightly. 'That's where the ghost is supposed to hang out.'

'There's no ghost,' Brody corrected her.

She gave him a playful push. 'Don't be boring. You know I've heard her, and even your mum says she's felt a ghostly presence in the attic. And everyone loves a ghost story for Christmas.'

By the look on Sophie's face, that wasn't true.

273

Tegan led the way up the stairs, with the guests in between and Brody bringing up the rear along with Harold, whose tail thumped against the banister with joy.

'I feel like I ought to hold up an umbrella or something!' Tegan trilled at the top of the stairs, clearly loving the attention.

'This is just like the National Trust,' Agatha declared as everyone squeezed onto the landing. Though spacious by most standards, it was cosy with ten people and an over-excited Labrador.

'Are you going to charge us twenty quid each?' Nico quipped.

'Is there a tearoom?' Una offered with a smile.

'No, but this is where Brody hands us the bill for all the food we've scoffed,' Nico shot back.

'Actually you can pay by doing all the washing up and mucking out the stable,' Brody said, more sharply than he meant to.

'I've done worse jobs,' Nico replied silkily.

'Shall we move on?' Tegan stepped in.

Brody caught Sophie's eye, but she looked quickly away. Tegan led the way down the hall.

'I haven't tidied up!' Brody said when she paused outside his room.

'Oh, we won't go in. I only wanted to show everyone the lintel over the door. They say the oak came from a shipwreck off Whitehaven.'

There were a few appreciative 'Oohs' from Una and the Smith half-sisters.

'Is it true?' Hugo asked Brody.

'Probably. We had a local historian round and she said it was documented in some archive in the Armitt Museum in the village.'

Una's attention was captured by something on a beam. 'Oh! Is that mistletoe?' she asked.

'I never had you down as a mistletoe kind of guy,' Nico said to Brody.

'There's greenery all over the house, after we hosted a Christmas party the other week. I didn't put it there,' Brody replied, aware that Nico was bringing out the grump in him.

'Who did then?' Nico asked.

'I did,' Tegan said. 'I found it downstairs and couldn't resist.'

'In that case, we'd better make use of it,' Una gushed and planted a kiss on Hugo's lips.

Tegan smiled at Brody, who flashed a smile back and tried to avoid Sophie's eye. She'd been almost silent on the way round the house so far. He longed to get the tour over with.

Agatha tutted. 'Now, now, we can't all start snogging each other on so slight an acquaintance. Apart from Una, Hugo and our hosts, of course.'

Nico smirked. 'I think we know each other pretty well by now,' he said to Agatha, playfully planting a kiss on the cheek.

'Cheeky boy!' Agatha replied with a girlish giggle and gave him a little push.

'Who wants to see the attics and meet the ghost?' Tegan asked, moving down the corridor, but Agatha lingered by the next door.

'That carving is beautiful,' she said, pausing to admire the oak door. 'It looks very old.'

Suzanne flattened her palm on the elaborately carved panel. 'Was that rescued from a shipwreck too?' she asked.

'Yeah, the *Titanic*,' Nico quipped and Amber giggled.

'It was carved by a local carpenter in Victorian times, but the oak was from a table that was much older,' Brody said, joining them by the door. Not only was he conscious of sounding grumpy, but also a bit pompous. Yet he was finding it increasingly difficult to ignore Nico's sarcasm.

'It's gorgeous,' Suzanne said. 'Reminds me of one in a hotel we used to stay in when I was little . . .'

Brody saw her glance at Amber, who simply looked back at her with sadness in her eyes. Whatever might have happened the previous night, it seemed like they were putting it behind them.

'You should see the carved panels in my room,' Tegan commented. 'Mind you, the wind howls under the gap in the door. I reckon that's why Brody puts his guests in there, so they don't outstay their welcome . . .'

Brody froze. That 'my' resonated like a clanging bell. Had people noticed? He glanced over to Sophie, but her expression was unreadable.

'Shall we move on, darling?' Tegan said hastily, realising too late what she'd said.

'Yes, though it's really very boring up there,' Brody cautioned.

'On the contrary,' Nico replied with a grin, clearly having picked up on it, 'it's *way* more interesting than I'd ever expected.'

'Hey, Brody, have you got a full trainset up in the attics or something?' Hugo asked jovially.

Everyone laughed, including Sophie and Tegan.

No, thought Brody, but it might be fun to lock an annoying Italian up there for a while. In the dark. 'I wish,' he said to Hugo, forcing a smile to his face.

Somehow everyone made it up the narrow staircase to the attics, whose rooms were accessed via a long corridor. Brody switched on the light, which only illuminated the cobwebs and dust up there.

'This is the maid's room,' Tegan said, pushing open the door to the second room, with glee.

'Allegedly,' Brody muttered, desperate for the tour to be over.

The door opened into a room with a sloping roof. Brody flicked the switch, amazed to find that the single naked bulb hadn't blown yet. It was piled high with junk: an old pram, chairs, tea chests from the days when people used such things for moving house. There was a child's bike – not even his, but his Uncle Trevor's – plus boxes full of dusty books, most of them his father's. The James Herriots were his, of course.

It was like opening a portal onto his childhood, and his

parents' childhoods. On a day that was meant to be special, he was painfully aware of the absence of his father, and felt bad that his mother was on her own. Instead he was leading a bunch of strangers around his home, and was worrying about Tegan and Sophie.

'Wow!' Una said, at the front of the group as they crowded into the small space by the doorway.

Amber stopped dead, pointing. 'What's that? On the top of that chest?'

Brody followed her gaze. All he could see was an old porcelain doll, which had been his grandmother's, its dress now tattered and dusty.

'The doll? It was my granny's. Mum didn't want to throw it away, but I find it – a bit creepy, if I'm honest, so I put it up here.'

'The eyes follow you everywhere.' Tegan shuddered.

'Quite,' said Agatha.

'Dad gave me one like that,' Amber said. 'Not an old one. A reproduction, but exactly like that. She had a pink dress. I've still got her.'

'And me.' Suzanne exchanged a glance with her. 'Only mine had a lilac dress. Mum said she was too valuable to play with, so I just plonked her on a chest of drawers. She's in my spare room at home now.'

Brody was worried this hadn't been a good idea, when Nico swore out loud and Tegan let out a piercing shriek. A bumping noise made almost everyone cry out in unison.

'What the hell was that?' Nico demanded.

'The ghostly maid dropping her ... tray?' Agatha suggested.

'It was Harold,' Sophie piped up from the rear. 'He's knocked over a vase.' She picked it up. 'Luckily it's still in one piece.'

Harold wormed his way through everyone's legs, tongue lolling, making everyone laugh except Nico, who glared angrily at the perpetrator.

Brody caught Sophie's eye and she smiled briefly, as if she'd forgotten she was disappointed and angry with him. He grinned back, and for a second she seemed to smile in return, transporting him to the moment when they were on the cusp of taking their friendship to something more.

Sophie's smile faded. 'I'll put this back on the table,' she muttered. 'And I think I'll go downstairs. I feel a bit cold up here.'

'I think we should all go back down,' Brody said, the chill seizing him too. He'd found the day trying enough, without reminding himself of how much he'd lost.

'Thank you so much for your hospitality.'

'Thank you! I've really enjoyed it.'

'Watch out for the ghost!'

'Happy un-Christmas!'

'Whoops! I think I've had too much mulled wine.'

With Tegan beside him, Brody bade farewell to his unexpected guests with a broad grin on his face.

Sophie was the last to go. 'Thank you again,' she said. 'Both of you.'

'You're welcome,' said Tegan, 'I hope it wasn't too awful?'

'It was lovely, but I think you'll be very glad to have the place to yourselves again. I hope your belated Christmas dinner goes well.'

'Thank you,' Tegan replied graciously. 'I'm looking forward to seeing my parents. My dad's not at all well and he's actually waiting for an operation, so it will be nice to be together.'

'Oh?' said Sophie in surprise. 'I didn't know. I'm sorry to hear it.'

Was Brody imagining it or did Sophie catch his eye with a shocked glance. She must be thinking he was even more of a bastard.

Outside, the cold rain was falling softly. It was clear that a rapid thaw was under way, and the drive was slushy. Agatha had linked arms with Hugo and Una, though for whose benefit Brody wasn't sure, as they were all slightly unsteady. The porch light lit them as far as the road, but they were relying on torches for the rest of the journey.

Sophie led the way, a torch in one hand and two bags of food in the other.

'Whoa!' She slipped and almost fell, but Nico was there in an instant, his hand at her elbow, steadying her. He didn't remove it immediately, either.

Brody thought Sophie didn't need any man's help, but it hurt that she seemed happy to accept Nico's. He watched until his porch light clicked off and they'd all vanished into the darkness, before shutting the door.

The house was suddenly shockingly quiet. He didn't know whether to breathe a sigh of relief or panic. Today had been stressful at times, but while he'd been rushing around, he'd at least been kept busy. Helping the Nowak children had been an unexpected highlight. Now he was alone with Tegan, with nothing to distract him.

'That wasn't so bad after all,' she decided. 'Reminds me of the old days. Do you remember your last birthday party? Carl and his friend didn't leave here until three in the morning and you had the hangover to end all hangovers.' She laughed.

Brody did remember. It had been one hell of a night and one hell of a morning after. He'd been happy then; at least he'd thought he had, from what he could remember.

'Sophie was so brave to move here on her own. Did she split up with someone before she took over the guest house?'

'What makes you think that?' Brody asked.

Tegan shrugged. 'I don't know. She seems – sad somehow. Don't get me wrong, she's a nice person and she's very pretty, but why else would you move to a place like this in the middle of nowhere, if you weren't running away from something? She'll really feel it when her guests leave after Boxing Day.'

'She'll be OK,' Brody said. 'Hopefully the power should be back on soon too, now the weather is clearing up'

'I didn't mean the power. I meant it will be awful for her being alone again.'

'Maybe she'll be glad to have some time to herself,' Brody replied. 'She's used to looking after herself.'

Tegan frowned. 'You sound as if you know her well.'

'Not *that* well.' He gave a yawn, trying to change the subject, hating how Tegan was making assumptions about Sophie, but knowing it was raising her suspicions to keep defending her. 'I don't know about you, but I'm knackered. I need a shower, then I have to get some decent sleep in case I'm called out overnight. The snow's melting now, so I'd have no excuse for not attending.'

Tegan rolled her eyes. 'Not that you need an excuse – I know you love your job. You couldn't stop helping people if you tried.'

That was his problem, she'd told him the other day. He was too kind and, by implication, a soft touch.

'Brody? Are you sure you're OK?'

He saw she'd put her hand on his arm and had a tenderness in her expression he hadn't expected. It was a waste of time to dwell on bitterness and anger. The past was the past and they needed to pull together to get through the next few weeks.

'I'm fine, apart from being tired,' he managed. 'Thanks for what you did today. It can't have been easy entertaining a bunch of strangers and missing out on your parents' special day.'

Tegan paused on the threshold of the doorway. 'It's weird, but now I'm back, sleeping under the same roof as you, it's almost as if nothing has changed between us.'

Brody replied with the very briefest of smiles. On the

contrary, he felt as if his whole life had been turned upside down in just a couple of days. And after they'd got through tomorrow's celebrations with her parents, he was going to find out exactly how much longer it would be until they could come clean.

Chapter Twenty-Six

Sophie was busy preparing the Boxing Day breakfasts – though not much prep was required, as the meal consisted of fruit loaf, cake and juice – when the power came back on.

With a little 'Hurrah', she immediately put the kettle on to make some tea and coffee. While her guests had been very tolerant about their makeshift breakfast, she knew how much they'd be missing a hot drink. She was desperate for caffeine herself.

She went into the dining room to find Amber and Suzanne sharing a table and chatting quietly, which was definitely one of the silver linings of the past few days. Hiding her surprise, she silently crossed her fingers that peace might have broken out. She served the drinks and apologised again for the lack of a hot breakfast, promising that she'd go out for fresh supplies for supper and the following morning's breakfast as soon as the supermarket opened in Windermere.

The mood was cheerful, with everyone making plans for the day, now that the snow had thawed enough for people to get out and about in their cars. Straight after breakfast Una, Hugo and Agatha headed to a local National Trust property. Nico had gone out alone, while Suzanne and Amber had left for a walk – together.

Sophie returned to the kitchen to run the dishwasher, tidy up and write a list of supplies needed to replace all the lost food. She had more than enough to do, and yet her thoughts turned far too often to Brody.

She'd felt sorry for him at times on Christmas Day. It was clear he'd found the day as awkward as she had and when they'd opened the door on the attic full of family possessions, she'd thought he seemed weighed down by the memories. On the other hand, Sophie had felt even more sorry for Tegan, who was clearly besotted with Brody and worried sick about her father.

That's where they'd be today, she thought, stacking the final few plates in the dishwasher. They'd be at Brody's future in-laws soon, to enjoy the traditional family Christmas that he and Tegan had missed out on.

'Need a hand?'

Sophie had just pushed the button on the dishwasher when she found Nico hovering at the door of the kitchen, a large camera and lens cradled in his hands.

'Thanks, but everything's sorted now. I've finished here and I'm going off to the village to get some fresh food.'

'It's a shame the power cut ruined your plans for yesterday,' he said.

'I'll have to consider getting a generator, like at Felltop.' She almost said, 'like Brody'.

'Might be a good idea.'

'How was your walk?' she asked.

'Good. I got some decent shots of the fells. Though I could hardly fail, given what's around me.'

Sophie was glad to see Nico look happy, rather than giving his usual arch smile. He certainly made a decorative addition to the kitchen.

'It's stunning, isn't it?' she said. 'When I first moved here, I couldn't believe how beautiful it was. I've even learned to love it in the rain.'

'Even so, it was a big step. I read on your website that you only bought the place in the spring.'

'Yes . . .' She paused, unsure why he wanted to bring this up.

'Can I ask what you did before?'

Sophie decided to tell him the truth. 'Would you believe I ran a Christmas shop?'

His jaw dropped. 'No. You're joking?'

'Not at all. I ran it with my partner, but it didn't work out, so I decided to have a complete change.'

'That's some change . . .' He rested the camera on the table. 'I'm guessing it was the partner that didn't work out, rather than the business?'

'You'd guess right,' Sophie replied, about to deflect his question, but then she realised that her own guests had shared their stories. Nico hadn't revealed that much, if she was honest, but perhaps if she said more, he might reciprocate. 'I split up with my fiancé after he had a fling with my best friend. Actually it was more than a fling. They're together now and expecting a baby.'

Nico winced. 'Ouch! That's really tough. I'm sorry. Your ex must be a total twat, not to mention devoid of a brain.'

Sophie had to smile. 'That's one way of describing him. It

was horrible, I'll admit, but if he hadn't cheated on me, I'd probably never have moved to Sunnyside and made a completely new start.' And now she needed another fresh start, she thought.

'You're very brave,' he said archly.

'Am I? Some people thought I was running away, but actually I was doing something I'd always wanted to, and making new memories, so – here I am.'

'You certainly have made new memories: setting a new tradition with the "Escape for Christmas" break, helping to deliver babies and herding a bunch of frankly very quirky guests.' His brown eyes glittered with amusement. For the umpteenth time, Sophie acknowledged to herself that Nico was an incredibly handsome man. She loved to look at him and yet there was no knot in the stomach when she did so, no racing of the heart, like Brody caused her.

'I'll admit it wasn't quite the stay I'd imagined giving my guests.'

'Still, you handled it very well.' His eyes held hers, daring Sophie to look away. 'Do you mind if I say something I might regret?'

'That depends . . .'

'More accurately, I'll regret it if I don't say it. I wondered if I can see you again – after my stay ends.'

Wow! Sophie hadn't expected that. She had been propositioned not long after she'd taken over the guest house, by a man who'd turned out to be the owner of an artificial-lawn company. He'd wanted her to replace her garden with plastic grass. She'd politely told him where to shove his grass and was determined she'd be fully booked if he ever tried to stay again.

'That's very flattering,' she said lightly, but firmly. 'But I don't date guests.'

'I won't be a guest soon,' he said, with a teasing smile. 'And it doesn't *have* to be a date or any kind of commitment, if that's what's bothering you.'

'Um, that's very presumptuous of you,' Sophie murmured.

'What's the point in pussyfooting around? We're two attractive people. We're both single, and probably never going to meet again. You said yourself you wanted new experiences, so why not?'

Sophie gasped again. 'I'm flattered, but I'm not interested.'

'Life's too short not to seize the moment. Or are you still not over someone else? Someone whose name begins with a B?'

'What?' she said, shocked that he knew about Ben.

He frowned. 'I was thinking of the neighbourhood vet. Brody.'

'Brody is engaged to Tegan, who you met yesterday.'

'But that didn't stop him trying to look at you,' Nico said teasingly.

She shook her head in disbelief. 'Come on, how can you be jealous when you've only known me two days? And Brody and I are nothing more than neighbours and friends.'

'I'm sorry if I've offended you, but if you're waiting for

Brody to have a change of heart, I'm not sure he'd ever break away from Tegan, no matter how much he wants to.'

Sophie wasn't sure what he meant by that. 'I need to go to the shops.' She scooped up her car keys to emphasise her point.

After he'd left, Sophie drove down to the village, concentrating hard on the roads following her encounter with Nico. The sun was out and water was flowing down the lane. The fellsides were criss-crossed with becks, swollen with meltwater gurgling its way down to the lake. Pockets of snow remained where the sun hadn't yet reached and she had to negotiate the slushy areas carefully. The farm shop was closed until after New Year, so she headed to the small supermarket in Bowness to stock up on food for Boxing Day supper. The guests were looking after themselves for lunch, thankfully.

She gave a thought to Brody at his in-laws'; and to Ben, who was probably celebrating their happy news with his new partner's family or was cosied up with Naomi. Her stomach knotted. The past couple of days had brought so many emotions to the surface. Seeing a new life born in front of her eyes had reminded Sophie that she'd once hoped to have a family with Ben. And Brody had been so great with the Nowaks' kids.

He'd been great in so many ways. Capable, strong, kind, gorgeous . . . yet she must harden her bruised heart again.

She'd put him on a pedestal he didn't deserve.

Chapter Twenty-Seven

'There. That wasn't so bad, was it?' Tegan said as they returned to Felltop Farm later that evening, after spending Boxing Day with her family.

Brody wished he felt the same.

He locked the front door behind him. 'It's good to be home,' he sighed, relieved that he didn't have to keep up the pretence any longer.

Brody's mother had joined them for lunch and he'd made a big effort to set aside his misgivings and make the day as happy as possible. Tegan had played her part too, although they'd both been reminded of how fragile her father's health was. Brody felt his mind was elsewhere, constantly drifting off to thoughts of Sophie and wondering how she was getting on.

'I think I'll make a tea,' Tegan cut into his thoughts. 'Do you want one?'

'Yes. Thanks. I need a shower first.'

Brody showered in his en suite as quickly as he could, hoping the effect of the warm water and his previous broken nights would result in a swift and deep sleep later on. He walked into the bedroom to find Tegan sitting on the end of the bed in silk pyjamas and a robe.

'You shouldn't be in here,' he said, acutely aware of being naked.

'Why not?' She rolled her eyes. 'It's not as if I haven't seen it all before.'

'Because . . . you know why. What would Wes say?' he added, unable to keep the bitterness out of his voice.

'I'm not thinking about Wes,' she whispered, standing up and trying to move closer to him.

Brody walked around the other side of the bed, reaching for a pair of little-used pyjama bottoms from the chest of drawers.

Tegan looked intently at him. 'Don't you normally sleep naked?'

Keen not to make a big thing of it, he laughed. 'The farmhouse does tend to be cold this time of year, if you hadn't noticed.' To emphasise the fact, he pulled on a sweatshirt. 'I thought you were making a drink?'

She sighed and played with her hair. 'I came in to ask if you wanted anything with it. Brandy? Whisky? Now you're off-duty you can relax.'

That was impossible, Brody thought. He hadn't truly relaxed for days, weeks – maybe even longer, since he'd been part of this charade. Apart from at the lantern parade, and at the party with Sophie. She made him feel good about himself and they got on so well, having gone through similar experiences. 'No, thanks. Just the coffee will be fine. I'll come down now,' he added firmly, keen to get rid of Tegan.

When he got downstairs, Tegan was curled up on the sofa. 'What did you think of Dad then?' she asked. 'I was

291

shocked when I saw him. He's looking thinner and like he hasn't slept. He didn't eat much dinner, either.'

'He's probably worried about the surgery. That's understandable,' Brody reasoned.

Tegan stretched and yawned. And at that point her phone rang. She pressed her lips together. 'Sorry. I need to get this.'

She walked off, and he heard the stairs creak under her hurried footsteps. 'OK, Wes. Just because you're three thousand miles away doesn't mean you need to shout!'

He stayed in the snug longer than he'd intended, keen to avoid overhearing Tegan's conversation with her boyfriend. He neither wanted to hear them arguing nor getting 'lovey-dovey', both of which only brought him pain and made him feel helpless. Tegan might have hurt him and no longer be a part of his romantic life, but he still cared about her as a friend. He couldn't bear to think of her throwing her life away on a man who was clearly an absolute tosser.

Harold deigned to shift himself from the carpet and licked his hand, and Brody realised how cold he'd grown in the unheated room.

'OK, boy. Hint taken. Let's go up to bed.'

'Harold! Harold! Come back here!'

It was a hopeless cause. Harold hared off across the field towards Sunnyside.

'Ha-Rold!' Brody bellowed, but by now the Labrador was out of earshot. Brody had taken him for a walk as soon as the sun was up. A few drifts of snow had stubbornly stuck around, but mostly the fields were slushy and muddy.

Harold was already filthy and also wildly over-excited to be out. All the strange people, smells and disruption of his routine had turned him into an unruly toddler again, not the four-year-old almost-sensible dog he'd become.

Brody started to jog after him, slipping in the slush in his wellies. He reached the gate that opened from the footpath to Sunnyside's garden just in time to see Harold slip inside the rear door to Sophie's flat, which was slightly ajar to let the smell of frying bacon out.

'Sh-h-hit . . .' Brody muttered, breaking into a run.

He reached the open back door.

'Oh, Harold! No!'

He marched inside to find chaos. A tray of sausages was scattered on the floor, with Harold happily hoovering them up. Muddy paw-prints were smeared all over the tiles.

'Oh God,' Brody muttered, before grabbing Harold's collar.' I'm sorry! Harold, you so should not be in here.'

Sophie's hair was piled messily on her head, her cheeks were red and her apron was smeared with tomato ketchup. She'd never looked more beautiful or more stressed out.

'You can't blame the dog,' she said sharply, implying that she very much blamed Brody, as his owner.

'He must have been attracted by the smell,' Brody said, holding on to Harold for grim death. 'He ran off. It's my fault for not keeping him under control. Harold!' Brody tightened the lead as the Labrador lunged for another sausage. 'I'm so sorry about the mess. I'll take him outside, and I'll pay for the sausages,' he said, knowing the offer sounded ridiculous, yet desperate to help in some way.

He shooed Harold out of the back door and into the porch. 'Now stay there!' he said sternly. Harold settled down on the mat in the porch. 'Here, have this.' He gave the Labrador a rawhide bone from his coat pocket. It was wrong to reward the dog for pinching food, but he wanted to make it up to Sophie. 'I'll be back for you – you reprobate,' he said, wagging a finger.

Back in the kitchen, Sophie was tipping the sausages into the bin.

'Was that someone's breakfast?' he asked. 'I mean, obviously it was someone's breakfast.'

'Well, yes. They were for Amber, Suzanne and Agatha.'

'And Nico?' he asked.

Sophie frowned. 'Nico had a continental breakfast, because he wanted to go out early to take some photos. Anyway you really don't have to pay for the sausages. I'll offer the others extra eggs and mushrooms. I'm sure they won't mind. After the other catastrophes, a few missing sausages won't make much difference at this point.'

'Even so, I feel responsible.'

Her eyes narrowed. 'For the sausages?'

For everything, he thought.

She looked away. 'I have to get on with the breakfast. Hugo and Una went for a stroll, but they'll be back any minute. Amber's waiting for hers, and I need to explain.'

Brody heard barking outside the back door, yet he couldn't leave.

'I know this is terrible timing, but I really need to talk to you.'

'You're right. You've picked the worst time, and I don't see what we have to talk about. Please, let me get the breakfasts. Ricky was meant to come, but he has the flu, so I'm on my own.' She picked up a frying pan.

'I can help. I can fry some bacon.'

'No, really. There's no need.'

'I have to do something.'

'For you or for me?' she asked. Brody thought that Sophie knew him far too well.

'Both. Where's the bacon? In the fridge? You go and talk to your guests.'

Sophie let out a sigh of exasperation, then said, 'If you really want to help, you can clean the kitchen floor. The mop and bucket are in the scullery. I'll sort out the breakfast.'

Brody found them and set about erasing the evidence of Harold's sausage raid. Sophie came back from speaking to the guests and started frying bacon.

Having come out with Harold first thing, before having any breakfast himself, Brody's mouth watered at the aroma of frying bacon and at the sizzle of the pan. Ignoring his hunger pains, he finished the floor, checked on Harold – who was happily eating his bone – and went back into the kitchen.

'Do you want this bacon?' Sophie asked, holding up a pan with two rashers. It felt like a peace offering. 'I've done too much.'

His stomach rumbled, yet he was also aware that Tegan would be wondering where he was. 'I shouldn't,' he said.

'Suit yourself. The bread's on the table if you change your mind.'

She waltzed out of the kitchen with the last two plates of breakfast, and Brody finally caved in. He slapped the bacon between two slices of farmhouse bread and bit into it. He was starving and he wasn't going to refuse Sophie's offer.

When she returned to the kitchen, he was upending the ketchup bottle onto the second half of the sandwich.

'Ah, you did change your mind then?' she said, rewarding him with a faint smile.

'Woof!'

Brody groaned. 'I'd better see what Harold's up to now, in case he's bothering your guests.'

Sandwich in hand, Brody hurried outside, still eating the last of his bacon butty. He didn't want Harold committing further misdemeanours with Sophie's guests. But he needn't have worried because Harold was still outside, lying on his back while Una Hartley-Brewer tickled his tummy.

'What a lovely boy you are. How handsome!'

Experiencing a momentary pang of envy that his dog was more popular than he was, Brody swallowed his last bite and joined Una and Hugo.

'Oh, here's your owner,' Hugo said, on seeing Brody.

'I think it's very much the other way around,' Brody replied. 'I hope he's not being a nuisance?'

Hugo scoffed. 'Harold could never be a nuisance. Could you, old chap?'

Sophie walked out with a bin bag and smiled again on seeing Harold rolling over and snuffling with pleasure at being the centre of attention.

'We were just coming into breakfast,' Una said.

'I'm afraid some of it is inside Harold,' Brody commented, with a stern look at the dog.

'He got into the kitchen and stole the sausages,' Sophie explained, exchanging a glance with Brody.

Hugo chortled. 'Did he? Who can blame him? I bet they smelt far too tempting. Sophie's breakfasts are amazing.'

'I'll do you extra bacon instead,' Sophie offered.

'That's kind, but please don't worry,' Una replied. 'I suppose we'd better come in and enjoy our last few hours. I don't want to leave.' She paused before sighing. 'I don't want to go home, if I'm honest. I know it's silly, but the house seems so empty without the kids and our best pal. Sorry. I'm being sentimental. It's just been so nice to be in a full house again.'

Sophie patted her arm. 'You're not being silly, and I understand. I don't know what I'd do without Jingle and Belle,' she added kindly.

Though Brody was used to being with bereaved pet owners, he was still moved. 'I feel that way about Harold too. He's one of my best mates. I know what it's like to lose a friend, be it a dog, a cat, a horse . . . Pets carve out a special place in our hearts.'

'Of course you must know that more than most,' Una said. 'I couldn't do your job.'

'I'll let you into a secret,' Brody replied, smiling. 'Sometimes I think I can't do it myself, but I want to do my best for all animals and, if I can help, then I will. I must.' He was surprised by how passionate he sounded. Una and Hugo had reminded him of the reasons he'd gone into veterinary practice in the first place.

'You're a lovely man,' Una said, making Brody wince inwardly.

'It's been a pleasure to meet you and Sophie – and Harold.' Hugo shook Brody's hand and smiled at Sophie.

'And Tegan, of course,' Una added hastily. 'I hope we see you again when we come back to Sunnyside in the summer. You'll probably be married then. Have you set a date?'

Brody squirmed. 'Er – not yet.'

'Take my advice,' Hugo said. 'Don't hang about. You'll be wanting a family soon. Can't be rattling around in that big place on your own.'

'Hugo . . .' Una said, though Brody guessed she fully agreed with her husband.

'I'd better go back in and sort out your breakfast,' Sophie said and slipped back into the kitchen.

'Come on, Harold!' Brody urged him glumly, picking up his lead.

The couple followed Sophie through the rear door, and Brody trudged home towards Felltop. He'd be glad to get back to work later, where he could focus on treating his patients and not think about his complicated personal life – even though it was a coward's way out of what he knew, in his heart, he ought to do.

Chapter Twenty-Eight

Sophie finished the breakfast service with a huge sigh of relief. With Ricky unable to help and then Harold creating mayhem – not to mention Brody – the morning had been a very hectic affair.

Now she stationed herself in reception, ready to see her guests off. Her first attempt at an alternative Christmas had gone anything but to plan, resulting in her guests having no heating, light or hot water, being snowed in, enduring an unexpected power cut and having to stay at a stranger's house while having a traditional Christmas thrust upon them. Not to mention one of them finding out that the person she seemed to hate was staying in the next room. Sophie could only hope they didn't leave bad reviews or ask for refunds.

Suzanne was first to leave, coming down the stairs with a suitcase that she dumped on the tiles.

'Hello!' Sophie said brightly. 'Ready to check out?'

'Yes, actually.' Suzanne's mouth turned down.

'I'm so sorry your stay didn't go as planned,' she said, readying herself for a string of complaints.

'It was . . .' Suzanne began. 'It was *life-changing*.'

'Oh? Um. *Really?*' Sophie couldn't hide her surprise.

'Yes. Not at first, of course. I was absolutely horrified when I initially realised Amber was here. It felt like some terrible coincidence – a punishment, on top of losing my dad.'

'Our dad,' said Amber from halfway down the stairs.

'Don't worry,' Suzanne went on, probably noticing Sophie's wary expression. 'We're not going to come to blows. And Amber is right. He was *our* dad. He fathered both of us, and it's not our fault that he lied. I guess our mothers were so angry with each other because they couldn't take it out on the one person who deserved it.'

Amber nodded. 'We've realised that blaming each other is pointless. Being forced to spend some time together in close proximity felt like a living nightmare at first but, in a weird way, it was probably the best thing that could have happened.'

'Was it?' Sophie said, hardly daring to hope their stay had worked out after all.

The two women exchanged a glance and Amber spoke.

'Yes, because we had to talk to each other. We both love our families, but we've also realised they are the source of our problems – not each other.' She glanced at Suzanne, as if to give her a cue.

'Our mothers are, perhaps understandably, at war with each other, and our other siblings are taking sides. Both our mums are feeling so hurt and betrayed, and rightly so, but we've realised that even though our families are at odds, we don't have to be.'

'It was a question of loyalty, you see,' Amber explained.

'Over Christmas we've understood that we actually have a lot in common and we both hate the conflict between us all.'

'There's definitely more that unites us than divides us. I just wish our families would see that too,' Suzanne said wistfully.

'Same. So we're going to go home and speak to our mothers and siblings,' Amber explained. 'And tell them that, no matter what Dad did, the two of us won't be scarred by it or left bitter. We've already arranged to meet up as soon as we can. And we'd like to stay here,' she went on. 'If you'll have us, after making a scene on Christmas Eve.'

'It was unforgivable.' Suzanne gave a wry smile. 'I bet you didn't need any entertainment, with us two around.'

'I was more concerned about your holiday being ruined,' Sophie replied, remembering Nico's popcorn comment.

Amber wrinkled her nose. 'I hope we didn't ruin it for the others.'

'Not at all, and I'd love to have you back, though I don't reopen until February. I'm having a break.'

'I don't blame you,' Amber said. 'Now I think I should settle my bar bill. Once we've checked out, we're going for a coffee and a talk before we both head home.'

'Of course,' Sophie said, handing them the bills she'd already prepared.

Both of them paid and were ready to leave, when Amber hugged her and Suzanne offered a warm smile.

'You must be exhausted. You must hear everyone's life story!' Suzanne said.

Not everyone's, Sophie thought, but she was privy to

some secrets that people would never dream of sharing with their nearest and dearest. In many ways she'd realised it was a privilege, and she loved that her little guest house could provide a safe refuge from the world, whether it allowed people to form new bonds or simply recuperate after a busy time.

'I could definitely get a job in the Secret Service,' Sophie joked, walking to the front door with them. 'Have a safe journey, and good luck. I'll see you in the spring. I'm think-ing of hosting an "Escape from Valentine's" break, so perhaps I'll see you for a weekend then.'

As the Smiths drove off, Vee's VW trundled onto the drive. Sophie walked out and greeted her with a big hug the moment she got out of the car.

'Boy, am I glad to see you!' Sophie told her.

'Same. I'm delighted to get out of the house,' Vee said with a chuckle. 'Honestly, I should head up the UN, for all the diplomacy I've had to carry out over the holidays. Between my family and Kev's, I've been close to throwing everyone out at times. His sister and brother almost came to blows over a game of bloody Monopoly! Then my niece was sick after eating almost a whole packet of Matchmakers, and we lost the TV remote for a full half-hour. I've catered for so many special diets, I ought to have a Michelin star!'

Sophie laughed. 'That sounds almost as stressful as my Christmas.'

'Oh, Soph. I heard about it from Kev. Bloody hell, you have had quite the time of it.'

'You have no idea ... All the plans went out of the

window. I got propositioned, helped deliver a baby, had to keep two warring sisters apart and ended up having to wear a party hat and pull crackers after all.'

'Wow!' Vee murmured. 'That beats Monopoly-gate.'

The bell dinged in reception. 'I'll tell you about it later. It's time for check-out.'

'I'll make a start on the vacant rooms, shall I?'

'Thanks!' Sophie said, walking back to the desk.

The Hartley-Brewers waited at the desk with matching cabin bags by their sides.

'Have you had a good time?' Sophie said, keeping things light. 'I apologise again for the disruption.'

'Oh, please don't apologise. We've loved every minute of it!' Una declared. 'Which is surprising because, as the day grew closer, we started to have cold feet, you see.'

'Oh?' Sophie hadn't heard any guest admit to dreading their stay before.

Hugo had a sheepish air. 'It did seem a little bit – mad to escape for Christmas. It's really not the sort of thing we do. We had to fib to our friends and families and tell them it was a normal Christmas break.'

'But now we're going to tell them the truth,' Una said. 'Because they won't believe that we were trapped in a snowstorm, helped to deliver a baby and spent the day at a stranger's farmhouse. Not to mention leading a salsa evening. We loved that.'

Sophie laughed. 'Everyone loved it. Thank you so much again for stepping in, and I hope you'll enjoy more dancing back home.'

303

'It was fantastic. And there's something else. After meeting Harold – and Brody – we're going to look into getting another dog. It's heartbreaking to lose a friend, and we've both been so terrified of going through the pain again.'

Una's eyes glistened. 'But Brody reminded us that if you can help an animal in need, then you should, so when we can offer a loving home to a rescue dog, it seems wrong not to do so.'

Sophie felt a little teary herself. 'I'm so pleased for you. Rehoming a rescue dog is a brilliant idea.'

'Harold melted our hearts,' Una said and exchanged a shy glance with Hugo. 'And I think we've both felt rejuvenated in other ways since we got here.'

'A power cut can be a good thing,' Hugo said, slipping his arm around Una.

'Hugo! That's far too much information!'

Sophie agreed. 'Erm, cash or card?' she asked politely, resting her hand on the payment terminal.

After they'd paid, the couple picked up their bags.

'I'm very happy to hear all that. I'm so glad you've enjoyed yourselves.'

'Oh, there's just one more thing,' Una said. 'Hugo and I have been racking our brains since we arrived. You remind me so much of someone.'

'Oh?' Sophie said.

'Yes, you're the spitting image of the woman who used to run the Christmas shop in Stratford.'

Preparing to fess up, Sophie smiled. 'Oh, really? Am I?'

'Oh yes,' Hugo said. 'Though you smile a lot more than she did.'

Do I? The words almost slipped out, but Hugo carried on.

'I never liked that skinny young chap who used to run it with her. He always seemed shifty to me.'

'Hugo. Come on! I want to get home before it's dark.'

'Have a safe journey,' Sophie said, warming to the couple even more. She'd thought they were rather an unadventurous pair, typical of couples who'd been together for ever and had resorted to matching anoraks because it was easier and safer. Now she thought they were the lucky ones, with their shared passion for dancing and for each other. They were comfortable together and loved each other, and that was more than millions of people were ever able to say.

She saw them off, aware they'd reminded her that she'd also made the right decision to change her life. Until Una had dragged Hugo away, she'd been fully ready to admit: 'Yes, that was me. I was that serious-faced woman with the shifty partner, except that I never realised how serious I'd become, or how devious he was. I'm so glad that I smile a lot more now, and that I took the plunge and bought Sunnyside.'

She had barely five minutes to herself before Agatha dawdled downstairs, carrying her case. Wearily she put down her bag next to the reception desk. 'I don't want to leave, but I've a hospital appointment tomorrow – nothing serious, so don't worry. I just don't fancy the thought of going back to an empty house.'

Sophie's heart went out to her guest. 'I've loved having you here.'

'Bet you say that to all the guests!'

'Oh, I really don't,' Sophie replied with a laugh. 'I absolutely don't.'

Agatha smiled. 'I want to thank you, too. I haven't had so much fun since Ron passed away. I worried I was turning into an old curmudgeon and I've rather retreated into my shell lately. It was only the prospect of spending Christmas with my dreary cousins that brought me here.'

'Thank goodness you *were* here to help with the baby,' Sophie said.

'Hmm, I only wish I'd kept off the party spirit, so I could have been even more useful at the business end.' She squared her shoulders. 'However, the experience has taught me I can still be useful. I've shied away from volunteering since Ron passed away. It felt ever so slightly desperate, and I couldn't find the energy until now . . . But in the New Year I might see if I can help out with a medical charity like St John Ambulance or the Red Cross.'

'They'd be so lucky to have you,' Sophie said encouragingly.

'I'm not sure about that, but I'll definitely look into it in the New Year.' Agatha patted Sophie on the shoulder. 'And you can be sure I'll be back, before next Christmas, and I'll tell all my friends what adventures I've had!'

Sophie laughed, not sure that she wanted too much detail about the adventures on the travel review sites.

There was only Nico left to check out now. Sophie was slightly dreading it, after yesterday's scene in the kitchen.

He trotted downstairs, a leather overnight bag in one hand and a scarf looped stylishly around his neck, looking effortlessly chic with his cover-model looks.

Sophie felt her body tense and he must have sensed her embarrassment.

'Don't worry, I'm not going to repeat my – offer – of yesterday,' he said. 'It was crass of me and I'm ashamed I even tried it, which is an emotion I rarely feel.'

'It's history now,' Sophie said, the tension easing.

'However, before I leave, I feel I owe you some honesty. I need to tell you why I'm really here.'

Chapter Twenty-Nine

'I thought your passport had expired . . .' Sophie said, wondering what he might say next.

Nico grimaced. 'Ah, well, it *is* true that I was meant to go to Italy, and I wanted somewhere to stay over Christmas a long way from anywhere. My passport hadn't expired, but I found myself in need of a place of – sanctuary, shall we say?'

'Sanctuary?' she echoed. 'That's an interesting word.'

'My family in Italy is expecting me to get married to a very nice, very beautiful woman who I've known for years. We've been dating on and off and it became more serious a few months ago. Our families are very traditional, and my parents – and hers – were clearly expecting us to announce our engagement over Christmas.'

'Ah. What about your girlfriend? Was she expecting that?'

'Carlotta and I haven't discussed it. It's the people around us who are piling on the pressure. I can't remember the last time I was home without someone – Mum or Dad or my sister – asking me when I'm going to "settle down with a nice girl and start a family". I used to laugh it off, but now I find it . . . upsetting.'

'Shouldn't you talk to Carlotta about how you feel?'

Sophie asked, sympathetic in one way, but also feeling sorry for his girlfriend.

'Of course I should, but I'm not a paragon. Not like Brody next door. I fear I'm not even a decent sort of man. I may be a very bad man.' He smiled. 'I'm joking about that, but I did decide to come here, lie about my passport and tell my family I was off to the back of beyond to a remote retreat.'

'I can't see you at a retreat. Did your family believe you?'

'Probably not.' He shrugged. 'Maybe I'm secretly hoping they'll realise I need to follow my own path, though it won't be to any kind of destination they'd approve of.'

'You have to be honest with them,' Sophie said. 'You can't keep hiding away from the truth. Why not just tell them – Carlotta, and your families – that you don't want to get married at the moment.'

'Ah, if only it was that simple . . .

'Isn't it?'

'If I were to be honest with them, I'd have to say that I don't want to get married for some time, perhaps not ever, and certainly not in the way they envisage marriage. I can't even imagine meeting one person I'd devote my life to. I don't want to "forsake all others".' He shuddered. 'I'm not gay or straight, or any label. I prefer to defy description. I simply like beautiful people. Of any variety.'

So he was struggling to accept his sexuality and explain it to his family, Sophie thought, feeling sorry for Nico that, behind his show of confidence, he was clearly battling to come to terms with who he was and to feel comfortable in his own skin. 'I'm sorry you feel pressured to act or be a certain way,' she said. 'But that shouldn't stop you finding one special partner one day.'

He shook his head. 'You are so lovely, Sophie. So certain of what's right and wrong, and with such high expectations of those around you. It's a shame you've been let down by this Ben – and now Brody. I'm afraid no one will ever be able to live up to your ideals because, as much as we try our best, we all make mistakes along the way.'

Nico had now crossed several boundaries, and so was uncomfortably close to the truth.

'I'm sorry you feel you can't be honest with your family or be your true self,' Sophie replied calmly. 'It must be making you very unhappy to be playing a part all the time.'

Something like regret flickered in Nico's eyes, and his cool smile wavered before he replied, 'Don't worry about me. I'll be fine. Now shall I settle the bill? I think I might have run up quite a tab on the honesty bar.' He paid swiftly and left, with only a 'Bye' before driving off in his Alfa.

Was Sophie also expecting too much of people? Of a partner? To be loyal and kind and faithful? Was she expecting something, and someone, who simply didn't exist? Yet no matter how naive or fantastical it seemed, she refused to give up hope of finding them one day.

As the clouds descended from the fells, a sense of sadness settled on the empty house. It seemed too large and echoing. It wasn't meant to be occupied by one person. Thank goodness Vee was there. Sophie could hear her singing as she stripped the beds upstairs.

There was no time to dwell on things. She would go and

help Vee. She was halfway up the stairs when she heard a shriek.

'Oh my God! Sophie! Quick!'

Sophie ran up the final steps to see the Hartley-Brewers' door flung open. Vee was standing by the bed with her hands over her mouth.

Sophie went in and her heart seemed to stop.

Her two beloved cats were lying limply on the duvet.

Chapter Thirty

Sophie flew into the room. 'Jingle, Belle!'

At the sound of her voice, they both stirred. Belle let out a pathetic miaow and Jingle tried to crawl off the bed, but then started retching. At least they were alive, though that was all that could be said about them. Sophie felt wobbly with shock.

'Oh dear,' Vee said. 'I'm afraid they've been sick all over the carpet and – er – have upset tummies too.'

'They must have eaten something bad. You poor, poor things,' Sophie said, stroking Belle's fur.

'Have they eaten anything different?' Vee asked.

'I don't think so, unless the guests have given them some treats.' She felt like crying, but knew that wouldn't help her cats now.

'I'll look around and see if I can find anything that might have upset them.' Vee hurried to the other side of the bed. 'They've been sick here as well – poor loves. Hang on a mo, there's something under the bed.' She pulled out a green sprig with white berries.

'Mistletoe?' Sophie cried in horror. 'That's toxic to cats!'

'Shit, I'd no idea. How did it get in here?'

'Una and Hugo must have brought it. They went to the

garden centre yesterday and were joking about how the holiday had revived their love life.' Sophie groaned.

Vee put her arm around Sophie. 'Right, get on the phone to Brody now. Ask him what you can do.'

'I don't know if he's in. He was meant to go to work today. Maybe I should call the surgery?'

'Try him first. It'll be quicker,' Vee urged.

'I hope he's still at Felltop,' Sophie said, uttering a silent prayer as she pulled her phone out of her pocket.

The call rang out, while her pulse skyrocketed. What if Brody wasn't there and she was too late by the time she reached the vet's? What if she lost both of her cats?

'Brody!' she cried when he answered the phone just as she was about to give up and rush the cats to the surgery. 'Thank God I've got you. The cats are really poorly! They've eaten some mistletoe that my guests left in a room, and they've been sick and worse – and now they're lying on the bed, drooling.'

'Mistletoe?' Brody said, then the phone went silent for a couple of agonising seconds. 'I'm at home, so I'll come round as fast as I can. Get their carrier ready. We'll need to take them into the surgery.'

Sophie wanted to sob, but pulled herself together and focused on finding their carrier and bringing it up to the bedroom. The cats were conscious, but still drooling. Belle was letting out pathetic miaows and Jingle had been sick on the bed again.

It seemed like an age before she heard Vee open the door to let Brody in and he rushed into the bedroom.

'They look bad,' she said, fighting back tears. 'Can you save them?'

'I need to get them to the surgery for some proper treatment,' he replied. 'Can you show me the plant, so I can see exactly what it is?'

Vee held up the innocent-looking green plant with its white berries.

'Yep, mistletoe. Sorry, but I had to double-check. Do you know how much they've eaten?' he asked, doing a quick examination of the cats.

'No. I didn't realise the cats had been in here. Una and Hugo stayed in here and must have left the mistletoe. We found it on the floor,' Sophie said, rubbing her hands together.

Brody gently stroked Belle's head. 'Come on, you two. Let's put you in your carrier, so we can look after you properly.'

Gently he helped Sophie place the cats in their carrier. They made no objection, which told Sophie how poorly they were. Plus, Brody hadn't answered her question of whether they would survive.

He took the cats out of the door.

'I'll stay here and look after the house,' Vee said to Sophie and patted her shoulder. 'Jingle and Belle couldn't be in better hands.'

Fighting back tears, Sophie carried Belle downstairs and out to Brody's Defender. With both cats on the floor in the rear, she strapped herself into the passenger seat. She could hear faint miaows from the back, which at least meant the cats were conscious, but what if they didn't make it to the surgery?

Brody drove swiftly out of the gates and down the steep lane that led to Bannerdale and the practice.

'Can you do anything for them?' she asked. 'Please be honest.'

'I've only treated one case of mistletoe poisoning before, and that was a small dog, which recovered well. Try not to worry; the cats may only have eaten a small amount, and you caught it quickly. The problem is that mistletoe contains all kinds of toxins that will irritate and upset their stomachs.'

'Could it – be fatal?' Sophie said, suppressing a shudder.

'In the worst case, it can affect their breathing and could cause a cardiovascular collapse.'

Brody put his hand over hers. It felt so good on hers, warm and strong and comforting.

'But we *can* treat them and we'll soon be at the surgery. I've phoned ahead, so they know we're coming. You're lucky you caught me, because I was about to leave the house on my way down there.'

'I've disrupted your life again,' Sophie said.

'You haven't. This is my job. It's what I spend my life doing.'

Twenty minutes later they were carrying the cats into the surgery. While Sophie helped Jingle out of his carrier, the vet nurse coaxed out Belle, who crawled out and flopped down on the treatment table. She made a pathetic attempt to bite Brody, then gave up.

'I know you don't want to tell me they'll be OK. I understand.' Sophie swallowed back her tears. 'But what can you do to help?'

'We'll need to induce vomiting, then give them activated charcoal to help mop up the toxins. They should pass that through their digestive systems. Please try not to worry too much. You did the right thing to call me.' He smiled reassuringly, but Sophie still felt sick to her stomach.

'You are in a sorry state, mate,' Brody said to Jingle. 'But we'll do our best to make you feel better. You won't think that for a while, though.' He turned to Sophie. 'The first thing to do is make them sick up anything inside them. You might want to wait outside or go for a walk or something. There's nothing we can do until they've vomited the full contents of their stomachs. I promise we'll call you in when there's anything you can do.'

Sophie nodded and stroked her cats, knowing it was best to give Brody and the nurse space to treat them. 'Get well, you two. I can't bear to be without you.'

Knowing she couldn't sit still, she walked into the chilly streets of Bannerdale, hardly knowing where she was going. It was only as she'd said, 'I can't bear to be without you' that she fully realised how much of a comfort her pets had been, after she'd split from Ben. Thank God he hadn't wanted them. Sophie would have never let him, anyway. She'd have gone on the run rather than part with them!

Yet now she felt guilty for bringing them to a strange place with hordes of strange people coming in and out – and all the unpredictability of the guests bringing stuff into the house that might hurt them. She'd have to be so much more careful in future, making sure the cats were kept safely in her flat, out of harm's way.

In the village the lights were shining and there were plenty of Christmas visitors in boots and coats, picking up supplies in the outdoor stores, queuing at the bakery and packing the tea shops. Life went on as normal for them, but all Sophie could think of was her poor pets feeling sick and in pain. She'd done a couple of circuits of the village and had somehow found her way back to the surgery. Despite Brody telling her not to worry, her heart rate rose as she approached the entrance, fearful of what she might find.

The nurse showed her into Brody's room, where the cats were lying on heated mats on the exam table.

'They've been sick again,' he said, 'and now we're going to give them the charcoal. They aren't going to be too keen on it, but the good news is that they're conscious, so we can syringe it into their mouths rather than using a tube. After that, we might have to repeat it every four to eight hours, and I'm going to give them some intravenous fluids to make sure they aren't dehydrated.'

'I'm staying.'

'There's no need. They'll just be resting in the pens, feeling sorry for themselves. I'll let you know if there's any news, but for now, I'm afraid, we have to let them recover. Please, go home and have a rest and some food. I promise I'll stay here overnight with them.'

'Are you actually on duty tonight?' she asked, feeling relieved Brody would be keeping a close eye on them.

'Not technically.' He shrugged. 'I was on evening late surgery anyway, and I want to stay. Now go ... No arguments.'

'OK, but please let me know how they are, and thank you. Again.'

'You won't thank me when your cats are doing black poos for a few days,' he said.

Sophie nodded. 'I think that's the least of my worries.'

With the heaviest of hearts, she decided that Brody was right, although she was still astonished that he'd offered to stay at the surgery overnight. She phoned Vee, who insisted on collecting her from the village and taking her back to Sunnyside.

'That's a forty-minute round trip. I'll get a taxi.'

'You stay where you are. I'll come for you. I won't hear any arguments.'

'Everyone is bossing me around today,' Sophie said, with an attempt at humour.

'Sometimes we all need bossing and to be looked after. Wait there and I'll see you soon.'

When they arrived back at Sunnyside, they found a large cardboard box in the porch.

Sophie picked it up. 'What's this? I didn't order anything?'

Vee opened the front door. 'Dunno. It wasn't here when I left.'

'It looks like a hamper,' Sophie said, carrying the box inside. She was surprised when she opened it to find the parcel crammed with festive treats, such as mince pies, chutney, wine and a mini-fruitcake. She found a slip of paper on top and read it. 'Oh, it's from the Nowaks – a thank you. They needn't have . . .'

'Yet they wanted to.' Vee delved inside. 'It's fantastic. Even if it is Christmassy.'

'I gave up avoiding Christmas some time ago,' Sophie mumbled. 'And really this should be for Kev and the mountain-rescue team who hiked up here in the terrible weather.'

'That's his job. Kind of,' Vee said. 'He was pleased as punch to be able to help.'

'Will you at least take this wine and the chocolates?' Sophie suggested, putting a bottle and some chocs on the kitchen table. 'And thank him from me.' The kindness she'd been shown brought her to the brink of tears again, but she held them back.

'If you insist,' Vee said.

'I do. And now I'm going to make us both some lunch. Sit down.'

Vee obeyed. 'Yes, boss.'

After they'd eaten, Vee left for home and Sophie went upstairs to clean up the room where the cats had been ill. She found it pristine, and ready for letting again when the guest house reopened. Vee had done it while she'd been at the vet's, which was beyond the call of duty.

Sophie sat down on the bed and finally the tears she'd been trying to hold in since that morning fell. After allowing herself an indulgent cry, she tried to keep busy, tidying the kitchen and doing some of her accounts, resisting the urge to glance at her phone every two minutes. Darkness fell not long after three-thirty, and so she lit the lamps in her flat and flicked through the TV, finding something easy to watch. Sunnyside seemed very big and lonely, and every creak and rattle of the boiler set her on edge.

She didn't fancy any proper dinner, so she took some unused cold bits from the fridge, trying not to look at the empty cat bowls sitting side-by-side by the door. She was picking at half a pork pie when her phone rang.

'Brody!'

'It's OK. They're still resting quietly. I'm going to give them another dose of charcoal—' He broke off and Sophie heard voices. 'Sorry, have to go. Emergency. Not with your cats.'

The phone went dead.

Sophie's heart went out to the owner whose pet was an emergency, but she was starting to feel more hopeful that Jingle and Belle were recovering as well as they could. Time ticked by and she flicked through the channels. It was now 8 p.m. and Brody's evening surgery would be over. He'd be spending the night there, probably on the tatty sofa she'd seen in the staffroom.

It didn't seem fair that he was watching over her cats while she was here. Surely she could do something?

Taking a plastic box, she went to the fridge and filled it with pork pies, cold sausages and quiche. She raided the hamper for mince pies, chutney and biscuits. She didn't know if Brody had eaten, but it didn't matter, and she figured the nursing team would enjoy the pies and biccies if he wasn't hungry.

She jumped in the car and drove down the dark lanes to the village.

The lights were all on at the vet's surgery, but there was only Brody's Defender parked behind it, so she guessed he was the only member of staff on duty.

Should she be here? In the circumstances?

She felt ridiculous, and out of place. She was bringing supper to a man who was engaged to another woman. Brody hadn't asked her to come – she was only a client. It felt desperate . . .

She glanced at the Tupperware box on the passenger seat and her shoulders slumped.

'Sophie?'

A face loomed in her car window. It was Brody, in scrubs, with a look of astonishment that was hardly encouraging.

Sophie opened the window.

'I shouldn't be here, I know. I ought to go home, but I thought: you're here all night because I let my cats eat something poisonous; and I was climbing the walls at home, so I thought I'd bring you some food in case you hadn't had any dinner . . . But now I feel really stupid for doing it.'

'You're not stupid, and I haven't had any dinner. I was about to order in a takeaway, but I'd much rather have what you've brought.'

'You haven't seen it yet.' She was opening the door. 'It's only leftovers.' Her pulse spiked. 'How are the cats?'

'Still sleeping it off. They're off the drip and they've both had a drink of water. That's a good sign.'

'And your emergency? I've been thinking about that too.'

'Spaniel hit by a car. Broken leg. He's on the mend and he's in here overnight too, so don't feel too guilty at me staying.'

Brody smiled and Sophie's heart did a double back-flip. Why, why, *why* had she fallen for a man who was taken by someone else?

'You said you had food?' he added.

'I can leave it with you. I don't want to get in the way.'

'You're not. You wouldn't be. Come in and have a coffee with me, at least. I could do with a break. It's been a very long day.'

After collecting the food, Sophie followed him into the staffroom. The sofa had a sleeping bag on it.

'Do you want to see Jingle and Belle and then we'll have a coffee?' he offered.

'Yes, please.'

Brody smiled. 'Come on then.'

He took her to the ward, where the two cats had cages set well away from the unfortunate spaniel. They were each lying down on soft blankets, with a bowl of water and the cat toys Sophie kept in their cages. Seeing them behind bars in such a clinical environment made her feel guilty again, but they both miaowed loudly as she approached.

'They look brighter,' she said, wanting to scoop them up and cuddle them, despite the fact that neither would enjoy such fuss, even if they were one hundred per cent well.

'I think so too,' Brody agreed. 'If they keep improving, they can probably go home tomorrow.'

'Oh, that's brilliant news.'

He opened the door, so that she could stroke them. Jingle licked her fingers and Belle started purring.

'I know they're only cats,' Sophie said as he closed the doors again. 'But I've been so worried.'

'They're not *only* cats. They're your friends.'

She smiled. 'I'm sure they don't think I'm their friend. I'm merely the human who provides the food and catnip.'

'They rely on you for a warm and loving home,' Brody said. 'And, I can assure you, I've seen plenty of cats who don't have that.'

He put the kettle on while Sophie washed her hands and decanted the food onto plates bearing the logo of a cat-flu vaccine.

'I hope you like pork pies,' she said.

'I love them. This looks great.'

Sophie's stomach rumbled. Now that she'd been reassured her cats were on the mend, her appetite had returned.

They sat down on the sofa with plates on their laps.

'I was so sad for Una and Hugo when they spoke about losing their dog. I know my cats will have to go some day, but I'd hoped that was a way off, after they'd lived long and happy lives. To go in this way – in some horrible freak accident – is just too horrible to contemplate. You said you understood how bad it feels?'

'Vets are as heartbroken as anyone when we lose our own pets. We even – and don't tell anyone – feel very upset when it's the end for someone else's pet. Maybe we don't show it in front of the patient and owners, although we're allowed to express some emotion, especially if we've known the animal a long time or it's a very traumatic death.'

Sophie felt strangely comforted by the genuine sadness in his expression. It meant that the animal – and the owner – really did matter to Brody.

'So many times I, or a colleague, have held it together with patients, then gone to the staffroom and had a big snotty blub. Why do you think we keep such a large supply of tea, biscuits and tissues?'

Sophie smiled, then said, 'We spend so much time holding back our real emotions. It takes its toll. The things I hear from guests – funny stuff, outrageous secrets and some heart-rending tales. Like Agatha told me how lonely she'd felt after Ron died, and that helping with the baby had given her a new sense of purpose.'

He paused. 'What about Nico?'

'Nico?' Sophie hadn't expected Brody to bring him up. 'He . . . is an unusual character,' she said. 'I hope he doesn't book again, to be honest.'

'Why?'

She suddenly wished she hadn't said anything about Nico. 'Various reasons.'

Brody pressed his lips together. 'I thought he was a bit of a tool, to be honest.'

She burst out laughing, then realised she should probably be a bit quieter, with the sick animals recuperating next door. 'Oh, I'm sorry. It's the relief.'

'Don't apologise. I like to see you laughing again.' He put his plate on the floor. He looked at her so tenderly that it sparked a ray of hope in her heart that Brody genuinely cared about her. It was a ray that she had to extinguish quickly.

'Thank you for staying here, but I have to go home,' Sophie said.

'Of course. I have work to do too. Thanks for the food. Very thoughtful of you.'

'You're welcome. Bye.'

Sophie hurriedly grabbed her coat and rushed out of the vet's to the safety of her car. She never wanted to be the 'other woman'. Even if she hadn't kissed or slept with Brody, she'd wanted to – she wanted Tegan not to be his fiancée, and that was wrong. It was exactly what had been done to her, and she could never inflict that kind of pain and humiliation on Tegan, no matter how much she herself would love to be with Brody.

From now on, she would resist all and every temptation to interact with him, beyond that of vet and client. In fact once the cats were fully recovered, it might be for the best to find another vet. However difficult it might prove, with them being neighbours, the more distance she put between her and Brody, the better.

Chapter Thirty-One

Brody made it to Tegan's parents in time for dinner the following evening. He'd stayed the night at the surgery before handing over to his colleague, leaving her in charge of discharging Jingle and Belle, who thankfully were on the road to recovery.

Once again, he'd come so close to doing something he'd regret: confessing all to Sophie.

Tegan hadn't been impressed that he'd rushed off to help Sophie, and was even less impressed when she found out he'd decided to do an unscheduled overnight shift at the surgery. God knows what she would have said if she'd found out that Sophie had made a special journey to the practice with a food parcel . . . Tegan had decided to stay at her parents' last night instead, and he'd had to promise to go over there for dinner today after work. It meant they'd have to share a room, but there was no getting out of it.

Brody greeted her father and mother, handing her some flowers that he'd picked up on the way over. Alan went into the kitchen to help Fiona with dinner, leaving Brody alone with Tegan in the lounge.

She stared at him. 'You look tired,' she said. 'Tough night?'

'Not too bad. I had to operate on a dog that had been in a car accident and he stayed in overnight.'

'Poor thing,' Tegan murmured. 'How are the cats?'

This seemingly innocent comment set him on edge instantly, thinking it best not to tell her about Sophie's visit. 'They're on the mend. It was touch and go, but they'll be OK.'

'I'm sure Sophie's relieved.'

'She is.'

'And very grateful. You're making a habit of rescuing her.'

'I've hardly rescued her. I'm her vet, so I've treated her cats, like I'm paid to do. And it wasn't Sophie having a baby,' he replied, more brusquely than he'd intended.

'OK, there's no need to be so touchy.' Tegan moved to stroke his arm and made a soothing noise, making him feel like one of Sophie's cats.

She then burst out laughing, on her father walking into the dining room. A smile lit up Alan's face too, yet Brody's spirits plummeted. He shoved his hands in his pockets, feeling tired of playing the happy couple.

'Sorry for interrupting, only your mother says the food is ready. I've laid the table, if you want to come in?'

They ate dinner, chatting about the annual New Year's Eve ball that was held on one of the lake steamers.

Tegan tutted. 'I think you'd be better with your feet up in front of the fire, Dad, than at a wild party. I'm worried it'll be too much for you.'

Alan patted her hand. 'Thank you for your concern, sweetheart, but I'm already absolutely sick of having my feet up, and I'll be stuck inside for ages after the op. And since when has the Steamer Ball ever been wild?'

'There's no point in trying to stop him,' Fiona said with a shrug.

Alan rolled his eyes at Brody. 'They want to keep me wrapped in cotton wool. Can you please tell them I'm tougher than they think?'

Brody held up his hands. 'I'm staying well out of this, Alan. Sorry!'

'Coward,' Alan teased.

The talk turned to Tegan's brother, and how he and his ex had had to share the children over Christmas, which was why Harry hadn't been able to see them yet over the festive period.

Fiona tutted. 'Poor wee lambs. I don't think they know whether they're coming or going, this first Christmas.'

'They'll get used to it. Kids are very resilient.'

Brody felt Tegan squeeze his knee under the dinner table, though he wasn't sure if it was for comfort or as a warning not to get involved.

'Tegan says you've been up all night with an emergency?' Fiona queried as they finished eating.

'Two, actually. We had a dog who'd been in a road-traffic accident, and I was on lates anyway, so I stayed over.'

'She says your neighbour's cats were poisoned by some mistletoe? Poor things. How bizarre.'

'Two of her guests left the plant in their room. Cats are curious creatures, so it was just a freak accident. Luckily I was able to help them.'

'Can it be fatal?' Alan asked.

'Oh yes. It can cause cardiac failure at its worst.' Instantly Brody could have kicked himself for his choice of words and quickly modified them. 'In this case, it only caused them to have an upset stomach and feel very sorry for themselves.'

'Sophie was lucky that Brody was on hand. *Again*,' Tegan said.

'You are quite the hero, saving your neighbour's cats *and* delivering a baby at the same address. Must be something about that house,' Fiona joked. 'I hope we don't have any drama like that here.' She gave her husband a meaningful look. 'Your father's been overdoing things again. Can you believe he was in the shed looking for a snow shovel this morning, before I stopped him!'

'Dad!' Tegan cried. 'You weren't!'

'I was fetching the shovel for your mother,' Alan said innocently.

Fiona rolled her eyes. 'I practically wrestled it off him and cleared a bit of the drive before our neighbour offered to help.'

'I'm still well enough to wash a few dishes, so leave me be,' Alan insisted, after Brody joined him in the kitchen, having offered to dry up. 'Being a hero must be tiring,' he went on, scrubbing at a pan. 'If you don't mind me saying so, you look done in.'

'You get used to unsociable hours in my line of work.'

'You'd have had an easier life selling garden machinery.'

Brody gave a wry smile. 'You sound just like my dad

would have done. Are you sure? I don't think I'd have slept well, being responsible for millions of pounds worth of stock and keeping the business afloat. Uncle Trevor seems to have managed very well without me.'

'He's cut out for it, although the vet's is a business, isn't it? You have the same concerns about profit and loss, and staff.'

'We have a very able practice manager who deals with all of the admin, thank goodness. The animals can't phone me up and complain their new tractor isn't what they were expecting.'

Alan laughed. 'I can't imagine you doing anything other than working with animals – you have a great way with them. Your father would have been proud. He knew you wanted to be a vet. He knew you'd never take over the business.' He placed the pan on the drainer with a sigh of relief.

'I hope so,' Brody said quietly, paying special attention to drying a colander.

'I know so.' With a grimace, Alan stripped off the Marigolds. 'Why do they never make them big enough for people with massive paws?'

Brody laughed. He had the same problem. At six feet three, his feet and hands were hardly on the petite side. 'I dunno. I nearly dislocate my wrist pulling off some of the gloves I use.'

Alan took a seat at the table while Brody finished drying the pots. He guessed he was in for a 'proper chat'. It seemed to be the day for it, and while Brody would much rather have avoided any deep conversations, he felt he owed it to Alan to listen.

'I know your mother wasn't best pleased with your choice of career, but she is very proud of you. You should hear the way she talks about you.'

'I'm not sure I want to,' Brody replied lightly.

Alan shook his head. 'It's all good. You're a great son and a decent man. You try to do the right thing. Too much so sometimes.'

'What do you mean?' Brody asked, hearing an echo of Tegan's own comment about him being 'too nice'.

'I've seen you tie yourself in knots trying to keep everyone happy: your mother, your patients – even our Tegan.'

Brody froze, his heart beating faster.

'She's our daughter, and we love her and want the best for her. For both of you. You do know that?'

'I know.'

'So if there's anything troubling you, or her, you do realise you can always reach out to us? I know Tegan worries about us – about me – too much lately. She wants everything to be perfect. I know damn well it can't be. I think you do too.'

Brody felt he owed Alan a degree of honesty. 'Well, you know I lost Dad to a heart attack, so we're both worried and want to help your recovery in any way we can.'

'Yes, our Tegan would do anything to make me happy . . .'

Brody's blood ran a little colder. Did Alan know something was up? They'd been so careful to keep up appearances since she'd got back.

'And I'm not sure Tegan realises that the one thing that *would* stress me out is if I thought people were keeping things from me. If they were being less than honest with me, to spare my feelings. Trust in a relationship is important, and I'm a grown man, I don't need to be wrapped up in cotton wool.'

With his stomach churning, Brody polished the saucepan with the tea towel.

'I think that pan is dry,' Alan observed and held out his hand for it.

'Yeah. I think it is.'

Alan looked him straight in the eye as he stood up to put the pot back in the cupboard. 'I'm strong enough to hear the truth and to know when something is wrong,' he said. 'And if I'd had another son, I'd be proud that it was you. Don't think that means you have to be my son-in-law.'

Jesus! Brody had a lump in his throat the size of Mars. He wished Alan would leave off, stop tormenting him with honesty and kindness. He couldn't cope. This was his chance to come clean too. Alan was holding out a lifeline, so why couldn't he take it?

He murmured a thanks and, for once, was delighted that Tegan chose that moment to interrupt.

'How long does it take to wash up? I came in to make the coffee.' She put her arm around her father.

Alan kissed her cheek. 'We're done, and the pans are gleaming, thanks to Brody.'

He gave a weak smile. 'I'll make the coffee, if you like.'

'We both will,' Tegan offered. 'You go and sit down, Dad.'

*

'What do you think of Dad today?' Tegan asked on the drive home to Felltop. 'Is he looking more tired? I thought he didn't eat so much at dinner.'

'I thought he looked the same as Boxing Day. It's a tiring time of year, but he seems to be doing pretty well to me, all things considered.'

'Really? I hope you're right. I only hope he doesn't deteriorate before the op comes round. I couldn't bear him to have any shocks.'

Brody stopped the car. 'I'm sure he'll be fine.'

Tegan turned to him. 'You can't promise that.'

'I can't promise anything, but your dad's fully aware of the situation. He's sensible and resilient. He'll be OK. But you might have to go easy on him – I think he's started to get a bit tired of all this fussing around him.' Brody thought back to their conversation. Alan must sense that all was not as it should be between him and Tegan. He was giving Brody the chance to say how he felt, although Brody would never have dreamed of doing that without discussing it with Tegan first.

He felt anxious, yet also relieved that the time might finally have arrived when all the deception could end. Tegan had realised it wasn't working and, while no situation was ideal, the best plan was surely to be honest.

His chest tightened from the cold the moment he got out of the car. Frost coated the ground and the stars twinkled above him in the great bowl of sky. Below, the village gleamed in the valley, yet across the field Sunnyside was in darkness. Sophie must be out or having an early night with the cats as they continued to recover. Brody wanted to call her to see how they – and she – were, but daren't with Tegan nearby, particularly after her comments about him always playing the hero around Sophie. Maybe Tegan would phone Wes later and he could find somewhere quiet to give Sophie a quick call.

Look at him: sneaking around in his own home. It was another reason he really had to sort out this situation, as he couldn't carry on walking on eggshells like this.

'Shall I make a drink?' Brody offered when they were inside, greeted by Harold bounding up to him for some fuss.

'Good idea.'

They sat in the snug, with Tegan curled up on the sofa, Brody in his father's chair, thinking back on what Alan had told him. As far as Brody could recall, his father had never told him he ought to be a vet. They'd never discussed it. Perhaps he'd assumed Brody would take over the business and grow out of his own dreams . . . or perhaps his dad was afraid he wouldn't.

The chair creaked under him and the springs dug into his backside. He thought of his mother's offer to have it repaired. If he did, he would never feel the shape of it again; never feel the hollow worn by his dad and by him; never hear the springs creak as they groaned under their collective weight. Renovating the chair felt like betraying his father, and yet Brody knew he had to do something or the whole thing would collapse.

Both options were unthinkable and, right now, he wasn't sure which was more unthinkable than the other.

Chapter Thirty-Two

'So how was Ye Olde Stratford-upon-Avon?' Vee asked, after the waiter had delivered two Poinsettia cocktails to their table on 30 December.

They'd arranged to meet at Raffaelo's Café Bar, after Sophie had returned from a flying visit to her parents. She'd been knackered after the holiday and had enjoyed two nights of being cooked for by her parents, and pub meals with Lyra and a couple of old friends who hadn't gone over to the Dark Side with Ben and Naomi.

'Still "Olde",' Sophie joked. 'Boringly flat compared to here, and very busy with tourists.'

'You didn't have any awkward run-ins then?' Vee said.

'No, thank goodness. I didn't really go to any of our old haunts. To be honest, I think even if I had seen Ben and Naomi, it wouldn't have spoilt my trip back; and it's good to be feeling like that's ancient history at this point.'

'Well, after the last few weeks, you've had other things to worry about,' Vee sympathised, sipping her cocktail.

'You could say that. It's certainly been a rollercoaster.'

'I know, but you can make a fresh start again from tomorrow. A new year awaits!'

'I can't wait,' Sophie said. 'One of my old mates has

335

invited me to go to Gran Canaria at the end of January and
I've said yes.'

'Lucky you,' Vee declared. 'Some winter sun is exactly
what you need. What I need too – can I stow away in your
suitcase?'

Sophie laughed, and the reminder that she had friends –
old and new – lifted her mood. She'd made her new life here
and, whatever happened, this was her home now.

Vee sipped her cocktail. 'Talking of the New Year,' she
said, 'what are you doing tomorrow night?'

'Tomorrow? Er, staying in with the cats,' Sophie replied.

'Sounds wild. How about you come to the Steamer
Ball instead?'

Sophie had seen the event advertised and had heard
people in the village talking about it. 'Is that the one raising
money for the mountain-rescue team? I thought it was sold
out, though. I won't be able to get a ticket at the last minute.'

'Yes. It's the biggest night of the year in Bannerdale.' Vee
smirked, 'It is sold out, but I've got a spare ticket because
Kev's mate can't make it, and he asked me to find someone who might like to go. It's a shame to waste it. Plus,
it's free . . .'

'Oh, but if I did come – and it's a big "if" – I'd have to pay
for the ticket,' Sophie insisted.

'Kev's mate has already paid, and he doesn't want any
money because it's in aid of the mountain-rescue team. Now
come on, how many times will you get to spend New Year's
Eve at a posh do on a lake steamer?'

'Isn't it an annual event?' Sophie asked.

'Yup, but after the year you've had, you've got to take chances when they come along,' Vee urged her.

Sophie caved in. 'OK, you've persuaded me! But I'm still going to donate the cost of the ticket. I'm so grateful the team came up here in the snow to help Anna Nowak.'

'Hurrah!' Vee clapped her hands in delight. 'It'll be a blast. My mum is babysitting and it's been ages since Kev and I had a proper night out. It will be even better with you coming along too.'

'Thanks for asking me.' Sophie smiled. 'Mind you, I don't know what I'm going to wear.'

'Tell me about it. Kev is *not* impressed by having to wear black tie. I got him a suit from the online Oxfam. I'm sick of tatty jeans and a tabard, so I'm really looking forward to glamming up!'

Sophie had to smile. 'You deserve it.'

'So do you,' Vee said and raised her glass. 'To us! And to Sunnyside!'

'To us, and to Sunnyside!' Sophie clinked glasses with Vee. She ought to be so proud of what she'd achieved – and she was proud, and looking forward to the ball. She pulled her phone from her bag. 'I'd better book a taxi before it's too late. Don't fancy driving back in the small hours.'

'You'll be lucky to get one at this short notice. We've already got a cab booked. I could ask them to come up to Sunnyside before collecting us.'

'Thanks. You really are a star,' Sophie replied, chinking Vee's glass again. The ball would be the perfect chance to let her hair down and forget about all her problems. Although, she suddenly realised, Brody and Tegan might be there too . . . That prospect felt like a thorn in the delicate flesh of her happiness. No, she mustn't let it spoil the evening or dampen the mood. If the event was as popular as Vee was saying, hopefully she'd be able to avoid Brody all night.

Vee moved on to asking Sophie more about her flying visit home. It had only been for two nights – and she'd taken the cats with her in their travelling crates. They hadn't been terribly happy to be uprooted, but there was no way she was leaving them. In the end they'd spent the time being cosseted by her parents and having far too many Dreamies.

Sophie went home and examined the contents of her wardrobe. So much of what she'd brought with her was still undisturbed on the rails, in the same place as when she'd first unpacked it. There wasn't much call for kitten heels and sundresses up here. When the weather was good, she'd been busy working, and her nights out invariably involved the pub or Raffaelo's, both of them casual affairs where she wore her trusty jeans and a nice top.

She pulled a couple of dresses out of the wardrobe: a short red shift-dress and a slinky black number that she'd last worn to the premiere of a play at the RSC. That had been on a balmy June evening, and while the dress still fitted and looked nice, it would be very chilly on the boat. Her cardigans and padded jacket hardly did the dress any favours, but Vee's comment about Kev's suit had given her an idea.

By 10 a.m. on New Year's Eve, Bannerdale was bustling with visitors who'd arrived for the 'Twixmas' and New Year celebrations. Even though Sophie could probably have filled Sunnyside, she was more than happy with her decision to close and take a long break herself. Reopening in February would give her time to do a few of the odd jobs around the guest house that she'd put off, and it also meant that she was free to celebrate tonight, not having to worry about serving breakfast to guests in the morning.

It was nice to immerse herself in the pre-party atmosphere, like everyone else, taking in the aroma of cinnamon lattes and gingerbread wafting out of the coffee shops and bakery. She browsed the charity shops, hoping to find something suitable to go with her dress. As she'd hoped, there were a lot of post-Christmas donations of festive season outfits from people having clear-outs. After some rooting around, she found a faux-fur bolero that would be perfect. That was as long as the cats didn't find it and nest in it, before she needed to wear it tonight.

Sophie bought an amaretto latte and a cinnamon bun to enjoy in the park. Sitting on a bench, she ate her late breakfast with a view of mountains still dusted with snow. It felt as if she was on holiday and could finally breathe a sigh of relief as her first year at Sunnyside was drawing to a close.

Putting the awkwardness with Brody aside and focusing on the positives, she realised quite how far she'd come: staying afloat in her business, surviving a festive season that many had said would be a flop, handling a power cut, a snowstorm and a baby being born on the premises – and her beloved cats were recovering well after their ordeal.

No matter what lay ahead, she would celebrate tonight,

with the new friends she had made. Vee's taxi was coming to pick her up first, after a job in Townend village, and then down to Bannerdale to collect Vee and Kev, before dropping them all off at the jetty to catch the steamer. There was going to be a buffet and live band, followed by a disco on board, before the taxi was booked to bring her home to Sunnyside again.

She was on her way back to the car park when a display in the window of the gift shop caught her eye. Carl's 'emporium', Magpie, was the most tempting shop in Bannerdale, crammed with presents and goodies, from beautiful cards and stationery to artwork and jewellery. All were locally made by different craftspeople, and Carl had great taste. Sophie's eye had been drawn by a silver wirework necklace set with semi-precious stones that were like chips of blue ice. Its price tag was, as expected, quite a bit more than she'd ever contemplate paying.

On the other hand, it had been a tough year and she was going to a fancy ball – having a proper night out for the first time in a long while. She could treat herself to the necklace, which she'd surely wear again . . . And it was exactly the type of item that Bloody Ben would have said was 'a rip-off' and its price would have been 'hiked up by the retailer'.

Sophie went inside, to find several customers browsing in the shop's nooks and crannies, and one buying a child's toy at the counter.

After they'd gone, Carl greeted her with a warm smile. 'Sophie! How lovely to see you. What can I do for you?'

Sophie knew she was taking a risk in engaging with Brody's best friend, but she now wanted the necklace *badly*. 'I saw a silver necklace in the window and I'd love to take a look at it, please.'

'Ah, you mean the one with the pale-blue stones? They're made in the Lakes by an artist in Hawkshead. They're so beautiful – I don't blame you.' Carl had such a lovely way with his customers.

'That's the one.'

'Come with me to the window and I'll get it out.'

After Sophie had pointed out the necklace, Carl handed it over to her. 'Is it for a special occasion?' he asked.

'Yes. I'm going to a ball tonight.'

'Not the mountain-rescue thing on the lake steamer?'

'Er, yes . . .' Sophie's skin tingled.

'I'm going too! I think this will look fabulous. What are you wearing?'

'A long black dress and a cream faux-fur bolero. I wanted something sparkly to brighten it all up.'

'This will definitely do that. Did you know there are earrings to match? And a bracelet? Would you like to see those too? No obligation, of course.'

She nodded and Carl whipped the matching pieces out of a cabinet by the till. All Sophie could think about was that if Carl was going, then Brody might be too. She was wary about asking, though, because then Carl would tell his best friend, and it would surely get back to Brody.

She lingered over the bracelet and earrings as Carl chattered about the ball and the buffet, and the steamers. Don't ask about Brody, Sophie reminded herself, even as every fibre of her wanted to know whether he'd be there.

'Vee and Kev have invited me,' she said, in an attempt to provoke a response. 'They had a spare ticket. We're sharing a taxi.'

'I'm walking down to the jetty. A bonus of living in the village,' he said. 'My flat's over the shop, you see.'

'Oh, that's convenient,' Sophie replied, waiting for him to mention who else would be there.

'It is.' Carl paused. 'So have you decided on the bracelet and earrings?' He lowered his voice. 'I can do you a twenty per cent discount if you want them all. As you're a friend.'

Sophie hesitated for a moment. It was a beautiful set and would go perfectly with her outfit, plus all of her money had gone into the move and business, so she deserved to treat herself for a change. She smiled. 'OK, I shouldn't, but why not? I haven't splurged for a long time.'

'Wise decision!' Carl replied. 'I can't wait to see you wearing them.'

While he was busy wrapping her purchases and taking the payment, Sophie's mind worked overtime. Dare she ask him outright? She sensed other people queuing up behind her.

Carl handed her the gift bag. 'See you later then and, for your information, Brody is going tonight. So are Tegan and the oldies.'

Her stomach churned. 'Are they?' she said, feigning polite interest.

'And I shall be very, *very* cross if knowing that fact puts *you* off.' He grinned. 'After all, you've got a beautiful dress to wear and some gorgeous new jewellery to go with it; you absolutely *have* to show up.'

Chapter Thirty-Three

'Are you sure you should be going tonight, Dad?'

Tegan was retying her father's bow tie at her parents' house.

'Don't fuss, please,' Alan pleaded. 'I won't be overdoing it by spending a few hours out of the house, and I need it, after being cooped up for so long. And let's face it, if something goes wrong, half the bloody boat is packed with medics.'

'I hope we won't need them,' Tegan said.

Brody resisted the temptation to take off his own narrow black tie. He wasn't used to formal wear, and he hadn't worn his tux since a veterinary-awards do in London more than two years previously. He secretly longed to be at home, in front of the fire, with Harold for company.

Fiona appeared in a long dress, with a sparkly clutch bag under her shoulder. Brody was struck by how alike Tegan and her mother were: the same blonde hair, same slight figure, same air of brittle tension, except it was better disguised in Fiona's case. They must both be worried sick about Alan, though he seemed jovial enough.

Tegan stepped back from her father, having finally fixed his tie. 'There. Done. You look very smart.'

'As does your mum. You both look absolutely smashing. Don't they, Brody?'

Brody nodded. 'Yes, they do,' he agreed, adding, because for once he could speak the truth with a clear conscience, 'stunning.'

'I just need to touch up my make-up and then we can go,' Tegan said. 'I won't be long. Brody?'

'I'm coming. I need my wallet and phone from upstairs.'

'Please don't tell me you're on-call?' Tegan cried.

'Not tonight,' he promised. Although that meant there was no chance of him being called away and saved.

He followed Tegan up to her old bedroom, where they'd been getting ready for the party. Brody had come straight from work. He'd had a busy day catching up with patients and, in between his regular round of vaccinations and health checks, he'd extracted four teeth from a Miniature Schnauzer called Bentley and had microchipped a Hermann's tortoise – a procedure he'd had to google. But none of the animals' problems had even come close to stressing him out the way humans did.

Tegan sat down at the dressing table, topping up her lipstick.

Her grey satin dress had a draped back that showed off her bare shoulders. He'd seen it before; it was the same dress she'd worn on the night he'd first asked her out. Then, as now, she'd piled her hair on top of her head, and she wore sparkly studs in her ears. He'd turned up at a mutual friend's posh birthday party, in his brogues and Barbour, after attending the difficult birth of a calf. He'd only meant to

345

look in and hand over a gift, but he'd stayed, looking scruffy and probably a bit smelly, like a servant gatecrashing the aristos.

Yet Tegan had said he looked sexy, and Brody still had no idea why she would think that.

Just because his father and Alan were close didn't mean that he and Tegan were predestined to be together, though that's how people around him viewed it. That's why it was going to be so hard to tell their families the truth, because he knew they were all willing them to have a happy ending.

He'd loved Tegan. He still cared for her – beyond friendship, nothing like the love for a brother or a cousin, yet not in any of the ways he should feel, for a partner in life. Perhaps he never had. Perhaps he'd been afraid, at thirty-five, to accept that he might never find a special someone.

'You're quiet,' she said, talking to the mirror. 'You might have shown more enthusiasm for my outfit. You were a bit cold and distracted downstairs and you need to be more affectionate, so my parents don't start worrying something is wrong.'

'You look fantastic,' Brody muttered. 'You always do.'

'Thanks. It's always nice to be told.' She picked up a perfume bottle and sprayed it on her wrists.

'Tegan . . .' he began, steeling himself. 'We need to talk about – this situation. Later, when we're on our own, obviously.'

' "Talk?" ' Her eyes widened in alarm, making Brody's pulse rocket. She swung round to face him and heaved a deep sigh. 'Yes, actually, I think you're right. You see . . .' she

346

chewed her lip. 'I have something I need to get off my chest.' Her eyes glistened with unshed tears.

Brody sucked in a breath. Had she finally come to the same conclusion as him? That they had to be honest with her parents now? With everyone? 'I'm so glad we're on the same page then.' He felt a rush of relief.

She nodded. 'I know. It's killing me too.' She walked over to him and put her arms around his neck. 'But, you see, it doesn't *have* to be a lie. We can make it real again.'

His heart almost stopped. 'How?'

'I've made a terrible mistake. I want us to try again.'

The shock robbed him of words.

'I could try to win back your trust. I know you were devastated when we split up.' She touched his face, and Tegan touching him like that made him tense up. 'I took you for granted. I was so lonely when I first went to work in New York. I was overwhelmed, and the pressure was huge. I didn't think I could make it, and Wes was . . . supportive. Charming.'

A tear trickled down her cheek and dropped onto the lapel of his jacket. 'Or so I thought, but I was simply confused and alone. Now I realise that he isn't a fraction of the man you are. I've made a huge mistake, Brody, and I want to put it right. This may come as a shock, but I've finished with Wes. I told him last night that it was over. I told him that,' she gulped back a sob, 'I was – am – still in love with you.'

'Tegan . . .'

She held both his lapels. 'So now we don't have to pretend any longer.'

Brody was so numb with shock, he could barely frame a response. The situation was now even worse than before. He didn't have feelings for Tegan any more, and he couldn't believe that she thought she could come back and everything would be OK, just like it was. He realised that Tegan thinking he was much too nice meant she thought he was a pushover, but he wasn't going to be. Not any longer.

He cleared his throat. 'We can't keep deceiving your parents, my mother – everyone. It's wrong.'

'It is, and I guessed my dad and mum were starting to suspect things hadn't been right for a while. I decided to come clean, before you got home from work. I mentioned that we've been having some problems, but we're back together now, so everything is going to be OK. And now Dad knows that, it means he can rest easy and not feel stressed.'

She leaned forward and kissed him on the lips, but Brody pulled away.

'And we *will* be OK, Brody. I know we will. I'm truly sorry for what I did, and I hope to earn your trust again. As long as you're willing to try and make it work. It's up to you.'

Chapter Thirty-Four

The taxi dropped them off at the jetty where the steamer was waiting, windows blazing and festooned with coloured lights like a mini version of an old-fashioned liner. The band was already playing, with the sound of jazz drifting over the quay, and there was a queue of excited passengers waiting to board.

Sophie got out, and the cold hit her after the warmth of the taxi.

'Oh, this is so beautiful!' Vee cried, while Kev paid the driver.

'I feel like I'm about to board the *Titanic*,' he grumbled, adjusting his collar.

Vee playfully batted him on the arm. 'I bloody hope not! I don't fancy my chances in the middle of the icy lake.'

'No. It's two hundred feet deep in the middle, you know.'

'Oh, don't say that,' Sophie protested. 'It gives me the shivers.'

Vee was rocking a red jumpsuit and a sparkly black jacket. She stamped her gold platforms. 'I'm shivering anyway. I hope we get on board soon.'

They joined the queue at the brightly lit boathouse. It was a clear night and the moon shone down, reflected in the black waters of the lake, along with the shimmering fairy lights looped along the lamp posts on the boat pier.

'Although I'm freezing, I'm glad I made an effort,' Vee said, and Sophie agreed. It was strange to see so many people in tuxes and dresses, when most were usually bundled up in thick coats and jeans.

Luckily the queue moved swiftly and they were soon stepping aboard the Windermere steamer, the largest in the company's fleet. The guests were, of course, always using the boat service that plied the whole length of the lake and criss-crossed it. However, Sophie had been so busy that she'd only experienced it a couple of times, to reach the far side of the lake for walks on rare days off.

The boat was decorated with fairy lights and tinsel. Dealing with Christmas decorations no longer seemed such an issue to Sophie, set against her other troubles. Besides, the festivities would be over tomorrow and packed away for another year. If only her feelings for Brody could be packed away so easily. If only they could be sealed inside a cardboard box and hidden in a loft.

She forced her attention back to the moment, if only for Vee's sake. Her friendship was precious, and Vee deserved a happy evening, not a moping companion killing the mood. The band was playing in the saloon, on the main deck. As they walked inside, they were handed glasses of fizz by the crew. She recognised a couple of faces: traders from the village and one of the GPs, and two people who collected the trade waste from Sunnyside. They nodded and smiled.

Kev was immediately swept off by members of his mountain-rescue team, who had pints in hand. He disappeared down the steps where, judging by the number of people coming up and down, the bar was situated.

Vee linked arms with Sophie. 'That's it. We won't see him again for ages.'

Sophie laughed. 'Let's find a seat.'

The music stopped and an announcement was made. 'Ladies and gentlemen, welcome on board! Before we get the party started, we'd just like to run through some safety information . . .'

Once that was over, the captain told everyone they were edging away from the jetty and the boat started moving. Vee and Sophie got chatting to – or, rather, shouting down the ears of – the couple who ran the bakery. The band started up again, playing pop favourites.

'The band isn't bad,' Sophie said, sipping her second glass of fizz.

'It's played at Raffaelo's a few times. The guitarist is a friend of Kev's – Seb. He works in the music shop.'

'He's really good,' Sophie said, impressed by Seb's guitar solo.

'That's his brother, Travis, taking photos.'

Sophie nodded. She'd passed Travis's gallery many times and knew he was married to Freya, who ran a local cottage management company.

It seemed as if everyone was here, apart from Brody.

'Oh, I love this one!' Vee said. 'Let's dance. Kev's too shy unless he's had a few drinks!'

For a while Sophie lost herself in the music. It had been so long since she'd danced like this. The volume ramped up and the dance floor became packed. Briefly she thought she glimpsed Tegan, but realised she had the wrong woman – much to her relief. Carl was also on the floor, with a man Sophie recognised from the mountain-rescue team, and gave her a little wave.

They danced to four tracks in a row, and finally the band took a break while the buffet was served. Warm and a little out of breath, Sophie and Vee left the floor and went to collect their food.

Surely, *surely* they would bump into Brody's party at the buffet, but there was no sign of them. She was beginning to wonder if they had come after all. Perhaps Tegan's father wasn't feeling well. She sat down at the table with Vee, and Kev joined them.

'I knew you'd come back when the food was served!' Vee said, and Kev grinned.

'I'm not daft. Are you having a good time? Sorry, I got cornered by one of the team in the bar.'

Vee rolled her eyes. 'Course you did.'

Someone Vee knew passed by and started talking to her and Kev.

Sophie carried on eating her sausage roll and nodded at points in their conversation to pretend she was listening. Out of the corner of her eye, she saw the tall frame and mop of dark hair of Brody, who was making his way up the stairs from the lower bar with a tray of drinks. If she hadn't been sitting down, she might have needed support at the sight of him in a tux and a slim black tie. Her whole body tingled with desire. She turned away because there was no point in tormenting herself like this, when he was with someone else.

She wished she could sneak away to avoid seeing Brody and Tegan, but it was impossible. She was trapped on the boat until it docked at 1 a.m. and she'd have to make the most of it.

Before she could move her chair around, Brody seemed to have spotted her. His eyes widened in surprise, as if he hadn't expected her to be there, and gave her a brief smile. Sophie died a little inside. How had she fallen so fast, so hard for such a lost cause?

He was walking their way and had paused by their table, still holding the tray. 'Hello. This is a surprise.'

'Is it? Vee gave me a last-minute invitation. I would have thought Carl would have told you,' Sophie replied.

He frowned. 'Carl? I don't understand.'

'I popped into the gift shop earlier and bought some jewellery.' Before she realised it, her fingers were touching the necklace, feeling how cool the stones were against her flushed skin. 'He mentioned that you would be here tonight with Tegan and her parents.'

'No, Carl didn't say anything to me, but I haven't had a chance to catch up with him. I was working before I came here. The necklace is very nice,' he said and hesitated before adding, 'You look very . . . nice.'

Sophie could hardly meet his eye. 'Thanks,' she muttered, wanting to say so much that she could barely reply at all.

'Right. Yes. I should take these drinks back to the others,' he mumbled awkwardly, still lingering by the table.

Sophie nodded. 'Yes. Nice to see you.'

With another uneasy smile, Brody walked towards the rear of the boat, presumably to where Tegan and his future in-laws were sitting. Sophie pushed her plate away.

Vee touched her arm. 'You've gone quiet. Are you OK?'

'Fine. Fine. I think I'll pop to the Ladies before the dancing starts again,' Sophie said, forcing herself to sound cheery.

She made her way through the packed saloon and down the stairs, to find a long queue for the Ladies. There were at least six people ahead of her, so she resigned herself to the wait. It was impossible not to think about Brody, how gorgeous he looked and how uncomfortable he'd seemed to see her. His compliment about her looking 'nice' had made her cringe. She'd rather he hadn't said anything at all.

She'd barely moved when Tegan emerged from the Ladies and waved at her.

'Oh, hello again!' She was wearing a gorgeous grey satin dress. 'How are your cats?' she asked. 'Brody told me they'd eaten some mistletoe and he'd had to treat them.'

Sophie hid her surprise that Brody had said anything about the incident. 'They're fine now, thanks.'

'Good . . . And your anti-Christmas break went well?'

Sophie thought it wasn't worth arguing about what the

break was, having grown tired of explaining it to people. 'Yes, I think everyone enjoyed it. Thank you for having us all on Christmas Day. It was really kind of you.'

'Oh, you're welcome! Actually it was a lot of fun. I was just worried it might be a bit too Christmassy for you all.'

Sophie kept her smile in place while being desperate to escape, hoping that the queue would move faster. 'In the circumstances, I think some turkey and tinsel were the least of our worries.'

'Yes, I s'pose so. Well, I'd better get back to Brody and my parents. I think I mentioned that my dad's not well, but he still insisted on coming here tonight. He never misses the New Year's Eve do.'

Sophie recalled the conversation with Tegan on Christmas Day and it made her feel sorry for her all over again. 'It's great he could make it. Vee was telling me that this was one of the big nights in the Bannerdale social calendar. I'm sure your dad will be OK,' she went on, wondering if she was talking rubbish. Surgery of any kind didn't sound like a trivial thing and she could understand why Tegan was concerned.

Tegan sighed. 'It is great . . . and I hope he's going to celebrate many more of them. People keep telling me it's a routine op these days, but that's not true. He has angina too.' She held up crossed fingers. 'Brody keeps trying to reassure me it will be fine. I don't know what I'd do without him. He's so supportive. I'm very lucky.'

Sophie gave a weak smile. 'I really hope it all goes well,' she said. 'I'd better go back too. Vee will be wondering where I've got to.'

'Brody will too. See you on the dance floor maybe? If I can persuade Brody to dance. It's not really his thing, but we're celebrating tonight.'

Tegan waltzed off, holding up her dress to avoid tripping on her silver heels. Sophie felt terrible that not only had Brody kept quiet about his fiancée, but he'd done so when she was already dealing with so much. No wonder Tegan seemed rather brittle and clingy at times.

After visiting the loo, Sophie decided not to go straight back to her table, but instead headed for the exit. Although the night was calm, the cold took her breath away. There were half a dozen people out there, though it was so cold that most of them were shivering and hastily going back inside.

'Sophie!'

Brody's voice. Had he followed her? She hadn't noticed him when she was talking to Tegan. She wrapped her arms around her body.

'Why are you out here?' he said. 'You must be freezing!'

'I don't want to go inside.'

'Then have this.' Even as he spoke, he was shrugging off his jacket.

He draped it around her shoulders, his fingers brushing her bare collarbone as he did so. She didn't know which goosebumps were from the cold and which were from the touch of his hand on her bare flesh. Far too large, the jacket was warm from his body and smelled of his aftershave, and the silk lining caressed her body the way she wanted him to.

Moonlight shimmered on the unruffled surface of the

lake, and the fells were black against the night sky. It felt incredibly romantic, and even more wrong that she was out there with Brody.

'I don't think this is a good idea.' Sophie tried to pull off his jacket and held it out. She didn't care how cold she was.

Brody sighed. 'Please put it back on. You'll freeze out here.'

Reluctantly she did so. 'Tegan won't be happy if she comes out and sees this, though. Brody, she's your fiancée.'

'Actually she'd have no reason to be mad. We're not engaged any more. We're not even a couple.'

'What?' Sophie shook her head, disgusted at what she'd heard. 'This is a new low, Brody. I wouldn't have expected a line like this from you. She clearly seems to think you're still together.'

'It's not a line. It's the truth. We split up months ago. Tegan met someone new in New York, not long after she started there, and broke off our engagement. We only pretended we were still together for the sake of her father. Tegan didn't want to upset him. Neither of us did,' he qualified. 'Alan took a turn for the worse after her brother announced he was getting divorced last year. Tegan is petrified another shock might make Alan have a relapse before his op.'

Could it be true? Could she really trust what Brody was saying? He had no reason to make up such a story. Sophie tugged his jacket around her, shivering with the cold. 'And Tegan's going along with this? Because she didn't even hint to me that anything was wrong just now. The opposite, in fact.'

He shoved his hands through his hair in frustration. 'Initially it was Tegan's idea. I wanted to make a clean break as soon as she told me about her affair, but I agreed to keep up the charade until her father was recovering. I genuinely thought I could do it, while she was on the other side of the Atlantic. Only a couple of people had known about the engagement, and not having to face them and tell them we'd broken up was easier to begin with too. I didn't factor in how hard it is to deny your real feelings. I didn't factor in falling for someone else. For *you* . . .'

Sophie could feel her heart beating faster. Suddenly the cold didn't matter, and yet . . .

'I've always liked you,' Brody went on. '*More* than liked you, but obviously I suppressed my feelings. Then Tegan dropped the bombshell that she'd been having a relationship with her boss. I was stunned and hurt. I felt humiliated.'

'I know that feeling,' Sophie murmured, hardly daring to believe that what Brody was saying was true. 'After I first split with Ben, I realised that it was a good thing we'd parted before we were married. Anyone who could have an affair with my best friend behind my back – and blame me for it – was better off out of my life. I needed something to blame, and I blamed Christmas. Even though I knew it wasn't rational, I needed something to hang my insecurities and my grief and anger on.'

'I understand. I always did.' Brody took her chilled hands and held them between his own warm ones. 'Even if you were having doubts about a relationship, a betrayal like that knocks you off your feet. Maybe it served me right; maybe Tegan could sense that I wasn't as committed as I should have been, but even so I would *never* have hurt her in the way she hurt me. It's why I've tried so hard to stop myself even thinking about you.'

'After the lantern parade and then at the party that night, I realised how much I liked you,' Sophie told him. 'I was just starting to feel brave enough to open up to someone else, but then that . . . stable moment happened and made me terrified in case I got hurt again.'

'No, please believe me. I'm nothing like your ex. Even growing close to you felt like betraying Tegan, and I hoped I might feel differently over time. Unfortunately, the more I saw of you, the more I realised that I couldn't go on pretending.'

Sophie was torn between joy and fear. She'd longed to hear Brody say these words. She'd lost all hope that he really was the lovely, gorgeous, nice guy she'd originally thought. It was miraculous to know the truth, and yet she couldn't get past the fact that he was still engaged to another women, even if in name only.

She took her hands out of his and moved apart from him. 'I – I do like you, Brody. More than like. You must know that, but I could never be part of breaking up a relationship. Tegan clearly hasn't accepted it's over between you, and I don't want to be part of some agonising love-triangle. Until and unless she accepts that you two are over, there can't be a future for us. Don't let me be the reason you hurt someone.'

Brody's fingers brushed hers for the briefest moment, setting off fireworks through her whole body. 'Sophie, no matter what I do, I'm going to hurt someone. Sometimes you can't avoid it, if you want to do the right thing for the ones you love.' He took her hand again. 'I can't tell you how much I want to hold you. Kiss you. *More.*'

Sophie had no need of his jacket. The heat rose in her body and every nerve ending zinged. She longed to be in his arms, and alone with him.

'Not until you're truly free,' she insisted. 'Only you can make that happen.'

'I know, and I *will*.'

'Brody!'

Tegan ran up to them, tears running down her face. 'I've been looking for you everywhere! You have to come. It's Dad. He's having an angina attack.'

Chapter Thirty-Five

Brody apologised as he carved a path through the drinkers in the bar. The floor above thumped with dancers and the bass pulsated from the disco, which was now in full swing. He'd had no choice but to leave Sophie and immediately follow Tegan inside.

It seemed an age before he made it to the upper deck, where Alan was sitting at their table, bow tie hanging loose, with Fiona fanning him. The man did look pale, though it was hard to tell with all the flashing disco lights.

'Dad!' Tegan knelt on the floor in front of her father. She had to shout above the music.

Brody joined her at his side. 'Alan. How are you feeling now?'

'You can tell my wife and daughter to stop fussing,' Alan replied firmly. 'I've taken my medication and I'm already feeling better.'

'Can we help?' A couple of people from the mountain-rescue team approached them, and the grey-haired man of the two spoke to them. 'I'm a doctor, and Deep here is a paramedic. Can you tell me what happened?' the doc asked, sitting down on a chair next to Alan.

Brody helped Tegan to her feet, so that the doctor had more room.

'I'm fine. I felt breathless and an attack coming on, but I've had my pills now and I'll be OK. Please, I don't want a fuss!'

'Alan . . .' Brody pleaded, his own heart pounding when he recalled the moment his head teacher had called him out of the classroom to break the news about his father. 'Best to let them help.'

Fiona put her hand on her husband's shoulder. 'Yes, you should. How often do you get to see a doctor within two minutes of feeling poorly?'

'I'm not poorly. I have angina and I have my pills. They *will* work.'

'Do you mind if we just sit here with you for a few minutes and chat?' the doctor said. 'So we can make sure you're on the mend?'

'If you like,' Alan replied, grudgingly. 'Though you both should be up there and dancing.'

'I've got two left feet. You've given me an excuse to avoid making a prat of myself.'

'I hate Abba,' Deep agreed, standing by Fiona.

Alan rolled his eyes. 'If you say so.'

A few people were staring. Brody smiled but said firmly to them, 'Shall we give Alan a bit of space, if you don't mind?' His glare did the trick.

Tegan squeezed Brody's hand. 'We shouldn't have let him come,' she murmured, while the doctor checked her father over.

'This could have happened at home,' Brody replied, as reassuringly as he could. 'I think he's looking perkier already.'

'I hope so,' Tegan said. 'Because if anything happens to him, I'll never forgive myself.'

'It's not your fault that he chose to come here tonight. Your dad makes his own decisions.'

Tegan said nothing, but let go of Brody's hand.

He glanced around, hoping to find Sophie, but there was no sign of her. He'd had to abandon her by the rail of the boat. She'd understand, he knew that – but what timing!

A short while later, the doctor said he was happy enough to leave Alan to recover at home.

'Someone's offered to give us a lift,' Fiona said to Brody and Tegan. 'You two stay here and enjoy yourselves.'

'Oh, we're not leaving you!' Tegan declared. 'Are we, Brody?'

'We'll come home with you,' he agreed.

Fiona shook her head. 'Your dad and I don't want to cut your evening short.'

'It's already pretty late,' Brody began, unwilling to leave the family on their own, even though he had hoped to find Sophie again.

'We *are* coming with you,' Tegan said firmly. 'I'll find my coat.'

Brody picked it up from the bench by their table, while Fiona helped Alan on with his, much to his annoyance.

'Please, stop treating me like I'm ninety-nine.'

Tegan stood, waiting for Brody to slip the coat over her

shoulders, as she always did. 'Thank you,' she said and smiled at him, though her eyes were like chips of ice. 'Don't you think you should go and fetch your tux jacket?'

It was only then that he remembered Sophie must still be wearing it.

Brody woke on New Year's Day with Tegan next to him. He'd already known he'd have to share a room with her, when they'd decided to stay with her parents.

Alan had seemed OK when they returned home and he'd gone up to bed. At Brody's urging, Tegan went to bed at the same time as her parents. She looked exhausted after the stresses and strains of the past few months. Brody had stayed up, watching the spectacular fireworks in London. He'd never felt less celebratory and yet, at the same time, he knew that the turning of the year was his chance finally to lay the past to rest, no matter what the risks.

Tegan had been asleep when he went up and it seemed petty for him to kip on the floor, so he lay on top of the duvet and pulled the eiderdown over him. It was a good while after that before he finally fell asleep, thinking of the past, the people he loved and the future, with all its possibilities, if he only had the courage to grasp it.

He was dressed by the time Tegan woke up, and her long blonde hair had spread over the pillows like a halo. He sat on the bed watching her for a moment until she started to stir.

'Morning,' she said, blinking and pushing herself up the pillows.

'Morning.' Brody looked her in the eyes and felt a rush of

tenderness, the kind you felt for a very dear friend. 'Tegan, there's something we have to do, and we have to do it very soon.'

She was silent for a few seconds, picking at a thread on the eiderdown.

Slowly she nodded her head. 'You're in love with Sophie, aren't you?'

He paused for a little breath, then said, 'I tried not to be. I wasn't until after we split up that it happened. A long time after we split up.'

'I know. I didn't want to accept it at first, but it's become pretty obvious over the past few days. Does she know?'

'Actually, no. She thought I was a bastard, and now she thinks – well, I'm not sure she knows what to think of me.'

Tegan shook her head and gave a small, sad smile. 'You couldn't be a bastard if you tried.'

Brody felt choked with emotion. 'Thanks. I wouldn't be giving myself any gold stars, though. I seem to have made a bloody mess of everything lately.'

She hugged her knees, staring at the duvet. With his heart in his mouth, Brody waited for her to burst into tears or start an angry row.

'I think . . .' Tegan began, still not looking at him. 'I think we've both made a mess.' Finally she lifted her eyes to his with the saddest of smiles. 'But I've made a bigger mess. I ruined everything the moment I decided to get involved with Wes. I deeply regret that now.'

'We can't change the past, but at least you can go back to him in New York,' Brody said gently.

'But I would rather not have fallen for him. Wes broke up with me. Turns out he's not a good guy, but at the time I fooled myself into thinking he offered something that was missing.'

'You were in a strange country and were worried about your family.' Brody surprised himself by how he felt the need to defend Tegan, and he did still care about her. But he also knew, finally, that it was over between them, and that nothing but total honesty would help either of them come to terms with it.

'It was more than me being needy,' she admitted. 'Deep down, I sensed that we – you and I – weren't the right people to spend a lifetime together. Not as anything more than close friends.'

Brody felt choked with sadness and relief.

'After Wes, I knew that our relationship was broken beyond repair. I just . . . didn't want to face up to it. The way I treated you was unforgivable – coming back here and trying to pick things back up again – even if you hadn't fallen for Sophie.'

He swallowed. He'd known, deep down in his heart, that Tegan had probably guessed the truth. He'd known she was worried for her father and was, perhaps, already regretting her decision to have an affair with Wes. Hearing it didn't make Brody feel happy or triumphant. It was merely sad that, despite not wanting to, they'd ended up hurting each other and those around them.

'You're a good man, Brody, just not the man for me, no matter how much I've tried to convince myself that you are.

I think it's best if we both start again, and I do really want you to be happy.'

It was all he could do not to hold Tegan's hand to comfort her.

'Thanks for having the courage to say that. The past few months have been pretty horrible for both of us, but I think we need to do the right thing, right now, and hope it will be OK.'

She sighed, then nodded. 'That's all we can do.'

Finally he picked up her hand. 'Come on then. Let's tell them together.'

Chapter Thirty-Six

Sophie chose the most direct path to the top of the fell above Sunnyside, climbing until her lungs were fit to burst, because the effort distracted her from the ache in her heart. It was the first day of the new year and she was determined to shake off the shackles of the old one.

Finally she made it to the summit cairn, shrugged off her rucksack and heaved in some breaths. Wow! It was great to be alone at last and to relax in the stillness of it all. No people, no chatter, only the sound of the wind blowing, to disturb the stillness.

The fell was a very modest one, in the grand scheme of Lakeland hills, yet no one else could be bothered to climb it on New Year's Day, when many people would be nursing their hangovers. Far below her, in the shifting mist, Lake Windermere glistened in the valley. The mist would burn off by lunchtime; she'd learned enough about her surroundings over the past ten months to know that. No smoke spiralled from the fat chimneys. Gabriel must be inside his shelter, although the sheep, with their curly horns, were munching away in the fields.

Brody would be at his future in-laws', she thought. She'd

seen them all hurriedly leave the steamer the previous evening. Tegan's father, Alan, had seemed well enough to walk off the boat after it had called in at Bowness jetty to let him, and a few other passengers, off early. She'd no idea what had happened after that, and she could only hope he'd been OK.

Hot chocolate from her flask and a brownie from the farm shop were very welcome. She felt both at home here and out of the place, at the same time. She was just finishing the last of the brownie when she heard barking from below. A few seconds later Harold trotted over, woofing and snuffling with delight to see her.

Sophie's stomach knotted and her pulse quickened. She hadn't dared contemplate what would happen with Brody, after last night. They'd seemed to be so near to being together, and yet so far away. She couldn't see any way of them being together without causing pain to Tegan and her family.

Brody appeared at the top of the path, breathing hard and heading straight for her, once he spotted her. He looked gorgeous, but Sophie suppressed the urge to run to him.

'Hello,' he said with a grin. 'Fancy finding you up here.'

'It does seem a big coincidence,' she said.

'Apart from the fact that I did see you – or thought I saw you – halfway up here, when I got home just now. It's that red coat.' He gave a sheepish look. 'I'm afraid I got out the binoculars to check . . .'

'You've been spying on me through binoculars?'

'Well, I didn't want the wasted effort of coming up here to find that you were some pensioner on a New Year's Day hike.'

'Do I look like a pensioner?'

'Not close up, no.'

She gasped in mock horror. 'Thank you for that!'

Brody broke out in a smile – the old kind of smile that she used to see a lot, before Tegan had come back. She dared to imagine that he was standing taller, as if a weight had been lifted from his shoulders. It did feel like they'd slipped back into the way things had been between them, with a lightness and ease to their conversation.

'I came to ask you if I could have my jacket back,' Brody said.

'Your jacket?' Sophie was confused.

'Do you still have it?'

'Yes, I brought it home with me last night. You can have it back,' she said, wondering for a moment if her hopes had been misguided and Brody really had hiked up here because of his coat.

'No. You keep it, if you like. It looks so much better on you anyway.'

The smile on his face lit the flame of hope in Sophie's heart all over again. When it melted into a look of such tender concern, she needed to sit down.

'I came to find you as soon as I could. I came to tell you that Tegan and I spoke to her parents this morning. We agreed to tell them the whole truth, that it's over – officially over – between us.'

'Oh!' Her hand flew to her mouth. This was what she longed for, yet dreaded to hear. 'But what about Alan? Is he OK? I was so worried that you might not tell him, that you might stay with Tegan. I was even more worried that if you did break it off, Alan might take a turn for the worse. That I might be the reason for it.'

'No, Sophie. None of this is your responsibility. It was always mine and Tegan's. Alan is doing much better. Obviously he and Fiona are very sad about the situation but, to be honest, they were also not that surprised. In fact they seemed quite relieved.'

'Really? It can't have been easy.'

'It was one of the hardest things I've ever had to do, but now that I have, I feel as if a burden has been lifted from my shoulders. Alan told us he felt far more stressed worrying about what the heck was really going on between us than hearing the truth. He told us he knew that we were trying to protect him, and it was kind, but that it was kinder to be honest.'

'Alan and Fiona seem like lovely people.'

'They are. They've always been like a second mum and dad to me.'

'Love isn't a game with a winner or a loser, is it?' she said, wanting to reach up and touch his face.

'No, but without being brave and following your heart, everyone loses. There will be someone for Tegan. A far better partner than I would ever have been.'

'Would you have been? Would you have married her?' she asked.

'Being brutally honest, I hope not. I'm glad Tegan left me initially, for so many reasons.'

'You only ended it with her this morning.'

'Yes, but we've had a lot of time to come to terms with it. And she'd already moved on. And that's what I want to do now.'

Sophie's heart raced and she hoped Brody meant it – that he wanted her like she wanted him.

'If you need time, or if you want me to take some time, then I will,' he told her, 'but I know what I want, and that's to be with you. You always listened to me, even after I'd had the worst day. However ironic it seems, I always felt I could be myself with you.'

'Now you can,' Sophie replied.

'Yeah.' He heaved a huge sigh. 'Don't laugh, but I feel as if I've finally come home.'

'I'll never laugh at you.' She grinned. 'Well, unless you're wearing a grubby Santa hat in the surgery, or trying to convince me that a python is cute.'

'Pythons are cute. All my patients are.' He laughed. 'Does that mean that next year you might actually allow a party hat on the premises?' he asked, holding her gently around her waist. It felt amazing and natural.

'Hmm. That might be going too far,' she said. 'I'm joking ... but I've also learned that there are plenty of people who find Christmas stressful or lonely, or just can't face the pressure to have a perfect day. It's OK to love Christmas, and it's also OK to want to spend it quietly or simply do something different. But the spirit behind it – people coming together and celebrating life – that's what we should hold on to and nurture, whether it's over turkey and tinsel or paella and flamenco. I've learned something else too,' she continued. 'You might be able to escape Christmas, but you can't avoid facing up to your fears, or blaming them for you holding on to the past. I also learned a lot from my guests.'

He laughed. 'Even from Nico?'

'In a way. He can't be himself with his family. He's struggling to find the courage to tell them about his true self. Everyone came along looking for an escape, when what they really wanted was a fresh start.'

'Did you?' Brody asked, holding Sophie's gaze.

'Yes, although I bought Sunnyside for *me*, and not to run away from Ben. It was my baby, my business that I could create and manage completely for myself. I wasn't looking for anything else, least of all love.'

'And yet . . . you didn't count on finding such a handsome neighbour next door?' said Brody, pulling her closer.

Though she had no words, Sophie realised that she loved every fibre of him, inside and out. His scruffy, wind-tumbled hair, his muddy walking boots, his ancient Barbour, even a wayward dog that stole the breakfast from her guests.

They were kissing. This time she was able to give herself, enjoy every second, every sensation, the touch of his lips on hers, the warm pressure of his mouth, the scent of him. It could go on for ever and no one could stop them.

'Woof!'

Sophie burst out laughing. 'Harold!'

'Thanks a lot, buddy,' Brody tutted. 'And would you mind taking your nose out of my crotch.'

Sophie laughed. 'He's probably embarrassed at all this lovey-dovey stuff.'

'He probably wants to go home for a nap – it was a good walk up here.'

'And do you?' she asked.

'Right now, a nap is the last thing on my mind.'

He took her hand and they walked down the fellside towards Sunnyside. Harold barked and raced on ahead. And Sophie wasn't sure who was more eager to get home: the dog or both of them.

Epilogue

Four weeks later

On a Sunday morning at the start of February, Brody woke up with a cat on his head and one on his feet. Sophie was used to it, but he stirred in his sleep and let out a cry.

'Oh my God, I dreamed I was being attacked by a grizzly bear!'

'Worse. Jingle is trying to lie on your head. Shoo!' Sophie gently ushered the cat off the pillow. He sprang across the bed, by way of Brody's bare chest.

'Ow! Those claws are sharp!' Brody rubbed his chest.

'Welcome to my world,' Sophie told him.

Brody peered down the bed. His feet were poking out and Belle was licking his toes.

'She thinks you need a wash.'

'Woof!'

Harold trotted into the bedroom and licked his hand.

Brody sank back onto the pillow. 'You know, sometimes I think there are five of us in this relationship.'

Sophie laughed. 'Eight, if you count Gabriel and the sheep. I brought coffee. Now shoo, you three – let Brody get up.'

He pushed himself up, revealing his toned and naked torso, a sight that almost caused Sophie to spill the coffee on the duvet. She placed the mug on the bedside table.

'Brrr,' said Brody, suddenly cold now that his body was out of the warmth of the covers. 'Has it snowed?'

'A little bit, though not enough to cover the snowdrops.'

Sophie was wearing a sweatshirt over her pyjamas, and furry bootees. It wasn't the most attractive outfit, but she'd had to put on something in the early-morning chill. The guest house was still closed to visitors and she hadn't had the heating on. By day, she'd been working up a sweat doing some maintenance on the guest house, preparing to reopen; and at night she and Brody had kept more than warm enough, without the need for radiators. They'd alternated between spending nights at Felltop and at Sunnyside since the New Year, and then after she'd got back from her trips to Stratford and Gran Canaria.

Sophie sat next to Brody on the bed and he put his arm around her. Harold gazed up at them from the floor. The cats lounged on the window ledge, staring at them all.

Brody sighed. 'Harold does not approve of long lie-ins. This face means he thinks I ought to take him for a walk.'

'And I need to feed the cats,' said Sophie, as Belle jumped deftly onto the bed with a plaintive mew.

Brody stroked the cat's head. 'The animals come first.'

Sophie nodded. 'Always.'

'On the other hand, it *is* Sunday and I'm not on-call, so after we've done our duties we have the rest of the day to ourselves . . .' He reached for her hand.

'Woof! Woof!' Harold barked on cue.

'OK, OK. Let me finish my coffee and put some clothes on, then I'll take you out, boy.'

After breakfast they took Harold out for a walk in the fields. Christmas might be only a memory, yet the scene was still as festive as ever, with snow-topped fells and the lake glinting in the valley below.

Brody threw a ball for Harold and then chased after the dog himself, when Harold decided to roll in something unpleasant. Sophie watched them both, finally able to reflect on the twists and turns her life had taken since the previous Christmas. The path ahead was straight and clear now and she felt at ease with herself.

She'd recently been back to see her parents and friends, and her brother and his family. They'd pulled crackers, worn party hats and played 'Twister', and Sophie had enjoyed every minute. She'd also met up in the rooftop bar of the RSC with Lyra, who'd bumped into Ben's mother earlier that day in town.

'I told her you were seeing a vet,' Lyra had said with a grin.

'She must think I've got distemper,' Sophie had joked, and they'd both laughed so loudly that the people at the next table had frowned disapprovingly.

Lyra had raised her glass. 'And I'm so happy for you. Even though I miss you, I'm absolutely delighted for you, and I can't wait to come up and visit again in the spring.'

'I can't wait either,' Sophie had said.

They'd then moved on to talk about the guest house and her plans for the future. Lyra had decided to borrow one of Sophie's ideas and had organised a Stratford version of the 'Escape from Valentine's' break, which was already fully booked at Sunnyside. Single guests or groups of friends could come to Sunnyside to enjoy an early-spring nature break of walks, wildlife-spotting and forest-bathing with like-minded people. Lyra had arranged a theatre visit and a wine-and-food tour around the local area and was also fully booked.

As they'd raised their glasses again, it was to the future.

A gust whistled off the fells now and blew a flurry of drifting snow into her face, but Sophie embraced it, tasting ice-crystals on her tongue and the sharp bite of the wind against her cheek. She would celebrate every season from now on, no matter what it brought.

Brody had started walking back towards her and, when his phone rang, a grimace crossed his face.

Sophie held her breath as he listened and spoke.

'OK. Right. Oh my God. Oh . . . that's a huge relief. I'm very pleased to hear it. Thanks for letting me know. Bye.'

His smile returned when he ended the call. 'That was Fiona. Alan had surgery yesterday. They had a cancellation, so he was able to go in a couple of days early. It's gone well and he's back on a general ward, recovering.'

'I'm so glad. That's good. It must be a big weight off Tegan's and Fiona's minds.'

'Yes. I'll call Fiona later. Tegan's back in the States, working out her notice. Fiona told me she's coming back to the

UK. Some company in London has head-hunted her apparently, so at least she'll be in the same country as her parents and able to visit more often.'

'I'm glad, for her family's sake,' Sophie said and meant it.

'Me too.' He put his arm around her. 'You know, this morning got me thinking. How is Harold going to deal with two cats all the time?'

'They seem to get along OK,' Sophie replied. 'Wait, why? Are you suggesting . . . that we move in together?'

'In theory, yes – it's what people do – but I suppose there's no rush, when we already live next door.'

'Plus, I have the guest house to run,' Sophie pointed out.

'And we already have all the perks of living together,' Brody said, with a twinkle in his eye.

'You're forgetting that we don't need to be too traditional and rush into anything. I already have a reputation for doing things differently,' Sophie joked.

'True.' He smiled. 'Come back to the farm. I have something special to show you.'

'So you said you had something special to show me,' Brody's mother said, when he took her coat in the hall later that afternoon.

'Come with me,' Brody said.

'This is all very mysterious . . .'

He led the way towards the snug, where the fire was glowing in the hearth on the chilly afternoon. It looked bare, now that the decorations had been taken down and the tree long turned into mulch at the recycling centre. But there were daffodils in a jug on the coffee table and a pot of hyacinths in the window, both courtesy of Sophie.

However, it wasn't the fire or the flowers that caught his mother's attention. They were not what stopped her in her tracks and made her gasp and hold her hands to her mouth and start to cry.

'Oh, Mum! I'd never have done it, if I'd thought it would have this effect on you.'

'No, you should have. It's only that . . . it's so beautiful, and so – so perfect, and I'd no idea and—'

'Do you think Dad would have approved?' Brody asked nervously.

'Approved? He'd have loved it.'

'Why don't you try the new chair for size?' Brody offered. 'I'd love to.'

His mother sat in the armchair. 'Where did you get this made?'

'At the furniture workshop in the village. They did a rush job. Turns out I saved their chihuahua last year, and they said they owed me a favour. They didn't, but I wanted the chair, so I took them up on the offer.'

She ran her hands over the arms of the chair. 'It's identical.'

'Practically, though the upholstery is slightly different. They couldn't find an exact match.'

She rested her hands on it. 'Silly of me, but I can almost feel Ralph's hands have been here.' She glanced up, her eyes suspiciously bright. 'Dare I ask where the old chair is?'

'In the dining room, with a cover over it. Harold loves it.

I expect it will fall apart pretty soon, but I couldn't bear to part with it.'

'What a brilliant idea.' Louise got up and hugged him warmly. 'It's perfect.'

'Now, would you like a cup of tea?' he asked, filled with relief and pleasure that his mother approved.

'I'd love one.'

Sophie walked in. 'Shall I make it? Hello, Louise.'

'Hello, Sophie.' Louise gave her a peck on the cheek. 'It's nice to see you.'

'So do you like the chair?

'It's wonderful.'

Brody took Sophie's hand. 'Some things should stay the same, and some should change. We treasure the old traditions and make some new ones of our own.'

Her warm fingers curled around his own.

'Which is why I'm so happy to tell you that Sophie and I are officially a couple. We've been keeping things low-key until now, but it's time to go public.'

Louise smiled. 'I'd kind of worked out that you were close, but I hadn't realised quite how close. I'm so pleased. You both look happier than I've ever seen you.' She gave them a hug.

Harold woofed joyfully and everyone laughed.

'Quite right, Harold,' Brody said, knowing that in that moment he'd never felt happier or more certain of anything in his life.

Acknowledgements

I owe a huge debt of thanks to all the people who helped me with the research for this book. I am not a vet. I am not a midwife. I've never run a guest house and, if I did, all the guests would leave after five minutes!

The problem is that when an idea grips you – as the idea for the 'Escape for Christmas' did – you don't think about the research involved until it's far too late. You simply launch in, feet first, and then realise that you've got to find and pester a lot of busy people with some frankly outlandish questions. Imagine asking a veterinary surgeon, 'How would you deliver a baby, if you had to?' I cringed when I asked that one! I also had to ask the vet numerous other questions about her non-human patients, and I want to give a huge thank-you to Jessica Carmichael for her patience. Any mistakes are entirely my own!

As for how to deliver a baby in a snowstorm . . . Luckily for me, one of my best friends in the world was a midwife, and is now an author of vintage murder mysteries. Dear Nell Dixon (aka Helena Dixon), I can never thank you enough for your help.

Equally, my friend Lyn McCollough Fegan was wonderful

in relating her stories as a guest-house proprietor and in playing the game of 'managing' Sunnyside for me.

Then there was the small matter of caring for a donkey. Who, I thought, has a donkey? Fortunately I realised that my accountant, Barbara, does! Thank you, Barbara. I had no idea donkeys weren't waterproof.

One part of this book was easy: the animal characters. I asked my reader group to tell me about their pets and their trips to the vet, and I was crushed in the rush! They came up with hundreds of stories about pets and vets, some funny, some sad, some bizarre: all touched my heart, and a few of them have made it into the book.

Even when a story is finished, the work is only just starting for the team of editorial, production and marketing professionals at Century Books. Firstly, I want to thank Katie Loughnane, not only for editing this book, but for persuading me to make my new home at Century; and Claire Simmonds, publishing director, for her ongoing support. Also Mandy Greenfield and Rose Waddilove, in the managing editorial team, for their meticulous eyes, tact and patience. Thanks also go to Emily Griffin; to Hana Sparkes in publicity; to Issie Levin and Lucy Hall in marketing; and to Jess Muscio and the whole Century sales, editorial and production team. They have been simply sensational.

This November I will have been writing fiction for twenty years; and for the last nineteen of them I have had the support of my amazing agent and friend, Broo Doherty. She has championed my work and been by my side, and I appreciate it more than I can ever say.

ACKNOWLEDGEMENTS

This year has also been uniquely special, thanks to my family: to Mum and Dad, and to my husband John, and to Charlotte and James: ILY.

And just as I was editing this book and writing about the birth of the fictional baby, my own granddaughter arrived – two weeks early! I hung on with the dedication and acknowledgements, for her to make her debut in the world.

So let the very last word of this book be the biggest, most wonderful welcome to her: **Romilly**.

Sign up to

Phillipa Ashley's

newsletter for all the latest news,
exclusives and giveaways!

www.penguin.co.uk/authors/298314/phillipa-ashley